FANGIRL
Down

FANGIRL
Down

A Novel

TESSA BAILEY

AVON

An Imprint of HarperCollins*Publishers*

FANGIRL DOWN. Copyright © 2024 by Tessa Bailey. All rights reserved. Printed in the United Kingdom. No part of this book may be used or reproduced in any manner whatsoever without written permission except in the case of brief quotations embodied in critical articles and re-views. For information, address HarperCollins Publishers, 195 Broadway, New York, NY 10007.

HarperCollins books may be purchased for educational, business, or sales promotional use. For information, please email the Special Markets Department at SPsales@harpercollins.com.

FIRST EDITION

Designed by Diahann Sturge

Golf illustrations © RNko7/Shutterstock

Library of Congress Cataloging-in-Publication Data has been applied for.

ISBN 978-0-06-337420-1 (paperback)

27 26 25 24 CPI 10 9 8 7 6 5 4 3 2 1

For Mac

ACKNOWLEDGMENTS

I ramble through a lot of story ideas on social media, but they don't always get made into a book. This is one of those rare times a brainstorm kept me in a chokehold and every once in a while, a reader would message me, asking when I planned to write the book about the grumpy pro golfer and his superfan who disappears. *Thank you* for the encouragement. In this case, it really pushed me to write Wells and Josephine's story . . . and it turned out to be an all-time favorite.

This book is dedicated to my daughter—and also anyone out there without a working pancreas. But it's not a book *about* type 1 diabetes, in the same way people living with T1D are about so much *more* than the condition. This is a love story. With a side of insulin. Someday this will be the first book of mine that my kid reads. Please, for the love of God, may she skip over the butt stuff.

Thank you to Nicole Fischer for editing this book with love and honesty—you're going to be truly missed. Thank you to my husband for answering my golf questions. And as always, thank you to my readers for being the best in the business.

FANGIRL
Down

CHAPTER ONE

I am the number one Wells Whitaker fangirl.

Sure, golf's resident bad boy has seen better days, but that's the thing about being a fangirl.

Be in it for *life* or keep walking, pal.

There are three qualities one must possess to make an impact as a fangirl.

Number one: Enthusiasm. Let them know you're there, baby. Otherwise blend into the polo shirts and khakis like everyone else.

Number two: Persistence. Skipping tour stops in one's home state isn't an option. Fangirls show up and show *out*.

Number three: Bring snacks. Food at a golf course is expensive and no one is cheerful after shelling out fourteen dollars for a hot dog.

To be fair, it hurt to drop *five bucks* on lunch these days, but Josephine Doyle wasn't thinking about that now, because Wells Whitaker himself was making his way to the tee box of the ninth hole. And oh, he was in rare form today. Surly as a snake, unshaven, ignoring the outstretched hands of spectators hoping for a high five from the once-promising golfer. He raked a hand down his handsome face, shook out a tattooed forearm, and yanked the driver out of his bag with all the ceremony of a lint flick.

Utterly majestic.

Josephine popped in one of her AirPods and tapped on the

tournament livestream, her ear flooded by the jocular tones of the commentators, Skip and Connie.

Skip: *Well, it's a beautiful day here in Palm Beach Gardens, Florida. Unless, of course, you're Wells Whitaker. In which case the sunlight is probably irritating your hangover.*

Connie: *This year's tour has presented quite a challenge to the golfer, who has already seen better days at twenty-nine. He swung into the tour on a wrecking ball five years ago, won three majors. Now? Most weeks, he's lucky to make it past the opening round.*

Skip: *Today . . . well, let's put it bluntly, there isn't a chance on God's green earth Wells makes it through to tomorrow. And frankly, Connie, I don't think he cares.*

Connie: *Not if his nocturnal activities are any indication, Skip. Take to the internet for proof that golf is the furthest thing from Whitaker's mind. A mere six hours ago, he was questioned by police after a bar brawl in Miami—*

Josephine plucked out her AirPod and shoved it into the pocket of her official Wells Whitaker brand pants. It wasn't so long ago that Skip and Connie worshipped Wells. In the fangirl business, they were called Fair Weather Fans. They showed up for a player only on his best day. When the window into success wasn't even a smidgen grimy.

That's fine. Josephine would more than compensate for those Judases.

And today?

Today she would finally get the chance to tell Wells she hadn't counted him out. Down? Sure. But never out. She'd look right into those bloodshot eyes and remind him that his greatness wasn't something that could go away. It had simply gotten hidden beneath self-doubt, alcohol, and a frown that could scare the feathers off a duck.

Josephine still couldn't believe she'd won the contest.

Even if she had entered it sixty-one times.

Lunch and Lessons with Wells Whitaker. One lucky fan would share a meal with the once-great and soon-to-be-great-again Wells, followed by a putting lesson. Technically, Josephine didn't *need* the lesson, as she'd grown up on a golf course, worked in a pro shop, and spent her days teaching proper techniques to customers.

Golf was her life. She was more stoked for her chance to shake some sense into the defeated athlete. No one else seemed inclined to take on the task. Especially his caddie, who appeared to be watching *Vanderpump Rules* on his phone.

Really, the sparse crowd that had followed Wells to this hole seemed inclined to knock off early or find a more popular player to watch, a couple of them breaking from the pack and wandering toward the clubhouse before Wells even took his shot. A bunch of Fair Weathers if Josephine had ever seen them.

Unfortunately, Wells looked like he was considering dropping out of the tournament altogether, too. On one hand, that would mean Josephine would get lunch sooner. Her waning blood sugar could use the boost.

On the other, she'd rather see him finish the day on a high note.

Time to make an impact.

Josephine reached down deep for her fangirl wail and set it

loose, startling many a khaki-pants-wearing man in the process. *"Let's go, Wells. Put it in the hole!"*

The golfer gave her a stone-faced look over his generously muscled shoulder, affording her a view of his light brown eyes and square jaw. "Oh, look. It's you. Again."

Josephine gave him a winning smile and held up her sign, which read WELLS'S BELLE. "You're welcome."

A line popped in his stubbly cheek.

"You got this," she mouthed at him. Then couldn't resist adding, "I'm excited about our lunch today. You remember that I won the contest, right?"

His sigh could have knocked over a small child. "I tried to forget, but you tagged me in your Instagram story. Eight times."

Had it been eight times? She could have sworn she'd limited herself to six. "You know how the important things get swallowed up on that app."

"Well. It didn't." He prodded at a lip that looked suspiciously split. "Do you mind if I concentrate on this shot now? Or do you want to go over the specials menu?"

"I'm good. *Great*, actually." Josephine pressed her lips together to stop the smile from bursting straight off her face and held up her sign with renewed purpose. Everyone in the crowd was gaping at her—something that used to be a lot easier when she had her partner in crime. Her best friend, Tallulah, used to accompany Josephine on these fangirl outings for moral support, but she was currently on a research trip out of the country, leaving Josephine to hold down the sidelines alone. But Josephine was okay with that. She was thrilled her friend had gotten the once-in-a-lifetime opportunity. Didn't mean she didn't miss her terribly.

Swallowing the goose egg in her throat, Josephine ignored the man furiously brandishing a paddle at her that read QUIET

PLEASE and shouted, "Keep it in the short grass, Wells, you absolute legend!"

"Ma'am," the paddle man snapped.

Josephine winked at him. "I'm done."

"Good."

"For now."

Wells watched the exchange while shaking his head, then turned back around, shifted down into his stance, and . . . look, there was simply no ignoring the gas in the man's tank. Glute strength gave a golfer driving power and Wells's posterior was the one part of his career that remained a champion. Bounce a quarter off that thing? Nah, try two silver dollars. They would rebound off his well-rounded booty and knock a fangirl out cold. And she'd go down smiling.

"Once upon a time, Whitaker would have birdied this hole in his sleep," a man standing behind Josephine whispered to his son. "Shame he let it all go down the drain. They should take his tour card before he embarrasses himself more than he already has."

Josephine glanced back over her shoulder, giving the spectator the most disdainful look she could muster. "He's right on the verge of a comeback. Too bad you can't see it."

The man and his son issued an identical scoff. "I'd need a microscope, honey."

"To those with an untrained eye, maybe." She sniffed. "I bet you guys spend fourteen dollars on hot dogs."

"Ma'am," begged the paddle guy. "*Please.*"

"Sorry."

Wells flexed his grip around the club, squinted out at the fairway, and hauled back, his once-famous drive missing its former finesse.

The ball sailed straight into the trees.

Disappointment rippled all the way down to Josephine's toes. Not for herself, because she hadn't gotten the privilege of witnessing something great, but for Wells. She watched the way his shoulders tensed, his head dropping forward. The hushed murmurings of the crowd might as well have been cymbals crashing. The last remaining spectators wandered away, off to find pastures that didn't need so much watering.

But Josephine stayed. It was the fangirl way.

CHAPTER TWO

How did that saying go?

You're the hardest on the ones who love you the most?

Apparently, it was true. Because Wells had one fan left—one single, overzealous, and annoyingly cute fan—and his first instinct was to blame his botched shot on her. That wasn't fair; he'd botched plenty of shots lately without her standing on the sidelines. Maybe he'd finally reached his capacity for self-disgust. Or maybe he was simply the shithead so many friends and admirers had written him off as over his two-year decline.

Whatever the reason, the fact that she remained there even now, steadfast and smiling encouragingly after he'd shot straight into the fucking trees? Wells couldn't bear it. She needed to go, like the rest of them. Get lost. This auburn-haired sideline warrior wearing his merch was the only thing that had gotten him out of bed this morning—because she was always at his Florida tour stops. Always. Without fail. Didn't she know they'd discontinued his clothing line last year? He'd been dropped by Nike, too. At this stage, he would be lucky to get a sponsorship from a dandruff shampoo brand.

His mentor, the legendary Buck Lee, wouldn't even return his texts.

The world had counted him out long ago.

Yet, there *she* stood, holding the sign.

Wells's Belle.

Jesus Christ. He needed to put this girl out of her misery.

The only way to do that was to put himself out of it first. Otherwise, she would show up next week, next month, next year. Fresh and unfailing and staunchly supportive, no matter how low he finished on the leaderboard at the end of the day. She kept coming back.

Therefore, Wells kept coming back, not wanting to disappoint her.

His last remaining fan. His last remaining . . . anything.

Josephine.

But he didn't want to do it anymore. Didn't want to show up and try uselessly to recapture the glory days. He'd lost his magic and would never find it again. It was somewhere out in the trees with his ball. She needed to go, so *he* could pull the plug. So he could stop waking up every morning trying to locate his missing optimism. He could finally drink himself to death in peace and never see another golf green for the rest of his life.

None of which would be happening if he followed through on this ridiculous contest.

"Go." Turning on a heel, he ripped off his glove and waved it in the general direction of the fans streaming toward the clubhouse. Looking her in the eye was hard, which was ridiculous because he didn't even *know* her. Not personally. And he never would. They'd had many brief exchanges on the course, but all their conversations were golf-related. Quick, if somehow . . . meaningful. More important than the average interaction with a spectator. He couldn't dwell on that, though. It was over. "Go. I'm dropping out." Finally, he found the balls to lean across the rope and meet her widening green eyes. "It's over, belle. Go home."

"No."

Laughing without humor, he chucked his glove down the fairway. If only he could play a ball that straight. "Well, you're going to be cheering for a ghost, because I'm done."

Slowly, she lowered her sign.

The sight made his chest lurch, but he didn't let himself flinch outwardly.

"You're down but you're not out, Wells Whitaker."

"Listen to me. I'm out. I'm quitting the tour. There is no reason for you to come here anymore, Josephine."

All at once, her smile brightened and, God help him, she went from cute to *stunning*—an observation that could mean absolutely nothing, since they were cutting ties right here and now. "You called me by my first name. You never have before."

He knew that fact well, didn't he? He'd refrained from calling her anything but her self-selected nickname, because anything else felt too personal. And there was nothing personal here. They were athlete and number one fan—and they needed to be done. *Over.* He had to sever this remaining tie to golf or he'd never be able to get on with the rest of his miserable has-been existence. At *twenty-nine.*

Goddamn this sport.

And goddamn her for making him want to show up and try.

Utterly ridiculous, considering this was the first time Wells had even said her name, despite the fact that she'd been cheering him on from behind the rope for the five years he'd been on the tour.

"What about the contest?" she said, folding up her sign and holding it to her chest. "Lunch and Lessons with Wells Whitaker. I won."

He gestured to the trees. "Obviously I'm in no position to give you a lesson."

She stared off down the fairway for a moment. Then said, "I'm a coach, myself. Maybe I could give you one."

Wells did a double take. "Excuse me?"

"I said, maybe I could give you one." She winced, as if she'd finally run that presumptuous suggestion through a filter. "My family owns a little pro shop nearby and I know everything there is to know about golf. My first pair of baby shoes had spikes on the bottom." She took off her visor and now . . . her eyes looked even bigger. More compelling. And he didn't know why, but letting this loyal girl down wasn't sitting well. "You don't love the sport anymore. Maybe I can help you love it again. That's what I meant by giving you a lesson—"

"Josephine, listen to me. I don't *want* to love it anymore. I've lost my soul to this game and it has given me nothing in return."

She gasped. "Nothing except three majors titles."

"You don't understand. The titles start to mean nothing when you're incapable of doing it again." He closed his eyes and let the truth of those words sink in. First time he'd said them out loud. "The best thing you can do for me is leave. Pick some other golfer to harass, okay?"

His only remaining fan tried to keep her features stoic, but he'd inflicted some hurt with that suggestion. *Keep going. Get it over with.* Even if the idea of her cheering for another player made him want to impale himself on his wedge.

Wells bit down hard on his tongue so he wouldn't take it back.

"It's a bad day. Shake it off and get back out here tomorrow." Her laugh was incredulous. "You can't just quit golf."

He laughed as he turned and strode for his bag, his caddie nowhere in sight. "Golf quit me. Go home, belle." There was a note stuck between his clubs. Frowning, he plucked it up between two fingers to find a resignation letter from his caddie. If one could call a scrawled note on a bar napkin a resignation letter. Instead of being angry, Wells felt nothing but relief.

Excellent timing.

That saved him having to fire the son of a bitch.

"Wells, wait."

His back muscles tightened at the sight of Josephine ducking under the rope and jogging in his direction, her deep, reddish-brown ponytail swinging side to side. Such a move was wildly against the rules, but there was no one left to care. He'd leave the club and no one would even notice, would they? Except her.

"There are people who still believe in you," she said.

"Really? Where?" He hefted the bag onto his shoulder. "All I see is you."

Again, hurt trickled into her gaze and he ignored the impulse to throw down his bag, tell her everything. How his mentor had abandoned him after one bad season and he'd realized his support system was all smoke and mirrors. At the end of the day, he was alone, like he'd been since age twelve. All anyone cared about now was how well he hit this little white ball and *God*, he resented that. Resented the game and everything about it.

"I'll stay right here until everyone comes back," she said.

Frustration raked down his insides like a pair of fingernails. He just wanted to throw in the towel and she was the only one preventing him from doing it.

Wells steeled himself against the urge to set down his bag and select a club one more time, for this person who unwisely continued to believe in him. He reached for her sign instead, calling himself ten times a bastard as he tore it straight down the middle. He threw the two sides onto the grass, forcing himself to look her in the eye, because he couldn't be a bastard *and* a coward. "For the last time, I don't want you here."

Then it finally happened.

She stopped looking at him as if he were a hero.

And it was a million times worse than hitting into the trees.

"Sorry about lunch," he said thickly, wheeling around her. "Sorry about everything."

"What about your green jacket?"

Wells stopped in his tracks, but didn't turn to face her. He couldn't let anyone see what those two words—*green jacket*—did to him. Especially her. The tournament held in Georgia every year was widely regarded as a kingmaker. You win the Masters Tournament? You are an automatic icon. The winner was traditionally awarded a very distinct green jacket and lorded over anyone who didn't have one. Aka the dream. *"What?"*

"You said once that your career wouldn't be complete without winning a green jacket at Augusta. You haven't done it yet."

A shard of ice dug into his gut. "Yes, I'm aware of that, Josephine. Thank you."

"Goals don't just stop being goals," she said adamantly. "You can't just stop wanting something after working so hard for it."

"I can. I have."

"I'm calling bullshit, Wells Whitaker."

"Call bullshit all you like. I won't be here to listen."

With that, he left the course for the final time—and he was right, no one noticed.

No one except for Josephine. The last person on planet Earth pulling for him. He would very likely never see her again. Never overhear her defend him in the crowd or see her signs pop up reassuringly among the baseball caps, her unusually colored hair a perfect complement to the green surrounding her.

Acknowledging that was a lot harder than he expected, but he kept walking. Halfway to the parking lot, he dropped his golf bag and let the clubs spill out, not giving a shit what happened to them. The lack of weight should have made him feel lighter.

The sense of freedom would come eventually. Right?

Any second now.

But when he looked back at the course and saw Josephine still standing in the same spot, facing away from him, the heaviness intensified so swiftly that his gait faltered. Still, he commanded himself to get into the driver's side of his Ferrari, giving the ivy-covered establishment the finger as he peeled out of the lot.

Wells Whitaker was done with golf and everything that came with it.

Including green-eyed optimists who made him wish he could win again.

CHAPTER THREE

Three weeks after quitting the tour, Wells cracked open one stinging eye and had no idea what day it was. It might have been June or December. For all he knew, he'd gone *backward* in time. He'd disconnected from reality as soon as he left that golf course in Palm Beach Gardens and returned to his condo in Miami. Drinking. Lord Jesus, there had been so much drinking, his lungs and guts felt like they were caked in fresh tar.

Despite the wicked stepmother of headaches currently crushing his skull beneath the toe of her boot . . . his limbs were kind of jumpy. An indistinct memory poked the back of his neck like a bony finger. He needed to get out of bed and do something. But what? There was no tee time, no practice round, no press conference. Nothing to do but get lit again.

Hurricane Jake.

"Fuck."

His arm shot straight out to grab the remote control, his body twisting around in the sheets to sit up. There was a hurricane last night. Apart from some strong winds and lashing rain, he hadn't really felt the effects in his high-rise condo. Last thing he remembered, it was going through Palm Beach and goddammit, he'd thought of her. Josephine. She lived there, right? *My family owns a little pro shop nearby.* He recalled her saying that. So if she didn't live in Palm Beach, then close. Close enough to get hit.

And he must have been a stupid level of drunk, because he'd

had the irrational worry that she might still be standing on that golf course watching him leave when the hurricane landed. A ridiculous notion that he wasn't any less stressed about in the light of day.

He had no obligation to that woman.

It wasn't as though he'd formally invited her to be his number one fan.

His *only* fan.

At this point, she'd probably started cheering for someone else.

Good.

Stomach gurgling with acid, Wells turned on the seventy-inch flat-screen opposite his bed and flipped to the news, his heart sinking like an anchor when the destruction appeared. The coast had been clotheslined by hundred-and-fifty-mile-an-hour winds, torrents of rain. Blackouts and flooding. Cars overturned. The sides of buildings had been ripped clean off.

Was she affected?

Wells muted the television and fell back against the headboard, his finger tapping anxiously on the remote. This wasn't his problem. There were emergency services who helped people after weather disasters. Not to mention, he wasn't in any shape to help anyone.

He needed the help.

Cautiously, he turned his swimming head and glanced around the room. Discarded clothing, bottles, glasses, and plates holding half-eaten food. He'd gone full rogue, abandoning his protein diet and exercise routine. Also, shaving and showering and productivity. A few nights ago, he'd forced himself to venture outside, but that decision had led to yet another bar fight with some clown who'd lost fantasy sports money thanks to Wells's bad performance. So his right eye was purple and swollen. It provided little comfort that the other guy looked worse.

Getting sucker punched hurt like hell, but the brawl itself was a relief. He'd grown up fighting. In school, he'd spent more time in the principal's office than the principal herself. An angry kid—that's what he'd been. Resentful over being abandoned by his parents. Turbulent and hot-tempered.

Then Buck Lee had gotten ahold of him.

The summer Wells turned sixteen, he'd scored a job shagging balls at the local golf course and mainly, he'd been excited for an opportunity to silently mock the rich kids while he earned a few bucks. Where would he be now if he'd never picked up that driver and smashed a ball three hundred yards while Buck watched from the clubhouse?

Probably not sitting in a five-million-dollar condo.

Stressing about a girl he barely knew.

Wells's Belle.

A pressing sense of responsibility had him growling and reaching for his phone. His manager had quit weeks ago and they'd had zero communication, but he'd bite the bullet for some information. Otherwise, he'd always wonder if something bad had happened to her on his watch—

On his watch?

"Stop acting like she's your girlfriend. She's a *fan*."

Big, optimistic green eyes shining up at him.

I'll stay right here until everyone comes back.

"Dammit." Was his head pounding with the force of his hangover or was it something else? Wells didn't know, nor did he care to explore the reason he felt a responsibility to a certain redhead. So he just dialed.

His ex-manager, Nate, answered on the third ring, sounding groggy. "You better not be calling me to bail you out."

"I'm not." On the screen of his television, the news was showing a shelter full of people displaced by the storm and he furiously scanned the faces for one full of hope and humor. "Listen, remember that contest? People entered to have lunch and a putting lesson with me."

"The contest only eighty-one people entered?"

Wells winced. "I'm not sure it was necessary to give me that number."

He could almost see his old manager giving a negligent shrug. "Why are you suddenly concerned about the contest? The clubhouse restaurant called to let me know you'd blown off the reservation. I'm telling you, *I was shocked.*"

"You shouldn't be. Their food sucks." He pictured himself sitting across from Josephine in the brightly lit clubhouse restaurant and felt his stupid pulse move just a little faster. "Christ. I could have taken her somewhere nicer."

"The quality of their niçoise salad is neither here nor there, because you didn't hold up your end of the bargain, my man."

"You don't need to remind me," Wells snapped, triggering an ache behind his eye.

Had Josephine been really disappointed he didn't take her to lunch?

Of course, she had. He'd done nothing *but* let her down. For years.

"Just give me the winner's number and I'll leave you alone," Wells rasped.

"What?" Nate laughed. "I can't do that. Ever heard of privacy laws?"

The pinch of panic he experienced really didn't agree with him. "I'm taking her to fucking lunch, all right? I don't like the loose end."

"She doesn't want lunch. She doesn't want anything from you."

Wells's hand tightened around the remote, the sound of the

news reporter's voice turning muffled in his ears. "What the hell does that mean?"

"It means . . ." Nate groaned, followed by the sound of bed springs creaking in the background. "I don't like loose ends, either. After I found out you pulled a no-show on the reservation, I called the winner and offered to set up the same deal—lunch and a lesson—with another, less grouchy golfer."

"You *what*?" His hangover leaked out of his ears, leaving him so painfully sharp and clearheaded, it was almost disorienting. "She's *my* fan."

"Not anymore. I offered to send her some Wells Whitaker memorabilia and she turned that down, too. Your beer koozies hath no power here."

Wells was out of bed and pacing now, but he couldn't remember standing up. Was the floor tilting or was he still drunk? "I don't give a shit about privacy laws. Just give me her number."

"Not a chance. I escaped your employment without getting sued and I don't intend to open myself up for those legal ramifications, especially now that I'm *not* on your payroll."

"This is crazy," Wells shouted into the phone. "I'm trying to do the right thing."

"It's too late, man," Nate said back, his voice elevating to match Wells's. "You've ignored obligations and behaved like a royal prick for two years. You've *always* been a royal prick, but now that you don't have the golf game to back it up, no one has to deal with you. Especially me. Goodbye, Wells."

Silence swam in his ear.

God, he needed a drink. Badly.

But he couldn't seem to make the move to the kitchen to get a fresh bottle of scotch. Everything Nate had said was true—he had behaved like a relentless prick his entire career. Trash-talked the other pros instead of making friends. Been indifferent toward the fans. Either outright ignored the press or gave them answers they couldn't air on television.

More than anything, he wanted to give the world his middle finger and go back to bed. No one expected anything from him. He had no family to let down. No real friends to piss off. No mentor to disappoint.

But as loudly as oblivion called to him, the crystal-clear memory of *her* sang louder.

God, it was annoying.

"We're getting lunch, Josephine," Wells shouted on the way to the shower. "Dammit, *we're getting lunch*."

CHAPTER FOUR

Josephine hung up the phone with a shaking hand, a wounded sound escaping her mouth as she surveyed what used to be her family's pro shop. When law enforcement had officially declared it safe to drive on the roads, she'd jumped into her ancient Camry immediately, steeling herself for the worst the entire way. Yet she still hadn't been prepared.

Half of the inventory of clubs was gone. Floated away in the flood waters or possibly looted. The cash register was on its side in a bank of sludge. The display of rangefinder binoculars she'd arranged only last week was sticking out through the broken back window.

All she could do was stare at the mess. She had no idea where to begin cleaning up. If there was a place to sit down, she would do it now. In her haste to get out of her apartment, she'd forgotten to eat breakfast and the beeping on her phone reminded her of that now. Her low-blood-sugar alert was going off.

Movements lethargic, Josephine rooted in her purse for her plastic roll of glucose tabs and popped a few into her mouth, chewing, willing the sugar to bring her back up quickly, though the movements of her jaw felt unnatural. At least the deafening buzzing in her head had one advantage—it was drowning out the conversation she'd just had with the insurance company. The one who was no longer providing coverage.

She centered herself with a deep breath and called her parents.

"How bad is it, kiddo?" asked her father right away.

"It's bad, Dad."

Her parents both let out breaths that brushed up against her eardrum. She could picture them standing right beside each other in the kitchen, sharing the single phone they owned. Her mother would still have a pink towel on her head from the shower, her father sans pants. "That's okay, you two. We knew it was going to be a challenge, but the Doyles are up for it," said her mother, always the optimist. Forever finding the bright side. "We have flood insurance on the shop. It'll take a while to come through, but that'll just give us time to plan our grand reopening."

Josephine's legs turned so rubbery, she almost sat down in the foot-deep water.

She could see the late notice in her hand, remember reading the order to renew four months ago. Where had she stuffed it? Was it floating in the debris somewhere?

Oh God. *Oh God.*

Josephine looked around, swallowing hard at the sight of black-and-white pictures stuck in the sludge, their frames shattered, along with the frame holding the first dollar bill ever spent inside those walls. Her grandfather had opened the Golden Tee Pro Shop in the mid-sixties. It was attached to Rolling Greens, a landmark golf course in West Palm Beach that was open to the public. The little shop, where customers could rent clubs, buy merchandise, and talk golf, had seen much better days, before the ritzy private clubs had started popping up all over southern Florida, but Josephine had aspirations to change that in the coming years.

A putting green out front, more on-trend merchandise, a beverage bar.

She'd been giving extra lessons lately to save up the money to make those dreams a reality, but in one fell swoop, those possibilities had been swept out to sea by Mother Nature.

The Golden Tee belonged to her family, though she largely ran it solo these days. She'd been a late-in-life baby for her parents and they'd retired a few years ago. But the shop was still their very heart and soul. How would they react if they knew business had dwindled so drastically that she'd used the insurance money to buy insulin, instead?

She absolutely, 100 percent, could *not* tell her parents that. They were hoverers by nature. Throw in the fact that she'd been diagnosed with type 1 diabetes at age six and she'd grown up with two full-time human helicopters that watched her every move. In her late teens, she'd managed to convince them that she could take care of herself. They'd stopped following her on the app that allowed them to see her blood glucose number. They'd trusted her to make *good* decisions.

Failing to renew flood insurance in Florida was *soooo* not a good decision.

Nor was forgoing her own private medical insurance at age twenty-six so she could afford the monthly rent on the Golden Tee. Buying insulin out of pocket did not fall under the category of smart moves. Sure, several drug companies had capped insulin at thirty-five dollars recently, which was a tremendous help, but those vials were small and the costs added up. And insulin was only one component of living with diabetes in the age of smarter technology. Medical devices, such as her glucose monitor, had an astronomical price tag out of pocket. Necessary trips to the endocrinologist weren't cheap, either, without that little white card with numbers on it.

She'd hoped to skate by for a super brief period of time without a policy, borrowing supplies from the doctor when possible, but she'd leaned on that goodwill too long . . . and now her chickens were coming home to roost.

"Joey?"

She gulped at the sound of her mother's voice. "Yes, I'm here."

"Do you want us to come down?" asked her father.

"No." She molded her palm to her forehead. "You don't want to see it like this. I'll, um . . ." She turned in a circle, ordering the prickle behind her eyes to *cut it out*. "Let me clean up a little before you come by. Maybe a few days?"

"Joey, you don't have to take this on alone," her father said sternly.

"I know."

That's what she said out loud. However, the truth was that she took on *everything* alone. She didn't know any other way to feel like a capable adult. Growing up as a diabetic meant a lot of people assuming she was incapable of certain things. *Are you okay? Do you need a break? Should you eat that?* That constant concern from others had led to Josephine's being determined to prove she could do *anything* without issue or assistance. And she *could* do mostly anything—except for be in the military or fly a plane.

Unfortunately, staring at the mess that was her family's shop and having no clue if she'd be able to salvage it, she didn't feel capable of diddly-squat.

"I'll call you guys back in a while, okay?" she said brightly. "Love you."

"We love you, too, Joey-Roo."

That prickle behind her eyes got stronger and she hung up, blowing out a pent-up breath. She'd give herself five minutes to gather some courage, then she'd come up with a plan. Surely the government was allocating funds for disaster victims, right? Although she knew from past experience with hurricanes that it could take *years* to see that money—

"Hello?"

Josephine froze at the sound of that voice, calling from outside the shop.

She would know that raspy baritone in the middle of a monsoon.

It sounded like Wells Whitaker, but she had to be mistaken. Low blood sugar tended to make her slightly dizzy, her thoughts fuzzing together like cotton. The man who had fallen off the face of the planet three weeks ago was not knocking on the last remaining intact window of the Golden Tee Pro Shop.

"Belle, you in there?"

Belle.

No one called her that but Wells.

No. No way.

No.

She turned around and nudged the door open with her toe, which wasn't very difficult, since it hung by a single hinge. "Uh . . . hi? Whoever you are?"

A rush of breath. "Josephine."

None other than Wells Whitaker's face appeared in the doorway. Also, his body. It was there. All of him was there. He wasn't dressed for golf, as she was used to seeing him. Instead, he wore a black hoodie, jeans, his signature backward ballcap, dark hair sticking out from every side. His sideburns were overgrown, on course to collide with his unshaven facial hair where it scaled the sides of his sculpted face. His eyes were bloodshot and the smell of alcohol was basically the third occupant in the room.

Yet, despite the fact that he currently looked like human roadkill, he somehow retained his mystique. His Wells-ness. This was the guy who would lead the ragtag group of strangers in a dystopian universe. Everyone would just follow him without question. No one would be able to help it, because he had this way of moving and observing that said, *Yeah, okay, civilization is dead, so what?*

And he was *here*.

"What . . . is going on?"

His eyes moved sharply over her body, as if assessing for injury. "You're okay." A beat passed, his gaze meeting hers and holding. "Right?"

Physically, she was fine.

Just a little worried about the obvious hallucination taking place.

"Yes. I'm . . ." She blinked several times, trying to get her eyes to stop playing tricks on her. "What are you doing *here*?"

He rolled a single shoulder. "I just happened to be staying with a friend, not too far away. I remembered you saying something about your family owning . . . a pro shop? While I was out walking around, looking at the damage, I kind of just stumbled on this place by accident."

Josephine gave all of that a moment to sink in and none of it made the remotest lick of sense. "But . . . really? You came to stay with a friend in the direct path of a hurricane? And . . . this course is two *miles* from any residential area. You'd have to walk—"

"Josephine, you know a lot about me, right? Probably way too much."

"A Sagittarius raised in southern Georgia, you were discovered by one of golf's most legendary masters, Buck Lee, while—"

"Then you also know I hate answering questions."

That was the understatement of the century. Wells had once spent a full thirty minutes scrolling on his phone during a post-tournament press conference, completely ignoring the rapid-fire questions about a shouting match that had ensued with his caddie on the sixteenth hole. When his time was up, he'd calmly gotten up and swaggered out of the media tent, earning himself the nickname the Media unDarling.

"Yes, I do know that about you."

"Good."

Leaving that single word hanging in the air, Wells waded into the water left standing in the shop, charting the damage from beneath a furrowed brow. Josephine was grateful for the break in conversation, because now that her initial shock over Wells Whitaker appearing out of the blue had worn off, she was remembering all the reasons she'd made the painful decision to relinquish her fangirl status.

True, fangirls didn't quit. They were loyal to the end. But that day on the golf course, when he'd torn her sign in half, he'd ripped apart something inside her, too.

Apparently there came a point when a fangirl needed to be *more* loyal to herself.

And she didn't deserve to be treated like yesterday's garbage.

Her faith in that decision was stronger than ever that morning, faced with the potential loss of something that truly mattered—her family's legacy and livelihood.

"Have you called the insurance company yet?" Wells asked, hands propped on his hips, slowly bringing his attention back to her. "Were they able to give you a timeline?"

"Um." Oh no, her voice was shaking. She swallowed the thick feeling in her throat and looked down at her hands. "Um . . ."

"Hey." He stabbed the air with a finger. "Uh-uh. Are you *crying*?"

"I'd give it a sixty percent chance," she said on a sucked-in breath, blinking rapidly at the ceiling. "Can you please go?"

"Go?" She heard him shifting in the water. "I see what you're doing here. You're telling *me* to leave this time. You've gotten it out of your system, okay? We're even."

"I'm not keeping score. I just have a lot of important things on my mind and you are not one of them."

He caught that statement on the chin, his jaw giving a sharp flex. "Tell me the important things on your mind," he said in a lower tone.

"Why would I do that?"

"I'm asking you to."

"Do you even remember what happened last time I saw you?" Her curiosity was genuine. Did he think he could just walk into her shop and demand that she detail the way her life had taken a catastrophic left turn? She couldn't even tell her own parents. "Do you?"

Briefly, his gaze flickered down to the water. "Yes, I remember."

"Then I don't think it should come as a surprise that I'm kicking you out." How symbolic that her attention should be drawn to a framed poster of Wells on the other side of the shop. His image was water damaged to the point of distortion. "I'm not your fan anymore."

CHAPTER FIVE

Wells stared down at the green-eyed girl who was—very inconveniently—even prettier than he remembered, a corkscrew winding into his chest cavity. He kept his jaw tight, gaze unconcerned, but let's face it, he was starting to get pretty damn concerned.

Unusual for him. To say the least.

Wells Whitaker didn't *need* anybody. After his parents got jobs on a cruise ship and started sailing nine months out of the year, he'd been raised by his NASCAR promoter uncle, who didn't take much of an interest in his nephew beyond allowing him to sleep on the pullout couch in his one-bedroom apartment in Daytona Beach. Wells had engaged in a lot more than the typical childhood mischief growing up, shoplifting and fighting his way to two school expulsions, and his behavior only escalated when his parents decided he wasn't worth the constant aggravation.

After getting caught with a stolen bike he'd intended to pawn in order to buy a new pair of sneakers, he'd ended up in juvenile court and the judge had given him one more chance to turn his act around. Since he was sixteen, that included getting a job. Looking back, that judge could have come down a lot harder on Wells, and he appreciated what the man had been trying to do. Getting that job shagging balls at the local course had led to his career, his mentor-apprentice relationship with Buck Lee, and eventually his spot on the PGA tour.

And he'd let himself begin to need that friendship. That *bond*.

He'd allowed himself to need the roar of the crowd after sinking a putt.

But their attention had been quickly diverted to the newest hotshots on the tour.

At the end of the day, though, Wells was pissed only at himself. For believing that people were capable of *anything* unconditional. There were always contracts or understandings that allowed your colleagues and "friends" to wiggle out, if you turned up lacking one day. He'd fallen victim to the classic has-been plight and that, more than anything, pissed him off.

This fierce girl, who'd gone from holding back tears to looking like she wanted to grind a golf cleat into his guts, couldn't be any different than anyone else. She'd dropped him, too.

Something inside Wells refused to let him put her into the same category as the ones who'd come and gone, though. Josephine was in a class by herself and goddammit, she wouldn't seem to budge from it. Not an inch.

I'm not your fan anymore.

"Yes, you are. You're just having a bad day."

She started to blink very rapidly. He shuddered to think what she might have said to him if a series of beeps hadn't filled the room in that moment. She sighed, reached into her pocket, and pulled out a small plastic tube, emptying two quarter-size tablets into her mouth.

"What's beeping? What are those?"

Absently, she lifted her arm until her elbow was pointing up at the ceiling. For the first time since he'd "known" Josephine, he noticed a small, gray, oval-shaped button on the back of her arm. "The beeps are letting me know my blood sugar is low." She dropped her arm. "I'm a diabetic. Type one."

"Oh." He should have known that. Why didn't he know

that? Wells searched his mind for any knowledge whatsoever that might be lurking about diabetes and came up empty. They weren't supposed to eat anything with sugar, right? "Are those things . . . all you need right now?" he asked, tipping his head toward the tube as she stowed it back into her pocket.

"Yes. Right now." Under her breath, she added, "Better to have low blood sugar than high."

"Why is that?"

She pushed a hand through her hair, turning away from him slightly to survey a damaged display rack. "High blood sugar requires me to give myself insulin to come down and I need to spread my supply out." A slight flush appeared on her cheeks. "My health insurance isn't up to date at the moment."

"Oh."

The knowledge that this person was so much more than his most loyal fan came crashing down on Wells's head like a ton of bricks. Josephine had problems to contend with. Serious ones. Her family's shop was underwater and she had to worry about blood sugar going up and down. And he'd ripped her fucking sign in half? *What kind of a monster am I?*

Wells cleared his throat hard. "Health insurance seems like it might be pretty vital when you're a diabetic."

"Trust me, it is. But . . ." Her throat worked. She paused, coughed, and kept her voice even. Brave? Or was she just trying to avoid getting emotional in front of him because he'd demanded it? Both? "Everything just snowballed so fast, you know. Ironic in Florida." Why did that joke make him want to splash through the water and . . . hug her? Jesus, he was not a hugger. He wasn't even a shoulder patter. "I fell behind on rent payments for the shop. At first, it came down to paying for rent or the commercial insurance . . . like, flood insurance? I paid the rent."

A weight sank in his stomach. The shop wasn't covered.

"Shit, Josephine."

"Mega shit." She closed her eyes, shook her head a little. "Last year, I put my health insurance on pause so the payments wouldn't be a burden on the shop. Started taking on more golf lessons, so I could just buy my medical supplies out of pocket. But like I said, everything just seemed to snowball and . . ." She trailed off. Took a breath, lifted her chin, and pasted on a determined smile. "I'm going to figure it out, though. I always figure it out."

He hadn't deserved to have this girl in his corner for the last five years.

That fact was growing more obvious by the moment.

Someone should have been cheering for her, instead.

"I can give you the money," Wells said, easing the worst of the pressure in his chest. Okay. Yes. He had the solution. She wouldn't have to spread out her insulin or be forced to take any other measures to remain healthy. He might not be the number one golfer in the world anymore, but he had tens of millions banked from those earlier, successful days. Might as well give the cash to someone who needed it, before he spent it all on scotch. "I'll write you a check. Enough to repair the shop and cover your health insurance for a year. Just until you're back on your feet."

She stared at him like he'd suggested they take a vacation on Mars. "Are you serious?"

"I don't say things I don't mean."

Silence passed. "Neither do I. So believe me when I say, there isn't a *single chance* I'm taking your money. I'm not a charity case. I can take care of myself. *And* my family."

"What is this? A pride thing? You're too *stubborn* to accept?"

"Are we really pointing out each other's flaws, because I don't think you have that kind of time on your hands."

"I have nothing *but* time on my hands."

"Fine! Then your backswing is timid."

"My—" His neck locked up like a prison cell. "*What* did you say?"

"I said . . ." She stomped through the water and got right in his face—and damn. It had been a very long time since he'd wanted to take a woman to bed this badly. In fact, maybe he'd never wanted that outcome more in his life. At this exact point in time, it would have been the angry kind of sex that ended with nail marks down his back and her in a stupor, because yeah, she'd just taken a shot at his technique. And she wasn't done. "You used to swing like you had nothing to lose. It was glorious to watch. Now, you handle the driver like you're worried the ball might yell at you for hitting it too hard." She stabbed him in the chest with her index finger. "You swing like you're scared."

No one had spoken to Wells like that. Not since Buck.

Not since those early, early days when he'd picked up the club and felt magic race all the way up into his shoulder and a sense of purpose in his fingertips.

It was like coming up through the surface of the water and taking a deep breath.

Her honesty was oxygen.

But breathing it? That part was terrifying.

"You think *you* could show me better? I had no idea you were a professional."

"I might not be a professional—"

"No. Because if you were, you would know that once you lose your stroke, getting it back is like trying to find a needle in a haystack. I've *looked*, Josephine. One day, a player has formula and the next, he's forgotten how to pronounce the ingredients. That's why these greats go on winning streaks that seem endless, but they *always* end. Success in golf is finite."

"Do you really believe that or are you just making excuses to be a quitter?"

"I don't need this shit."

"Then leave."

"Oh, don't worry. I will."

He didn't move an inch. The dumbest, most harebrained idea of his life was occurring to him and the more he allowed it to invade his mind, the more oxygen he breathed. Her oxygen. She was an endless supply, standing right in front of him and, Jesus, he couldn't walk out of there knowing the obstacles she'd have to face by herself. Leaving her to deal with everything alone would haunt him day and night, along with her . . . mouth. God, her mouth. It was the most stubborn and kissable mouth he'd ever seen.

Whatever you do, don't voice this ridiculous idea out loud.

It probably wasn't even possible. The longest of long shots.

But maybe . . .

Maybe one last time, he'd swing like he had nothing to lose.

"If I can get back on the tour, if they'll allow me back on, why don't you put your money where your mouth is and caddie for me? Since you know so goddamn much."

Josephine went so perfectly still, she might have transformed into a mannequin. "Wait . . . what? Wh-what did you say?"

"You heard me. Next stop on the tour is San Antonio. You in?" He crossed his arms in defense of her shock. Hell, his *own* shock. "If you won't just take my money, earn it, instead."

She stepped back from him, her chest rising and falling. "Are you messing with me?"

"Let's get one thing straight, belle. You will never wonder where you stand with me or if I'm bullshitting you. You get exactly what you see. I don't mess around with people, but especially you."

Heat singed the back of his neck.

Fuck.

That last part had slipped out.

"Because I'm potentially going to be your caddie," she tacked on, mercifully. "There can't be any secrets or pretenses between a golfer and his caddie. A caddie is a chauffeur, coach, and priest all in one package."

"Is that a yes?" Wells asked gruffly, holding his breath.

"I . . ." She looked around the flooded pro shop, as if searching for someone to talk her out of his wild idea. "I mean, I would have a couple of conditions."

"Name them."

"I can't caddie for you indefinitely. When and if I make enough money to remodel the shop the way I've always wanted, I'll have to . . ."

Wells waited. And waited. "You can't even say the word 'quit' can you?"

She made a face. "I'll have to come *home*, is what I'm saying."

"Got it. What else?"

Green eyes zeroed in on him and he sensed the gravity of what came next. "I meant it, Wells. I won't be pitied. Okay? I've been coddled and treated like a charity case many times before, all because of my T1D. But I'm not one. If we make this agreement, it's because it'll benefit us both. Not just me."

Whether this arrangement would benefit him remained to be seen—nothing he'd tried to bring his game back on line had worked, so why would this? But he'd bite. Hell, he didn't want her to feel like a charity case, either. "Done."

"Then . . . I don't think I can say no."

Wells tried not to be obvious about his breath escaping. "Fine." He shrugged. "Good."

"Do you really think you can get back on the tour?"

"You let me worry about that. You just show up and carry the bag."

Several beats of silence passed while she looked at him, almost appearing bewildered.

"What is it, Josephine?"

"You didn't even . . . consider that diabetes might make it hard or impossible to carry your bag all over a golf course for eighteen holes."

"You've done harder things than carry a bag. Haven't you?"

God help him, the sheen that appeared in her eyes made him utterly fucking determined to get his ass back on the tour, even if it meant swallowing his pride—and he'd be doing that by the mouthful. "Yes," she finally answered. "I . . . yes. Thank you."

Before Wells could do something out of character, like ask if she perhaps needed a tissue or a comforting shoulder pat, he turned and stomped out of the water.

"Wait!" She splashed after him. "I have one more condition."

"What now? A kidney?"

"Maybe later," she responded, without missing a beat. "For now, let me take you to get a haircut and shave. I'm not being seen on national television with a guy who looks like he just survived six months in the Amazon."

Wells cast her a dark look over his shoulder, despite the bubble of amusement lurking near his collarbone. Honestly, he shouldn't have given up any more ground, but the PGA wouldn't allow him onto the green looking like an ungodly mess, anyway, so might as well concede the point to Josephine. "Is that the *final* item on your list?"

"Yes."

He sighed. "Fine. Let's go. I'll give you a ride."

"A ride? Didn't you say you walked here?"

"What did I say about questions?" Sliding on his shades, he unlocked the door of his Ferrari with an expensive-sounding beep. "Get in and hold on."

CHAPTER SIX

Watching the barber whip a teal cape around Wells's shoulders and fasten it behind his neck was nothing short of surreal. Wells was a mysterious celebrity creature she observed from a safe distance or on television. Now she was watching him gripe under his breath about being required to take his hat off. A moment later, it became obvious why.

He looked like he'd miraculously survived a trip to the electric chair.

His chocolate-bark hair was flat in some places, pointing like a broken spring in others.

And still, *still*, he managed to retain his beastly attractiveness.

Not that she would let him know that.

"Wells." Josephine walked to the front of the barber's workstation and laid a gentle hand on the reflective surface. "Let me introduce you to this incredible, new invention called a mirror."

He flashed her his teeth. "Did I hire a caddie or a comedian?"

"Seriously." She let her hand drop. "When is the last time you brushed your hair?"

"I've been busy." He waved a hand at her, disrupting the fall of the cape. "Sit down and be quiet, would you? You're distracting the barber."

Josephine remained standing. "I'm going to take a shot in the dark and say you don't have a woman in your life."

"Thank God."

"What does that mean?" she asked, tilting her head.

Wells glanced around. "You're answering your own question by dragging me to get a haircut."

"I should have let you be your own worst enemy in peace?"

"Exactly."

She hummed while trading an amused glance with the barber. "Don't forget to shave his neck."

A few beats of silence passed, the spritz of the spray bottle filtering in between the sound of hair dryers and muted conversations throughout the salon. Wells flicked her a curious look and sat up a little straighter, earning him a sigh from the barber. "What about you? You got a boyfriend, or what, Josephine? I'm guessing not."

The barber whistled under his breath. "Brave."

Josephine covered her wave of embarrassment with an eye roll.

"What?" Wells jerked a shoulder. "I'm not saying she isn't . . ." He trailed off, visibly searching for a new direction. "I'm not saying she doesn't have one. But if you had a boyfriend, I'm guessing he wouldn't love the fact that you spend entire afternoons cheering me on so enthusiastically. That's all I meant by guessing you're single."

"You're saying I can't be an avid spectator *and* have a boyfriend?"

He gave a brief headshake. "Not if I was your boyfriend."

"No chance of that," the barber commented. "You're digging a pretty deep hole."

"Could you mind your own business and just cut my hair?" Wells griped, before shifting in his seat and retraining his attention on Josephine. "Boyfriend or not, belle?"

"Not," she said sweetly. "Thank God."

Why did he seem weirdly pleased by that? "Now it's my turn to ask what *you* mean."

"I don't really know what I mean," she said honestly, after a short sifting of thoughts. Snippets of time she'd spent on dates or attempting relationships that never quite entered a comfortable phase. "I guess . . ."

Wells was watching her closely. "What?"

"Women are expected to be kind of . . . demure. Or grateful. Most of the time I'm neither of those things."

"How is that?"

Josephine braced her shoulders against the wall and looked up at the ceiling, trying to put into words why she'd slowly let dating take a back seat to her job for the last couple of years. "I think it's partly that I learned to challenge myself growing up, because no one was going to do it for me. I talked myself into trying things people cautioned me against—like playing sports or entering a dance contest. Challenging myself and succeeding made me feel good, so . . . I don't know, maybe I falsely expect people to appreciate when I challenge them—"

"Trash-talk them, you mean?"

"Sometimes." She wrinkled her nose at him. "Also, I grew up on a golf course where the love language is trash talking. That's how I communicate. And guys can dish it out, but they can't take it."

Wells snorted.

"What?"

"Nothing."

"No, really. What?"

The barber had stopped trimming Wells's hair so he could listen to the conversation. Wells leaned back and raised a lazy eyebrow at the man, and he promptly got moving again. "You claim you want a guy who trash talks you, but your feelings would get hurt."

"It sounds like you're speaking from experience, Whitaker. Exactly how many women have you sent to therapy?"

"No idea." He winced as the barber sharpened his blade. "I don't conduct exit interviews."

"Maybe you should start. It could be enlightening."

"I've got a pretty good idea what they'd say. I don't need to subject myself to—"

"Trash talk?" She let her smile expand. "Oooh. Yet another one who can't take it."

He let out an indelicate snort. "I can take it."

She pursed her lips.

His features transformed with disgust.

A laugh wiggled around in her chest, begging to burst out of her mouth, but she put a lid on it. She'd wholeheartedly meant to needle him and wouldn't be jogging back any of her statements anytime soon. However, she *was* having fun. Which was a lot more than she could say for the last, hmmm, eight men she'd gone on dates with. And there had been only eight, total, in her life.

She'd traded words with Wells on occasion at tournaments and their exchanges had been interesting. Snappy. Memorable. She couldn't help but be kind of pleased to know they shared the same dynamic in real life. Not because she wanted to *date* him. Or because he was a shade sexier when he was in a foul mood— fine, several shades—but more so because his crabby disposition made her feel . . . open to challenge him. She'd never really experienced that before.

"Beyond that, I had this *thing* growing up. None of the other kids had it. So I doubled down to prove I was not only the same as everyone else, but stronger."

Josephine couldn't believe she'd said that out loud.

Actually, she wasn't really sure she'd even acknowledged that truth to *herself* before. Now that she'd plucked at the thread, though, she felt compelled to keep tugging until the thought had been fully realized. "One time, in sixth grade, my class went on an overnight camping trip in Ocala. No parents. I think my mom and dad secretly got a hotel room nearby, actually, in case of an emergency, although they've never fessed up." She shook her head. "Anyway, this one kid, Percy D'Amato, claimed he'd seen a black bear in the woods and everyone was freaked out." She paused to remember. "I took out my flashlight and went out into the woods by myself. And you know what? There *was* a bear."

Wells did a double take. "No, there wasn't."

"Yes. There was. I screamed bloody murder, and it ran in the opposite direction."

"It's starting to make a lot more sense why you're not intimidated by me." This time, she couldn't quite hold in her laugh—and the briefest of smiles carried across the lips of Wells Whitaker, before he quickly went back to frowning, heaping more shades of sexiness on top of what was already a veritable mountain. Even in a barber's chair, while having shaving cream dolloped onto his jaw, he looked more like an angry gladiator than a golfer.

"Is it your goal to intimidate people?" Josephine asked.

He didn't answer right away. "It's not something I think about."

"Your impenetrable darkness just comes naturally."

"Sort of like your brightness."

That caught her off guard. "You think I'm . . . that I have brightness?"

"Better . . . better . . . ," murmured the barber.

"I . . ." He opened his mouth and closed it, making an irritable gesture that sent the edge of the cape flying. "You would have to have a certain brightness. On the inside. To keep showing up with a smile on your face for a losing player. Not that I was paying attention."

Josephine felt an unwanted, possibly dangerous tug in her throat.

She rubbed the spot to make it go away.

"Of course not," she said.

"Maybe, initially, I intimidated people on purpose. I grew up without a dime, walked to school when everyone else was getting dropped off by parents, lunches packed. Birthday invitations in their backpacks to hand out at recess. I wanted them to know I didn't give a shit."

This time, there was no ridding herself of the throat tug, so she didn't bother trying to massage it away. "But you did? Give a shit."

He stopped just short of confirming, visibly uncomfortable with the direction they'd taken. "Maybe. I don't know." He transferred his glare to the barber. "Could you please stab me in the neck to get me out of this conversation?"

"Texas ought to be fun," Josephine said cheerfully.

"There's no fun in golf, Josephine."

She swiped a finger through the shaving cream and tapped the dollop onto his nose, trying valiantly not to consider the perfect slope of it. "You've never played with me before."

CHAPTER SEVEN

Wells swiped a gym towel down his sweaty face, tossed it onto the bench press, and took another lap around his home gym. All week, he'd been subjecting himself to grueling workouts. Seven days later, the alcohol was still seeping out of his pores. Apart from the overall need to get himself back into playing condition, he'd been using exercise as a means of distraction. A way to stall. It was now or never, though.

The tournament started in two days and Wells wasn't yet back on the roster.

He needed to call Buck.

Otherwise, he'd hired Josephine as his caddie for no reason and his new set of clubs had been shipped to the resort in San Antonio in advance of nothing.

"Quit being a coward," he commanded himself, picking up the towel once more to wipe away the perspiration on his chest. "Make the damn call. What's the worst that could happen?"

Buck could tell him to fuck off.

Technically, his mentor had already done that. There was nothing to lose here. Nothing but his pride.

Wells stared at his reflection in the wall mirror for long moments, caught off guard by the trepidation in his face. When had he become so indecisive? Before he'd been lauded as the next Tiger Woods, he'd never second-guessed himself. He'd made every decision, even the bad ones, with full confidence. *What the hell happened to me?*

Wells didn't know. But apparently when he'd told Josephine that golf had stolen his soul, it wasn't an exaggeration.

Josephine.

His other reason for distracting himself with exercise.

Women didn't usually get under his skin. It was fucking annoying, was what it was. Last night, while in the shower, he'd had an imaginary conversation with her. Out loud. Defending his backswing. When he thought of the tournament, she was the first thing that popped up in his mind. How she'd be wearing a caddie uniform with his name on it in big, block letters. And how he liked that image a little too much.

Wells had no time for romantic bullshit. Occasional, casual hookups were part of his bachelor lifestyle, but anything beyond that only led to making plans, enduring long-winded phone calls, and taking on responsibilities he'd never asked for. He'd learned that early on in his career after three *very* short-term relationships. Being on television, making millions of dollars, had made him something of a magnet for people with a single motive: get a slice of that money pie. Relationships tended to move very quickly in the golf world. Because players were on the road so often, they were pressured into making commitments. To offset the doubt.

Not Wells. Not ever.

The fact that Josephine had been more than happy to wash her hands of Wells altogether—and seemed to kind of *dislike* him—was somewhat . . . reassuring. Hell, she'd tried to throw him out of her pro shop. She wouldn't even take his money without working for it. He *definitely* wouldn't have to worry that she had some secret plan to make a rich, devoted husband out of him.

Cool.

Great.

Wells realized he was staring at his own thunderous frown in the mirror and shook himself, snatching the phone out of his pocket and pulling up the contact for Buck Lee.

One deep breath and he dialed, hating the way his pulse raced.

Buck answered on the third ring, the older man's voice as distinct as ever. A soft boom.

"Wells."

"Buck."

"I suppose if you're calling me, you must be alive," drawled the legend. "The question is *why* are you calling, Wells? We've got nothing to say to each other."

Two years had passed since his mentor had washed his hands of Wells, but the memory still had the ability to sting. "I had no other choice but to call you. I'm asking you to hear me out."

"Son, if you wanted to quit, you should have gone through the proper channels, instead of lighting on out of there without showing an ounce of respect. There is nothing anyone can do for you now."

"Now that's a lie, Buck. You could cancel the tour with a phone call, if you were so inclined."

His mentor scoffed. "If you think flattery is going to get you anywhere—"

"We both know I don't flatter anyone. It's the truth."

A long sigh on the other end. "What do you want from me? Hurry up, so I can tell you no."

Panic moved like an ice cube slipping down his spine. "I want back on the tour."

"Never going to happen," Buck said, without hesitation. "But I am curious to know why. Why do you want back on the tour? You're embarrassing yourself out there. I don't know what happened to the Wells Whitaker I coached to greatness, but he's long gone."

Pressure spread behind Wells's eyes, his head pounding.

This was humiliating. He wanted nothing more than to hang up.

The only thing that prevented him from doing so was Josephine. She would be on her way to Texas soon. For him. Because he'd asked. Because she needed help and caddying was the only way she'd take assistance from him. "There's a . . ."

Girl? No, that sounded cliché. Or made it seem like there was a romantic connotation to his relationship with Josephine—and there definitely wasn't. Even if he wouldn't mind a good, long taste of her. Just one, to appease his curiosity.

"I have a new caddie," Wells settled on, attempting to banish the thought of kissing the spirited redhead. "Something about the way she speaks about golf, my game in general, that makes me think . . . she could . . ." *Make me love it again.* "Make a difference."

This time, the pause was so long, Wells checked to see if Buck had hung up.

Then finally, he said, "I'm sorry, did you say your caddie is a *woman*?"

Wells frowned. "What about it? You think that means she can't be qualified?"

Buck let out a breath in his ear. "Qualified or not, you've already become a joke out there. Now you're proposing a tour comeback with a woman carrying your bag? Have you thought about how that's going to look, son? If another player made the same attempt, he'd probably be called progressive. But you? They're just going to think it's another way for you to mock the establishment."

The word "mock" in the same sentence with Josephine made him want to throw a dumbbell at the mirror and shatter it to the ground. "First of all, Buck, I think you're forgetting that I don't give a flying fuck what anyone thinks." *Draw back the irrita-tion.* His mentor was his only hope. He'd be screwing himself *and* Josephine over if he lost his temper. He'd gone into this phone call knowing it would be hard, hadn't he? "Second . . . she needs this."

That wasn't what he'd planned to say.

But when it came down to making the request about him or Josephine, his pride prevented him from asking for himself. Wells might not care what anyone thought about him, but there was still a significant part of him that wanted to make Buck proud. And that meant keeping his pride intact. Josephine *was* the main reason he was attempting to get back on the tour. He wouldn't really allow himself to hope for some fairy-tale return to greatness, so he went with the simplest truth.

Besides, that information wouldn't go any further than Buck and the tour chairmen.

"Her family's pro shop was devastated by this storm and she's just . . . good. All right? A good person. But I can just tell she's also clever at reading the course." Wells's mouth nudged up at one corner. "She used to whisper conflicting advice to me from behind the rope. One time, she outright argued with my caddie—"

"Wait. Whoa whoa whoa, slow down. You're talking about that fangirl who used to hold up signs for you down in Florida?"

"She's not just some fangirl. She's smart. And dedicated. Or . . . she *was*." The throb behind Wells's eye intensified. "Look, she's in a bind. If I can finish in the money a few times, she can see her way out of it."

He could practically hear Buck processing the whole explana-tion. "Let me get this straight. You expect me to believe you're coming back on tour . . . purely out of goodwill. You want to help a fan rebuild her pro shop?"

Yes.

And maybe, on some level, she makes me want to try again. One last time.

Wells made a sound in his throat.

Buck's fingers tapped on an unseen piece of furniture. "I'll tell you something, but you didn't hear it from me."

"Done."

"The tour has been quiet this year. Viewership is down. There's no . . . Cinderella story. You know how the fans eat that kind of thing up. After all, you *were* the Cinderella story once." He paused. "Against my better judgment, I'll take this to the commissioner. Down-and-out golfer makes his return for a good cause."

Wells dug his fingers into the center of his aching forehead and rubbed. "If that's the story you need to go with to get me back in the lineup, so be it."

He ignored the voice telling him he'd live to regret that decision.

Bright and early on Tuesday morning, Josephine set down her suitcase on her parents' front stoop and willed herself to ring the doorbell. She had so much to tell them—and they weren't going to believe a word of it. Probably not until they saw her on television, broadcasting live from the Texas Open in San Antonio in two days' time.

It had been one week since Wells Whitaker blew back into her life and possibly changed it forever. Being offered a caddie position on the PGA tour was not something that happened to everyday people. In the golf world, caddying for a professional golfer was like finding a pot of gold at the end of the rainbow. Golfers made, in scientific terms, a *fuck-ton* of money. Winning a major tournament, such as the Masters, paid out *2.5 million dollars* for first place. Heck, coming in fortieth place earned thirty grand.

Caddies took 10 percent of the cut, in addition to their salaries.

Every night this week, she'd lain in bed well past midnight staring at the ceiling, spinning fantasy scenarios in her head. What if she could *actually* help Wells get his missing stroke back? What if he finished high in the money a couple of times? Not only would she be able to afford to rebuild the Golden Tee, but she wouldn't have to beg her endocrinologist for spare medical supplies. She wouldn't have to choose between groceries and rent money.

This unexpected fork in the road could be life changing.

Or, leaving Palm Beach when she could be finding a *realistic* solution to her family and personal problems could make things exponentially worse. She was putting her faith in Wells and it could cost her a lot of valuable time and effort.

There must have been part of Josephine that still believed in Wells, though. A piece of her that had never lost hope or counted him out, because staying home felt like a bigger risk than leaving. And *man*, she wanted him to win again so badly, the possibility was like a chocolate bar with almonds dangling in her face. Eating it could throw her blood sugar out of whack, but indulging in the anticipation tasted so good, she couldn't help but reach for it.

Her mother opened the door, pink towel in place around her head. "Joey-Roo. What are you doing standing out here?" Evelyn Doyle leaned to one side. "Is that a suitcase? Did you come for a little staycation? I have sugar-free cookies in the pantry."

She kissed her mother on the cheek. "No, not a staycation." Josephine picked up the suitcase and followed her mother inside. "But, obviously, I'll take some cookies."

"I always keep them on hand!" Evelyn yelled, hustling through the über-Floridian living room toward the kitchen. The entire house was decorated in various shades of yellow and green, indoor plants in abundance, ceiling fans whirring lazily. A moment later, her mother emerged from the kitchen, shaking a white-and-blue box. "Yum yum!"

Josephine snort-laughed and took the box, hesitating to open it. "Is Dad here?"

"He's in the backyard. Honey!" shouted her mother, pausing to listen. "Honey! Joey is here. Come inside. The man can't hear a damn thing, I swear."

"I can hear just fine," Jim blustered, ambling into the living room while folding the newspaper under his arm. "Hello, honey."

Cheek kisses were followed by her father gesturing to the suitcase with his folded-up newspaper. "What's that?"

"I have some news." Bold understatement. Her parents were golf fans—and knew quite well about her past devotion to Wells Whitaker. They were likely going to faint from shock. "Maybe you should sit before I tell you."

Evelyn and Jim exchanged a look, plopping down on their plastic-covered couch simultaneously. They were already smiling, because they trusted that whatever she said was going to be positive. They were all fired up and ready to be supportive, just like always.

If only they knew how much she'd let them down.

A notch formed in her throat while she prepared to speak.

She'd let the insurance lapse on the Golden Tee. Hadn't been taking care of her health, the way she'd promised to do in exchange for some independence.

Now she was betting on a long shot to fix everything. Would it pan out?

Yes. No.

Maybe.

Please. Let this work.

"Some volunteers helped me clean up the shop this week. It's still waterlogged and damaged, but the ruined inventory has been thrown away and we pumped out the water." She smiled at her father. "I think there's a chance we'll still be able to use Pop Pop's old register, once it dries out a little bit."

"That is *excellent* news, honey."

"Yes." She looked down at her suitcase, briefly wondering if she'd hit her head during the hurricane and this was an elaborate coma dream. "It's going to take some time before we . . . have the money to repair the shop. But once we do, I'm going to meet with a contractor about finally making the additions we've been talking about forever. It's going to be more functional and modern. We'll have the drive-through window and consultation lounge. The putting green outside. It's going to be bigger and better than ever. You'll see. We just have to be patient."

Her mother blew a raspberry. "Those darn insurance companies. They'll take your money easy enough, but God forbid you try to get some back."

"What your mother said."

"Yes. That's all very true." No more stalling. Josephine opened her mouth to continue, but her phone buzzed in the pocket of her jean shorts. "Er . . . hold on. Someone is texting me."

"Who is it?" Evelyn asked. "Is it the insurance company?"

"They don't text people, Mom."

Josephine's stomach jolted at the name on her screen: Wells.

Wells was texting her.

It hadn't stopped being weird.

The afternoon she'd taken him downtown for a haircut, they'd exchanged numbers out of necessity. After all, she was going to be working for him. Since then, however, he'd texted only once with her flight information and seven measly words.

Be in San Antonio by Tuesday night.

She'd reread and analyzed that single sentence all week. Did that mean he'd succeeded in reinserting himself into the tour? Because that was not going to be easy. The PGA tour officials took tradition and sportsmanship very seriously. Walking off the course in the middle of a round without consulting anyone, followed by a highly publicized disappearance from the public eye? Not very sporting, indeed.

Josephine tapped on her second text from Wells, hoping it would provide more insight than his last message. Perhaps what she could expect once she reached San Antonio, a tee time for Thursday morning, his overall feelings about the course itself.

Nope.

Wells: Bring a dress.

"A dress?" she muttered.

For what? Certainly not to wear while caddying. All she'd packed was the proper attire for spending four days traipsing around in the hot Texas sun. She'd have to swing home on the way to the airport in order to pack something fancier.

Josephine: Why?

Of course, he didn't answer. Wells Whitaker didn't like questions.

Josephine sighed. "While we're waiting for the repair money, I'm going to be out of town a lot. Traveling."

"Traveling?" Her mother lost some of the color in her face. "Where?"

Jim patted his wife's hand. This was going to be hard for Evelyn. Sudden changes to the daily routine of a diabetic meant adjustments up the wazoo. Mainly meal planning, but the change in time zones also meant rearranging her long-acting insulin schedule and preparing for big fluctuations in her blood sugar numbers. Diabetes was a bucking bronco of a condition and it didn't like change, which made traveling a challenge. While Josephine was growing up, they'd rarely gone anywhere outside of Florida as a result.

"This week, I'll be in San Antonio. Texas."

"Oh, I see." Jim beamed. "She's going to watch the tournament. Good for you, kiddo."

"Well," Josephine drew out. "I will be watching it in a *sense*. But I'll also be caddying for Wells Whitaker."

Evelyn and Jim looked at each other. And how they *laughed*.

"You really had us going for a second there, Joey-Roo," said Evelyn, dabbing tears of mirth from her eyes.

Josephine had seen this reaction coming. "Guys, I'm serious." She shook her phone at them. "Look, he's texting me right this second."

"Sure, he is," her father said with an exaggerated wink. "Ask him how he managed to birdie the fifth hole at Pebble Beach back in '21. Did he go into the rough on purpose?"

"Wells doesn't like questions."

Evelyn and Jim fell back against the plastic couch cushions, laughing.

"I knew you weren't going to believe me," Josephine called over their guffaws.

"She brought a suitcase as a prop and everything!" Evelyn hiccupped, before turning slightly serious. "Oh, Roo. It's not that we don't think you *could* caddie for Whitaker, but how in the world would that ever happen?"

Josephine debated telling them he'd arrived at the Golden Tee out of the blue, but they wouldn't believe that, either. Frankly, *she* was still trying to decipher the logistics of his unannounced arrival at Rolling Greens. "Just watch the tournament kick off on Thursday morning, okay?" She pointed at their entertainment center, which was used primarily to hold plants, but there was a television somewhere among all the greenery. "You're going to see me on TV. It'll be live coverage, so I won't be able to answer phone calls. Okay?"

"You're too much." Jim chuckled. "Where are you really going?"

"Did you pack an extra test kit?"

"Yes."

"What about your emergency shot? Are you traveling with someone who knows how to use it?" Her mother stood, hands clasped beneath her chin. "Are you meeting Tallulah somewhere? She's always so good about making sure you have a sugar stash for lows."

"Tallulah is in Antarctica, remember? And I'm good, Mom," Josephine called over her shoulder, already wheeling her baggage to the front door. If she stayed, Evelyn would inevitably beg her to open the suitcase so she could perform a medical supply checklist and it would never suffice. Packing an actual *doctor* in her carry-on wouldn't be enough to make Evelyn stop worrying. "Don't forget. Thursday morning."

"Ohhhh-kay!" Evelyn and Jim singsonged simultaneously.

"You betcha," tacked on her mother.

Josephine gestured to the Uber waiting for her at the curb. "I'm leaving for Texas now. As soon as I stop at home to get a dress, I'm going to the airport."

"To caddie for your idol, Wells Whitaker," Jim said, with an exaggerated wink.

"That's right."

She closed the door of the Uber on the sound of their laughter.

CHAPTER EIGHT

Wells had done it.

Somehow, he'd convinced the golf gods to bring him back on tour.

When Josephine arrived at the resort in San Antonio, she went straight to the clubhouse with her carry-on—now containing a dress and heels—because she wasn't going to bother checking in to her room if Wells hadn't succeeded. The ornate, Spanish-style building with high-domed ceilings was a hive of activity when Josephine walked in, sports reporters everywhere, caddies she recognized from television commiserating in groups—all of them men.

Imposter syndrome blocked her progress and she almost turned around and ran straight back out the door. It helped to remember that she'd yelled *you suck* at some of those caddies at one time or another while watching them on television. And she'd meant it. Thoroughly.

Garnering her courage, Josephine moseyed up to the desk clearly marked CADDIE CHECK-IN, relieved when the woman behind the computer monitor gave her an open, friendly smile. "Hello. How can I help you?"

"Hello." Josephine pushed down the handle of her carry-on suitcase. "I'm checking in. I'm caddying tomorrow for Wells Whitaker."

A good half of the conversations in the room seemed to die at once.

The woman's kind expression froze on her face, her eyes ticking to the rest of the room briefly, before landing back on Josephine. "Wells Whitaker. I just want to make sure I heard you correctly. The acoustics in here can be a challenge."

"That's all right. Yes, I said Wells Whitaker."

"Oh." A jerky nod. The poor woman was probably pressing a button beneath the table to alert security. Silence was spreading in the room like a ripple in a pond and all Josephine could do was stand there, bite the inside of her cheek, and let the fire climb the back of her neck. What had she done? Flown all the way to San Antonio after two text messages? To caddie for a highly unreliable man? "Okay, let me just pull up his information . . ." The woman reared back in her seat. "Oh! Here he is. I thought . . . well, I didn't know he was competing." She scanned the screen for a moment. "You're Josephine Doyle?"

The air flat-out vacated her lungs.

It was real. This was really, actually happening.

"Yes, that's me."

The woman nodded, giving her a once-over that was almost . . . proud? "Well. I'll definitely be tuning in to watch tomorrow, Josephine." She turned to face a rolling file cabinet behind her, seeming surprised to find a blue folder with Josephine's and Wells's names printed on the top. She handed it across the desk with a flourish. "Here is your schedule for the next five days. Your official pass should be in there, to be worn around your neck at all times during competition. You'll need it to gain access to the caddie locker room, where you'll find your uniform tomorrow morning. There's also the almighty scorebook in the folder, course yardage charts, and some drink tickets for the welcome cocktail party tonight."

"Welcome cocktail party?" Josephine repeated. That explained the dress.

"Why yes, it's tradition. We have to give the golfers a chance to rile one another up before they tee off. Makes things interesting." She reached across the desk and gave Josephine a conspiratorial arm squeeze. "Don't let them rattle you."

"I won't." Easier said than done. She could still feel a dozen sets of eyes piercing into her back. "Do you know if Wells has arrived?"

"Impossible. I would have heard everyone gossiping like middle schoolers."

"Or alerting the local authorities." Her new friend laughed, and Josephine gave her a grateful look. "Thanks for your help."

"There's more where that came from. I'm Beth Anne and I'll be here all week."

Josephine turned from the desk to find the entire room full of caddies staring at her.

Some of their smirks were curious, others were an obvious intimidation tactic, but they were *all* smirking in one way or another. If they'd overheard she was caddying for Wells, their reaction wasn't the least bit surprising, since he'd won the unofficial award for Biggest Dick in Golf five years running.

One of the reporters had noticed interest spiking in Josephine's direction and was furiously flipping through her notes, obviously trying to make sense of the newcomer, and Josephine's head swam at the very idea of being questioned by the press, so she tucked the folder beneath her arm, yanked up the handle of her carry-on, and beelined for the exit.

Josephine arrived at the buzzing hotel lobby a few minutes later, intending to check in and get the key to the cheapest room in the resort, which she'd booked earlier in the week. Leaving that sort of thing to Wells didn't seem wise and she wasn't going to lose this opportunity over a few hundred dollars.

But when she gave the clerk her name, he only looked at her in confusion.

"I have two reservations for you, Miss Doyle."

"Oh." A tiny bit of pressure ebbed from her chest. "He did it. He booked me a room."

"Yes . . ." The young man's eyes ticked between her and the computer monitor. "I'm going to go ahead and give you the room I think will make your stay most . . . comfortable."

"Great."

Five minutes later, Josephine stepped into the most palatial, over-the-top hotel room she'd ever seen in her life. No, it couldn't even be termed a "room." It had three seating areas.

"Three?" She let go of her suitcase just inside the door and wandered through the suite in a daze. "But I only have one butt," she muttered.

Her toes sank into the soft, rich burgundy carpeting. Soothing music played from the television, the air-conditioning taking her nerves away on an unseen breeze. A giant, jetted tub called to her from the bathroom and she made a short, breathy sound, her hands flying to her mouth. She bypassed the rustic four-poster bed sitting in *its own separate room* and went straight to the tub, twisting the hot water nozzle and stripping off her travel clothes. One did not simply pass up the chance to soak in a tub when one's apartment shower was the size of a shoebox and had all the water pressure of a limp handshake.

Once the tub was filled to a steaming 60 percent, Josephine shook the black elastic band out of her hair, massaging the ponytail tension headache from her scalp, and stepped into the porcelain haven. She dunked straight under and emerged from the surface with a moan that could easily be interpreted by her neighbors to mean something else entirely. But so be it.

This was paradise. Traipsing all over a golf course and dealing with Wells's surly attitude would all be worth it if she could return to this room at the end of each day. Josephine stayed in the bathtub so long, the water started to cool. So she added a little more hot, the soothing temperature enticing her loudest, most appreciative moan yet—and the noisy gurgle of running water muffled the sound of a door opening and closing.

Josephine shut off the nozzle with a frown, her head turning toward the bathroom entrance. Surely, that had come from next door.

Those footsteps, too. They were coming from the hallway, right?

All six feet two inches of Wells appeared in the bathroom entrance.

Josephine screamed, the piercing wail echoing off numerous marble surfaces.

"Jesus Christ!" Wells boomed, turning around quickly to give her his broad back.

But not before he saw her naked breasts. Looked right at them. Oh God. *Oh God!*

She lunged over the side of the tub for a towel and stood, wrapping it around herself. "What are you doing in here?"

"Funny," he said evenly, despite the muscular tension in his shoulders. "I was just about to ask you the same question."

"This is the room they gave me at check-in." Finished securing the white, luxurious terry cloth about her body, Josephine smacked her forehead. "Once I saw the room, I should have known it was yours. I'm . . . this . . . *ughhhh.*"

Still facing away, Wells crossed his arms. "What the hell does that mean?"

"I mean, obviously this room is yours. The bathtub bamboozled me. Drew me in like a gator to a roasted ham or I would have pieced it together—"

"Can I turn around yet?"

"If you don't mind that I'm in a towel?"

Briefly, he tipped his head back. "I think I can suffer through it, belle."

"Then . . ." She glanced at her reflection over the bathroom sink and winced at the black half-circles of mascara beneath her eyes, the wet hair dripping onto her shoulders. "I guess so."

A beat passed before he turned around again, focusing on a spot over her shoulder before finally making eye contact. Were his pupils bigger than before or was the steam distorting her vision? Because she could almost feel her own dilating to the size of salad plates over being in close proximity to this tall, sinewy athlete in the intimate setting of a bathroom. Wearing no clothing while he was fully dressed. Something about that contrast was sending an unwanted ripple of goose bumps down her spine, as was the fact that he looked *a lot* healthier than the last time she'd seen him. The cords of his colorfully inked forearms stood out like he'd gotten back into lifting weights, a very distracting biceps vein disappearing up the sleeve of his shirt.

Stop looking.

"I booked us the same kind of room. Yours should look exactly like this." Did his attention drop to the knotted towel between her breasts, pricking every inch of skin below her neck? Or were her nipples puckering from the air-conditioning? "My name was on both reservations, so they must have given you my key by mistake."

"Oh." So . . . he *had* booked her this extravagant suite? Why? "I would have been happy with a normal room."

"All that moaning you were doing in the bathtub suggests otherwise."

Indignation snapped in her throat. "If you heard me moaning, why did you walk in here?"

"Did you hear yourself? You sounded like an injured animal. I thought someone was on the verge of death." His gaze ticked to the tub, back to her. "Is this your first bath?"

"Says the man who almost needed a chainsaw to cut his hair last week." They smirked at each other. "Women don't just miraculously appear in your room."

He propped a forearm on the doorjamb and raised a single eyebrow at her.

"Oh, I see. They do."

Something about the realization made her skin shrink. But it wasn't jealousy. No way. Sure, she couldn't help but have a healthy appreciation for an attractive athlete with a prolific posterior, but that wasn't why she'd supported him all those years. She'd been his number one fan because, at the height of his success, there was no one more exciting than him on the course. No one more daring and irreverent. He'd never been in it for the accolades—she'd witnessed love for the game in his every move and it had drawn her in.

Women could come stocked in his mini fridge for all she cared.

That spike lodged in her neck was simply a product of having her bath cut short.

"For some absurd reason . . ." Wells pushed off the door frame, running a hand down the back of his neck. "I feel the need to clarify. Women have appeared in my room twice—and both times, I called security. It wasn't a welcome surprise, unlike a moaning redhead in my tub—"

"What are we going to do about the mix-up?" she interrupted, alarmingly relieved while still being distinctly embarrassed. "Should I call the front desk?"

Wells regarded her levelly for several moments. "No. You stay here. I'll go down and get a key to the other room."

Josephine pondered that. "But if the other room was meant for me, there could be a man waiting in my bathtub." Batting her eyelashes, she slipped between Wells and the door frame, staunchly ignoring the butterflies that scattered in her stomach when he gave her mouth a prolonged look. "I should probably take it."

He turned to face Josephine where she now stood in the living space, a muscle popping ominously in his cheek. "You're here to focus on golf." He gave her a meaningful look. "So am I."

All at once, she became very aware that this man was now her boss—and he was right. They were in Texas to play golf. Getting into a bickering match with a golfer who could change her life by winning was not the wisest move, was it? And being that Wells was her boss, she should spend as little time as possible standing in front of him in an extremely brief towel. "I'm focused."

"Good," he said, back to having his arms crossed. Aloof.

"Are *you*?"

"I'm always focused. It just hasn't translated into winning lately."

"What are you focusing on?" she asked, even though she should probably shut up and get dressed.

"Golf," Wells spat out. "I thought we established that."

"What part of it? Your swing? The leaderboard? The shot you're taking? The next hole?"

"We talked about the questions, Josephine," he snapped.

She held her ground. "You're going to have to start answering them or I won't be able to do my job, Wells."

He adjusted his stance, leaning forward a little, wafting his scent in her direction. He smelled like pine and a hint of something else. Like the interior of a new car. Warm leather? She couldn't quite put her finger on it, but she shouldn't be envisioning things. Things like dragging her nose along the curve of his strong neck to further study the origin of those leather and pine notes. "My *old* caddie didn't ask questions," Wells pointed out.

Josephine squared her shoulders and took a step in his direction. "I wouldn't have taken advice from your old caddie two inches from the hole. He was a banana brain."

"A . . ." Was he holding back a laugh? "You're going to have to learn some meaner insults if we're going to be spending time together."

"Fine. He was human-shaped shit stuffed into some khakis."

"Better."

"Thank you. Answer the question. Which *part* of golf are you focusing on?"

"All of it. At once." The words clipped their way out of him. "My pathetic world ranking, the possibility of another shitty finish, the disappointment from everyone, from . . . Buck, the fact that the fucking club feels like a foreign object in my hand now, when it used to feel like an extension of my arm." He tilted his head, took a step closer to Josephine. "Does that answer your annoying question?"

His honesty created a sharp ache in the center of her chest, but she refused to let it show on her face. "It's a starting point," she managed.

Wells snorted. "A starting point to where?"

They were toe-to-toe now.

Close enough that she could feel his breath on her face.

When had that happened?

His fingertips were near enough to the edge of her towel that it seemed almost natural for him to brush those digits along the fronts of her thighs. But it wasn't natural. Not with her boss. So she suppressed the urge to inch forward and find out how his thumbs would feel digging into her hips. And yeah. Wow. She didn't need any more proof that her dry spell had turned into a dry era.

"I guess we'll find out where you're headed . . . together," Josephine whispered.

"Together." This time, there was no mistaking the way his light brown eyes tracked down to her mouth, his chest expanding. Enough that it almost touched the knot of her towel. Ever so briefly, his attention strayed to the bedroom located over her shoulder and his eyelids sagged. But just as quickly as it happened, he locked his jaw and stepped back. "I'll meet you outside your room tonight at seven."

"For what?"

"The party, belle. We're going together."

Stupid pulse. Please stop racing. "Why?"

The glint in his eyes was sort of . . . dangerous looking? "Because I'm not going to give the other caddies a chance to eat you alive."

"I can handle myself," Josephine insisted.

"Yes, but if they came for you, it would piss me off."

"Does anything *not* piss you off?"

Wells ignored that. "And we need me calm and focused, right? We've already decided that." He backed up until he reached his suitcase, picking it up with a very distracting biceps flex. "You're not one of these women who takes a million years to get ready and makes us late, are you?"

"No."

"Great."

Wells started toward the door, then stopped, changing directions toward the mini fridge. Josephine watched curiously as he yanked open the door, observed the contents, and slapped it shut again. "There are juices in there, if you need them. Apple and orange. Do those work for you?"

It was embarrassing, really, the way she had a hard time finding her breath in order to answer that gruffly delivered question. This man was rude to her one second, and in the next, he was considering her blood sugar needs. What complicated corner of the universe had he come from? "Yes. And I brought stuff, too. Glucose tabs and . . . thanks."

He left the room with a grunt.

Josephine sat down slowly in one of the many needless seating areas. She'd known joining Wells on his comeback was going to be an interesting ride. One hour in and she was already positive she'd underestimated exactly *how* interesting.

CHAPTER NINE

She *was* one of those women who took forever to get ready.

Wells stood across from Josephine's door, his back against the hallway wall, and attempted to glare her into emerging. He could hear her jogging back and forth in there. Between what and what? Why were the things she needed to get ready spread out all over the room? It didn't make any *sense*.

Maybe after he'd left, she'd taken another bath, since she'd loved the first one so much.

The memory of her moaning made him curse, a weary hand raking down his face. That sound was never going to fade away, was it? All husky and uninhibited. If she reacted that way to a tub full of water, he wanted to know what kind of noise she'd make if he went down on her. Just . . . spread her thighs open and fucked her with his tongue. His goal wouldn't be to make her moan, though, it would be to make her scream.

Wells cleared his throat hard and started to pace.

He never should have gone into that bathroom. As a man who had been around the block a few times, he should know the difference between a moan of pleasure and a moan of pain. But some intuition had informed him that Josephine was inside that bathroom—and the mere possibility that she could be hurt had propelled him forward without a second thought. His impulsiveness had cost him. Big-time.

Now he'd seen her pale, round tits and those berry-colored nipples.

Life was going to be a lot harder from now on.

Harder. Yeah, that about covered it.

Knowing her naked body rivaled the temptation of her mouth . . . was going to be taking up a lot of space in his head. There was no way around that fact. No way to forget her thighs, slippery from a bath. Or her skin, softened and dewy from the heat.

"Fuck my life," Wells muttered, right as Josephine dove through the hotel-room door.

"Sorry! Sorry. My parents called."

"Your *what* . . ."

He'd been all prepared to complain. To give her a hard time about taking eight hundred years to throw on some clothes. Unfortunately, as soon as she came out of the room in a strapless minidress, he forgot the state they were in, let alone remembered to be angry she'd taken so long.

Nothing had ever been more worth it.

He'd never had a favorite color before, but the deep emerald of her dress instantly became the one. It covered more than the towel had earlier, so why did it make her skin look so different? Almost . . . glowing? She'd done something to her hair, too, because it was usually up in a messy knot. Now it was down and sort of flowy? Shiny, too.

Oh shit, and then she looked up at him, rubbing her red lips together.

Red.

Maybe that was his favorite color.

Focus, man. "A call with your parents took an extra half an hour?"

"It does when they think you're experiencing a delusional episode."

"Come again?"

"They don't believe me. That I'm here caddying for you." She fiddled with something in her purse. Was that a purse? It was the size of a wallet, yet it appeared to hold a hundred items. Chapstick, a mini comb, eye drops. A green, cylindrical pen-like object and alcohol swabs. Was that her insulin? He'd done some research on type 1 diabetes before coming to San Antonio, enough to know that there were more ways than one to administer insulin. Since she didn't appear to have a pump, he assumed she took shots. "At first, my parents thought it was funny," Josephine continued, recapturing his attention. "But my father is now speculating that I suffered a concussion during the hurricane. My mother's theory is that I met a man and eloped, but that might just be wishful thinking on her part. Either way, they're ready to call the FBI."

"You know, I can easily clear this up." He waved a hand at her purse-thing. "Let's go. FaceTime them."

"Really?" Hesitantly, she opened her bag again. "Right now?"

"Yes, right now," he said, impatiently. "Unless you'd like to spend another half hour brushing your hair or something."

"Thank you for noticing." She pressed her lips together, seemingly to trap a laugh, and he found himself wishing she would just let it out already. It had been a long time since he'd heard her laugh and it had probably been at something someone *else* said, while she was standing in the crowd behind the rope. He wouldn't have minded being the reason for that laugh just once. "Okay, here goes," she said, the distinct ring of FaceTime connecting filling the hallway. "Hey guys, there is someone here who wants to speak to you."

Wells took the phone, frowning down at the screen. "You've raised a daughter who can't be ready on time, even though she had a full four hours. I hope you're proud of yourselves."

One of the people staring back at him had pink curlers in her hair.

The man was wearing an apron.

Something sizzled on the stove behind them.

"You're . . . ," the man started, setting down the spatula in his hand. "You're actually there with Wells Whitaker, Joey-Roo."

"Yes, I know, Dad. I told you."

Joey-Roo? Wells mouthed at Josephine.

She rolled her eyes at him.

"How did you manage to birdie the fifth hole at Pebble Beach back in '21? Did you go into the rough on purpose?"

Wells thought back. "Yes. I didn't like the angle after my drive landed, so I bypassed the rest of the fairway and gave myself a better position to the green."

"Brilliant! I *knew* it," whooped Josephine's father, before he promptly lost his grip on the phone and it went crashing to the ground, giving Wells a sweeping view of their über-Floridian household.

He squinted an eye. "Dear God, that is a lot of plants."

"Be careful how you speak about my brothers and sisters," Josephine deadpanned. "They can hear you."

The golfer shook his head at her. "As you can see, she hasn't eloped or suffered a brain injury. But she might get fired if she keeps me waiting this long ever again."

With that, he hung up the phone and handed it back to Josephine.

"Ready?"

Appearing dazed, she took back the device. "You didn't even say goodbye."

"Yes, I know." He put his hand on the small of her back and ushered her toward the elevator, trying very hard not to move his thumb, even though it itched to memorize the spot. "When you draw out goodbyes on the phone, there are inevitable promises to call again soon. I'm not falling into that trap."

"Who hurt you, Wells?"

He ignored the twinge in his chest and stabbed the down button for the elevator.

Surprisingly, one of six sets of doors opened almost immediately. Wells sighed when he saw half a dozen other people were already occupying the car. They were obviously staying at the resort specifically for the tournament, because their jaws hinged open when they noticed Wells. He was inclined to wait for the next elevator, but Josephine stepped inside without hesitation, and since he wasn't about to let her go down alone, he was left with no choice but to follow suit.

The lack of space put them in close quarters. Enough that when the elevator jolted and began traveling downward, he had to brace a hand above Josephine's head or risk their bodies colliding. From his vantage point, the bow of her upper lip was even more distinct. There was also a little freckle buried in the right side of her hairline. And God, her skin . . .

Christ. Get it together, man.

Now would be a good time to recognize one very important fact. Technically, Josephine worked for him. Meaning, he needed to stop wondering if she had a sensitive neck. Or if she'd touched herself in the bathtub. Shit like that was off limits. He might not be the most ethical of golfers—or human beings—but he would *not* take advantage of his position as her boss.

So if she could stop smelling like flowers and sneaking looks up at him with her beautiful green eyes, that would be fucking amazing.

"What pit of hell did the nickname Joey-Roo come from?" Wells grumbled.

He regretted his tone when she choked a little. "Oh. Well, they started calling me Joey when I was a baby, which as you know, is what they call a baby kangaroo. Hence, Roo."

"Ridiculous."

"It's better than all of *your* nicknames."

"Which are?"

"The Prick of Putting, the Doomsday Driver. And my personal favorite, Unhappy Gilmore."

Someone behind him snorted. Another coughed.

Josephine bit her lip, her body shaking with mirth. Would she still be laughing if he backed her up tight to the wall and took over the job of sinking his teeth into that lip?

You're not going to find out.

Although . . . was she thinking the same thing? His caddie's gaze skated down to his lips, before zipping away, a flush creeping into her cheeks. Was he utterly insane for putting himself into a situation where he would be spending hours upon hours upon days with a woman he found this attractive, while also having her on his payroll?

"Wells," she said huskily. "It's our turn."

He shot a look over his shoulder to find the entire elevator had been vacated and they were the only remaining occupants. Meanwhile he was still towering over Josephine in the corner. Music and laughter from the party had invaded the tiny space and somehow, he hadn't heard a thing. Cursing inwardly, he backed up, gesturing for her to precede him.

"After you."

"Oooh." She sailed by with a smirk. "Careful, they'll start calling you the Gallant Golfer, the Princely Putter—"

Wells snorted, catching up to her in one stride and walking

beside her down the lantern-lit hallway. "I just don't want to deny you the fashionably late entrance you so desperately wanted."

"How long exactly are we going to dwell on this? Until you find something else to tease me about?"

They paused outside of the entrance to the ballroom, waiting for the group in front of them to give their names to the clipboard-toting young woman. "That sounds about right. Got anything good?"

"I'm a treasure trove of material, Whitaker, but you're going to have to work for it."

Wells suddenly wished he'd blown off the pointless party and taken Josephine to dinner, instead. Maybe it wasn't too late? Sharing a meal with one's caddie was the furthest thing from unusual. In fact, it was normal. Expected. And Wells was dead positive that he would enjoy talking to her more than anyone on the other side of those doors. "Listen, the food in there is going to be fancy and bite-sized. Maybe we should—"

Josephine gasped and gripped his forearm, her attention focused on something inside the event. "Oh my God, it's Jun Nakamura."

He was forced to switch gears. "What about him?"

"What *about* him? Oh nothing, just a couple of major titles." Stars sparkled in her eyes. "His precision is incredible."

She was . . . fangirling? For *another* golfer?

Envy dug into his throat like a rusty nail.

"What happened to Wells's Belle?" he half-shouted.

"Maybe if he has an earlier tee time than us tomorrow, I'll go see him in action. What do you think I should write on his sign?"

"*Nothing*, Josephine. You're not making him a sign."

Slowly, her mouth spread into a grin. "I thought you said you could take a little trash talk. The vein in your forehead leaves me skeptical."

Wells stared down at her.

His heart dislodged itself from behind his jugular, moving back into place, but still pumping at an uncomfortable rate.

She'd been teasing him about cheering for another golfer.

And he'd swallowed it, hook, line, and sinker.

A lot of things occurred to Wells at once. The fact that he really liked Josephine, probably too much, was first among them. Second, he started to wonder if he might grow to trust her. Like, actually *trust* her. One of the reasons he never kept a caddie around for long was his inability to believe that (a.) someone might know more than him. Or (b.) want the best for him.

The one time he'd experienced those things was with Buck Lee. The one time he'd trusted anyone had been with his mentor, too. But Buck's friendship had been conditional. Dependent on Wells's continuing to win.

Wells swore he'd never place that kind of faith in anyone again.

And he wouldn't.

But for the first time in a long time . . . he was tempted.

In more ways than one.

CHAPTER TEN

Walking into the welcome party for the Texas Open was Josephine's version of going backstage at the Grammys. It was a veritable who's who of golf. The athletes she'd been watching either on television or from the sidelines were suddenly inches away, yucking it up in business casual, surrounded by tasteful sconce lighting and vases of lush, white peonies. In the interest of being honest with herself, no one revved her fangirl engine like Wells Whitaker, her perpetually aggravated escort, but he didn't need to know that.

Now that she was his caddie, any fanlike behavior would be unprofessional.

After five years of devotion, however, she couldn't quash Whitaker fever completely, so she'd painted a tiny tribute on her toenails, just to keep the spirit alive. Which was safe, because there would never be a situation where he saw her barefoot.

Er . . . *another* one, anyway.

She'd make sure of it.

Caddying on the PGA Tour was a once-in-a-lifetime opportunity and she wouldn't blow it by noticing . . . *things* about Wells. Things about him she never would have known before spending some time with him. For one, he was very sensitive about his former mentor. When the topic of Buck Lee came up in conversation, he looked down at the ground. Like an automatic tic. Another trait she'd noticed was that Wells did nice things, like accompany her to the party, offer her a dream job, check her mini fridge for juice . . . but he seemed to feel the need to balance out those kind deeds with a lot of growling and complaining.

Josephine's thoughts were interrupted when Wells plucked a glass of champagne from a passing tray and handed it to her, gruffly asking the waiter for a nonalcoholic beer. He raised an eyebrow at Josephine, as if inviting a comment, but she only returned his stare.

"Thank you," she said, setting the flute down on a nearby table. "But I'll pass tonight. There's a dance floor and no one wants me to end up there."

"Oh," he said, coughing. "I disagree."

"No, really. It's a whole situation."

"As your employer, I should know up front what we're dealing with."

They traded a silent look over the word *employer*. Their relationship, as it was now, didn't necessarily feel like a boss-employee relationship, but that could very well change in the morning once competition started. Josephine let out a breath. "There is only one musical act that can make me dance. If that group comes on, it's finger guns and hip thrust city."

This was the closest to laughing that she'd ever seen Wells. "You know I'm going to ask which band."

"And I told you, you're going to have to work for things to tease me about."

"It's the Spice Girls or something, isn't it?"

"Cold."

"Timberlake."

"Freezing. You'll never get it. Sorry." Josephine pursed her lips and looked around the room, noticing for the first time that nearly every head was turned in their direction. "I guess it's going to be up to us to mingle, since none of your friends are approaching."

Wells accepted the nonalcoholic beer from the waiter and tipped it back, drawing Josephine's attention to the strong lines of his throat, before she determinedly dragged it away. "You think I have friends?" He used the back of his wrist to swipe moisture from his upper lip. "That's adorable."

"There isn't even one person in this room you can tolerate?"

"I'm tolerating you, aren't I?"

She couldn't possibly be sensing a flutter in her belly over that. Tolerating someone didn't pass as a compliment. "Besides me."

"Nope."

Surely this man wasn't a total lone wolf. "Do you have any friends *outside* of golf?"

Wells shrugged, rubbing at the back of his neck. He started to set his beer down, then changed his mind, keeping it in his hand. *Look at that.* She'd landed on something.

"Few years back, during a charity pro-am," he started, referencing the tournament where a professional golfer gets paired with an amateur, who is usually a celebrity in some capacity, "I got stuck with this hockey player as my teammate. Have you heard of Burgess Abraham?"

Josephine started. "Uh . . . yeah. I don't even have an interest in hockey and I know who that is. Isn't he constantly going viral for being somewhat . . . volatile?"

"That's him." Wells rolled a shoulder. "Anyway, he lives in Boston, but he shows up occasionally to spectate when I'm in California, since he's got a vacation home in Monterey. I've gone to one or two of his games, too. We go for a beer—maybe. Nothing is set in stone. But I wouldn't call us *friends*, so if he shows up, I never said that."

She shook her head. "Why are men like this?"

"Let me guess, you have someone you call *bestie*." He shuddered.

"Proudly."

"Who?"

"Tallulah." Saying her best friend's name made her throat sting, so she swallowed hard. "She's a future marine biologist who wants to specialize in winter wildlife. Ironic for a Florida girl, right? She's been studying penguins as an intern in Antarctica for almost a year." Pride in her friend brought a smile to Josephine's face. "You might remember her. She came with me to cheer you on a few times."

Wells shook his head. "Must have been too distracted by your aggressive chanting."

She hummed.

Why was he studying her so hard? Was the concept of friendship so foreign to him? "You . . . miss her. A lot."

"Yes," she said, pressure creeping in behind her eyes. "A lot."

After a long moment, Wells nodded.

He started to take another sip of his beer, but he hesitated to press the bottle to his lips when a group of men entered the room doing a lot of laughing and back-slapping.

One of them was Buck Lee.

Now in his mid-sixties, the legend himself didn't spend a lot of time in front of cameras anymore. He'd retired two decades ago, but his indelible mark on the game kept his influence strong in the golf world, as evidenced by the room quieting at his entrance.

He wasn't tall or short, falling somewhere in between, his bald head covered by a tweed newsboy cap. He walked with several tour golfers, all of whom Josephine recognized, since they were all leaderboard regulars, including Chance Montgomery, Ryan Kim, and Buster Calhoun. As one, they slowed to a stop in the middle of the room and basked in the crowd's undivided attention, before breaking off into smaller groups.

Buck's eyes settled on Wells and Josephine, as if he'd known they were there all along, but was simply taking his time acknowledging them. Wells didn't move a muscle, but there was a sudden electrical charge in the air.

"Are you two on speaking terms?" Josephine ventured.

"Sure." Wells's tone was one of forced nonchalance. "He ran interference with the powers that be to get me back on the tour."

You got your answer. Let it drop. "Things just seem a little strained."

Or just invade his privacy.

"I'd rather not talk about it, Josephine."

She nodded. That was fair. "Okay."

"I guess I just expected my mentor to be a little more . . . constant. In my life. But I guess my losing streak was making him look bad. Can't really blame him for wanting to keep up appearances," he finished dryly.

"It sounds like you do. Blame him."

Wells cut her a look. "He knew what he was getting into. The day he met me, I had a black eye and two pockets full of silverware from the country club restaurant. I've never pretended to be anything other than exactly what I am."

Josephine chewed that over. "Good to know. What are you planning on robbing from the premises tonight?"

"What?" He snorted. "Nothing."

She quirked a brow. "Why not?"

"Because I'm not the same person . . . I was." A low whistle from Wells. "Wow. I walked right into that, didn't I?" Slowly, he rocked back on his heels. "Are you implying that what happened with Buck was my fault?"

"No," Josephine said firmly. "How could I do that? I wasn't

there. And if I'm being totally honest, I'm always going to default to being . . ."

"What?"

"On your side," she said as fast as possible, trying not to enjoy the way the lines around his mouth softened. "I just think hurt feelings might cause a person to see a situation differently."

"Do I strike you as the kind of guy who gets hurt *feelings*?"

"I am very sorry to inform you that everyone has feelings."

"I'm going to deeply regret hiring you."

"No, you're not." A lot like they'd done in the hotel room earlier, Josephine and Wells seemed to gravitate toward each other when having a conversation, until their toes were pressed together and she had to tilt her head back. And she couldn't help but wonder if it looked . . . intimate to the rest of the party.

Of course it did. Because it was.

There was no other word for feeling his body heat through her clothes.

And reacting to it with skips of her pulse.

In the interest of professionalism, Josephine eased away, ignoring the way he frowned over the move. He regarded her curiously for a moment, then said, "You told me trash talk doesn't hurt your feelings. What does?" A thought seemed to occur. "And please say something besides 'bitter assholes who rip my signs in half' because I just stopped seeing it every time I blink."

He really just let that roll off his tongue. Like it wasn't a big deal that he'd been dwelling. "You're nicer than you think, Wells."

"No, I'm not." He grunted. "What has hurt your feelings? He better not have a name."

"Okay, do you want to make me a *list* of unacceptable responses?"

"Go ahead. I'm done."

Josephine shook her head at him, then took a moment to

think. "The summer I turned twelve, my neighbor wouldn't let me help with her garden. She'd just moved in next door to us and immediately, she had a tractor come dig up the concrete slab in her backyard. All these white trellises were installed and she tied purple bougainvillea to them, so they would climb the side of her house. It was like an explosion of color happening outside of my bedroom window. So I went over one day and asked to help. I wanted to learn how to garden so we could make our backyard just as pretty—and she said no. That hurt my feelings. It's why my parents went out and bought a hundred houseplants. They made me an indoor garden."

She didn't expect Wells to be hanging on her every word, especially over a story about flora that was long dead by now, but he appeared to be . . . rapt? "So, what? Your feelings get hurt when someone rejects your help?"

"Yes," she said simply, remembering the way her neighbor had noticed her glucose monitor and gotten nervous, like she didn't want to be responsible for a medical emergency.

He hummed in his throat and continued to watch her. "Are you good at *accepting* help?"

"No." Heat slowly built on her cheeks. "Wow. I walked right into that, didn't I?"

He tipped back his beer with a little too much gusto. "Afraid so."

"You don't have to look so smug."

"I'm sorry, I have no control over my face right now."

"Maybe I'll lose control of my finger and poke you right in the eye—"

"Wells," came a voice to their left.

It was Buck Lee. Holding out his hand for a shake.

Wells cleared his throat. "Buck."

It wasn't lost on Josephine that when Buck eyeballed the nonalcoholic beer label in Wells's hand, he appeared somewhat skeptical. He didn't bother to hide it, either, and she couldn't help but be disappointed in the legend. She definitely wouldn't be mentioning this to her father, who owned a commemorative set of Buck Lee pint glasses laser-engraved with the man's face. "This must be your new caddie," said the older man, extending a hand in Josephine's direction.

"Buck, meet Josephine Doyle," Wells drawled, his smooth tone contradicting his tense demeanor.

They shook. "Looking forward to tomorrow," Buck said. "Ought to be . . . interesting."

Josephine willed the champagne glass back into her hand. Weirdly, it didn't appear. "Yes. Heard we're getting a little rain tonight. The ball should be sticking."

"Indeed." Buck gave her a blithe smile. She worked on a golf course, so it was far from the first time in her life that she'd been discounted straight off the bat because of her gender, but just like always, she would let her results do the talking. "Mind if I have a word alone, Wells? Nothing major, just a little business."

Wells glanced at Josephine, a vein ticking in his temple. "It can't wait?"

"Already too busy for the old friend who installed you back on the tour?"

"I didn't say that," Wells countered firmly, still appearing conflicted.

That's when it occurred to Josephine that he didn't want to leave her alone. Even for a few minutes? He'd said something about the caddies eating her alive, but they couldn't possibly be *that* bad. Even if they were, she was woman enough to handle it and then some.

"Go." She tipped her head toward the lantern-lit terrace. "I want to grab some air, anyway. Nice to meet you, Mr. Lee."

"Please, call me Buck."

She nodded and gave Wells a quick smile. "Catch up with you later."

Without giving Wells a chance to protest, she wove her way through a sea of recognizable faces, feeling a little bit like she was dreaming. A week ago, she'd been standing in knee-deep sludge, stuffing ruined inventory into black garbage bags, praying an alligator wasn't lurking in the water—because Florida—and now? Wearing her best dress at a lavish party full of golf studs. Life never stopped throwing curveballs.

Josephine almost gasped out loud when she stepped onto the terrace.

The branches of a giant magnolia tree stretched overhead, flickering, jewel-tone lanterns dangling low. The conversation was more hushed outside, perhaps because it overlooked the manicured golf course and the setting predisposed people to silence. The air was balmy, breezy, and fragrant, whispering over her bare shoulders like silk. Someone approached her with a champagne flute, and she took it to be polite. Or maybe because she needed a prop with which to float through the elegant crowd, many of whom were watching her pass with curiosity. Fastening a serene expression onto her face, she continued until she reached the rail of the terrace, the green spreading out in front of her, buttered in moonlight.

Within seconds, a man approached from her left. He was roughly the same age as Josephine and sporting a necktie patterned with lizards, and he had a genuine smile, deep brown skin, and mirthful eyes. "Well, if it isn't the hot gossip item herself," said the young man, leaning his elbows on the railing beside her. "I'm Ricky. Nice to meet you."

"Hey. I'm Josephine."

"Oh, I know." He winked at her, then went back to looking out over the golf course with obvious adoration. "Don't worry, something scandalous will happen tomorrow and they'll move on. A pro will smash their putter into three pieces or mix plaids. You'll be off the hook."

She glanced back over her shoulder, catching a woman in the act of gesturing at her with one of the hors d'oeuvres. Were people interested in her because she'd joined forces with the villain? Or was it because she was the only female caddie on tour? Maybe both. "When will I ever get another chance to be whispered about at a party that's serving caviar on tiny pieces of toast? This is once-in-a-lifetime stuff."

"Now that's the right attitude." Ricky gave her a conspiratorial look. "You know, our golfers are paired up for the next two days. We're going to be seeing a lot of each other."

"Are you bringing the communal ibuprofen, or am I?"

Ricky ducked his head on a laugh and reached over to shake her hand. "Tomorrow isn't looking so rough after all, Josephine."

She couldn't agree more. Knowing there would be a friendly face in the vicinity dulled some of her spikiest nerves. "Which player are you caddying for?"

Pride squared his shoulders. "Manny Tagaloa."

Josephine sucked in a small breath. "Oh wow, the new guy."

"Yup. He's already upstairs asleep for the night. The man's got a powerhouse drive, but he's boring as hell. Makes my job a lot of fun." They shared a snort. "I'm only doing this caddying thing on the side until I can get my reptile business up and running."

"And that is the dead last thing I expected to come out of your mouth."

"Excuse me for interrupting," a man said from behind Josephine, his voice smothered in the South. "I just had to meet the woman of the hour."

"Oh boy," Ricky muttered for her ears alone. "Here we go."

A ripple carried all the way down to Josephine's ankles when she turned around and looked directly into the face of none other than the tour darling, Buster Calhoun, his sandy-blond hair lying artfully on his forehead. This guy never failed to be humble on camera, giving the media the *Aw shucks, I'm just grateful to be here* moment they craved. For the briefest of windows, Josephine couldn't help but be starstruck.

"You must be Josephine Doyle," he drawled, lifting her free hand and kissing the air just above her knuckles. "An honor and a pleasure."

"It's nice to meet you, Mr. Calhoun."

"Oh." He feigned surprise. "My reputation precedes me, I see, but I'm far more interested in yours, as is everyone else." He encompassed the terrace with a sweep of his martini. "Where *did* you come from Miss Doyle?"

She smiled brightly and said, "Florida."

A brief pause was followed by a charming chuckle. Three other golfers joined him.

When did *they* get there?

Calhoun took a slow sip of his martini. "And what are your thoughts on the course tomorrow?"

Josephine thought back to the research she'd done over the last week. The kidney bean–shaped sand trap on eleven, the water surrounding seventeen. "I think the two forced carries on the back nine are going to make a bunch of grown men cry."

For an extended moment, Calhoun appeared dumbfounded. Then he and his companions erupted with amusement. "Well, I'll be, Miss Doyle." Something new, like interest, took shape in the Southerner's eyes. "I might just have to steal you from Whitaker."

"I highly suggest you don't try that," Wells said, shouldering his way through the group of men and pinning Josephine with a hard look. "If you're done being cornered by these preening windbags, I think we've stayed long enough."

"Aw, don't take her from us so soon," Calhoun complained, clapping a hand down on Wells's shoulder. He removed it just as quickly when Wells gave him the famous death glare. "She's the most interesting thing at this party," he said, voice weakened slightly.

"She's not the entertainment."

"At least let her stay for the fireworks." He gestured to the night sky. "They're just about to begin." He gave Josephine a sly wink. "I sponsored."

Wells rolled his eyes so hard, Josephine was surprised when they didn't pop out of his ears. He looked as though he wanted to respond to Calhoun's boast, but a loud boom overhead prevented him. Pink sparkles plumed in the sky, raining down shimmery lights, followed by another one in green, then white. Based on the increase in conversation, guests were emerging from inside to witness the spectacle on the terrace, leading to limited space and everyone crowding toward the rail that overlooked the green.

Calhoun started to sidle closer to her, but Wells cut in, surprising her with a firm hand on her hip. He turned her to face the railing, then planted his fists on the stone barrier on either side of her, bracketing her in neatly. The position went beyond friendly. At the very least, it was an intimate way to be standing with her boss. And the crowd was pushing forward at such a rapid rate, more and more space was being swallowed up by the second.

Sensing eyes on her, Josephine sent a sidelong glance at Ricky. His eyes sparkled with knowing humor.

Great. He thinks I'm with Wells. Like with him, *with him.*

But the other caddie was totally misreading the situation. Obviously, Wells wasn't interested in her romantically. Their arrangement was purely business. Like, come on. He wasn't even *nice* to her. The arm trap he'd created to keep the other golfers away was nothing more than a necessity, thanks to the surging crowd.

"I leave you alone for five minutes," he growled beside her ear, "and somehow you manage to find the worst possible company."

"The jury is out on that. I'm still trying to get a read on Calhoun."

"Close the book, belle. You're done reading."

Josephine's spine straightened. "Am I?"

She could hear him grinding his teeth. "Don't forget I've spent five years on tour with the man. His golden-boy image is exactly that. An image."

"One could say the same thing about your bad-boy image."

"No, *that* is accurate."

Overhead, the fireworks picked up the pace, booming and breaking apart one after the other in explosions of color. Thus, more guests crowded out onto the terrace, giving Wells no choice but to inch closer to Josephine. Her back molded slowly to his chest, his measured breaths stirring her hair ever so slightly. It was lucky that he couldn't see her face, because his heat, the strength of him made her lashes flutter, her lips parting to drag in the magnolia-scented air. "So what are you doing? Warning me away from him?"

"That about sums it up."

"Don't bother sugarcoating it."

"I never do." Wells cursed beneath his breath. "Josephine, I need to know you're mine, so I can concentrate."

Her vision split into two, before swerving back together. "*Yours?*"

"My teammate," he clarified in a low voice, after a moment. "The last thing I need is to worry about you defecting to some other camp."

Josephine whirled around—and it was a huge mistake.

Huge.

Wells towered over her, his arms caging her against the railing. And his mouth, his body, all of him, was very, *very* close. So close that her breasts dragged across the hard ridges of his stomach when she turned around, her head tipping back automatically so she could meet his gaze. A firework lit his face and she saw exactly how heavy-lidded his eyes were as they watched her breasts press up against his chest, a low rumble emitting from his throat.

Oh dear.

As quickly as possible, she twisted back around, grateful he could no longer see how the contact had affected her. So much that she struggled to locate the things . . . the . . . what were those things called you said out loud? Words?

"Is that what you're worried about? Me ditching you?" Frankly, after years of rooting for him on the sidelines, that hurt a little. "I guess I haven't made it obvious enough that I'm the sticking around type."

"I've made that assumption about someone before," he said near her ear.

Wells was referring to Buck Lee, right? After seeing them together inside, that didn't even feel like an assumption, just fact. "Well, I guess I'll just have to prove I'm different." The hard heat of his chest against her back was making her mouth dry, so when she spoke again, her voice sounded a little scratchy. "I won't give up on you as long as you don't give up on yourself again."

Did the pace of his breathing pick up slightly in response to that?

She watched as his right arm dropped away from the railing.

It remained at his side for three fireworks, four, until his fingertips brushed—just once—over the pulse of her wrist and she shivered. That small but deliberate touch made her so light-headed, she would have pitched sideways if Wells's body wasn't propping her up from behind, his pecs against her shoulder blades, her butt dangerously close to his groin area.

Could he see the goose bumps on her neck? Was that low rumble in his throat an appreciative one? She didn't know, but when his thumb pressed hard into the small of her wrist, she nearly liquefied into hot oil, ears ringing—and it was almost galling that she could no longer pretend she found him attractive in an objective way. Her body rioted when his came close—and it wasn't letting her ignore that very inconvenient fact. A thumb on her wrist was giving her that down-deep pretzel twist that begged to be unknotted. No doubt, if they were alone, she would have taken that final backward step by now, fitting herself to his lower body.

Teasing her bottom side to side.

Oh no, you don't. That's not why you're here.

The fireworks had hit their finale now, an explosion going off every millisecond, and despite her mental warnings, her pulse matched that frenetic tempo. Maybe something about the magnolia had dosed them with romance-laced air and this gravitational pull was just a side effect. It was almost like she could feel the night, the atmosphere, their closeness roping them together, along with her vow that still hung in the air. She'd meant it. His heart beat at a fast pace against her back, letting Josephine know without words that the sentiment had meant something to him. Maybe even a lot.

Her head seemed to tip to the left all by itself. Consciously or unconsciously showing him her neck? No idea. But when that sensitive area was bathed in a warm breath, she stopped caring and started wondering what his mouth would feel like. His teeth.

Wells's chest dipped and rose dramatically, once, twice, and his hand found her hip, squeezing where no one could see, slowly beginning to draw her back . . . back—

As suddenly as they started, the fireworks cut out. As one, the crowd ebbed, their attention dropping from the sky, and reality roared back. The guests receded, heading indoors with a lot of excited chatter, giving Wells no choice but to step away from Josephine.

Clearly trying to get his breath under control, he stared at something in the distance beyond her shoulder. "We've been here long enough. Let's go."

"Yuh . . . yeah. Yup, okay."

Smooth.

Wells jerked his chin at the ballroom, indicating she should go first. The movement was so flippant, especially after what had almost just happened—right? Had she imagined the whole thing?— she laughed under her breath a little, but the sound died in her throat when he leaned in as she passed, inhaling the air just above the slope of her shoulder, his elbow brushing against the curve of her side.

Walking was a challenge after that.

They left the terrace, walked through the party full of gawkers, and rode the elevator—empty this time—upstairs in silence. At least until they stepped off, covering the distance between the elevator bank and the door to her room.

"Josephine . . ."

"Yes?"

He braced his hands on his hips, shifted as he appeared to search for the right thing to say. "What happened downstairs is not going to happen again."

Wells Whitaker: not a mincer of words.

"Right. Okay. Good," she said on reflex, staunchly ignoring the ripple of disappointment. "I mean, really, nothing actually happened."

"Nothing is *almost* going to happen again," he corrected.

Stop nodding so hard. "I mean, where could it have led? Kissing? Under the romantic moonlight? Absolutely not. That isn't going to happen."

"Right." He looked thrown by the words *romantic moonlight.* "No kissing. No anything."

"Good."

She definitely hadn't come to Texas with the intention of forming a romantic entanglement with the professional golfer. It hadn't even crossed her mind. Fine, she was attracted to him. And baths made her feel more sensual than usual. The fact remained that this was *not* on the agenda. There was the not-so-little matter of rebuilding her pro shop.

Furthermore, they had this man's career to resurrect.

When he had said near kisses wouldn't happen again, she should have been *relieved.*

"*Good?*" Wells echoed, before quickly shaking his head. "I mean, right. Good. Our arrangement might be unusual, might be temporary, but the fact remains that I am employing you, Josephine. How I perform determines your paycheck."

"I agree. The lines are blurry. Nothing good can come from blurring them even more."

"I wouldn't say 'nothing good,' but I get what you're saying."

"I wouldn't say 'nothing good,' either. Maybe kissing *would* feel good. Who knows? Maybe I'm the best kisser you've ever met in your life. You're not going to find out."

"Definitely not," he rasped, clearing his throat hard. "Hold on . . . what?"

"Let's get a good night of sleep and kick some butt in the morning."

She held up a hand for a high five. He observed it with a look of pure disgust.

"Eight fifteen tee time, belle. Don't you dare show up late."

He backed down the hallway toward the elevator. "And don't you dare arrive cheerful, either, or I'll send you home."

"No, you won't."

He stopped at the end of the hall. "No, I won't," he said, without turning around.

Then he was gone. Leaving Josephine staring after him in a daze.

CHAPTER ELEVEN

Sleep never came easy for Wells the night before a tournament—and last night was no exception. As soon as the digital numbers read 5:00 A.M., he swung his legs out of bed, sat up, and dragged his hands down his face. *Can't believe I'm back here.*

What happened to being done with this sport?

It was the wrong question to ask himself when he'd spent the last eight hours trying not to think too hard about Josephine. Also known as the reason golf had dragged him back in.

He could still feel the shape of her hip in his hand.

He'd been tempted to kiss his *caddie* in front of players and association members alike because he'd been completely oblivious to their surroundings. That kind of romantic gibberish didn't happen to him. *Especially* sober. But the thing he couldn't seem to stop wondering was . . . would she have kissed him back? *God,* most of all, how did that mouth taste?

Maybe I'm the best kisser you've ever met in your life. You're not going to find out.

Wells groaned on his way to the bathroom, going through the motions of shaving, showering, and finger brushing his hair before slapping a hat down over the whole mess. He'd go out and walk the course, clear his head, acquaint himself with the terrain. Sleep would serve him a hell of a lot more, but rest wasn't in the cards.

Not with the redhead on his mind.

Not when he'd be back in front of the cameras today—an experience that had become more and more humbling over the last two years. This time, though, there was more than his career and finances on the line. He was playing for Josephine, too, and that added a whole, scary level of responsibility that he'd been flat-out reckless to take on. Because there was every single chance that he was going to let her down.

He'd been letting everyone down for two years. What made him think this time could be any different? He wasn't going to step out onto the green and find his stroke had magically been restored.

I won't give up on you as long as you don't give up on yourself again.

Those words rang in Wells's head as he descended in the empty elevator and strode through the sleepy lobby. A couple of organizers were running around setting up cardboard advertisements for luxury cars and wealth management groups. Not a Coca-Cola or Bud Light sign to be found.

Wells rolled his eyes at a floor-to-ceiling banner depicting Buster Calhoun behind the wheel of a Mercedes and walked faster out of the lobby, exiting into the humid morning air. The sun was creeping up over the horizon, ready to wash the course in Texas gold. A few staff members and the odd caddie were watching it happen. They looked at Wells curiously as he passed, probably noticing that his polo shirt didn't have a sponsor logo on it, since nobody wanted to put their money behind him.

"Aren't you glad you put your trust in me, Josephine?" he muttered, stepping onto the dewy course and wading into the mist, slowly inhaling the scent of freshly cut grass.

I won't give up on you as long as you don't give up on yourself again.

His chin jerked up when a figure appeared in the mist in front of him, a person coming in off the fairway for the first hole. As they came closer and took shape, he realized it was a woman—and unfortunately, he knew that shape very well.

"Belle?" He moved into the mist, intending to meet her half-way. "What are you doing out here by yourself?"

When they drew even, she blinked, obviously surprised to see him. Rays of sunshine stabbed through the moist air around her, like they were harkening the Second Coming. "Walking the course. What are you doing?"

"The same, obviously."

"Oh."

He flicked his gaze downward, taking in her sleep shorts and T-shirt. They were covered in smiling giraffes. "You're wearing pajamas, Josephine."

She winced. "I thought I would sneak back into my room before anyone saw me. Couldn't you sleep?"

"No," he half shouted at her, since his lack of rest was largely due to her mouth, how she'd looked in that green dress, and a million other annoying reasons, most of which originated with her.

"Well." She moved to stand at his side, so they were both looking out over the course, though their height difference meant her view didn't reach as far. "If you have the jitters, this is a good time to remind yourself that it's about the game." Man, her voice was . . . soothing. "Not the people and shouting and cameras. Try to remember the course just like this when all the noise starts. A big, quiet field. It's here to be enjoyed, not feared."

"Are you my caddie or my Zen master?"

"Get you a woman who does both, Whitaker."

He snorted and the sound almost, almost, turned into a chuckle.

They stood in the silence for a few moments, watching the sun rise in the distance.

"You know . . ." She tucked a stray piece of hair into her ponytail. "If you have something on your mind, now would be a good time to let it off. We have golfer-caddie confidentiality. Legally, I can't repeat anything you tell me."

"That's not a thing, Josephine."

"I just made it a thing."

"I have nothing on my mind."

This time, she snorted.

He turned a frown on her.

Damn, she was annoying. And the rising sun was picking up secret strands of gold in her hair and amber flecks in her eyes. Annoying. All of it. "Why don't you tell me what I'm thinking, since you woke up with so much wisdom this morning?"

She pursed her lips and Wells had to look away. Or risk reaching over and tracing the bottom one, so he could know once and for all if it was as smooth as it looked.

It is. You know it is.

Those lips would slide down his stomach like chocolate sauce on a scoop of ice cream.

The exact last thing he should be thinking about right now. Or ever.

She wasn't there to hook up. She was there to save her family's shop.

Her *health* was on the line, goddammit.

If he didn't take this tournament seriously, that made him a bastard.

Since when did he care about being a bastard?

Wells cleared his throat hard and let words leave his mouth unplanned. "Buck was there last night. And I guess every time I see Buck, I remember how he gave me this opportunity to be great and I pissed it away. To the press, he used to say, 'All the kid needed was a chance,' but maybe . . . I don't know, maybe I take chances and set them on fire. Buck isn't the first one to get sick of my shit and bail."

"Who else was there?"

He laughed without humor. "You never see any proud parents standing on the sidelines cheering me on, do you? No, because I was nothing but a delinquent growing up. They couldn't wait to get work on a cruise ship and sail away. I don't blame them for it, either." He paused to drag in a breath. "Maybe I don't have the right . . . tools to handle success, you know? Maybe I have this skill—and that's it. None of the character that makes me deserve it. Nothing . . . else."

At first, he was simply trying to distract himself from inappropriate fantasies about Josephine's mouth, but he was shocked to find a knot inside him loosening as his confession wore on. A knot he'd been completely unaware of.

"Wow," she whispered, staring straight ahead. "That's a lot to unpack. I thought you were just going to tell me to shut up."

He narrowed his eyes at her.

"That's not to say I'm unhappy that you told me," she rushed to add, reaching over to squeeze his elbow. Regarding him in silence for a beat. "Wells, don't you realize? You did a *lot* with your chance. Getting a tour card in itself takes a miracle. It's not always about the next thing you do. Sometimes it's about what you've already done."

His chest knit together and pulled, compromising his vocal cords. "Garbage."

"It's not garbage. And that whole thing about having parents on the sidelines . . ." She shook her head. "I have that in my life. So, I can't really see things from your perspective. But I know for a fact that character doesn't come from one single place. Success is more complex than that, and we're in control of it. Do you think I was your number one fan solely because of your golf game?"

That drew his attention sharply. Mainly because of the way she'd phrased the sentence. *Was your number one fan. Was.* "Weren't you?"

She grinned over piquing his interest, a dimple popping up in her cheek, as if he didn't already have enough to deal with. "The first time I saw you play was at a charity invitational. Down in Orlando for the children's hospital. You acted like a big grumpy bear the whole time. But you . . ." She trailed off, as if needing a moment to compose herself. "I saw you give your whole bag of clubs to one of the kids in the parking lot. After all the cameras had gone home and no one was watching." She dropped her voice. "I caught you displaying more than enough character."

Wells remembered the kid's smile like he'd seen it yesterday. "Must have been another golfer. That never happened."

"Yes, it did. That's why I started coming to watch you." She nudged him with her shoulder. "Everyone drifts from their path once in a while. But your path is still there waiting. It's a perfectly good one."

This woman was like one of those farm tools that churned up the hardened earth, turning over soil that just wanted to be left alone. Or thought it did.

"Should I expect one of these unbearable pep talks every morning, Josephine?"

"Only if I'm feeling generous." She paused, fiddling with her ponytail again. "What did Buck want to speak to you about last night?"

"You mean, while you were off charming the masses."

"Why, yes."

Wells cursed. "He told me to play nice with the press. It's one of the conditions for letting me back on the tour."

A giggle bubbled out of her, turning into a full-fledged laugh.

"It's not funny, belle," he muttered. "I'd rather hammer a rusty nail into my forehead."

She sobered. Sort of. "Do you even know *how* to play nice with the press?"

"You already know the answer to that."

"Forget golf, we should practice smiling."

He stabbed a finger into the air. "I am *not* smiling. I'm here to play golf, not become the next spokesman for Mercedes."

"Oh, I think we can mark ourselves safe from that hellish possibility," she murmured, before clapping her hands together. "Are you up for a quick challenge?"

"Did you forget why we're here?"

"Not golf. Not exactly. Something else." She gripped his wrist and tugged him into the lifting fog, toward the green of the first hole. Why he was allowing this freakishly positive woman to drag him around, he had no idea, except that he didn't want to be anywhere else and he was reluctantly enjoying himself. So confusing. "Okay," Josephine said, positioning him approximately ten yards from the hole. "Take out your phone and close your eyes."

"No."

"Do it," she growled.

"Fine. Jesus." Sighing with irritation, despite the ridiculous lightness in his sternum, Wells took out his phone and shut his eyes. "Now what?"

"Without opening your eyes, put your phone into the hole."

"Sounds perfectly normal." He tipped his head back to implore the heavens for patience, then gave in to the absurdity of it all, taking a few strides forward in the direction of the hole. When he judged himself reasonably close, he slowed down and shuffled forward at a slower pace, before bending over and—

"Mmmm," Josephine hummed behind him, the noise dissolving into what sounded suspiciously like an appreciative sigh.

His lips twitched. "What was that, belle?"

"Nothing," she said, way too quickly.

Wells tucked his tongue into his cheek to subdue a grin. Josephine was an ass girl. Good to know. He might not be the best golfer on this tour, but hell if he didn't have the best butt.

"Set the phone down," she instructed. "Let's see how close you came."

He dropped the device onto the grass and opened his eyes, dismayed to find himself a full two feet from the hole. "I already know I'm going to regret asking, but what was the point of this little exercise?"

She appeared in front of him, stooped down, and picked up his phone, placing it in his hands with a slap. "You could have walked past the hole, if you wanted. You didn't have to stay between the pin and where you started. You're not in the box. Look at this whole giant field . . ." Passion flickered in her green eyes and he couldn't help but feel an answering spark inside himself. "Don't limit yourself. Don't live in a stressful little box. Go as far as you want. That was the point."

With that, she gave him a cheerful smile, folded her hands behind her back, and walked away. Just dropped that mindfuck on him and skipped off toward the resort lobby entrance, like she hadn't just dropkicked his brain.

"I'm going to get a muffin, if you want one," Josephine called over her shoulder.

Goddamn right he wanted a muffin. After that eye-opening lesson, he wanted to eat enough carbs to kill an ox. And then another, equally pressing thought occurred to Wells and he found himself stomping after her in something of a daze. "You shouldn't be by yourself when you're wearing pajamas."

Without halting her stride, she spun around, giving him a look that implied he was smoking the good stuff. "Giraffe pajamas are probably a great conversation starter."

"You're *my* caddie. I'm the only one you need to have conversations with."

"Sounds bleak." She pushed through the double doors that ran along the side entrance to the lobby, sauntering toward the coffee counter, where the employees were still in the process of setting up. "Can you order me a muffin while I do my stuff?" She scanned the glass case. "Cranberry orange."

"They invented that flavor in hell, but sure."

The kid behind the counter asked Wells what he'd like, but he was distracted by Josephine swinging around the small cross-body bag and taking out the green object that looked like a pen. When she uncapped it, he could see that it was a needle. Insulin. She was eating, so she had to give herself insulin so her body could process the carbs. How easily he'd thought about consuming a mountain of them without worrying how it would affect his body, the way it would Josephine's. Biting her lip, she clicked a wheel on the end to a certain setting.

His heart lurched up into his mouth when she lifted her shirt and jabbed the needle into her stomach, two inches to the right of her belly button.

"Sir?"

"Uh . . ." Why couldn't he swallow? Did taking the shots hurt? He'd never actually seen her—or anyone—do it before. "One cranberry orange muffin, one blueberry, and . . ." *Coffee?* he mouthed at her.

"Water," she said back, smiling, tucking her tool back into her pouch.

A moment later, Wells handed Josephine her breakfast, wanting to offer her a lot more. Anything. Needing badly to make her life easier.

Maybe . . . he could?

Not that he would let her know. If Josephine realized he cared as much as he apparently did—according to the heart still stuck behind his Adam's apple—things could get messy and complicated. His focus needed to be on winning for her.

"Listen," he said, before they could part ways in the elevator. "Text me your father's number. I forgot to tell him something about that shot I made at Pebble Beach."

She fumbled the muffin. "You're going to . . . call my dad to talk golf?"

Wells shrugged. Bit into his muffin. "Purely to brag about my genius play."

"Right. I'll text you." Backing away, she gave him a little wave. "See you at tee time."

"Yup." He tipped his chin at her as they parted ways. "Is it Rihanna that makes you dance?"

"Nope."

"Something disco era, like the Bee Gees?"

"Wrong."

He cursed as she disappeared. Which freaking band?

The text arrived as Wells was crossing the threshold into his room. Of course, it was accompanied by an abundance of smiley face emojis. He waded through the cheerful yellow circles and tapped the number, holding the phone to his ear. Both of Josephine's parents answered on the second ring. Was this a . . . landline?

"Yes, hello. This is Wells Whitaker."

Silence.

"Is everything okay with Josephine?"

Oh God, they thought he was calling with bad news. Not surprising, since he sounded like an undertaker with bronchitis. Which probably had something to do with how unnatural it felt to do something for purely *un*selfish reasons.

He hadn't always been this self-centered, had he? No, toward the beginning of his career, he'd routinely volunteered at local after-school programs, mostly for troubled youth, since he'd been one of them once upon a time. He'd sent tour tickets to his uncle every time he was in Florida. At the very least, he hadn't snarled at everyone he met. But when his game started to decline two years ago, he'd taken a wrong turn. Well, maybe being around Josephine was pushing him back in the right direction.

Sure, he was out of practice caring about anyone but himself. But he couldn't help but watch Josephine give herself insulin and wonder if she couldn't use a second set of eyes. Not *help*, necessarily. Just some backup. Even if he was totally out of his depth.

Maybe he needed to walk past the hole a little, instead of being so limited.

"Josephine is fine, apart from her terrible taste in muffins." He walked to the window and looked out over the course, his gaze dropping to the hole where he'd stood only minutes earlier with his caddie. "First of all, please don't let her know I called about this. As far as she knows, we talked about Pebble Beach."

A slight pause. "Sure, son," her father replied.

"Second . . ." He swiped off his ballcap and scrubbed at his forehead. "Could you tell me what I need to know to help her take care of herself? Please."

Josephine's mother burst into noisy tears.

Great. I'm already regretting this.

But he didn't, really. Not even a little.

CHAPTER TWELVE

Josephine stood outside of the door to the "bag room," so marked with a golden plaque, where caddies arrived to retrieve their golfer's clubs before tee off. Loud laughter reached her from the other side of the door. All men. Obviously, she'd known that would be the case—there were no other women caddying on the tour. Having grown up on a golf course, this male-dominated world was familiar territory. But she wouldn't be working behind the counter of a pro shop today or giving someone's teenager a golf lesson.

This was the highest rung on the professional ladder.

She'd absorbed every ounce of knowledge there was to soak in on this sport. She'd lived, eaten, and breathed it for years. Technically, though, one could make the argument that she hadn't quite earned a spot this lofty—and she was positive that argument had already been made by the other caddies. Possibly even expounded on.

Deep breath.

Deep breath.

She would earn the right to be there. Starting today.

Josephine ran a finger over the golden plaque and started to push the door open—

"Hey."

At the sound of Wells's voice, her insides joggled. She turned to find him approaching, obviously having come from the player's locker room, located on the other side of the clubhouse . . . and wow, time was doing nothing to dull the impact of him. She'd seen him only a matter of hours ago. And she'd seen him a ton over the last five years. But there was something about having all of that glowering energy directed at her that made certain parts of her anatomy bat their eyelashes. "Hey," she responded. "I was just going to grab the bag and meet you at the starting point. I'm not late!"

A riot of laughter blasted through the door.

Wells looked at it. Then back at Josephine.

"Why are you standing out here?" Danger flickered in his eyes, muscles tensing, as though preparing for a fight. "Are they not letting you in?"

"No, nothing like that. I was just taking a second."

He relaxed. Slightly. "Why do you need a second?"

There was no way on God's green earth that she was going to tell her boss she was having a rare moment of intimidation. He needed to have full confidence in her now or he wouldn't be able to trust her out on the course. "I was admiring the plaque."

"Josephine, you're such a fucking golf nerd."

"I know." She took a hard swallow. "Meet you down there?"

"Yeah." He started to move, then stopped. "Do you want me to ask the tournament director for a separate bag room? No one would question it. And I guess . . ." He rolled a shoulder. "I would prefer it."

"Why?"

"Might be some shirtless guys in there." He glared at the door, then Josephine. "Just so we're clear, this is not a jealousy thing. I'm just trying to preserve your modesty."

"My hero," she breathed. "Protecting my innocent nature one hairy nipple at a time."

"Quit that." He adjusted his stance and hesitated before asking, "Do you not *like* hair on a man's chest, or . . ."

Why was he asking? Did he have a lot of the stuff?

Did he like it when a woman twisted it? Or would he rather twist a woman's hair?

The breath seemed to get trapped in her lungs until she could slowly let it out.

Whatever Wells had underneath his shirt, he probably owned it. Just swaggering around in unbuttoned jeans, wet hair, and bare feet like a cowboy after a one-night stand, the very picture of confidence.

"I don't deem men dateable or undateable based on body hair," she said, trying successfully to rid herself of that far too appealing vision. "But I *am* very picky about feet."

A dark eyebrow shot up. "Feet?"

"Yup."

Briefly, his attention dropped to his cleats. "What are your judging criteria?"

"It's not really something I can put into words," she mused. "Cleanliness is very key, obviously, but . . . I don't know. I guess I'm not *overly* partial to those long, skinny bones being visible at all times." She shivered. "It helps that every man in Florida wears sandals."

"That way, you can weed out the poor bony-footed saps."

"Precisely."

Frowning, he shook his head at Josephine. "Christ."

Ignoring his obvious disapproval, she tipped her head toward the door. "You know I have to go in there or I'm going to be called a high-maintenance princess for the rest of the tour."

Wells was already nodding. "That's the only reason I didn't already ask for the separate bag room when I entered us. It would have been bullshit, belle, but I didn't want you having to deal with that. And let's face it, I'd probably break someone's nose and get us booted."

For some reason, his use of the word "us" flushed her with warmth. As did his protectiveness of her. Funny, she always thought a man threatening violence on her behalf would be a turn off. Coming from Wells, it only made her feel embarrassingly giddy. "I'm glad you didn't ask for a separate room." She pushed at his shoulder. It didn't budge an inch. "Go take some practice swings. I'll try to survive the hairy-nipple forest."

"Is that before or after the bony-foot fountain?"

And so, Josephine was giggling like a middle schooler as she walked into the bag room. When a hush spread through the packed gathering of dudes, she wasn't thinking about their estimation of her. She was wondering if Wells had timed his visit and made her laugh on purpose, so she wouldn't be nervous entering the testosterone zone. That wasn't possible.

Was it?

Josephine scanned the wall for Wells's name, which would appear over a designated locker holding his clubs, along with her official uniform.

"Over here, Josephine," called a familiar voice.

Ricky, the caddie she'd met at the party last night. He stood toward the back of the bag room, indicating the locker beside his own.

"Thanks," she murmured, sidling up beside him and opening the door to find a fresh, white mesh vest with the name Whitaker on the back. Her inner fangirl must still have been lurking deep down, because a squeal threatened to burst from her throat. Forcing herself to be all business, she tugged the loose vest on over her head, satisfied that it paired well with her pleated black skort, and she shouldered the heavy leather bag. "Are you heading down?"

"As a matter of fact, I am," Ricky replied, grinning. "If we don't have a good round, at least we know there's a good round of drinks afterward."

"Amen to that."

All eyes were on them, the two newcomers, as they headed to the exit.

"Good luck with Whitaker," someone called behind her. It was a veteran caddie she recognized well. He carried the bag for Calhoun and got a lot of screen time while his pro cleaned up at every tournament. "His last three caddies hated his guts."

"She's going to need more than luck," said someone else. "She needs a miracle."

"Legend has it, Whitaker's game is still at the bottom of the lake at Sawgrass."

Snorts and chuckles filled the room.

"That's enough," one of the older caddies snapped at the men, before winking at her. "You're going to do just fine out there."

Josephine gave him a grateful look. "I will, thanks." She hesitated before walking out the door behind Ricky. Now would be a good time to show them they could push her around if they wanted, but she could give it back just as easily. "By the way," she called to the caddie who'd made the crack about Wells's leaving his game at the bottom of a lake. "I'm sure it's not your fault your golfer always ends up in the sand trap. But maybe if you like the beach so much, you should book a vacation, instead."

A roar of laughter carried Josephine out of the bag room.

Ricky fist-bumped her.

And that was the last good thing that happened that day.

Golf tournaments lasted four grueling days.

On the afternoon of day one, shit did not look good.

As a once-certified Wells Whitaker fangirl, she'd already been aware of his difficult attitude. But he must have shoveled cranky pills into his mouth by the fistful, because as soon as she handed him the driver at the first hole, he became a stone-faced gargoyle. Everything she suggested was greeted with a grunt or some sort of disagreement. He did so much cursing, not one, but two, officials had to roll up on their golf carts to warn him, and he'd broken his five iron by bashing it into a tree.

As soon as they finished, Wells stormed off the green to deliver his daily scorecard to the officials.

"Damn," Ricky said, coming up beside her. "And I thought *we* had a bad round."

Simultaneously, they looked over at Ricky's golfer, Manny Tagaloa. He was standing just off the green, utterly still, with a towel draped over his head.

"At least you finished even," Josephine muttered, throwing her bag up onto her shoulder. "We're going into tomorrow three over par."

"Drinks after we clean up?"

"The stiffer the better."

An hour and a half later, Josephine slumped onto her stool beside Ricky at the hotel's lobby bar. They were lucky to find seats, with sunburned and half-drunk golf spectators taking up every inch of real estate. When the bartender finally found a moment to take their orders, Ricky asked for a pint of lager and a lemon drop martini for Josephine. Normally, she would avoid something so sweet, but her blood sugar was flagging after walking all day and she desperately needed the boost.

"How did you get hooked up with Tagaloa?" she asked, after sighing into her first sip.

"He's a friend of my brother's from college, actually," Ricky answered. "We met at a bachelor party. Vegas. We were paired up for a round and something clicked. He got his tour card a week later. Right place, right time, I guess."

"Love that for you."

"Me too." The other caddie laughed quietly to himself. "What about you and Whitaker? How did that happen?"

"Well." She drew out the word. "I used to be a fan. Like, that's an understatement. I was a sideline warrior. Wore his merch to tournaments and cheered him on."

Ricky's eyes widened during her explanation. "Back when he was winning?"

"No, as recently as a month ago."

"Wow." He took a pull of his beer. "That's . . . admirable."

"Thanks. That's how we met, anyway. Then he quit." She peered down into the yellowish-white depths of her drink. "When the hurricane hit Palm Beach, he happened to be in the neighborhood and came to check on me. It kind of just . . . went from there."

Ricky blinked a couple of times. "He happened to be in the neighborhood?"

"That's right."

Another pause. "Doesn't he live in Miami?"

"Yes. He was visiting a friend."

"Huh." He watched the television behind the bar for several seconds, which, of course, was showing a recap of the day's best golf shots. Safe to say Wells would not be featured. "And this friend was . . . whom?"

Josephine wrinkled her nose. "I didn't ask and he didn't offer to tell me. Which probably means it was a woman."

"Right." He brought the pint glass to his lips again. "Not sure I would bank on that."

"Oh. Why?"

Before Ricky could answer, Josephine's phone started hopping around on the bar. She picked it up, expecting her parents to be calling with some heartfelt encouragement. But it wasn't her parents. It was Tallulah.

She gasped and snatched the phone to her chest. "I'm sorry, I have to answer this. My friend is calling all the way from Antarctica."

"Jesus," Ricky said, shooing her away. "Go."

"Be right back."

"Don't be surprised if your drink is gone," he drawled.

"It's yours." As soon as Josephine hopped off the stool, she tapped the screen to answer and held the phone to her ear, venturing into a slightly less populated section of the bar. "You're alive! I was starting to think you'd succumbed to frostbite or an angry walrus attack."

"The day is young." Tallulah sighed lustily. "It sounds like you're in a bar. I remember those. Vaguely. Are you on a *date*, Miss Doyle?"

"A friendly one, maybe. I'm in San Antonio at the Texas Open."

"And no one was shocked."

"Tallulah, you're not going to believe this." She hopped in a tiny circle. "I'm caddying for Wells Whitaker."

"*Yeeeessss*, Josephine." Her best friend drew the word out, clearly not believing her. "And I've joined the penguin colony. I'm their illustrious new leader."

Josephine gasped. "That's amazing. Do you get benefits?"

"Only the best. Dental and everything." Tallulah made a halting sound. "I miss you so much. I love what I'm doing, but they put me on assignment with three scientists who don't grasp the concept of sarcasm. When I leave the research center and tell them I'm going for a swim, they take me seriously. I mean, if I dipped in a toe, I would probably die."

"Have you tested that theory just to be sure?"

"I love you. Come to Antarctica. We have porpoises."

"I would, but I have to wash my hair?"

"And caddie for Wells Whitaker, of course," she said, in a very wink-wink-nudge-nudge tone. "What is he like one-on-one? And by *he*, I mean his derriere, obviously."

"Juicy as ever. You can't spell khaki without the 'a' and the 'h.' As in ahhhhh, there's that tight bubble butt."

"Oh yes." Her friend's muffled laughter made a smile bloom on Josephine's face. "*That* old slogan."

"It's a classic." She stepped aside to let someone pass on their way to the bathroom, her back bumping into something hard. "Sorry," she said, half turning, but failing to look at who was behind her. "Unfortunately, the butt doesn't make up for his temper. Or his lack of manners and inability to take helpful suggestions. Or his—"

The phone was plucked out of her hand.

Josephine whirled around, her gaze connecting with an unshaven jaw, before traveling upward to meet an unreadable pair of brown eyes.

Wells.

Was standing in front of her.

How much of her phone call had he overheard?

"I don't know what my caddie was going to say next, but I'm guessing it was something like, 'Or his tentative backswing.' She loves to give me shit about that."

Josephine could only gape.

"I might disagree with a few of her points, but everything she said about my ass is true. It's world-class." He ended the call and handed the phone back to Josephine. "Up to bed. I don't want you hungover in the morning."

Shock washed over her like an icy waterfall, followed by anger spouting like a geyser in her middle and shooting acid up into her throat. "My *best friend* was calling me from Antarctica, you donkey. I haven't talked to her in three weeks." If that was an instant flash of regret that moved in his face, she didn't care to acknowledge it. "And it doesn't matter if I'm hungover or chipper as a bluebird, I might as well be talking to a brick wall out there!"

His smile was tight. "At the very least, you enjoyed the ass show."

"Hang on to it with both hands, because right now, it's all you've got."

A lump moved almost discreetly in his throat. "Quitting already?"

Josephine's irritation graduated to the next level. "Is that what you were trying to do? Test me to see if I'd quit?"

He crossed his arms. "Are you?"

Something about his belligerence and the challenge in his eyes made her recall their conversation early that morning. *Maybe I take chances and set them on fire. Buck isn't the first one to get sick of my shit and bail.* Well, if he expected the same of her, he hadn't been paying attention. Nor would she give him the satisfaction of being like everyone else. "Nope! I'm staying. If for no other reason than to piss you off." She looked down at her phone helplessly, knowing she *could* try to call back the number, but it probably wouldn't connect. She'd tried several times in the past after getting disconnected. Reception was horrible where Tallulah was working and she was allotted only so much time on the landline.

Dammit.

A very dramatic bubble expanded in her chest and she needed to get upstairs before it burst. "For better or worse, I'll see you in the morning. Good night."

She shouldered past a stone-faced Wells on her way to the bar. After a brief apology to Ricky that he seemed to understand— since the entirety of the bar was now silent in the wake of her argument with Wells—she left some money for her drink and beelined for the lobby elevators. One of them opened right away, thankfully, and she stepped into the empty car.

Before the doors could close, a big hand slammed down between them, trundling them back open. Wells had followed her? Brave man.

After observing Josephine for the barest moment, he moved into the elevator beside her, both of them staring at the numbers overhead as they ticked upward, the air between them vibrating like the tail of a rattlesnake.

"I shouldn't have hung up the phone."

"We'll pile it onto your mountain of transgressions."

She sensed him wincing. "A whole mountain, huh?"

"By the end of the week, we should have a full range. We'll call it the Dumbass Alps."

"You really intend on staying that long?"

"I'm not going to answer that question again. If you thought I was going to quit so easily, why did you ask me to caddie for you in the first place?"

As soon as the doors opened on her floor, she practically leapt through the breach, leaving her question hanging in the air. Wells's heavy footsteps followed behind her. "Whether you're going to bail or not is a valid concern, Josephine. Hell, you're quitting this conversation pretty easily, aren't you?"

She threw her head back and groaned at the hallway ceiling. "Only so I don't put you on the injured list for the rest of the tournament." Having reached her door, she slid the key card out of her clutch and slapped it down on the sensor, making the green light flash. Her intention was to go inside and shut the door, restore her calm in the peace and quiet of the enormous bathtub or perhaps one of three seating areas, like Goldilocks's angry cousin. But something had been in the forefront of her mind for the last twenty minutes. She couldn't stop thinking about Ricky's skeptical reaction about Wells's unexpected arrival after the hurricane. So she stopped with a hand on the door and let her mouth take over, because anger had disengaged her brain. "Who were you visiting in Palm Beach? When you just happened to swing by Rolling Greens?"

A shutter dropped down, rendering his face expressionless. "What?"

"Who were you visiting?"

His cheek twitched. "I don't like questions, belle. Remember?"

Surely, fire was bursting from her ears. "Oh, really? Well I don't like this feeling that you're playing games with me."

That statement made him jerk back, visibly baffled. "I would *not* play games with you."

"All day, you ignored me and brushed me off because you *want* me to quit, because it would justify your whole screw-the-world philosophy. That's not a game?"

He blinked, staring at the wall for a moment, as if only now realizing what he'd done. "I . . . wouldn't. Not intentionally."

"Right." She exhaled sharply. "I'm just so glad I get to ruin that expectation for you."

"Everyone before you has quit," Wells said through his teeth, taking one purposeful step toward her. Then another. A third. Until he was so close, she could taste the soap from his shower when she inhaled. He cupped the back of her neck and turned her around, then slid his fingers up into her hair, tightening them around the strands and drawing her head back as his mouth moved closer from above.

Everything inside Josephine went on the highest of alerts, her nerve endings blaring like miniature alarms, her mouth parting with the sudden desperation to inhale his exhales, breathe him in, despite the argument taking place. His body was so firm and hot against hers, his height and strength making her wonder if he could do anything *but* manhandle a woman in bed. Would he try to be gentle and lose it toward the end? Or never bother with gentle at all?

"You don't want games? Fine. I wasn't visiting anyone in Palm Beach. I came for you." Those four words glazed her eyes and made her heart twist like a crank. "I'm sorry I hung up on your friend," he said, very precisely. "I was standing there listening to all the reasons I knew you were going to fucking quit, belle—"

"I'm not," she whispered, battling the urge to either bite his mouth or kiss it. Or both.

"We'll see."

Like, was he . . . *not* going to kiss her?

People didn't engage in mere conversations with their mouths an inch apart. Right?

Maybe he really wanted to drive home his apology?

Goodness. His eyes were . . . so beautiful and rich from this distance, his hand so assertive in her hair that she couldn't help wanting to offer him the whole package. Even if she was mad. Maybe *because* she was mad.

With his eyes fastened on her mouth, he slowly dragged his tongue along the inside of his bottom lip. The breadth of his chest dipped and swelled. "Get some rest," he rasped. "You have a long day of putting up with me tomorrow." He released her with obvious regret and stepped back. "I'll wear my tightest pants."

"Thanks," she said, dazed. "I mean—"

"Good night, Josephine." He turned and swaggered down the hall. "Enjoy watching me go. You earned it."

"I take it back. I quit."

His booming laughter echoed as he entered the elevator, then was gone altogether.

Josephine all but sleepwalked into the room, the words *I came for you* repeating in her head until she finally fell asleep.

CHAPTER THIRTEEN

Wells stood outside the bag room Friday morning, arms crossed, index finger tapping against his opposite elbow. Josephine was in there and he needed a word before day two got underway.

Well. Technically, he didn't *need* a word. He didn't owe anyone explanations.

So . . . what. After last night and the way she'd called him out in an eerily accurate manner, he *wanted* Josephine to understand him better?

That didn't make a lick of goddamn sense, either.

Except that if she understood him better, there was a chance their golfer-caddie relationship could become stronger. He'd never given a second thought to that kind of thing in the past. Wells played how he wanted. He didn't need a second opinion when it came to hitting a ball into a hole. He just got it done. Except that he wasn't getting it done anymore.

And that suddenly mattered a lot, because when he lost, so did Josephine.

Of course, that had been the same deal with caddies in the past, but he'd never taken anyone on exclusively. His caddies of tournaments past were well established and had financial security. Other options. This was different.

The other not-so-tiny detail that set Josephine apart from his former golf partners was that he wanted to fuck her so bad, he'd woken up growling her name and thrusting in his closed fist.

Imagining her auburn hair spread out on his pillow, her nails scraping down his back, her tits bare and bouncing. Damn, he'd come as hard as a bullet train. And truth be told, he'd felt guilty as sin about it afterward, especially considering he was her boss, for all intents and purposes.

But doubly so, because he'd ruined her night.

Hung up on her *best friend*.

Even now, thinking about what he'd done—and her devastated reaction—made his chest feel like a hollow cavity. He'd spent three hours last night tracking down an email for Tallulah at the research facility and God himself couldn't keep Wells from making up for that mistake. No matter how long it took. Otherwise, he'd be haunted by the memory of Josephine's unshed tears until the day he died.

A totally normal way for a golfer to feel about his caddie.

Wells dragged a hand down his unshaven face. One more minute of waiting and he was going in there to get her. Why was it taking her so long to collect his bag?

Finally, the door opened and there was Josephine, ducking beneath the arm of the man who was holding it open for her. Same guy she'd been sitting with at the bar last night.

Was something going on there?

His vision turned an alarming shade of gray, heat prickling his scalp beneath his cap.

"Oh." Josephine's gait halted when she saw him waiting. "Wells."

The other caddie split a look between them. "I'll see you down there." He stuck his hand out to Wells. "Good luck today."

Wells wasn't sure how he felt about this dude yet, but Josephine was watching him, her frown increasing with every second he hesitated. "Yeah," Wells muttered, shaking the young man's hand. "You too."

As soon as the other caddie was out of earshot, she goaded him. "Being civil wasn't so hard, was it?"

"Actually, I'm crumbling inside."

"Poor gargoyle." With a shake of her head, she started toward the course and Wells followed. He trailed behind on purpose, taking plastic rolls of glucose tabs out of his pockets, carefully unzipping various compartments on the golf bag, and stuffing the plastic tubes inside. Grape flavor. "I'm glad you're early. Some practice swings would be—"

"Is something romantic happening there?" Wells interrupted.

She blinked back at him over her shoulder, but thankfully he was done stocking the bag with sugar reinforcements, as Josephine's mother had suggested. "Is there something romantic happening where?"

Wells drew even beside her. "Between you and that kid."

"First of all, his name is Ricky and he's Tagaloa's caddie. We spent the entire day with them yesterday. Ringing any bells?"

"Barely."

She rolled her eyes. "Second, no. He has a girlfriend. Two of them, actually. Both of whom come second to his Komodo dragon, Slash."

"Good," Wells grumbled, the world comprised of colors again.

Josephine's cheeks deepened with a blush, ever so slightly. "Not for the second girl, I'm guessing." They walked in silence for several yards. "Was there something else you wanted to speak to me about?"

"Yes."

They continued walking.

Wells knew what he wanted to express, but he had no clue how to verbalize it.

"It's not that I don't want to take suggestions out there, Josephine. I'm not *that* fucking stubborn." That last part left her looking skeptical, which was fair, but he pressed on. "It's like . . . once my round becomes a dumpster fire, I just want to hurry up and burn it all down."

"You're self-destructive."

Despite that glowing sentiment, he really liked how Josephine just jumped into the deep end of the conversation with him, without any pomp and circumstance. "That sounds way worse than what I said."

Josephine stopped walking and backed off the path, so the pairs behind them could pass. Setting his bag down in front of her, she tightened her ponytail. In the . . . God, the *cutest* way. Why was everything she did so endearing? "*Why* do you want to burn it all down?"

"Honestly, I wasn't expecting to go any deeper with this explanation." His neck was getting hot. "Can we just leave it at dumpster fire?"

"Afraid not."

Wells cursed. He picked up his ballcap and dragged a handful of fingers through his hair before fitting it back on. "I'm only humoring you because I feel like a Batman villain after last night."

"Well," she said, without missing a beat. "You *are* the Bane of my existence."

Oh. *God.* Now she was making Batman puns? His heart was sprinting at the speed of light. What the hell was he supposed to do about this?

"Funny," he said, sounding somewhat strangled. "I . . . what were we talking about?"

"The fact that you're self-destructive."

"Still not a fan of that phrasing, but sure." He shifted, moving both hands to his hips. He felt like he'd been mule kicked in the solar plexus. "I guess I self-sabotage out there because I want to prove I don't care."

"*Do* you care?"

Wells opened his mouth and nothing came out.

Josephine stood silently in front of him.

An itch started beneath his collar.

"Do you care, Wells?"

"Yes," he said after several more beats.

"I guess a better question," she started quietly, "is why are you so reluctant to admit that you care whether you win or lose?"

Jesus. He'd only meant to explain to her that he wasn't a brick wall, as she'd described him last night. That he would do his best to try to listen, incorporate her suggestions. He didn't sign up for a therapy session. But with Josephine's clear, green eyes focused on him, he found the truth wanting to unravel in his throat. "I don't want to give anything that power over me. To make me . . ." *Out with it. You're in this deep, might as well keep swimming.* "If golf is going to make or break me, I'd rather break it first."

"Why?"

"Because then it's on my terms. I control what the sport does to me. If I'm going down the tubes, I'm going on my own raft."

"Your raft has holes in it," she said, patiently.

"I know, Josephine," he snapped. "That's why I gave you a chance to quit."

She threw up her hands. "Now we're getting somewhere. You played terrible yesterday to needle me into quitting."

"Not at first. But as long as I was setting shit on fire anyway, I guess I wanted to give you an excuse to give up on me, so I don't have to wait around for it." Good lord, there was a band around his chest that wouldn't stop tightening. "I brought you here with good intentions. I want to *win* for you. But hope is a fucking monster, belle, especially when that hope is pinned on me."

"No, it's not," she fired back.

"Buck had high hopes for me, right? As soon as I started stumbling, I lit a match and tossed it on everything." He stopped just short of bringing up his parents. Couldn't make himself dig quite that deep. "I fail people and they leave. I fail at this game, and it deserts me. It's easier to check out first."

"Is it? Is it easier or have you just gotten comfortable in a bad pattern?" Josephine stepped closer and flattened a palm on his chest. "Be brave, Wells. Let yourself care again."

Wells felt himself being pulled in two directions. Standing at a crossroads with a familiar wind pushing him down the path he knew. Where he could be alone, no one counting on him. That direction wasn't pretty. But it was comfortable. On the other path, there was . . . hope. Tempting, but dangerous. Especially when the possibility of *not* succeeding meant letting down this woman.

The sound of a golf cart buzzing closer interrupted his thoughts.

"Mr. Whitaker," one of the course officials said. "You're ten minutes to tee time."

"Thank you," Josephine informed him, with a strained smile. "We're coming."

The cart made a K-turn and zipped back in the other direction, leaving them in relative silence. Josephine stooped down and positioned his bag on her shoulder. He wanted to throw the damn thing on the ground, pick her up into his arms, and carry her to his room. He just wanted to bury his body and soul into her and delay playing the game that made him feel like a failure.

He wouldn't fail at making her moan. He'd be the fucking master at *that*.

"Wells."

"Yeah?"

"Stop looking at my boobs." She moved back onto the path, her feet eating up the distance to the course. "There is nothing sexy about this caddie uniform."

Wells followed, shocked to find he was . . . lighter. Despite the heavy baggage they'd spent the last five minutes wading through, he swore there was less tension in his neck. Even his legs were looser, to say nothing of his mind. Christ, was he open to . . . caring again, like Josephine had asked of him? "You're wearing a uniform with my name on it, belle. There is nothing hotter."

She pretended to gag. "How about this? If you eagle the first hole, you can . . ." Her mouth snapped shut, flames scaling the sides of her face. "Never mind."

His pulse picked up. "Oh, I'm going to need to hear the rest of that sentence."

"It's unprofessional. I was just . . ."

"Flirting with me?"

"No." She shook her head adamantly. "I wouldn't flirt with my boss."

If he wasn't careful, this whole exchange was going to make his dick hard and they were going to be on live television in the next couple of minutes. Unless his cock was auditioning for the role of stunt double to his nine iron, they needed to cool it. Although he didn't want to completely shut down the opportunity to talk about the nature of their relationship. What was allowed, what wasn't. Just to make everything really, *super* clear. "We need to have a conversation about this later, Josephine."

"No, we don't. It won't happen again."

"What won't happen again?" *Masochist.* "I don't even know what you were going to propose."

"It was silly. If you eagled the first hole, I was just going to offer to pose for a picture in my caddie uniform." Pink was rushing upward toward her hairline. "Since you think it's so hot."

His kingdom for that single picture. "You're on."

"I . . . no," she sputtered. "No, that's definitely not appropriate boss–employee behavior."

"No, it's not. And if I had been the one to propose this bet, I'd be at fault. But it was you, so I think we're staying on the right side of decorum."

"I'm shocked you even know the word 'decorum.'"

"You're the one suggesting a pantsless picture in your caddie uniform."

Her mouth fell open. "Who said anything about pantsless?"

"Sorry, the crowd noise is . . ." Wells tapped his ear. "The cheering really swallowed up what you were saying exactly."

Josephine smirked—and he knew. She was going to call his bluff. And his dick was *definitely* going to land the stunt double role. "Actually, I said pantsless *and* braless." She batted her eyelashes once. Twice. "You need to work on your listening skills."

His saliva evaporated into dust. "Hand me my driver."

CHAPTER FOURTEEN

Wells did, in fact, eagle the first hole.

She couldn't even look him in the eye as she collected his driver.

What had she been *thinking*?

What were they *both* thinking?

Was she actually going to send him a half-naked picture?

Since the moment they'd torn down the third wall between player and fan, they'd spent 90 percent of their acquaintance arguing. And 90 percent of those arguments were about pulling his head out of his ass. Was she attracted to him? *Yes.* No sense in denying it after the indecent thoughts she'd been having more and more lately, which were inexcusably heavy on butt biting.

Wells was *level ten hot*.

That wasn't in question.

But he was also her boss. And she was *all he had*. His mentor and manager had deserted him. Blurring the line of professionalism would be a terrible idea. Like, awful.

"I was thinking, Josephine," Wells said, coming up beside her, just outside the tee box on the second hole. "I shouldn't be the only one benefitting from a bet today. This calls for a fair trade off."

"We need to be talking about yardage," she blurted.

Did his lips twitch? "I wouldn't feel right if you didn't get something out of the deal."

"I have everything I need."

Very briefly, his attention dropped to her thighs. "Do you?"

A bead of sweat trickled down her spine. "Good thing you're not mic'd up right now."

He hummed in his throat. "What do you want in exchange for me taking par on this hole? The suggestion has to come from you."

"For decorum's sake? I'm not sure that word means what you think it means."

Wells let a beat pass. "I think I like flirting with you. I think you want to flirt back." His expression was serious when he looked down at her. "And as long as you know your job is safe and I would literally cut off my own legs before wielding my power over you, maybe we need to just fucking *flirt*, belle."

How did he manage to make the word "flirt" sound like an epithet? "That isn't what you said on Wednesday night."

"Now I'm qualifying what I said. As long as you're the one initiating . . ."

"The flirting?"

"And you know there's no pressure at all—"

"I do. I know that."

"Then we fucking flirt." He squinted out at the fairway. "Name the terms of your bet."

What was *happening* here? They were in the middle of a golf tournament laying down ground rules for *flirting*? How could she be having so much fun while being completely and totally caught off guard? Truthfully, though, she believed Wells when he said there was no pressure, because she felt none. He would never use his position to do anything that made her uncomfortable. Was her intuition enough of an excuse to take a tiny step forward? Safe enough to pose the mother of all bets?

His eyes challenged her to do just that, but there was reassurance there, too.

Josephine filled her lungs for courage. "If you par this hole . . ." She craned her neck to give his booty the tiniest peek, but couldn't bring herself to say the words. "Um."

Slowly, Wells's mouth edged up into a grin. "You want a picture of me dropping trou?"

And to think, she'd woken up this morning believing she led a mostly normal life. "I'm not sure there is any point in denying that I like your butt after you overheard my phone call last night."

"Juicy." He winked at her. "You called it juicy."

Josephine closed her eyes and released a withering sound. "Just play the shot, you clown."

Wells laughed.

He *laughed*.

Josephine's legs almost gave out. Her eyes shot open, hoping to catch the tail end of his laughing face, but he was already back to concentrating on the shot he was about to take, stepping right to left and examining the angle, feeling the wind.

His swing followed through, without the hesitancy he'd developed over the last two years, and the ball dropped down on the left side of the fairway. A smattering of applause rippled through the crowd assembled behind them.

Wells handed her the driver. "Good call, belle."

Josephine might have spent the rest of the morning driven to distraction by the fact that she'd just won a bet that guaranteed her a personal snapshot of Wells's rear end, but she was too transfixed by the glimpse she was getting of the old Wells. He consulted with her before every shot, both of them poring over yardage books and hunkering down side by side to compare notes on the angle of the green. He almost seemed to be having . . . fun.

But all that progress came to a screeching halt on the eighth hole.

Josephine and Wells were shoulder to shoulder, waiting for Tagaloa to take his putt, when Buck Lee appeared on the sidelines. He was just one face among the crowd, but his arrival was like a bucket of cold water tossed on Wells. His expression slowly grew shuttered, his movements less natural.

In no time, he'd dropped two spots on the leaderboard.

"Hey. It was a tricky slope. Shake it off."

When he didn't bother to respond, Josephine's stomach sank.

The next hole went worse.

Buck Lee left, as casually as he'd arrived.

And that's when her glimpse of the old, astonishing Wells Whitaker winked out completely.

At this rate, their chances of making the cut and continuing in the tournament tomorrow were slim to none. Not unless he managed to get through the rest of the afternoon without bogeying a single hole and that seemed about as likely as TSwift performing in her bathroom later tonight.

Keep trying. Don't quit on him. "The wind is picking up—"

"I don't give a shit about the wind, Josephine. I'm pissing into it at this point."

Her shoulders wanted to slump, but she wouldn't let them. "You're burning it all down."

"Sounds about right," he responded, tight-lipped, while examining the head of his club.

"Don't. Step back, recognize what you're doing, and balance yourself out."

His snort drew the attention of several spectators. "Oh Jesus, stop shovel feeding me your Zen nonsense, belle."

"Nonsense is allowing that passive-aggressive, condescending has-been to get in your head and letting him rearrange it. Letting him *win*. I thought you were more badass than that."

Wells's head turned slowly, pinning her with an incredulous look. "You met him for all of thirty seconds and you got all of that?"

"Yup!"

He really, truly looked like he was trying to claw his way out of the mental hole he'd dug for himself, but he just couldn't do it. The grimace of regret, the remaining light fading from his eyes, told her that much. "Let me take my drive, Josephine."

"Go for it. I'll be on the sidelines."

"*What?*" he shouted.

"I said, I'll be . . ." She fluttered her fingers at the roped-off spectator section. "Over there."

Panic slowly snuck into his expression. "What happened to never quitting?"

"I said I would never quit as long as you didn't quit on yourself. That's what you're doing." She whirled around, took a few steps, and ducked under the rope, a few feet to the right of the gallery—

And immediately her foot was run over by a golf cart.

Pain shot from her toes to her ankle, snatching the breath clean out of her lungs. It was such a shock, happened so quickly, she didn't even have a chance to make a sound. Her backside planted in the grass before she knew she was falling, her only necessity to get the pressure off her foot. Surely it was broken?

A roar of denial from Wells nearly deafened her. "*Josephine.*"

He was in front of her, his image momentarily blurred by the blood rushing to her head, but after a few seconds of taking stock, the shock wore off and the pain started to dull. *Just surprised. You were just surprised.* "I'm fine."

"What the fucking fuck," he exploded, dropping to his knees in front of her. "You got *run over.*"

"Just my foot."

"You ran over my caddie," he barked at the cart, which was carrying two officials. "I'm going to f—"

"Wells."

He made a sharp sound of frustration. "Where is the medic on this course?" Before she knew his intentions, Wells had picked her up off the ground to cradle her in his arms. "Where?"

The official stood up. "I've radioed them. The medical cart is on the way."

"Oh good," he responded. "Another cart. Maybe if we're lucky, it'll finish her off!"

"Watch yourself, Whitaker," the official shot back, jabbing the air with his finger. "We were headed over here to give you a warning about the profanity. *Again.*"

"Wells, it barely hurts anymore," Josephine said, trying to work herself free of the steel banded hold keeping her in place. "I was just caught off guard."

"Is this the wrong time to point out that this wouldn't have happened if you'd stayed with me, where you belong?"

"Yes, it's the dead wrong time to point that out." Her neck lost power, dangling back over the crook of his elbow. "Please God, don't let my parents see this."

"Here comes the medical cart," Wells said, still sounding far more anxious than the situation warranted. Three long strides and she was being settled onto a leather bench. The medic didn't even have a chance to climb out of the driver's seat before Wells knelt down again in front of Josephine. "I can't remember. Are you supposed to leave the shoe on when it's a sprain, so it doesn't swell? Or am I wrong?"

"It's not a sprain!" Josephine shouted.

"Sir, I can take over from here," said the medic patiently.

"Just a second. I'm going to check the damage."

Wells eased off Josephine's shoe and that's when everything started to move in slow motion. She thought back to the evening when she'd painted her toenails and denial swung inside her like a pendulum. "Not the sock. Leave my sock on."

"How am I supposed to see anything with your sock on?"

"There's nothing to see—"

Off came the sock.

There they were. Five freshly polished blue toes. With yellow letters on them. Spelling out W-E-L-L-S'. He went very still. Three seconds passed. Four. And then, ignoring her sputtering protests, Wells yanked off the other shoe and sock, revealing the word B-E-L-L-E.

He said nothing.

No movement.

He'd become a statue.

Josephine held her breath as he stood up, braced a hand on the top of the golf cart, and looked at her, long and hard, wheels turning behind his eyes.

His voice vibrated when he said, "We're making the cut."

Josephine jumped when he slapped a hand down on the roof of the cart.

"We're making the fucking cut, Josephine."

"Okay," she whispered, her embarrassment turning into something else. Pure hope. Hope and . . . connection. To this man.

For better or worse.

CHAPTER FIFTEEN

Wells watched the leaderboard shift on the television screen, his name slipping into the green bracket of players in the top sixty-four.

Unbelievable.

He fell back against the cushions of his hotel room couch and let out a gust of air. An odd, thick feeling crept into the space between his chest and throat, making it difficult to replenish the air in his lungs. He'd made the cut only once this entire season and it had been on a technicality, because the golfer ranked above Wells made an error on his scorecard.

But this?

This was legitimate.

And today's comeback could be credited to only one thing.

Or . . . ten to be exact.

Josephine's toes.

Wells dug his knuckles into his eye sockets and filled the suite with a semihysterical laugh. "You've lost it. You've completely lost it."

That might have been true, but there was no denying that an atomic bomb of relief and pride and hope, goddammit, had imploded in his stomach when he'd pulled off her socks and seen those little blue miracles staring back at him. There they were, proof that Josephine still had faith in him. She was still his num-

ber one fan. He *hadn't* lost her. And there had simply been no
way in hell he was going to let her regret that.

Wells pushed to his feet and paced to the bathroom, planting
his hands on the marble vanity and looking himself in the eye.
"Do *not* go to her room." He shrugged with forced nonchalance.
"Just don't."

It wasn't as though the mere act of going to her room meant
something sexual was going to happen. Strange things were taking place inside him, though. Every day that passed with this
woman in his life, he shed another layer of numbness and indifference. He was *actually* looking forward to playing golf tomorrow.

With her.

Near her.

Beside her.

Anywhere she happened to be.

Wells dropped his head forward. "Oh my God, get a fucking
grip."

He might have given her initiation rites when it came to
flirting, but the complicated power dynamic between them remained. Currently, Josephine was depending on him for an in-
come. She had a lot at stake.

His phone chimed in his pocket, dissipating his wayward
thoughts.

Speak of the . . . angel.

It was Josephine.

Trying valiantly to ignore the tightness in his throat, Wells
slid open the text message—and felt every ounce of blood in his
body race south. It was a bathroom selfie of Josephine wearing
her caddie uniform. And he didn't know where the hell to look
first. Because she'd definitely come through on her end of the
bet. Big time.

No pants.

No *panties*, either, as far as he could tell.

"Holy mother of God."

She'd tugged the hem of the pinnie down to cover her pussy, but the uniform was cut short by design, so he could see her hips, and there was no sign of underwear. Smooth porcelain as far as the eye could see, with a dusting of freckles in spots that made his mouth water. He was dying to grab and knead and lick her curves. Holy—she wasn't wearing a bra underneath, either, but it was a *fucking tease*, because of the mesh. It allowed for only tiny peeks at the flesh beneath, but he wasn't even going to pretend not to zoom in, trying to make out the dusky color of her nipples.

Right there. Puckered little circles.

He didn't even care if his horny brain was filling in the blanks.

"Baby." He raked a hand down the front of his pants and gripped himself. "*Fuck.*"

Josephine: Congrats on making the cut. Enjoy your new lock screen.

Wells took several deep breaths—and another five camera zooms—before texting back.

Wells: Fuck the trophy. I win. Forever.

Wells: The only thing missing is your face.

Her incredibly gorgeous face that he couldn't stop thinking about.

Josephine: Ah, come on. I don't mind if you leave your face out of mine.

Josephine: In fact, I prefer it.

He made an affronted sound, his head lifting to study his reflection.

Wells: I give great face, belle, and you know it.

Josephine: You're looking in the mirror, aren't you?

This woman had no right knowing him so well. No right. And he couldn't figure out what he'd done to get so lucky. For the first time in a long time, he wasn't alone. He had a . . . friend. A friend he couldn't stop looking at half naked. Jesus Christ, those *thighs*.

Wells: You still want it?

Josephine: Want what?

Wells: Your picture of this juicy peach, belle. You still want it?

Josephine: 😳 Yes. 😳

It was a good thing Wells was already unfastening his pants and turning around, so the mirror was reflecting his backside. He'd checked out his own ass plenty of times in the mirror, but he'd never actually taken a bathroom selfie of the damn thing. It took him a few minutes to (a.) find the right angle/lighting and (b.) flex without making it *look* like he was flexing. But in the end, ha, he got a shot that passed inspection and fired it over.

No response.

Yanking his pants back up, buttoning them, he waited. Waited more. Maybe she'd gotten in the shower?

No, she'd take a bath. She loved that tub.

His condo in Miami had a massive one that he never used, but for some reason, he was suddenly very glad it was there. No conceivable reason.

And now his dick was hard imagining Josephine in his bathtub, caddie uniform plastered to her body. He'd get in there with her. She'd probably make a beard out of the bubbles or some shit—and why did that make his windpipe feel eight times smaller?

He was aroused . . . both physically and emotionally?

What exactly was he supposed to do about *that*?

Willing his erection to subside, because they'd agreed to flirt and trade pictures, not *sleep together*, Wells stripped off the clothes he'd worn all day and took a shower, somehow withstanding the temptation to stroke away the frustration.

On one hand, he didn't have to live with the guilt.

On the other, his balls were stiffer than fucking doorknobs.

Great trade-off.

When he got out of the shower, she still hadn't answered his text.

All right, now he was starting to get self-conscious. Had she changed her mind about his ass? Better to go ask in person than send some thirsty text, right? Hair still wet, dressed in sweatpants and a hoodie, Wells found himself taking the elevator to Josephine's floor, because apparently, he just wanted to make the pain worse. Somehow, though, staying away from her was its own brand of pain.

"Someone, please, tell me what to do about this girl," Wells muttered, banging a little too loud on her door. "It's me."

After a beat, she answered. "Who is me?"

A vein throbbed in his forehead. "The only man you should be expecting," he shouted.

"Relax." She laughed, opening the door, skin looking *quite* flushed. Interesting. What had she been up to before he knocked? Oh, he had some idea. "I know golfers are weirdly territorial about their caddies, but you've really made it an art form."

Wells couldn't do anything but stare at the freshly scrubbed and shiny being standing in front of him. In bare feet and a bathrobe. He had a picture on his phone of this woman in nothing but a cropped mesh tank top. He'd sent her a picture of his ass. Were they just going to pretend that wasn't true? Wells didn't know. He knew only that, by some phenomenon, she looked equally incredible in the robe as she did half naked. "Uh . . . what?"

She shook her head at him. "Never mind. Are you going to come in?"

He held up his phone and pointed at it. "Well?"

"Well, what?"

"My ass selfie, belle," he exploded. "You didn't send back a single fire emoji. Are your thumbs broken?"

"I was . . ." She flapped her hands around. "I didn't know how to respond."

"You tell me it's a great freaking ass, that's how you respond!"

"You already know it's great!"

"I want to hear it from you!"

"Fine. Fine! It's firm and bitable and distracting. It's the kind of butt that probably makes other dudes too self-conscious to shower near you at the gym, because it puts all the other man butts to shame. If there was a harness on your back, your booty could be used as a seat on a roller coaster. Someone should whip it, honestly. It's an ass-whipping ass."

He immediately regretted asking for a response. Or maybe the problem was that he didn't regret it *at all* and would be thinking about her biting into his butt cheek like an apple for the rest of his life. "Better." He coughed. "You're in a robe, Josephine." Lord, he sounded like he'd been wandering in the desert for a week. "Do you want to put something on?"

Briefly, she looked down, then back up at him with an arched brow. "You've seen me in less now, haven't you?" she said dryly. "But let me know if you're going to succumb to the vapors. I'll ring the front desk for smelling salts."

With that, she let the door close, giving Wells no choice but to catch it and step inside, shutting it behind him. He'd made a mistake coming here. The room was fragrant from her bath, flowers and soap scenting the air. She'd turned on just a single lamp, lending a heavy intimacy to the room. Mood lighting that could only be termed as dangerous.

"Actually, I was going to get dressed and go to your room," Josephine said, taking a seat on the couch and tucking her feet beneath her. "You saved me a trip."

He hesitated at the end of the couch. "Why were you coming to my room?"

God man, try to sound a little less horny.

Easier said than done. He couldn't stop wondering what, if anything, she was wearing beneath that fluffy white robe. And how warm her skin would still be from the bath.

Did hot water make her limber?

Enough, asshole.

Something might very well be happening here, between them. Not that he had any idea what it was. But their positions as employee and employer made the tightrope they were walking on very thin, so he needed to navigate it carefully, for her sake.

"Well." She shifted her position, tucking a section of wet hair behind her ear. "What I was going to say . . . it seemed like a good idea when I was in the bath. But now that you're standing here in front of me looking like you just woke up from a forty-year coma and found out cars can fly . . . I'm second-guessing myself."

"Fuck. Sorry." Wells dragged a hand down his face. She had no idea how embarrassingly apt a description that was. He sat down on the opposite end of the couch. "Guess I'm still a little shell-shocked after that round today."

Her eyes twinkled. "I knew you had it in you."

"What did you want to talk to me about?" he said in a rush. It was that or kiss her.

"Okay. Okay." She folded her hands in her lap. Took a breath.

Oh, this was important.

Wells turned to face her a little more.

"I don't want to be too long-winded about the whole thing," she started. "But . . . you know, my parents were really protective when I was growing up. Because of . . ." She waved a hand at her insulin kit, which was sitting open on the coffee table. "You know."

Wells swallowed. "I follow."

"Like, my mother quit her job when I was diagnosed, so she could be home in case my elementary school called with an emergency. So, my parents were telling me everything was going to be fine, that I could live a normal, happy life like everyone else, but their actions said otherwise. I couldn't possibly be like everyone else if they felt the need to alert my soccer coaches or the parents of my friends. Or if they screamed, 'Do you have the emergency shot?' at each other every time we left the house."

A zipper had formed at the center of his chest and it closed one tooth at a time, tightening, tightening. "That was probably really scary."

Josephine nodded. Took a moment to keep going. "Anyway,

when I got older, I just needed to shut them out. When it came to my diabetes. For my own good. For *their* own good—I mean, the worry was going to kill them. They were doing their best. I love them. But I'm the one who has to live with it, you know? I'm the only one who understands. It's hard when other people get involved, because they remind me to be scared."

The air supply in the room had dwindled down to nothing. "Do you need to be scared?"

"If I overthink it? Yes. My life depends on this vial of insulin. But as long as I have what I need, I can live to be a hundred. People are told every day that they have conditions they *can't* live with. That makes me lucky in a sad, doesn't-have-a-working-pancreas kind of way, right?"

This wasn't the first time it had hit Wells how easily he could have chalked this woman up to being an overzealous fan. A face in the crowd. A beautiful one, sure, but a mere member of his cheering section, nonetheless. When, in fact, she should be celebrated everywhere she went. Wells ached to tell her she was so fucking brave, but intuition told him she wouldn't react well. It would remind her there was something to be scared about and she'd just told him she hated that.

He thought of the emergency glucagon shot back in his room, stored in his luggage.

The one her mother had overnighted him.

Should he send it back? How would Josephine feel knowing he had it?

"You are," he said, without thinking.

"I am, what?"

"Going to live to be a hundred. I demand it."

The dimple that formed on her cheek made him want to die. "You just don't want to find a new caddie."

Wells grunted.

She was sitting extremely far away.

Frowning at her, for some reason, he moved to the center of the couch, jerking his chin in a silent command for her to snuggle beneath his arm. "Come on. Before I change my mind."

Instead of cozying up to him, she reared back a little. "What is this? What are you doing?"

"Sealing this bonding moment with a hug, *Josephine*. What does it look like?"

"But that was only my preface!"

"There's more?" Was she trying to rip out his heart?

"Yes!" She stood in front of him, phone in hand, flipping it end over end. "I was thinking, you know . . . I've been expecting you to trust me *blindly* out on the course and you don't really have a reason to. Trust me. But what if I trusted you with something? I don't know. Maybe that would help."

Wells's raised arm dropped to the couch like a dead weight, his heart rapid-firing in his rib cage. "You're going to trust me with something?"

"*If* you want it. There is zero pressure."

"Yes." He was shouting again. "Whatever it is, belle. Yes."

"You haven't heard what it is yet."

"Yes."

"Wells."

"Yes."

"You really want to follow my blood sugar on the app?" Pink faced, she fumbled her phone a little and his entire body covered itself with goose bumps. "No one has ever followed me, besides my parents and Tallulah, but it has been years since then. You wouldn't have to *do* anything, obviously. You don't even have to turn on the alerts. I can take care of myself. But it's . . . I guess it's just something that's really vital to me. I thought if I trusted you with that, you might feel more inclined to—"

Wells pulled her into a bear hug.

He didn't even remember standing up, but suddenly, she was in his arms, her blue toes probably a good few inches off the ground. His blood raced in so many directions he felt dizzy. Among all the mental chaos, one thought occurred to him over and over again. If this incredible human being was willing to share something so important with him, he had to be worth a damn, right? He *had* to be worth salvaging.

"For the record, you didn't have to preface anything," Wells said against her forehead. "If you want something from me, ask, Josephine. You've got a standing yes."

She looked up at him and blinked a few times, as if surprised, before recovering. "I'll remind you of that tomorrow when you want to use a hybrid when we clearly should be using your five iron."

That mouth was inches away. Inches. "You bring this up during our bonding session?"

"Session adjourned," she murmured, her eyelids growing suspiciously heavy.

They couldn't have been any more obvious about staring at each other's mouths. He saw the pulse fluttering at the base of her neck. "Is it, belle?"

"Well, um." She wet her lips and his balls started to throb like a son of a bitch. "I was going to watch a movie if you want to hang out f-for a while."

I shouldn't. "Yeah. I'll stay awhile."

Wells didn't realize he still had Josephine locked in an embrace until she wiggled free, dropping down to the couch. When she reached for the remote on the coffee table and turned on the television, he noticed her fingers trembled slightly. Hell, so were his own. Sitting down with Josephine—in a robe—was a ten on the Richter scale of bad ideas. But there he went, taking a spot close enough to her that the cushion dipped, bringing her up against his side and allowing him to put an arm around her shoulder.

"Josephine."

"Yes," she whispered.

He held on to his willpower. "If you want me to leave, just say the word."

Her chest rose and fell, glassy eyes trained on the television. "It's just a movie, Wells."

He swallowed a pained laugh.

It's just a movie. Right.

And Josephine was just his caddie.

CHAPTER SIXTEEN

Josephine probably shouldn't have put on the movie *300*.

Going in, it seemed like a happy medium.

Action for Wells. Shirtless Spartans for her.

Right?

But she had forgotten about the scene. The *sex* scene. When King Leonidas is leaving for battle and makes very passionate love to his wife beforehand. An unbridled, slow-motion masterpiece that, frankly, she might have rewound a few times if she were alone. But she *wasn't* alone—and the atmosphere surrounding her and Wells was growing more charged by the second.

What was going on here?

Sure, they'd had their fair share of chemically confusing moments, where his closeness made her blood pressure spike and curled her toes in her shoes—the man was certifiably gorgeous. Sure, she'd stared at the incendiary picture of his hard-packed backside until her hormones had forced her fingers down the front of her panties. Before she knew it, said panties had come off completely. She *might* have been in the process of masturbating to a picture of her boss when he'd knocked on the door. Acting natural had been a challenge on par with pole vaulting with a piece of asparagus.

They'd settled into what could actually be a successful partnership. Some mild flirting, fine, but overall a respectful working relationship. More than she could have hoped for, actually!

But sitting beside him on a couch in the near-dark hotel suite—tucked up against his well-muscled side like they were on a date—while watching Leonidas *put it down* on his old lady was making pulses pound in places they had no business pounding.

Good lord. Don't think about pounding.

Was she making a bigger deal out of this than it was? Golfers and caddies tended to bond, didn't they? Many of them were best friends or even family, because of the trust factor being so important. Perhaps . . . they'd simply gotten closer, she and Wells. This was what they did now. They snuggled up and watched movies like a couple of ol' pals.

Merely hoping to confirm that plausible theory, Josephine snuck a quick glance up at Wells's face and found his expression strained, his gaze trained on her face instead of the movie.

Oh boy. Okay. Not just pals.

"I've been thinking," he started, in a low rumble that she could feel deep in her belly. "We're pretty good at this flirting thing, right?"

The temperature of her skin rose, face to fingertips. "Actually, I feel like I'm kind of bumbling my way through it."

He hit pause on the movie while arching a brow. "That picture you sent me was not bumbling. That was expert level."

"Oh." She bit down on a smile. "Good."

"*Good?*" He made a sound in his throat. "Belle. The earth moved."

The smile just kind of exploded across her face.

She heard him swallow. Loudly.

"Anyway, we have flirting momentum now. We should keep going. Do you agree?"

This man kept surprising her. She had to be on her toes around him, yet she also had this very distinct intuition that it would always be okay to let her guard down. How unique. "Yes. I agree,"

she said, trying not to sound breathless. "It would be irrespon-
sible to let the flirting momentum drop."

Wells nodded, took his time looking her over, his attention
eventually returning to her face. "What makes you smell so goddamn good, Josephine? Is it lotion? Perfume?"

"Lotion," she managed, bumpily.

"Thought so."

"It's a vanilla-lilac mashup. Very seasonal."

"Very *distracting*."

"How?"

"You show up smelling like that and I immediately think of
you . . . applying it." Never had the word "applying" sounded so
filthy. "That's how."

"Yes, I put it on in slow motion, slowly stretching each freshly
shaven leg out in front of me, toe in a perfect point—"

"Don't shatter the illusion," he teased, reaching over and tugging on the lapel of her robe, turning her body to face him more
fully on the couch. Her knee left the confines of the robe to rest
on top of his thigh and they both stared down at the contact for
a breath, until he said, "You like the way I smell, too?"

"Yes." She couldn't seem to get her voice above a murmur.
"Lotion or perfume?"

His lips twitched. "Aftershave." Gaze never leaving her face,
he brushed a thumb over her bare knee. "Why don't you come
sit on my lap and smell it up close?"

There was no oxygen to be had. "Okay."

Wells leaned toward Josephine, movements unhurried, his
mouth stopping a hairsbreadth away from her own, his big arms
locking around her middle and dragging her back with him to the
other side of the couch. And now, she was sitting on Wells's lap in
her robe, her butt on his muscle-packed right thigh, her exposed

legs draped over the left one. "Go ahead." His mouth moved in her hair, his hand fisting the belt of her robe. "Smell me."

Was the couch tilting? "Is this how you usually flirt?" she asked.

"Josephine." He lifted the hand wrapped in white terry cloth, using it to nudge her chin higher. And he looked her in the eye. "I never flirt."

What did *that* mean? She couldn't really find the wherewithal to decipher that statement, because she was nearly salivating with the need to smell this man. Up close like this, his aroma went from attractive to appetizing and she was powerless to do anything but dip her nose into his neck and inhale, notes of eucalyptus and almond oil rolling her eyes into the back of her head. Meanwhile, his hand, still fisting the fabric of the belt, was sliding up and down the valley of her thighs, stopping just at the border of indecency.

"Well?" he asked, his breath stirring her hair.

"I like it," she whispered, inhaling again.

A satisfied sound turned over in his chest. "I know something else you like, Josephine."

His gravelly tone made her shiver hotly. "What is it?"

Slowly and deliberately, he picked up the remote control on the arm of the couch and hit rewind, returning to the start of the movie's love scene. And then he hit play.

Josephine swallowed hard, trying not to be obvious about sneaking her knees closer together. Had he noticed she was paying a little too close attention to the scene earlier?

It started from the beginning, moans and drumbeats filling the living space.

Wells rested his mouth against her temple. "How hard he's fucking her. You like that, don't you?"

Arousal snaked through Josephine, starting at the buds of her breasts. They pebbled and grew sensitive inside the white terry cloth. And then lower, her stomach muscles knitting together one by one and drawing taut like shoelaces. She ordered herself to slow down her breathing and act normal, but Wells shifted in this sensual animal way beneath her, his right hand tilting her chin, his lips ghosting up the side of her neck—and the breathy sound she made in response to that featherlight touch more than answered his question.

He wasn't done asking questions, though.

"Did you pack your vibrator, belle?"

If he'd asked her that in broad daylight, she wouldn't have answered. Or she would have asked him if he'd packed his sense of privacy. But in the intimate darkness of the suite—with shadows playing on the wall and her backside planted in his lap—nothing seemed off limits.

"No," she whispered. "I didn't think it would be . . . necessary."

"Didn't expect me to send you pictures of my juicy ass, did you?"

Her laugh sounded more like a gasp. He knew exactly what she'd been doing when he arrived, the big jerk. Why was it so attractive that he'd said nothing until now? "Shut up."

The knuckles brushing her jaw firmed and there was no mistaking the hunger bracketing his mouth, his eyes. "Make me, belle."

A moan issued from the television. Maybe. It could have been inside her head or out loud, too, because God, she wanted to be kissed. Hard. Messy. Frantic. She was a bundle of concentrated nerves that were asking for appeasement. Friction. The touch of another person. And not just any person. Wells. "Just so we're clear, you want me to . . ."

"Make the first move and I'll take over." Their mouths were

touching now, lips damp from their mutual heavy breathing. "Or tell me to leave. And I will. But I need you to know there's no pressure, Josephine. You kick me out and you're still my caddie tomorrow and nothing changes. Not a damn thing. Understand?"

Had Josephine ever met someone who made her feel such a variety of emotions? Frustration, gratitude, belonging, anger . . . lust. "I understand," she said, sighing when his thumb traced the hollow of her throat, those glittering eyes studying her mouth like he was forming a strategy. "What happens after you take over?"

His chest vibrated, his mouth traveling along her cheek to rest against her ear. "After we're done kissing, you mean? Don't you dare skip past that. Finally going to get that taste I've been dreaming about."

"You've been wanting to kiss me? You're not even nice to me."

"You say that with a straight face from inside the presidential suite, belle?" He raised an eyebrow at her. "I already called ahead to the next place to make sure your room has the biggest bathtub—"

She kissed him.

A firm acquainting of lips that turned into three, four, smaller kisses. Like sampling each other and loving every taste even more than the last. Was that her imagination or could she hear his heart booming? Leaning into the kiss, she flattened her left palm on his chest and found the racing organ beating triple time and *that* turned her on more than anything. Proof that beneath his often jerk-like exterior was vulnerability. Need that matched hers.

They were kissing. Making out.

She was making out with Wells Whitaker.

Her boss.

But he wasn't really any of those things to her now. Not after getting to know him better. Now he was just Wells, her infuriating teammate who was also thoughtful and jaded and protective and hot-tempered and sexy. And he kissed like he wouldn't mind either of them running out of oxygen. He kissed her like she was a meal and he wanted to memorize every single flavor on his palate.

"I take over now, Josephine," he rasped, kissing her thoroughly. "You want it like that?"

Her answer was fervent and clear. "Yes."

"Good girl." He trapped Josephine's waist in his hands and turned her in his lap to face the television, which she could barely see now that she'd entered some sort of lust fog. "Lean back against me. I'm going to open this robe like a fucking Christmas present."

In the past, when it had come time to take off her clothes in front of a man, there was always a layer of self-consciousness. Wondering what they were thinking, not just about her body in general, but also the small gray circle on the back of her arm. There were none of those thoughts when Wells untied her robe with shaking hands and peeled it open, painting her nude body in the muted television light. God. She was hot. An inexcusable temptation. His rough groan told her so, along with the thick bulge beneath her butt.

She could feel him looking over her shoulder down the length of her body, could hear his breath growing thin in her ear, his hips pulsing upward slightly, grinding against her bottom, as if the moves were involuntary. Necessary.

"You let me into your room with no panties on?"

"I didn't think you would find out."

"Thank you, God, for Josephine's inappropriate movie selection." Her laugh turned into a whimper when he suctioned his mouth to the side of her neck, yanking the robe open wider, his fingertips dragging slowly up the sides of her rib cage. "You need me to be nice? I'll be the nicest person you ever met. Just to you. Only you. Jesus *Christ*, you're so beautiful."

That's how she felt. Totally and authentically.

Lusted after. Safe. Free to abandon any and all constraints.

Needy and daring all at once, she spread her legs into a V, draping them over Wells's hard thighs, encouraged by the groan that gathered in his chest.

"*Fuck yes*, belle. Is that an invitation to pet it?"

She let her head fall back against his shoulder and nodded. Ready to feel. *Dying* for it.

Not that he gave it to her right away. Wells took his sweet time, turning his head and licking into her mouth, luxuriating in every kiss. His palms scraped up and over her breasts, cupping them gently at first, the massage growing rougher and more adept with every slow, reverent squeeze of his hands.

"Were you rubbing yourself out when I interrupted? Were you on your tiptoes bent over the bathroom counter so you could look at my picture, fingers all slippery on your clit?"

"Yes," she admitted on a gasp.

His chest rumbled appreciatively. "Bet it's still wet, isn't it, belle?" He paused mid-kiss. They breathed hard into one another's mouth. "Go make sure."

Josephine's head swam, heat torching her body.

She couldn't stay still on Wells's lap and he really didn't seem to mind, grunting every time she moved her backside on top of his erection. She tilted her head in invitation and moaned as he took her permission, bathing her pulse with his tongue. She trailed her fingers down her stomach, delving the middle and index ones into the valley of slippery flesh, sucking in a breath when she encountered her swollen clit, no choice but to rub it. Rub it fast and tight.

"Wet," he said.

"Yes."

"Show me."

That directive might have been confusing if their bodies weren't speaking some kind of undiscovered language. Or maybe they were inventing a new one, unique to the two of them, because Josephine lifted up her fingers, seeing them glisten from beneath heavy lids, her eyes rolling back into her head when he bit her shoulder—*hard*—in response.

Approval.

She was given only a second to enjoy the perfect sting of pain before the robe was ripped away completely and she was thrown down, face up on the couch. Naked. Completely, blissfully naked while Wells was still fully dressed. So hot. So hot. Why was that so *hot*?

"You like being filthy with me?" he growled, before stripping off his hoodie, leaving him bare chested in sweatpants. This was not the man everyone saw on the golf course. Sure, he was still his hardy, rough-around-the-edges self, but he was dialed up to ten. His muscles were inked with WHITAKER across his collarbone, an all-seeing eye between his pecs, a snake slithering low on his right hip. His chest and abdomen strained with an almost furious energy. In short, Wells was magnetic. Harsh. Sleek. Beautiful.

He stroked the enormous ridge trapped inside his sweatpants, all while licking his lips and leaning down to drag his mouth side to side over the mound of her sex. Razing her inner thighs with his bared teeth.

"Oh my God," Josephine breathed.

Okay, she took it back. He was dialed up to fifteen.

"Tell me how you want to come," he rasped, kissing the inside of her right knee. Then left. Eyes blazing with need. "I can jerk off while licking this pussy. Bet I come quick as a motherfucker hearing you whine, Josephine. Or you can get it hard and fast on your back. What's it going to be?" He palmed his shaft through the sweatpants, squeezing. "Decide quick—I'm fucking starving for you."

That made two of them. It went both ways.

Her hips were restless on the couch, her nipples in pain from being so hard. She usually required more exploring of her imagination to get this ready. Like, she had to think of something arousing instead of simply being turned on by the reality of touching another person. But not with Wells. Every erogenous zone she possessed was gasping for air, especially her stomach muscles, which were tied in knots, pulling more and more taut by the second. *Decide quick—I'm fucking starving for you.*

It was simply the nature of their relationship—and her nature in general—to challenge him. Throw in the fact that she'd never been more sexually empowered and Josephine found herself crooking a finger at him, melding their mouths together slowly, sensuously, when he came closer. "No sex. Not tonight."

His head dropped forward, but he nodded. "Okay, belle."

"But if you don't lose your temper for the next two days and you finish under par . . ." She raked her fingernails down his chest and over his nipples, making him jerk and shudder. "You can come inside me."

True power was watching his pupils bleed into the brown of his irises, turning his eyes all but black, his right hand shoving into the waistband of his sweats to masturbate himself hard and fast. "Are you fucking kidding me, Josephine?" He growled behind his teeth. "God, I've never wanted to spank anyone so badly in my life."

"I'll let you do that, too," she whispered.

Wells cursed. "No condom. Nothing?"

"If it's safe for both of us?"

"It is. I'm up to date."

"Me too. And I have an IUD. It's the only thing that works well for me." She razed his jawline with her teeth. "It can work well for you, too. *Really* well."

"Ah fuck." He moved in a blur, dropping down to his stomach and pushing her thighs open, his mouth moving over her flesh like a pilgrim in prayer. He wielded his tongue like a sensual weapon, breathing filthy words and praise in between hot strokes, two of his fingers alternating between firm strokes of her clit and pumps inside of her quickening sex.

When had the ceiling of her hotel room been painted like the Sistine Chapel? Her inner thighs were the consistency of jelly, but they were tight at the same time, her sex pulsing faster, faster, until she had to clutch at the couch and grind her back teeth. "I'm close."

"Don't be afraid to wrap your legs around my head and grind on that tongue, understand? It was put there to lick this pussy. Finish hot."

Josephine's back arched off the sofa, tingles crawling up her shoulders, invading her scalp. Her nipples were throbbing, core flexing, robbing her momentarily of sight and sound; all she could hear was her own rapid heartbeat and shallow breathing. And then pleasure was washing over her in a terrible mind-blowing rapture of muscle spasms and bliss, her disembodied voice calling out Wells's name hoarsely.

"I'm here, baby. Baby, just let me put it in your mouth, just for a second." She opened her eyes to find him straddling her hips, sweatpants shoved down around his knees, his grip choking up and down those blunt inches without gentleness. "I'm one stroke away, swear to God. Please. Just need a little suck to get through the next two days."

The raw need in Wells's voice brought Josephine up onto one elbow, even though her vision was still hazy from her orgasm. And no sooner did she give Wells permission with her eyes did he walk forward on his knees and pump the smooth thickness of himself between her lips, groaning at the ceiling, then louder as she accepted more, more. But his voice cut off completely when she drew on him with enough suction to hollow her cheeks—

And with a vile curse, he pulled himself quickly out of her mouth and stroked a rope of moisture onto her breasts, followed by another, another, his abdomen flexed taut, his thighs shaking on either side of her and his eyes squeezed shut. It was the most erotic scene she'd ever been a part of or witnessed. In real life or in the movies.

King Leonidas had nothing on Wells Whitaker.

He dropped down on top of her, using his elbow to keep himself slightly elevated, his gaze unfocused as both of them struggled to catch their breath.

"Well," he said moments later, his voice like gravel as he scrutinized Josephine. "I guess this complicates the shit out of everything."

And with that, he got up and rearranged his sweatpants, then handed Josephine the robe. He jerked his hoodie back on over his head, paced around for a few moments while finger combing his hair and looked at her long and hard. What was he thinking? Had their impromptu hookup met his expectations? "You're not going to be weird with me in the morning, are you?"

She sat up, belted her robe, and ordered herself to be a grown-up about this. They'd exchanged pleasure and now he was leaving. He obviously wasn't a cuddler or an afterglow type of guy—and that was fine. She usually wasn't that type, either.

If Josephine kind of wished he'd held her for a little while afterward, she would get over it. "I'm not going to be weird. Are you?"

"Me?" He scoffed. "No."

Then nodded once and left the room.

With his hoodie on backward.

What . . . the heck had just *happened*?

CHAPTER SEVENTEEN

Wells replaced the squat bar in its cradle with a clang and turned to face the empty twenty-four-hour resort fitness center. Country music filtered into the air-conditioned space from an invisible speaker, a halogen light buzzing overhead. It was four o'clock in the morning and he really needed to be sleeping, but after three hours of dozing in front of the television, he'd woken up wired and knew there was no way he'd go back to bed.

He'd had two options.

Burn off some energy at the gym. Or go knock on Josephine's door and demand to know again if things were going to be weird between them now that they'd hooked up. Although "hooked up" sounded incredibly insufficient, considering he'd forgotten his room number, date of birth, and the current sitting president afterward. Waiting until a socially acceptable hour to make sure their relationship hadn't been compromised was making him restless.

He wanted to get it straightened out before their round got underway in the morning and they wouldn't have a chance to speak off camera until late afternoon.

Without some reassurance, his concentration would be fucked.

To be fair, it was going to be capital-F Fucked no matter what, because of Josephine raking her fingernails down his chest and challenging him to finish under par, so he could come inside her.

Wells groaned out loud, splintering the silence of the fitness center.

Yeah, safe to say their dynamic had changed a lot since yesterday—

And that scared the living shit out of him. If anything, he'd assumed he'd screw up on the golf course and send her packing. This? Was an entirely different ball game. He didn't have, didn't do, didn't understand relationships.

At all.

Way to dive right into the deep end with your caddie, man.

For the first time in his entire life, Wells kind of wished he could run this whole situation by another dude. He *could* try and call Burgess, but as far as Wells could tell, the ill-tempered hockey player was more emotionally stunted than Wells. Also, Burgess would almost certainly hang up on him, so yeah. No calls would be made today.

Buck was out, in terms of fatherly advice.

His own parents were God only knew where. Somewhere in Florida, last he'd heard.

Surprisingly, Josephine's father came to mind. If only Wells didn't need advice about *the man's actual daughter*, that might be an option.

Guess he'd have to figure this out as it came. Going it alone was nothing new for him.

He'd just never been in a *romantic* dilemma before.

And nothing had ever seemed to count this much.

This woman . . . she counted. Big-time. His gut wasn't in fucking knots over nothing.

Wells paced across the hardwood floor in the direction of the water cooler, but he drew up short when something outside the glass double-doored entrance moved, out of the corner of his eye. The resort pool was right outside the gym, glowing like a green jewel in the darkness, and a silhouette he knew very well stood peering through the gate.

Josephine?

He walked straight into the glass door.

The smack of his knee and forehead colliding with the glass, followed by a loud reverberation, made Josephine whip around, startled, then finally deflate with relief when she saw him. "Did you just walk into the door?" came her muffled question from outside.

"No. I *knocked* on it." Hastily, he exited, letting the door swing shut behind him, cutting off an elevator-music version of "Old Town Road." "To get your attention."

A twinkle danced in her eye. "Right . . ."

Just like he hadn't put his hoodie on backward after they'd nearly gotten busy on the couch. His entire equilibrium was off, thanks to her. Even his depth perception felt skewed as he approached her in the early morning fog. "I really wish you wouldn't go out alone at odd hours like this, belle."

She gave him a once-over, taking in his gym shorts and sweaty T-shirt. "You're out at odd hours."

"Yes, but I'm big and mean. You're short and sweet." Ignoring her pursed lips, he eyed the emerald pool lying beyond her shoulder. "Were you planning on going for a swim?"

"I didn't bring a bathing suit with me, so I was just going to stick my feet in." She reached out and rattled the gate leading into the pool area. "It's closed. I had a hunch it would be, but I figured I'd take the walk, anyway."

"Mmmm." Wells slipped the room key out of his pocket and approached the locked gate, taking a moment to study the mechanism. He lifted the handle slightly, then slid his card down between the slot and the metal tab, popping it open. " 'Closed' is a subjective term."

Josephine blinked. "Hotel security might feel differently."

"At this time of the morning, it's one guy in a golf cart and he's probably sleeping." He tucked his tongue into the inside of his cheek. "Do you want to get wet or not?"

"Wow." She pushed his shoulder. "Real nice."

"I was talking to your feet."

Lips twitching with mirth, she walked past Wells through the gate he held open, circling to a shadowed section of the pool and sitting down on the concrete edge. Wells watched her as he approached, enjoying the way she pulled her knees up to her chest, slipping off her sandals and setting them side by side. So neatly. She rolled her pajama pants up to her knees and tested the water with her big toe, before dropping both of them beneath the surface, sighing and tipping her head back, eyes drifting shut.

"Are you going to join me?" she asked.

Was that a real question? He'd only gone to the fitness center in the first place to prevent himself from waking her up too early. Just so he could be around her. *And* find out how she felt about last night. Right now, she was giving away absolutely nothing.

Watching her closely for signs of regret, Wells toed off his sneakers and peeled off his socks, tossing them into a heap in the middle of the walkway. He joined her on the ledge and sank his feet into the cool water. Taking advantage of the fact that her eyes were still closed, her head tipped back, he ran his attention down the front of her throat and literally felt his pupils expand. Did he have the freedom to lean over and sample that skin with his tongue or were they still figuring out when, where, and how it was okay to touch?

"I was going to come knock on your door," Wells found himself saying, with little to no prompting from his brain. Now she was looking at him and he had no choice but to qualify that with more words. "I wanted to make sure you didn't feel weird about what happened. Wanted to get on the same page before our tee time."

She leaned back on her hands, considering him. Outwardly, she was the picture of nonchalance, but even in the moonlight, he could see a slight flush on her neck. "Do I seem weird about it?"

"No," he said slowly. "Then again, you're out wandering the grounds before dawn."

She wet her lips, rolled her left shoulder. "All right, I'll admit I was a little caught off guard by the way you left so fast."

That admission made his pulse scatter like a bag of dropped Skittles. "I left so fast because I was caught off guard."

"By what?"

"How good it was." When relief showed up in her green eyes, his sweat turned clammy on his skin. Had his leaving her room so quickly caused her to feel insecure? "I don't know, my brain just kind of switched off when we started kissing. It's never done that before."

Were her cheeks rosier now or was that a trick of the moonlight? She looked almost . . . pleased by the fact that he'd lost his ability to think when her mouth touched his. At least one of them was cool with it. He might as well have ridden a roller coaster backward. "What do you usually think about during sex?" she asked, finally.

Red flags waved in front of his face. "Josephine, this conversation isn't happening."

"No, I really want to know." She folded her hands in her lap. "I'll go first—"

"Josephine, don't even think of saying another word." His blood pressure was now somewhere in the clouds. "Fine. I guess I concentrate on . . . not saying anything that might lead the woman on, while still making sure everyone has a good time." He tried to read her reaction to that and couldn't. "I've never been an asshole to women, Josephine. I just don't want to get stuck with one of them."

She put a hand on her chest. "I knew deep down you were a hopeless romantic."

"Hey, they probably didn't want to get stuck with me, either." He rubbed an impatient hand on his thigh, wondering how the hell he'd gone from squats to baring his soul in a matter of minutes. "What I'm saying is, I wasn't worrying about leading you on. *Or* getting stuck with you. I might have been surprised enough by that to leave a little abruptly. Believe me, it wasn't you."

Josephine was quiet for so long, her feet moving side to side in the water, that he almost begged her to say something, but she finally said, "You left out the part where your hoodie was on backward—"

"I have no idea what you're talking about."

Her laughter danced over the surface of the water. The silence was okay after that, but it lasted only until she tipped her head toward the gate he'd jimmied open. "Correct me if I'm wrong, but that wasn't the first time you've picked a lock."

"No. But it has been a while. Good to know I've still got it."

"Where did you hone these skills?"

He started to explain, then stopped. "I'm saying a lot of things this morning that make me sound like bad news."

"Don't worry, I already knew you were bad news." She smiled, letting him know she was kidding. *Thank God.* "I also . . . like you, anyway." She lifted her blue toes out of the water, wiggling them in the moonlight. "Remember?"

Josephine liked him.

You already knew that. She let you come on her tits.

Right. Maybe *every* time she said it out loud—or gave him proof—it would make him feel like a hero? That was something to look forward to. Recently, he'd been looking forward to a lot of things. Reassured that he wasn't making himself sound like a supervillain, Wells continued. "I didn't just fall in with a bad crowd growing up, I *started* the bad crowd. Kids who had too much freedom. Most of us got attention only when we landed in trouble, so we made a lot of it." He hesitated before telling her the next part. "On nights when my parents were using the house for a party, I used to break into my middle school to sleep in the gym. It was too loud at home. The party might end, but they'd fight after too much alcohol. I just . . . got really good at picking locks."

Josephine slid a little closer, until their hips were touching. "I wish you didn't have to do that. I'm sorry."

"It's okay." He rubbed a circle into her lower back, sort of entranced by the way their feet looked together in the water. "When I moved in with my uncle, I didn't have to sleep at school anymore. But later, I got caught with a stolen bike and the family court judge gave me an ultimatum. Spend time in juvie or get a job. I took the second option, but I wasn't about to let some judge teach me a lesson, so I started stealing the odd watch out of lockers, purely out of spite. Or maybe peeling a few hundred-dollar bills off a wad of them. That all stopped once Buck got ahold of me, but yeah . . . the pool gate wasn't even a challenge."

For a moment, there was nothing but the sound of their feet sluicing slowly through the water. "But you never totally stopped getting into trouble, did you? That fight a few weeks ago . . . and all the ones before that."

Wells sighed. "Yeah. I guess it's not something that has ever fully left me. The inner battle. I find that kind of comforting sometimes. Is that bad? I don't ever want to be a man who backs down from a fight."

"I think that's okay. As long as you're fighting for something worthwhile."

Mentally, he jogged back through the last few punches he'd thrown. "Let's say I'm sitting in a bar, minding my business, and some drunk stranger in a DraftKings hat starts calling me every name in the book for ruining his fantasy golf lineup. Then, let's say he throws a *very* saucy chicken wing at me. Would it be worthwhile to break his nose?"

"Obviously, yes."

They shared a growing smile, then went back to looking at their feet in the water. "What about you, belle? There has to be *some* trouble in your past. A school suspension or a little trouble with the cops. Public indecency. Give me something."

She squinted into the darkness. "Tallulah likes to party. More than me. She has this crazy high tolerance for alcohol and she's a fun drunk, so it never mattered how often I drank Diet Coke at the bars, she'd still make it fun. More often than not, she went out with casual friends or a guy and I stayed home and waited for an entertaining report the next morning. But this one time, she convinced me to go to New Orleans for her birthday . . ."

"I like where this is going."

"Do you? Because I smoked pot for the first time and went on a ghost tour, which, in case you're wondering, is the number one thing you should *not* do after smoking weed, probably right behind sky diving and attending a live birth. Especially in an unfamiliar city."

Wells's ribs were starting to ache from holding in his laughter. So he finally let it out on a shuddering gust of breath.

"We ended up in a graveyard, where I swore that bony fingers were poking up out of the ground." She gave him a solemn look that sent him over the edge. "Spoiler: it was grass."

"Ironic. Is that where the night ended?"

"No, as it happens. When the tour was over, I was so worried I might ruin everyone's good time with my freak-out that I doubled down and did two shots of tequila, just to show everyone that I was having a good time. And that I wasn't worried the ghosts had followed us from the graveyard—*even though* I really was. Literally, I was checking over my shoulder the whole night. But bottom line, the tequila kicked in and I ended up flashing a police horse. With a policeman on top."

Wells shook his head slowly. "There are so many twists and turns in this story, my neck is going to be sore. Tell me you didn't get arrested for that."

"Not in New Orleans, no. I just got beads."

"From the officer?"

"No, the horse. But that could have been the weed talking."

Wells had to bury his face in the crook of his arm to keep his laugh from waking up the whole damn resort. "That might be the greatest story I've ever heard."

"Thank you."

It wasn't until she glanced behind her, and down, that Wells realized he'd been rubbing her lower back in a circle the whole time she'd been speaking. Now, in the silence, she moved closer to him and he thought, *Yes, more kissing*, but she surprised him by laying the side of her face on his shoulder, instead. What *was* the feeling that swept through his chest like a storm wind? Some sort of combination of protectiveness and . . . gratitude that she felt relaxed and secure enough with him to use him as a pillow.

A series of beeps went off in his gym shorts—and her pajama pants.

Her blood sugar must be low.

Josephine lifted her head, her attention swinging from his pocket up to his eyes. "You downloaded the app and accepted my follow request? You didn't have to, you know." Worry clouded into the green of her eyes. "It beeps constantly. Like, it never ends—"

He kissed her.

It happened without any critical thought involved. Kissing her was like the words to a favorite song. He simply knew the lyrics.

"Of course I followed you in the app, belle. Soon as I got to my room last night and turned my hoodie the right way around." Chest tight, he reached into the opposite pocket of his shorts and fished out the roll of glucose tabs he'd put there, handing them to her wordlessly.

She stared at them for a beat before taking them. "You're carrying tabs?"

Wells rolled his neck, praying his behavior wasn't overkill. It's not like he'd even expected to see her this morning. He was just trying to get into the habit of carrying them, so he would never forget.

Josephine still seemed to be at a loss for words. "You just . . . did that? And you didn't make a big deal out of it." Uncapping the tube, she popped two purple disks into her mouth, chewing slowly. "Thank you, Wells. Really."

Ask me to walk on broken glass next. Watch me not even hesitate. Those sentiments wanted to dive out of his mouth, but he followed his gut when it came to this woman and he sensed, he *always* sensed, that she didn't like to dwell on the topic of diabetes too long. "Who makes you dance? Prince? Madonna. The Weeknd?"

A grin slowly shaped her mouth. "Nope. And stop trying to catch me off guard."

"It's only a matter of time before I figure it out."

"Keep dreaming."

As carefully as possible, so he wouldn't dislodge her cheek or cause her to sit up straight again, Wells put his arm around Josephine's shoulder. After a few minutes of silence, he looked down to find her eyes closed, her breathing deep and even. Was she *sleeping*?

Yeah. She was.

On him.

He allowed himself a moment of stunned pride before he gently lifted Josephine into his lap, turned, got onto his knees, and stood. He carried her to the row of white plastic lounge chairs arranged near the perimeter of the pool area and sat down, leaning back and closing his eyes with his caddie in his arms. Doing his best to memorize the feeling of her before his own eyelids grew heavy, as well. Just before he fell asleep, the most absurd thought occurred to him. What if the problem that morning hadn't been their inability to sleep?

What if they'd been unable to sleep . . . apart?

CHAPTER EIGHTEEN

The first two days of the tournament had been a roller coaster ride . . . if the roller coaster was on fire, and also got stuck upside down. Yet somehow day three ended up being the most remarkable of all. Wells shot his best round in two years. Over the course of the morning and afternoon, the crowd that followed Wells and Josephine from hole to hole grew bigger, more boisterous. A little while after that, the cheering started. They were *actually* rooting for Wells.

Not that he deigned to acknowledge it.

The Texas sun burned bright when they arrived on the fairway of the eighteenth hole. Wells took a long drink of water from his metal canteen and handed it to Josephine without looking. Too parched to question the move, Josephine let the cold water cool her throat, capped the canteen, and put it back in the bag, taking out her binoculars next and raising them to her eyes, surveying the green. She'd already given Wells her advice and was waiting for him to finish chewing it over.

"Where should I set it down?" he asked, referring to the ball. "Give me a landmark."

"Pitfalls of being short. I can't really see over the rise." She held out the binoculars. "You want to look?"

"Hop up on my back," Wells suggested, without missing a beat. "You won't be happy with the shot unless you can see it for yourself."

That *was* true. Still, the idea was absurd and *definitely* not happening. "I appreciate you wanting me to be satisfied with the strategy, but caddies don't just . . . climb on their golfers."

He arched an eyebrow at her.

"You know what I mean."

Wells hissed out a breath. "I'm afraid I need your opinion on a landing spot or I won't be confident in the shot, belle."

"Seriously?"

He hitched his chin toward his back. "Someone once said my ass could be used as a roller coaster seat. Test out the theory."

Her cheeks were growing suspiciously hot, but dammit, she really wanted to check their position in relation to the green. "I'm only going up for a second," she muttered, circling around back of him. Taking a tiny beat just to appreciate—

"Well, I know *one* thing you're satisfied with," Wells drawled.

Josephine begged the sky to keep her sanity intact. Then, settling her hands on his thick shoulders, she jumped, locking her legs around Wells's waist. The crowd laughed, followed by the sound of camera shutters going off. Josephine barely registered any of it because—*oh God.* She hadn't had a piggyback ride in a long, long time, possibly long before she'd become aware of her body or its sexual properties. Because she didn't remember piggyback rides like this—*at all.* The juncture of her thighs found the top curve of his buttocks, pressing oh so snugly, her inner thighs squeezing his waist. The clean aftershave scent of his neck was suddenly very close, along with the bunching of his back muscles against her breasts. And the air quite simply disappeared from her lungs.

"Uhmm."

"Binoculars, Josephine," he said hoarsely.

"Right. Okay."

She lifted the binoculars to her eyes with a shaky hand. "I

would say aim for the guy in the polo shirt and hat, but that doesn't really narrow it down. Um . . . the man in mint green." She passed him the binoculars. "See him?"

Wells looked. "Yeah. Put it down right there?"

"Yup."

He gave the binoculars back. "Check again." His hand, now free, wrapped around her ankle, his thumb sliding into her sock in a sweeping arc. Dug in roughly. "Take all the time you need."

At this rate, she'd need, like, thirteen seconds to orgasm. Tops.

In other words, it was high time to get down. Which she did.

"You ready?" she said breathily, smoothing her clothing.

"Some might say too ready." He inhaled deeply, visibly getting ahold of himself. Finally, he focused on the shot with a deep "mmmm" rumbling in his throat.

That's how Josephine typically knew it was time to get out of the way—when he gave a gruff "mmmm" and that crease appeared between his brows.

Silently, she backed up and held her breath, praying she'd given him good advice. She exhaled when the ball dropped in the exact place they'd chosen, around thirty yards from the man in mint, ten from the hole.

"Great shot," she said, taking the six iron and replacing it in the bag.

Wells started to respond, but the cheering around them swelled while they advanced to the green, preparing to putt. He looked momentarily surprised by the growing mass of people, but he hid it almost immediately, putting his head down and trudging on to the final shot of day three.

"Don't love the grass on this one."

"Bumpy in spots," she agreed.

"But I was thinking about that mindfuck lesson you gave me. The morning before the first round. Remember?" He hunkered down, putter in hand. "The course is bigger than the distance between the ball and the hole, right? What if I shoot past it a little to avoid that knotted grass and let it roll back in?"

"I love it," she murmured. "You can control that roll from here in a way you couldn't from the fairway. Make it delicate."

"Make it delicate," Wells snorted. "It's never been more obvious I have a chick for a caddie."

"Lucky you."

"We'll see."

She bit her lip to subdue a smile. "You good, then?"

"Mmmm."

That was Josephine's cue. She backed up, putting an unsteady hand on the bag. Today wasn't for all the marbles—that was tomorrow—but today felt . . . *big*. There was something exciting in the air. Wells hadn't lost his temper or gotten overly discouraged by bad shots. And she couldn't give the credit to their little wager. A man didn't resurrect his golf game in the name of sex. Right?

No.

That would be ridiculous.

Perhaps that was how it started this morning, but she'd been watching this man play for five long, storied years—and she could practically *feel* him coming back to life. Deep down, Wells Whitaker loved golf and finally, finally she could see him allowing that to be true again. Out loud. In his every action. What a glorious thing to witness.

Please let it continue.

The hard leather of the bag strap bit into the palm of Josephine's hand as Wells lined up the shot and fired gently, rolling the ball into the target, where it disappeared with a *clink*. The sudden roar of the crowd was tinged with shock at the daring play. Cameras jockeyed for the best position to film Wells as they passed through to the clubhouse. Commentators were recapping the shot on live broadcasts. It was mayhem.

For a golf course.

Meanwhile, Wells casually removed his glove and shoved it into his back pocket, as if he saw none of the stir he was causing. "Ready, belle?"

"Yes." She shouldered the bag. "Not even a single fist pump, huh?"

"We're better than that," he responded, loud enough to be heard over the crowd.

"Tell that to my fist." She shook out her hand. "It wants to pump so bad."

"Yeah?" Tucking his tongue into his cheek, he gave her a quick, but heated once-over. "I know how it feels, don't I?"

An embarrassing whoosh sound snuck out of Josephine, her legs wobbling ominously. *A lot* of cameras were trained on them. Not the most opportune time to be sporting stiff nipples.

"You're not just playing well because of my . . ."

"Sex-centive?" Wells deadpanned.

She shook her head. "As I've said before, thank God they know better than to mic you up."

He half-grinned, gesturing for her to stay close to him on their way up the path—and it was easy to see why. Hundreds of hands stuck out, begging for high fives from Wells. From . . . her, too? Yes. Every so often, someone shouted *Josephine!* Had her name been mentioned on the air or did they look her up—

"Stay close, please," Wells said briskly in her ear. "Belle, please."

"Okay."

"We've established that you're more than capable of shlepping my bag around for five hours, but I would very much like to take it now. Is that all right with you?"

"Why?"

"There are marks on your shoulder."

"Oh." She turned her head to one side, observing the series of red grooves buried in the place where her neck sloped into her shoulder. "They don't hurt."

"Looking at it is hurting *me*."

Josephine rolled her eyes, letting him take the bag.

Someone in the crowd made an *awwww* sound.

Josephine groaned, but after a few steps, she remembered what she'd been meaning to say to Wells. "You're not just playing well because of the sex-centive. You're enjoying the game itself again. I can tell."

A beat passed. "*How* can you tell?"

Josephine searched for the right words. "After you play a really good shot, you get this look on your face. Like you're really deep in thought. I think that's you trying to manage your feelings. Like, oh no. You wouldn't want to get carried away being too happy. So you stand there intellectualizing the shot or hunting for the negative side." She smacked his chest. "Don't *do* that, Wells. Let positives be positives."

"I'm looking at one," he said gruffly, visibly catching himself off guard, his step faltering subtly. "Did I enjoy today? Yeah. I guess I did. But I wouldn't have remembered how to enjoy it without you, Josephine." He cleared his throat hard. "Now if you're done being emotional, I need to turn in my scorecard, so I don't get disqualified."

"Y-yes," she stammered, stopping at the bottom of the ramp in an area that, thankfully, was cordoned off from the still-cheering spectators. "Do you want me to hold the bag?"

"Shoulder marks," he growled, storming into the clubhouse.

As soon as the door closed behind Wells, a woman in a PGA tour jacket and an earpiece ran up beside Josephine. "Miss Doyle?"

"Yes."

"As soon as Mr. Whitaker is finished turning in his card, his presence has been requested in the media tent."

"Really?" The blood drained from Josephine's face. "Oh God."

The woman's polite smile faltered. "I'm . . . sorry?"

It was on the tip of Josephine's tongue to inform the official that Wells wouldn't be making an appearance in front of the sea of sports reporters. But wasn't one of the conditions of him being allowed back on the tour that he play nice with the media?

"He'll be there," Josephine assured her, weakly.

This ought to be interesting.

A few minutes later, Wells exited the clubhouse, bag still perched on his shoulder. "We're going to eat, belle."

"Hold that thought. They want you in the media tent."

"Fuck my life," he grumbled, without missing a beat. "Why?"

"Probably because you just played your best round in two years."

He hissed an exhale between his teeth. Seemed to ponder the situation for a moment. "If that's the case, you're doing it with me."

Those words did not compute. "I'm sorry, what?"

"Straighten your ponytail." He took Josephine's hand, pulling her along behind him toward the tent. "You're doing the interview with me."

She gaped. "My ponytail is crooked?"

"Since the eleventh hole." He jerked a shoulder. "It's cute, so I didn't say anything."

"*Wells.*" She tried to slow him down, but her heels only skidded in the grass. "Golfers don't bring their caddies to the media tent."

"This one does."

"Why?"

"I don't know, Josephine," Wells fired back over his shoulder.

"I just . . . have this pretty intense need to make sure everyone knows you're very fucking important. *Okay?* Could you kindly just go along with it?"

Josephine's mouth snapped shut.

What was she supposed to say to that?

She couldn't think of a single thing. Not when she suddenly felt . . . buoyant. Like she could float up into the cloudless sky and bask there in the sunshine, never coming down. *Was* she? *Very fucking important* to him? She'd been harboring the hope that her assistance on the course was making a difference, but having Wells say it out loud unlocked something inside her. Something like . . . pride.

A young man with a clipboard waved them into the big, white media tent as soon as they arrived—and dear lord, it happened so fast. One second, they were outside in the blazing sunshine and the next, they were embraced by shade and ice-cold air conditioning. Also, lighting crews, television cameras, and reporters, interspersed with boom mics.

A table waited for them at the front of the room, complete with several microphones proclaiming all the major networks. Her parents were 100 percent going to see this.

"Hold up. Come here," Wells said, turning her around by the shoulders.

Before she could question his intentions, he tucked a few strands of hair into her ponytail and tightened it gently, making her eyes blink at a very rapid rate. "Thanks."

In response, he pulled her toward the stage with a grunt, ascending the stairs . . .

And stopping short.

There was only one chair.

Relieved in the most indescribable way, Josephine started to back down the stairs. "I'll just catch you later—"

"Nope."

Wells pulled out the chair, guiding her down into it.

Then he stood directly behind her, frowning, with his arms crossed.

"*What?*" he shouted at the tent.

A sprinkling of nervous laughter followed. Face on fire, Josephine watched the reporters exchange glances, some of them amused, others aghast. Finally, one of the brave ones stood.

"Mr. Whitaker," said the middle-aged man, holding a notepad. "Congratulations on a successful round of golf today. Would you mind giving us some insight into what led to you returning to the tour?"

"The question is would I mind? Yes."

Josephine didn't think. She just elbowed him. Hard. It just came naturally.

The tent erupted in laughter.

She couldn't see Wells's face, but she was relieved when he spoke again, dry this time, rather than hostile. "Does that answer your question?"

The reporter rocked forward on his toes, eyebrows elevating. "Your caddie had something to do with your return?"

"That's right. She bullied me into it."

Josephine leaned forward to speak into the microphone. "That's a lie, your honor."

More laughter, louder this time, echoed in the dim tent.

Wells bent over, nudging her aside to amplify his own voice. "Meet Josephine Doyle, folks. She's meaner than she looks."

"Only when you claim the wind speed is irrelevant."

"That's when you get run over by a golf cart to make a point, if I recall."

Josephine smiled broadly. "It was a welcome reprieve from you, Wells."

No one was holding back on the laughter at this point.

"Thanks for keeping me humble, Josephine."

She smiled up at him, surprised to find his usual stone-faced countenance held a glimmer of . . . affection. Her heart pounded in response. "Anytime," she said, breathily.

The media stared at them in silence for several seconds.

And then everyone started shouting questions at once.

Wells and Josephine didn't get much of a chance to speak during their late lunch.

Or on the trip through the lobby toward the elevators.

People kept stopping them for pictures and autographs.

Now, she stumbled back against the elevator wall after punching the button for her floor and stared straight ahead, shell-shocked. "What was that?"

"I don't know," Wells muttered, looking at his phone. "But my ex-manager called me three times in the last hour and he doesn't get out of bed unless someone offers him a boatload of money."

"Are you going to call him back?"

"Eventually." A muscle moved in his cheek. "I need to talk to you first."

The doors of the elevator opened on Josephine's floor and they stepped off, moving side by side down the hallway toward her room. And it was really saying something that she could feel the electric pulse of anticipation when she needed to shower and change *this* badly. Was he going to come into her room again? How could she miss the scrape of his jaw on her cheeks so badly when she'd experienced it only once? "What do you need to talk to me about?"

"Safety." He whipped off his ballcap and raked five fingers

through his hair, throwing a glance back toward the elevators. "When I said I wanted everyone to know how important you are, I didn't think ahead far enough. If you could just stay put in this room unless I'm with you, belle . . ." He patted the air with both hands. "My stress level would appreciate it."

"Wells, come on." She rolled her eyes. "They're just asking for my autograph because I happened to be there. They were just being nice."

"Golf fans are mean as sin, Josephine. I once had a child in a Callaway hat give me the finger. And he was with his grandma. Who told me to shove a club up my ass."

She slapped a hand over her mouth to keep from laughing.

"It's not funny. I'm asking you *nicely*—since nice shit is apparently so important to you—to please not go traipsing around the resort before sunrise anymore. Call me and I will come get you. Please."

"Wow. I don't know if *traipsing* is the right word . . ."

"*Josephine.*" Wells advanced on her, hesitating with a curse when their bodies were a breath apart. But then he pushed forward the remaining distance, flattening her against the door, making both of them exhale shakily, their bodies shifting together. Closer. "Let me be careful with you, belle. Let me worry without asking a bunch of questions, okay?"

"You hate questions," she whispered.

"Yeah. But I really, really don't hate you." Eyes closed, he rolled his forehead against hers. "Deal with it."

Why was it that this man saying he didn't hate her was the equivalent of another man promising to build her a kingdom? "When you retire from golf, you could consider poetry."

He made a frustrated sound, kissing her hard as he slapped both of his hands down on the door above her head. "If you make me wait one more second to hear your agreement to be careful, Josephine, I swear to *God*."

"I don't know," she said, her breath beginning to shallow, need causing her thoughts to run together in one high-pitched, continuous note. "It's kind of fun making you wait."

Going still, he searched her eyes, and laughed low under his breath at what he saw.

Challenge. Excitement.

Wells looked up and down the hallway. Clearly checking for other guests.

Making sure they were alone.

Then in one swift move, Wells lowered his hips and pressed up roughly between her thighs, lifting her feet off the floor. "You like teasing me?" he rasped into her neck.

Did she?

Yeah . . .

"Maybe a little."

"I could bring you inside," he said, circling his hips slowly, making sparks dance in front of her eyes. "Convince you to give me my prize a day early."

"You could try," she gasped, the thick base of him rubbing her clit.

He stayed right there, pressing tight. Tight. Tight. Until she screamed in her mouth.

"I could succeed." He swooped down and consumed her lips in a hungry kiss, drawing her tongue into his mouth with suction, then giving it back and licking deep, groaning with fervent approval. Snagging her bottom lip between his teeth with a growl before letting it go. "But I want to look you in the eye while I'm coming and know I fucking earned it. And I'm not talking about money, I'm talking about . . . you being proud. Of me."

She could only stare at him, shaken. In fact, he seemed a little caught off guard himself. "I'm already proud of you."

"Then I want more of it, Josephine." He kissed her softly and tensed, wincing as he let her feet meet the floor again. "A lot more," he said, stepping back and adjusting himself with a pained laugh. "I need to go before I change my mind. Are you going to stay put or not?"

Her nod was unsteady, thanks to all her bones transforming into gelatin. "You're lucky there's a bathtub."

"There will always be a bathtub, Josephine." He plowed his fingers through his hair again and turned, groaning up at the ceiling on his way to the elevator. "Good fucking night."

The corner of her lips tilted. "Good night, Wells."

She drifted into her room in a daze and plopped down on the carpet, staring into space, replaying the kiss while her fingers traced her lips. Was she falling for Wells Whitaker? Like the real man and not the persona she'd always admired from afar?

Yes.

Safe to say she was definitely slipping down a steep slope with no brakes.

There had to be good reasons to put them on, but in that moment, she couldn't fathom a single one. Maybe she wouldn't until one was staring her right in the face.

CHAPTER NINETEEN

Wells knew something was wrong as soon as Josephine answered the door the following morning. Her ponytail was crooked and she sort of mumbled good morning. None of her chipper, insightful encouragement or words of wisdom. More like a muffled *g'mornhey*. Once again, she was wearing her white hotel bathrobe and her lack of actual clothing was going to make them late for their designated practice period. Intuition told him not to mention that.

Not this time.

This was not the Josephine he'd left blushing at her door last night.

"Everything okay?" Wells asked cautiously, entering and closing the door behind him.

"I'll be ready soon," she called from the bathroom.

Then she said something under her breath to the effect of *some of us don't get to just put on a fucking hat.*

Wow. Tough but fair.

There was a lot of truth to that complaint.

Despite the risk of having a hairbrush leveled at his head, he rested his shoulder on the inside of the bathroom doorframe, watching in the mirror as Josephine fashioned another ponytail and ripped it back out, her arms falling back to her sides like they weighed a hundred pounds each. "Yes, but is everything *okay*, Josephine?"

"It's stupid. I should know better." She spoke very concisely. "I ordered room service last night and I didn't give myself enough insulin for the burger bun. I always underestimate the carbs in burger buns. *Always*. And I woke up with my blood sugar in the three hundreds."

It took a serious effort, but he didn't let his alarm show. "Is that dangerous?"

"I mean, it *can* be if sustained for a long period of time. But really, it's just life with diabetes. The three hundreds happen a lot more than I want them to, because I'll never be able to perfectly mimic a pancreas. It's impossible." She closed her eyes, breathing in through her nose and out through her mouth. "High blood sugar makes me feel on edge and . . . glitchy, sort of. My head aches. Concentrating is hard."

If Wells could have taken over the condition from her in that moment, he wouldn't have hesitated. Not for a single second. In fact, *fuck* his working pancreas. It had a lot of nerve. To have to worry about a burger bun? Not to mention, every single meal. Honestly, he wasn't sure how anyone could do this every day of the year and *not* be in a constant state of frustration. "That's how you're feeling right now? Your head aches and you're glitchy."

"Yes."

"How do we fix it?"

"*We* don't do anything. *I* do."

"Okay, that's fair."

Silence landed hard.

A combination of things were happening with her—that he could see, anyway. Regret for snapping at him, anger with herself, overall aggravation, physical distress. So many emotions crossing her face at once, like watercolor paints running together—and it was probably a private moment, but Wells couldn't seem to make himself leave.

"Can you handle this alone . . . without being alone?"

Her eyes slowly climbed to his in the mirror. "Sure," she answered, guarded.

Relieved, Wells nodded.

"I know I'm making us late," she said.

"That's not important right now."

She let out a breath, picked up the hairbrush, and put it back down. "I've given myself a correction, so I'm just waiting for my number to come back down. It will, but sometimes it's slow. I can still function, though, so let me just get ready."

"Let's say we didn't have to worry about making our practice time, because I'm a fucking golf god and practicing is for mortals. What else could you do to feel better?"

There.

A hint of a smile.

His pulse beat easier.

"I mean . . ." She shrugged. "Drinking water helps. And it'll come down really fast if I run."

He raised an eyebrow. Tipped his head subtly toward the main door.

"If you're implying that you'd like to go for a run with me, no you don't."

"Why?"

"If you think I'm irritated now, watch me perform the activity that should be an option only if someone is chasing you with a hunting knife. Do you know your lungs release a little bit of blood when you run? *They* know it isn't right."

"I won't say a word. We'll just run." He turned away from the bathroom and started to stretch, pulling his right heel up to his ass. "I'd really like you to feel better, belle," he said casually, when he actually wanted to shout, *Please feel better immediately.* "You think I'm scared of a little irritation? There is a picture of me in the *dictionary* next to the word 'irritation.' And I've never once tried to save anyone from it, so why should you do me any favors?"

"That is a pretty good point." She turned and leaned back against the bathroom sink, hesitating. "There is probably already a crowd outside. They'll be watching us, wondering why we're going for a random jog before tee off."

Wells didn't give a flying fuck what anyone thought, but . . . Josephine did. When it came to some things. Like her capabilities. Her strength. Needing a run for the sake of her health fell under both of those headings. She was strong because of her struggle, not in spite of it, but that was *his* belief. It didn't necessarily match how she felt in a vulnerable moment. "Let's run in the hallway. You don't even have to change."

She huffed a laugh. "Run in the hallway in a robe?"

"If it makes you feel better, I'll go shirtless."

A shoulder shrug from Josephine. "It wouldn't hurt," she mumbled.

"Stop trying to seduce me with flattery," he said dryly, tossing his hat on the bathroom sink and stripping off his polo. "Come on."

"My lungs are bleeding from excitement."

Despite her irritable state, he didn't miss the way she cataloged his chest and stomach. He might have even flexed a little, in the name of making her feel better. Whatever it took to get her out of the room and toward a fix—and he was not taking it for granted that she was allowing him to be part of the solution.

They positioned the brass hook to hold her door open, then stood side by side in the carpeted hallway, Josephine barefoot, Wells in the leather sneakers he usually wore until it came time to put on his spikes. "You ready?"

"No," she said, starting to jog.

Hiding his smile, he caught up and kept pace with her. Down to the end of the hallway, where they touched the wall, turned and started back in the direction they'd come.

"Depeche Mode."

"No," she answered without missing a beat.

"Bad Bunny."

"You're casting a very wide net."

"Give me the decade, at least," he complained.

"Only because you're shirtless." She glanced over, lips pursed. "The sixties."

He growled. "That would have been helpful in the beginning."

She hip checked him, briefly interrupting his stride. "I help you more than enough."

Truthfully? He kind of loved Josephine in a bad mood. "That's true. You do."

They tapped the hallway wall, turned, and continued, jogging in companionable silence for a few minutes. Until, "It's the Beatles, isn't it?"

"Nope."

Wells groaned.

"You're getting closer."

"There's that."

"There's also this." She knocked on a random hotel room door and then sprinted ahead at three times the speed they'd been jogging. Leaving him in her dust. Making it look like he was the one who'd knocked. Wells boomed a laugh, but it cut off abruptly when the door Josephine had knocked on opened a few yards behind him.

"Uh . . . yes?" called an older man into the hallway.

Without turning around, Wells picked up speed.

Josephine had disappeared back into her room.

No. She wouldn't. She would *not* close the door on him, leaving him out in the hallway shirtless, caught red-handed as a doorbell ditcher.

Spoiler: yes, she would.

Wells skidded to a halt outside her door and grabbed the handle, rattling it violently. Locked. "Oh. You are *so* wrong for this, belle."

Her gasping laugh reached him through the door.

"Open it."

"Son, did you knock on my door?" called the man on the other end of the hall.

"Sorry about that." Wells gave a stilted wave. "Wrong room."

Dude wouldn't leave it at that. "Aren't you that Whitaker fellow?"

Josephine was all but dying on the other side of the goddamn door. "You've had your fun," he ground out, though he was also . . . smiling? "Let me in."

The door clicked open and Wells stormed inside, letting it shut behind him while he watched Josephine huddle against the far wall of the room, face buried in her hands, shoulders shaking with mirth.

"Looks like you're feeling better," he remarked, wishing he could taste that laugh, feel it against his mouth.

"Much." She scooped her phone off the bed, tapped the screen, and held it out, so Wells could see the dots sloping downward, her number beginning to come down: 267. Still high, but going in the right direction. "It'll keep going down now that I've given it a kickstart."

"I'm glad, baby."

All right. That just . . . slipped right out.

They stared at each other for a few heavy moments, before heading for the bathroom at the same time, pausing in the doorway to search each other for objections, then going in together. Slowly. Wells pulled his shirt back on and replaced his hat while Josephine began another attempt at a ponytail.

"You know, it looks the exact same every time you do it."

She hummed. "To the untrained male eye, maybe."

"Give me a go."

She paused in the act of gathering her hair, revealing that very edible neck. "You want to do my ponytail?"

"I want to do a lot of things to your ponytail."

"*What?* Gross."

Smooth, guy. "That didn't come out the way I meant it to." He moved to stand behind her, shaking out his hands. "I'm nervous about my first hair gig."

"Seriously. I've seen you less nervous about a twenty-yard putt."

Wells took the brush in his right hand and started pulling it through her auburn strands. At some point, he knew he needed to begin forming the tail, but holy shit, this was soothing. "How do women get anything done? I'm not exaggerating when I say I could do this for hours."

"Throw in that ponytail comment and I think we're working with a fetish here, Whitaker."

Considering how it started, this morning was turning into the most fun he'd had in a really long time. Maybe even his entire life. Just being around her was . . . eighty experiences rolled into one. Relaxing, arousing, comfortable, arousing. Fun and interesting and right. And arousing. Was it a weird time to mention that he'd like to take a bite out of her neck? In fact, he was dying to untie her robe and look at her naked in the bathroom mirror, but now wasn't the right moment. Not when she'd woken up feeling shitty.

"All right, here goes."

Biting down on his bottom lip enough to draw blood, he used

the brush to sort of urge sections of hair into his fist. When he was satisfied he'd gotten them all, he panicked, because he had no way to keep them in this perfect formation—

She held a black rubber band above her shoulder. "Here."

"Thank Christ." He blew out a breath. "This part is stressful."

"I know!"

"There are bumps no matter what I do," he growled, wrapping the band, twisting, wrapping again, feeling like he was using someone else's hands.

"Yup. They look like shark fins."

A laugh bounded out of him. "Oh my God, Josephine, that's exactly what they look like."

Their gazes locked in the mirror and his heart whipped around like a car doing donuts. "You feel better, belle?"

"Yeah." She turned her head slightly and kissed the inside of his wrist. "Thanks, Wells."

No. He should be the one thanking *her*, right? She'd already started transforming him into a better golfer, but allowing him to help this morning? With something so personal and important to her? Fuck. That made him feel like a human. A human worth his salt.

Her faith sat welcome and heavy on his chest. And he wanted more of it.

Not knowing what to say, Wells leaned down and kissed the side of her neck, breathing through the need to do more. Touch her everywhere. His eyes closed on a rough exhale when she pushed her butt back into his lap. He gripped her hips and—

His phone rang in his pocket.

No. *Noooooooo.*

In tandem, they slumped, Josephine's sweet ass ending its temptation campaign as she smirked at him in the mirror, moving slightly out of his reach.

Grating a curse, he pulled out his phone. Nate was calling. Again.

There could only be one reason.

Comeback.

Wells could already hear the word curling in his ear. Did he *want* to hear it?

For Josephine's sake, yes. He did.

But for him? All that attention and accolades were fleeting. He knew that all too well now.

What had Josephine said to him a few days ago? *It's not always about the next thing you do. Sometimes it's about what you already did.* He'd been thinking about that a lot. And maybe . . . she was right. Maybe he could learn to let go of the pressure that came from comparing his rank to everyone else. Being critical of his swing. Stressing about the next tournament before he even finished the one he was playing. Maybe he could be in the moment, enjoying the game for what it had once been for him.

An escape.

"It's my manager," he explained.

"Take it."

Wells flipped his phone over in his hand a few times, then called Nate back. Finally.

"It's about time, champ!" greeted the bastard.

"Okay, that greeting was transparent, even for you. What do you want?"

"Is that how you talk to an old friend?"

"Last time we spoke," Wells drawled, his eyes locked on the pulse of Josephine's neck, "you called me a royal prick."

"Ah, ah, ah. I said you *behaved* like one."

Wells implored the ceiling for patience. "My practice round is starting. Why are you blowing up my phone?"

"You want to get down to brass tacks. Sure." Keys clicked

in the background. "I bring you a wealth of opportunities this morning, young man. And just to get the ugly fine print out of the way up front, I'll be collecting fifteen percent on all of these sexy opportunities."

"Wow." He ran a hand down Josephine's ponytail, smirking when she mouthed the word "fetish." "Too bad you don't work for me anymore."

"We can change that quite easily, comeback kid."

Wells sighed.

"Have you turned on the Golf Channel lately? Hell, even ESPN is putting coverage on you, man. The big turnaround story. You're hitting the ball like Wells of yore—and you've got a beautiful caddie, to boot? The media is lapping it up like hungry little kittens."

"They . . ." His pulse spiked like he'd just fibbed on a lie detector test and his arm wrapped around Josephine's waist of its own volition, pulling her back against his chest. "What are they saying about Josephine?"

"Nothing bad, obviously. There's nothing bad *to* say!"

Josephine turned in his arms and tipped her head toward the bedroom. "Going to get ready," she whispered. "Finish your call."

He kissed her forehead, nodded.

Like a husband sending his wife off to work.

After the morning they'd shared, it just felt oddly . . . natural.

He waited until Josephine was out of earshot and he'd shut the bathroom door to continue the conversation. Because he knew Nate well and he'd recognized the man's tone of voice. "What are they really saying about her?"

"Ah. Well, you know, times being what they are, writers and commentators can't technically *call* her hot, but there's a lot of winking and nudging going on. 'If she was my caddie, I'd be practicing a lot, too.' Ha ha ha. Stuff like that. On the innocent end of the spectrum, they're calling her your good luck charm."

"Oh." Humiliating that he should get choked up over that. "Hmm."

A few moments passed in silence.

"Is there? Something going on there?" Nate asked.

"That's nobody's business but ours," Wells growled. "Got that?"

"Loud and clear, champ."

"I don't like them talking about her. She's . . ." *Mine.* He paced the bathroom. "She's all heart. She's authentic and perceptive and loyal. There is no way they could do her justice with a sound bite."

Nate didn't respond right away. Then he said, "Sorry, there's nothing I can do about them talking about her. Especially if you keep winning."

"I know, dammit. I just don't like it."

"Then I suggest you keep your television turned off."

Wells walked in a circle rubbing the back of his neck. "All right, let's get this over with. What are these opportunities?"

"The most magical of all opportunities, Wells." The manager dropped his voice to a reverent whisper. "Sponsorships. Two of them."

"Whatever."

"How does Mercedes sound?"

"Pass. Next."

Nate fake cried on the other end. "I knew you were going to say that. Figured we'd cross it off the list early." He paused, for dramatic effect no doubt. "Ever heard of a little brand called Under Armour? And get this, they want to sponsor you *and* the caddie."

That brought Wells's head up. He stopped pacing. "How much?"

"Five figures each. For now. They're being smart, picking you off cheap before your return to the tour can officially be called a comeback. That being said, they're only asking for two appearances in their gear, so they can be sure you're not going to self-destruct and leave them with egg on their face. They will have first right of refusal on your next sponsorship deal. Fine by us, right? It'll leave us a ton of wiggle room to negotiate terms if you continue on this trajectory. *Which you will*, my boy. Sound good?"

Five figures. A few years ago, the offer would have been in the tens of millions.

God, he wanted that so bad for Josephine. She'd be able to rebuild the shop, afford better health insurance, take care of her parents. Five figures would mean a lot to her, though, too. A hell of a lot. "Done."

"I thought you might say that. They've already sent over a selection of shirts and hats for both of you to choose from. I've taken the liberty of having them arranged in a conference room downstairs."

"You're a smug motherfucker, Nate."

"We're back, baby!"

Wells hung up.

Left the bathroom—

And stopped short, watching with mounting hunger as Josephine tugged on a sports bra, covering her perfectly perfect tits. A T-shirt next. Too many layers.

"Hey," she said. "Almost ready."

He was well past the point of ready. But Christ. Where was this going? His feelings for Josephine were expanding at an alarming rate, but he had no idea what *would* or *could* come from the painful attraction. Sex might mess up their entire dynamic and yet, at this point, he'd probably die if he didn't fuck her brains out.

And soon.

What happened after that? Did she become his girlfriend?

How long could that last with them working together—especially taking into account that he could be a class A dickhead on the course? She could get run over by a golf cart again.

Or worse.

Wells cleared his throat hard. "Look. We've got a sponsor. Congratulations, belle, you're five figures richer. We're going downstairs to pick out your outfit—and it better not be anything pink."

She turned so fast, she almost fell down. "I . . . me? I'm . . . five figures? *Me?*"

Not for the first time this morning, a lump built in his throat. "Yeah."

"B-but . . . ," she sputtered. "Why?"

"Because you're . . . you, Josephine. And for the record, you're worth a hell of a lot more. I just have to prove myself before that's possible—and I will. For you. For . . . us." Even from across the room, he swore he heard her breath quicken. "Okay?"

"Okay." Not a hint of doubt in her voice. What had he done to deserve her?

"Good, let's—"

She gasped. "Are we going to try to match outfits?"

"Hell no, Josephine. Absolutely not."

CHAPTER TWENTY

Oh yes, they *did* end up in matching outfits.

By accident.

Or was it?

After five years of being a Wells superfan, Josephine had the advantage of knowing the colors he favored—and baby blue was among them. As soon as they walked into the conference room and she did a quick survey of both tables, she knew the polo shirt he was going to pick off the men's side of the room. It was more of a glacial shade than baby blue, but it was the closest to his signature color. And as luck would have it, there was a skirt that matched the shirt exactly, down to the navy logo.

"Do you want to play a game?"

Wells narrowed his eyes at her. "This feels like a trap."

"Me? Set a trap?" She blinked innocently. "Come on. Say yes."

He crossed his arms and sighed but couldn't quite keep the amusement from his expression. "Explain first."

Josephine swept a hand over the wide array of garments. "We pick and get dressed in an outfit without letting the other person see it. But once we put it on, that's it. No changing."

"You're stuck with whatever you pick."

"That's right."

Wells stroked his chin. "Somehow, I know I'm going to regret saying yes to this. But the fact that it entails you getting semi-naked is putting me in an agreeable mood."

"Uh-uh." She walked over to the door and engaged the lock. "No peeking."

"Josephine," he warned. "You're making me hard."

Never could she have predicted that a man making blunt references to his junk could rev her hormones like a tank engine. "Better be careful zipping up, then, I guess," she breathed.

He laughed with a flash of white teeth, smile lines and all. Utterly gorgeous.

She tried not to make it obvious how that laugh made her heart beat at a dizzying pace.

Holy moly. If he ever laughed like that on camera, this was only the tip of the iceberg when it came to sponsorship opportunities.

Wells waved a hand in front of her face. "You alive in there, belle?"

"What? Yes," she blurted, turning her back. "Okay. On your mark. Get set."

"Go."

She didn't have to sneak a look over her shoulder to know Wells went straight for that glacier blue. But she did underestimate how clumsy her fingers would become knowing he'd stripped off his own shirt to put on the new one. The soft ripple of fabric sliding up his chest and falling to the floor nearly made her eyes cross, her knee bumping awkwardly into one of the conference-room chairs as she reached for the ice-blue skirt.

"You okay over there?" he asked.

"Oh yes," she said quickly, peeling down her leggings.

"Uh-huh."

She tugged the skirt up around her hips, chewing her bottom lip while selecting a white polo shirt. Off came her top. Before she could drop the new shirt over her head, warmth met her bare back. "I peeked, belle." Wells gripped her hips, slowly pulling her butt back into his lap, his open mouth trailing up the side of her neck. "Your ass looks so ripe in this skirt, I can't even be mad that you tricked me into matching."

Wells turned Josephine around to face him, settled his mouth on top of hers, and walked her backward, using his grip on her hips to boost her up onto the conference-room table. Josephine all but sobbed from the sudden storm of need. "Wells . . ."

"I know." He hooked his hands beneath her knees and yanked her to the very edge of the table, bringing their lower bodies flush—and ohhh. He hadn't been exaggerating about being hard. "I know we've got a round of golf to play before I'm inside you, but Christ, these fucking thighs make it so hard to wait." Fisting Josephine's hair, he tilted her head back and slid the very tip of his tongue up the curve of her throat. "At least let me eat your pussy." He wound her ponytail tighter around his fist. Tighter. "You like the sound of that, Josephine? I think you do, baby. Your legs are shaking."

"I . . . um . . ."

"You chose a skirt for a reason, didn't you?" Wells groaned into her neck, his mouth sweeping across her cheek to attack her mouth, kissing her roughly, growling when she returned the kiss in kind. "You were hoping I'd get on my knees and lick it."

Honestly, it hadn't crossed her mind that a skirt would provide . . . opportunities.

For *access*.

But mother of God, it was crossing her mind now.

Zigzagging, ricocheting, *and* tumbling.

"Yes, please," she whispered against his damp mouth. "Please."

"I'm going to eat it now and fuck it later, aren't I, belle?"

Her core squeezed so dramatically, her eyes started to water. "*Yes*."

"Josephine." His teeth closed around her earlobe and tugged, scraping down to her shoulder and back up, before he ground his erection once, twice, against her panties. "This is one stroke of mine that doesn't need any work. You think about that good and hard when I'm sucking your clit."

"Oh my God."

He took off the ice-blue shirt, snagged her mouth for an explicit kiss, then started to go down on his knees—

A knock came from somewhere. Her chest, maybe?

No.

The door.

Someone was knocking on the door of the conference room.

"Son of a bitch," Wells cursed, slamming a fist down on the table, using his wrist to swipe sweat from his upper lip. "*What?*"

A few seconds ticked by. "Wells Whitaker, it's Kip Collings." A pause. "The tournament chairman."

Josephine's jaw nearly dropped to her ankles.

Kip Collings? she mouthed at a visibly frustrated Wells.

If they ever made a Mount Rushmore for golf, Collings would be on there. He was the guy who basically showed up only to hand the trophy to the winner. He was *that* important.

And he was about to catch Josephine in a bra, making out with her golfer.

"Mind if I come in for a moment?" Collings chuckled. "I'll be brief. I know your tee time is approaching and you're busy preparing."

"Or something," Wells muttered, massaging the bridge of his nose.

"Go unlock the door," Josephine squeal-whispered, jumping off the table and tugging on the white polo shirt. "It's the chairman."

"I almost had those panties off, Josephine. Frankly, I don't care if it's the pope."

"Don't say 'panties' and 'pope' in the same breath. We're going to get struck by lightning out there."

"Fuck," he said, wincing. "Please don't make me laugh when my dick is hard. It hurts."

"But I *like* your laugh."

"I like every fucking thing about you," Wells rasped, sweeping her face with an intense look, before shooting his gaze down to the ground. Meanwhile, Josephine felt herself floating upward toward the ceiling on little white, puffy clouds. "You ready, belle?"

She gulped. "Yes."

"One second, Chairman," Wells called, yanking his shirt back on and leaving it untucked so it covered the . . . situation. Then under his breath, "You old cockblocker."

Josephine smacked him in the shoulder.

Wells took his time crossing to the door, unlocking it with a palpable air of resentment and holding it open for the chairman. The older man came through the entrance with brown eyes twinkling, set deep in his age-lined, russet face. "You've caused quite a stir, you two." Kip eyeballed Wells. "For the right reasons, this time."

"It's nice to meet you, Mr. Collings," Josephine said, trying to calm her flustered state.

"Nice to meet you, too, young lady." He jabbed a good-natured finger at Wells. "You're keeping this one in line, I hear."

She maintained her smile. "He's gotten this far. He can keep himself in line."

She felt, rather than saw, Wells turn a surprised look on her.

"Right." The chairman considered them both. "Well, whatever magic you two are making together, keep it up."

"Oh, it's up," Wells muttered.

Josephine kicked him in the ankle. "Yes, sir."

The chairman chuckled, obviously missing nothing, but far from scandalized. "Our viewership doubled yesterday with the news of this possible comeback. And I hope you don't mind me saying this, but a young woman as a caddie? Hell, people find that mighty interesting. I can't say I blame them after seeing you two in action, but it's more than that. Man or woman or otherwise, Miss Doyle, you're damn good at reading a course." Collings patted his pocket and pulled out a key. "Speaking of which, I personally saw to it that you have your own bag room going forward. I'm sorry you've gone three days without enough privacy."

She waved a hand. "Oh, that's not necessary, sir—"

"First of all, call me Kip, please." Brooking no arguments, he pressed the key into her palm, nodding when she closed her fingers around it. "Second, I'm sure you're worried about the others griping about double standards and favoritism and all that nonsense. If you catch wind of it, you send them to me. My granddaughters have schooled me well."

Oh, she really liked this man. As soon as she got a free moment, she was going to call her dad and tell him about this conversation word for word. Minus the innuendo from Wells. "Thank you, Kip."

Wells nodded, his expression one of rare gratitude. "We appreciate that, Chairman."

The older man nodded and turned for the door, but not before patting Wells on the back. "Hang on to that one," he said. "And give 'em hell out there."

They both stared at the door for a beat after the chairman exited.

"I don't suppose we have time to—"

"Nope." Josephine sighed, glancing at the clock on the wall.

Wells hung his head a moment, before hitting her with open curiosity. "When he asked if you were keeping me in line, you could have made some smart-ass joke about my temper, but you didn't. Why?"

"Easy." With a wink, she sailed for the door. "No one trash-talks my golfer but me."

She turned in the doorway to find him looking thoughtful—and maybe a little stunned—but he recovered quickly, forehead gathering in a frown. "And no one gets too close to my caddie but me. Stay beside me out there, Josephine."

"Oh, I will. How else are people going to notice our matching outfits?"

His groan boomed down the hallway, followed by a peal of Josephine's laughter.

CHAPTER TWENTY-ONE

When they arrived at the first tee, a familiar figure stood beside a caddie, instructing the man on how to clean his balls properly. The sandy-blond superstar's forehead was pinched in irritation, although when he turned to face the television cameras, his smile belonged in a mouthwash commercial. Buster Calhoun. What was he doing here?

"Please, belle. Tell me we're not paired up with this shithead."

"I . . . didn't think we were." Josephine gave the other caddie a sympathetic look as he cleaned the balls with a more vigorous approach. "There must have been a DQ. Or maybe a couple of dropouts? Something that made them restructure the pairings."

That wasn't true. Calhoun had dropped in the tournament ranks. Down to Wells's level. But she didn't want to say that out loud and remind him that, although they had a good chance of finishing in the money today, they had a long way to go before his name started appearing in the top ten again. Whereas the guys at the top of the leaderboard were going to walk away today with payouts in the millions or six figures, Wells would be doing well to take five. A far cry from his earlier days on the tour, but a *vast* improvement.

Now all she had to do was get him there. Get through this round without dropping a zillion shots and leave Texas with something he didn't bring with him. Optimism.

Wells plucked off his cap and plowed five fingers through his hair. "Over fifty golfers remaining, and it had to be *this* leftover prom king."

"I can hear you, Whitaker," Calhoun remarked dryly over his shoulder.

"That was the plan," Wells called back.

Josephine shook her head at Wells.

What? he mouthed, dropping into a stretch.

Dammit. This curveball was the last thing they needed this morning. Wells might be playing better by leaps and bounds, but his progress was shaky. Fresh. He was learning to walk again. Being paired up with the number one golfer in the world, whom he didn't get along with, was the obstacle she hadn't seen coming.

As Josephine filled in the pertinent details in her scorebook, a shadow appeared on the ground in front of her. Without looking up, she knew those perfectly white Nike cleats belonged to Calhoun. His name stitched into the swoosh sort of tipped her off. "Well, if it isn't the woman of the hour, the lovely Miss—"

"*Nope*," Wells shouted, coming up beside her. "She's busy. Forever."

Calhoun laughed. "Oh, come on now, Whitaker, I'm just making polite conversation." His voice was as smooth as glass, but an ugly glint lurked behind his blue eyes. "I'll admit to thinking you were some kind of gimmick when this tournament started. Or maybe bringing in an amateur caddie was just another way for Whitaker to belittle the tour. You're the real deal, though, aren't you, Miss Doyle?" He winked at her. "I've been paying attention."

"I'm only going to say this one more time, Calhoun. Put that attention somewhere else," Wells said in a very low, precise tone. "Fast."

The clean-cut pro wasn't finished. "What are you worried about? That she might jump ship and come to play for a winning team?" Another infuriating wink in Josephine's direction. "Offer's open, Miss Doyle."

She slid in front of Wells before he could lunge for the other man, his chest coming up against her back. "I'm good right where I am, thank you." She reached down and subtly rubbed her knuckle against Wells's fisted hand, letting out a breath when his fingers uncurled. It was an unconscious action that was meant to remain only between the two of them, but Calhoun's gaze was sharp—and he caught it, a knowing smile spreading across his face.

"Aha," he drawled. "Guess I might be playing better, too, if she was my caddie."

"See, now I'm going to fucking kill you," Wells growled, wrapping an arm around Josephine's middle, obviously preparing to physically move her out of the way.

Oh dear. This was bad.

She dug in her heels as firmly as possible, but those efforts quickly proved futile. Her feet were leaving the ground. But she couldn't, under any circumstances, let a fight ensue between Wells and Calhoun or they wouldn't just be kicked out of the tournament, Wells would be off the tour permanently. The fact that Calhoun goaded his temper wouldn't mean anything to the officials—all the blame would be on Wells, thanks to his track record.

Josephine twisted around to face Wells, sucking in a breath over the murder spelled out in his eyes. "Hey. Hey, hey, hey." She struggled to get her feet back on the ground for leverage and finally succeeded, grabbing the sides of his face. "You're letting him get in your head. That's exactly what he wanted."

"He disrespected you, Josephine."

"That says more about him than it does about us, doesn't it?"

A muscle popped repeatedly in his cheek. "I can't let it stand."

"No, you can't. So beat him on the golf course."

Wells continued to pin Calhoun with a death stare over her shoulder. "But I won't get to hear any of his bones snapping that way."

Calhoun let out a strangled cough.

An official approached hesitantly from her left. "Is everything all right over here?"

"Yes," Josephine said, firmly.

"No," growled Wells.

Josephine gave the official the sweetest smile she could muster, considering she was holding back a bull from charging at a red flag. "We just need a minute."

"One minute to tee time, folks."

"We'll be ready," she assured the official, before refocusing on Wells. "Listen to me. If that smarmy, self-important jackass is trying to rattle you, we must be doing something right."

"I can *hear* you," Calhoun complained.

"That was the plan," she called. Then, quietly, to Wells, she said, "Block out the noise. It's just you and me out here."

That wasn't remotely true. In the few minutes they'd been standing there, getting ready to begin their round, a crowd the size of a small army had amassed. Commentators were chirping into microphones, spectators were shouting for Wells. For *her*. If she listened hard, she could hear the buzz of a drone overhead, no doubt capturing a bird's-eye view of the course for the television audience. It was total and complete mayhem.

For golf.

"I don't like backing down from a fight," he said. "You know that."

"This one isn't worthwhile."

"I strongly disagree."

Getting nowhere, she had no choice but to play her final card. "Are you forgetting about our wager?" she whispered.

She'd never seen a car hit a brick wall at a hundred miles an hour, but she suspected it looked something like Wells reacting to her reminder. The momentum of his ire came to a screeching halt. "I've decided to wait until we've played eighteen holes to kill him," he said briskly.

"That's all anyone can ask for," Josephine said on a relieved exhale.

Wells held out a hand for his driver and she laid the club across his palm, smiling to herself as Calhoun snorted and swaggered back to his own camp.

One crisis down.

How many more to go?

One. One crisis to go, it turned out.

And it happened on the final hole.

Wells remained steady throughout the morning, managing to maintain his position on the leaderboard. Fifteenth place. To Josephine, they might as well have been in first.

All he needed to do was make par on the eighteenth hole and Wells would bank thirty thousand dollars. Ten percent of that would go to Josephine. *Three thousand dollars.* On *top* of the Under Armour sponsorship money. It was more money than she'd ever had at one time. But at that very moment, the imminent hope of rebuilding the Golden Tee and restoring her health insurance came second to Wells getting his professional footing back. Every time he swung the club, he did it with a little more of his old finesse.

The crowd had doubled since the morning—and they were *excited.*

She could practically hear her parents freaking out on the couch at home.

That being said, Josephine *was* allowing herself to anticipate the changes she would make to the family shop. The shine of new hardwood flooring, the wall of reference books, the technology she would incorporate to modernize the space. How she would take it from a necessary stop for visitors to an experience that would keep them coming back.

She'd dream more later, though.

Right here and now, she was focused on Wells. Finishing the day off strong.

Calhoun was sulking over in the rough after an average round, waiting for Wells to take his putt. Meanwhile, Josephine stood on the green of the final hole. One putt. A single putt and they could go home winners, at least in her book.

But Wells was . . . frozen.

They'd conferred on yardage, angle, wind speed. And he'd just . . . stopped.

"What's wrong?"

He rubbed the center of his forehead and blinked at the ball. "What happens if I miss this?"

"You can't think like that."

"What is the difference in the payout if I miss?" He closed his eyes. "God, I don't want to fuck this up for us, belle."

"You won't." She handed him the putter. "Visualize the shot."

"That's the thing—I can't."

"Okay. Let's say you *could* visualize the shot. What would it look like?"

His head turned slowly. "Where in God's name do you come up with this shit?"

She grinned. "It's good, isn't it?"

He made a grudging sound. "Better than good."

Laughter went up from the crowd. She could hear the electric whir of the camera, the dropped voices of the commentators. How much was being overheard? She had no idea, but it didn't matter right now. There was only her and Wells.

"What does it look like?" she prompted again.

She watched the life rekindle in his eyes, cogs turning in his head.

Then he got into position. Took a breath. And sank the putt.

You'd have thought they'd just won the Masters, based on the crowd's reaction. The resulting roar was so loud, the ground shook beneath Josephine's feet. Everyone moved at once, reporters rushing onto the green, security holding back fans, beer sloshing onto khaki.

Wells dropped his putter, walked straight past a reporter asking him a question, and scooped Josephine off the ground into a bear hug. She laughed freely into his neck, hot pressure building against the backs of her eyelids. So many emotions hit her at once. Joy. Relief. Pride—and not only in Wells, but in herself.

Maybe for the first time ever, the dream she'd been nursing for years took a more distinct shape. She could bring this firsthand experience of working with a professional golfer—no, the *best* professional golfer—and pour that familiarity into the Golden Tee. She could take what she'd learned and drag her family's business into the twenty-first century . . . with the knowledge and confidence to back it up now.

A little fissure formed under her skin at the reminder that she'd eventually have to leave Wells and the tour, but . . . that had always been the plan, right?

She was *thoroughly* distracted from thoughts of the future, of leaving, when Wells pressed his mouth to her ear, bathing it in a hot exhale. "Josephine."

"Yes?"

"Let's get out of here." His fist tightened in the back of her shirt, his chest beginning to heave. "Don't make me go another minute without you."

She looked around in a daze. "Every sports reporter in Texas wants to talk to you."

"Fuck 'em." He wrapped an arm around Josephine's shoulders and used his body to shield her as they moved through the raucous crowd. "It's just you and me."

CHAPTER TWENTY-TWO

There was only one thing Wells wanted in this life—and it was to fuck this woman.

He wanted to get her somewhere dark, tear down her panties, and bury his cock between her soft, sexy thighs. And for some infuriating reason, everyone and their mom wanted to stop him. A crowd followed him to the clubhouse when he turned in his scorecard. Reporters shoved microphones in their faces, using the C-word on a loop. Comeback. Comeback.

Is she responsible for your comeback?

Josephine, how do you feel about being a good luck charm for Wells Whitaker?

Will we see you at the Masters together?

If Wells was even remotely capable of responding with any-thing but *please I need to come inside my caddie*, he would have told them yes, Josephine was unequivocally responsible for his comeback. Two weeks ago, he was a corpse. He'd never expected to pick up another golf club as long as he lived. Now he had a beating pulse. A purpose. The potential revival of his career. His blood was flowing again.

He had *hope*, because of Josephine.

And he just wanted to worship her for all that he was worth. Praise her and get lost in her and . . . demand to know what the hell they were to each other.

That's right—he wanted specifics.

Were they a golfer and caddie who incentivized sex as a strategy? Stranger things had happened.

Maybe friends with benefits? Boyfriend and girlfriend?

Shit. He liked the sound of that last one. *A lot.* It was too soon, though, and what would it mean for their dynamic on the course? Would they have to keep their love life and golf separate in order to be ethical? In order to have a healthy relationship, in which she wasn't constantly having to refocus him and talk him out of killing people?

Labeling what they had could complicate everything.

Josephine would have to be out of her mind to want to be his girlfriend, really.

Still, it had a nice ring to it.

Oooh. Rings.

Wow. Pump the brakes, man.

They were almost to the lobby of the hotel when a crowd swelled through the doors, holding up their phones to take pictures of Wells and Josephine.

They traded a pitiful glance and reversed direction.

Josephine laughed, stumbling a little as he pulled her along.

"What could possibly be funny at a time like this?" he demanded to know.

"You're dragging me all over this family-friendly golf resort looking for a place to"—she waved a hand—"collect on our wager. There is something funny about it."

"I promise you, Josephine, there is not."

"Wait!" She yanked him to a stop on the path. Eyes wide, she slowly drew a single key out of the pocket of her skirt, holding it up to the light. Sun glinted off its majestic surface like the angels were ordaining it the new Holy Grail. "We're forgetting I have my own bag room."

"Where is that from here?" He pressed both thumbs into his

eye sockets. "Christ, I'm so fucking horny, I've lost my sense of direction."

"This way."

"Fair warning, Josephine, I don't even have two seconds of foreplay in me."

"Aw, honey." She batted her eyelashes at him over her shoulder. "I don't need it."

Wells's tortured groan would echo on the pathway to the clubhouse for the next century. And it only grew louder when they saw that it was blocked by a group of autograph seekers.

"I know it's wrong to wish for a flash flood to sweep them away, but . . ." Wells trailed off.

"Don't do it."

"Too late."

"For shame, Wells—" Josephine broke off on an intake of breath. "Wait. There's Ricky. I've got an idea." Josephine waved at the caddie as he left the clubhouse and he changed direction to approach them, glancing between Josephine and Wells curiously.

"Ricky, remember that rare bearded dragon you were hoping to buy if Tagaloa finished high enough in the money?"

The young man smacked a hand over his chest. "Ouch, way to rub it in."

"If you create a diversion for us, no questions asked, Wells will buy you that lizard."

"I'll buy you ten lizards," Wells deadpanned.

"Done."

Josephine's friend ran in one direction shouting about a wet T-shirt contest in the hotel lobby and, miracle of miracles, the crowd migrated with him. Distraction in place, Josephine and Wells wasted no time running the remaining distance to the clubhouse, veering around the corner to where her personal bag room was located.

Josephine's hands shook as she tried to put the key in the lock, so Wells took over, all but kicking the damn door open to get them inside. A couple of caddies caught them in the act of disappearing into the bag room together, but Wells couldn't care less about the gawkers when this woman was in front of him, stripping off her white polo shirt as soon as the door was locked behind them. Her sports bra followed and she let it drop, and shook out her ponytail like a goddess, her tits bouncing around with the sultry movement.

Son of a bitch.

I've never needed anyone like this.

A few strokes of his cock and he could have come. Just from *looking* at her.

"Josephine," he growled through his teeth, backing her toward the row of lockers, gripping her hips hard with both hands. "Your tits are ruining my life."

Her back hit the lockers, rattling them. "In a good way?" she gasped.

"The first time I saw them, they were all wet and covered in bubbles. Swear to God, the image is burned into my fucking brain." Massaging her hips in his hands, his tongue traveled the slope of her neck and shoulder, lips suctioning, teeth scraping. Her skin was like ripe fruit that had spent all day warming in the sun. Absolutely delicious. "It's a crime that I haven't had those nipples in my mouth yet, belle. Push up and let me suck them."

Josephine arched her back on a stuttering exhale, elevating on her toes, but she was still too low because of their height difference. Desperate to get her closer as soon as humanly possible, Wells wedged a thigh between her legs and dragged her all the way to the top, straight up moaning over the warmth of her pussy through his pants and her underwear.

"Tell me you've got a bad ache between your legs," he rasped, dropping his mouth to her tits and raking his tongue across one of the stiff peaks. "Tell me you need me to fix it."

"Fix it," she said, shivering. "Please. It's bad."

Gratification punched him in the middle. Honor. Responsibility. It wasn't a small thing, to be the one this self-sufficient woman asked for relief. She was a kingdom—and she was handing him the keys. *Make it count.* His hands snuck around to her ass, taking hold of her firm cheeks so he could ride her up and down his thigh, her resulting whimper making his balls draw up painfully. "How long have you been wanting me inside you, Josephine?"

She blinked at him with lust-glazed eyes, her inner thighs tightening around his leg. "More and more since I've gotten to know you, Wells," she whispered.

Oh.

Shit.

Invisible claws dug into his jugular, his heart hammering loudly in his ears. Maybe deep, deep down he'd wondered if Josephine was still harboring a star-crush on him. Maybe subconsciously, he'd worried that she was just fulfilling a fantasy. But that's not what this was. They knew each other now. And the closer they'd gotten, the more she wanted him.

Same. He felt the same way about her.

The more he experienced Josephine, the more he required.

His chest damn near burned with the need to cave in, she'd unlocked so much hope and happiness. Unable to look at her without saying every last revealing word rattling around in his head, he focused on her breasts. Her swollen nipples, which wanted to be sucked on so bad. They were smooth and firm on his tongue, tightening the more he drew on them. Josephine writhed around on his thigh, sobbing when he flexed rhythmically beneath her pussy, his grip on her taut butt pulling her up and back, up and back.

It was worth every second of waiting. Worth ten millenniums of waiting, this woman.

"I think I'm close," she hiccupped, a thread of disbelief in her tone.

"Mmmm. These nipples sensitive, Josephine?"

"Apparently, I . . ."

"You never had them sucked the right way?"

"Wells."

"Come on my thigh, baby. No one is stopping you." He dragged his tongue over to her other nipple and teased it with bats and licks, before pulling on it deeply and feeling her entire body vibrate against him. "You get to rub yourself off on my leg. I get to turn you around and hit that wet little pussy from the back for a while. Sound fair to you?"

She half laughed, half sobbed, her hips moving faster, shifting up, back, side to side. "Are you supposed to be talking to me like this?"

"I don't know." He delved his hands inside her panties, digging his fingers into the supple flesh of her backside, jerking her closer, closer, closer. "But if the way I talk gets you humping my thigh like a dirty girl, try and stop me."

Josephine sucked in a breath and gripped the collar of his shirt, bending back in a clear request for more of his mouth on her nipples, and lord, he was all too happy to grant that wish. His cock turned into a fucking pike between his legs as he licked at those rosy tips, one of his fingers sliding down the cheeks of her ass to press a finger to her back entrance, something animalistic ripping through his insides when she mewled and rode his thigh with more urgency.

Oh, fuck. Fuck. Fuck.

She's going to kill me.

"As soon as you're done coming in your panties, belle, I'm

going to put my cock inside you," he said an inch from her ear. Sensing how close she was, Wells pushed more firmly against that breach between her cheeks and felt her begin to shake, her mouth falling open on a gasp of his name. "You sure about letting me come in it with no rubber?"

Her breath caught. "Yes," she managed, before pitching into an orgasm, right there as he watched, her hands twisting in the front of his shirt, her mouth gasping against his lips—and he attacked it with a kiss, knowing she was in search of an anchor and honored, desperate, aching to provide her with one. Oh Jesus, she was fucking magnificent, grinding into his thigh and kissing him with a total lack of self-consciousness. In a way that made him feel like he'd dragged the world's greatest treasure into the dark to selfishly keep and experience for himself—and hell, that's exactly what he'd done, hadn't he?

Mine.

Josephine, you're mine.

Those big green eyes connected with his, nearly rocketing his heart out through his mouth. In a blind panic over what she made him feel, Wells slid her off his thigh, whipped her around to face the lockers, flipped up her skirt, and stripped her damp, twisted panties down to her ankles. "Kick them off, Josephine. Nothing to keep me from spreading your legs."

While she did as he asked, flattening her palms on the locker in front of her, Wells unfastened his belt and lowered his zipper, hissing out a breath while traveling over the aching inches of his erection. Shoving his pants and briefs down to his knees, he trapped Josephine's hips with his left forearm, drawing her up to the very tips of her toes, all while panting, *panting*, in anticipation of feeling this woman from the inside. He rubbed his cock against her slippery entrance, groaning hoarsely into the nape of her neck.

"Josephine . . ." He was almost afraid of the words that wanted to leave his mouth, but he closed his eyes and let them tumble out, anyway, because it was *her*. "This . . . you and me. We're about more than golf. Or some incentive to win. We're more than that. But tell me I earned you, anyway." He pressed the head of his dick inside her, groaning through a gentle thrust and knew, instantly, that he'd never want to fuck another woman as long as he lived.

Call it intuition. Call it whatever you like, but the way Josephine held her breath and looked back at him over her shoulder, like she sensed some kind of radical shift in the atmosphere, was nothing short of life changing. She looked him right in the eye and whimpered as he pushed in every inch, deeper, deeper, until she was closed-mouth screaming.

An image of her walking down the aisle short-circuited his brain.

Made his pulse zigzag through his veins.

What the hell?

"Tell me," Wells demanded raggedly.

"You earned me," she murmured, squeezing him. "Have me however you want me."

Wells didn't need any more encouragement than that. He bent her over and banged her motherfucking brains out. What else was he supposed to do when her pussy felt like tight silk and she'd given him permission to come inside her? When she was using her leverage from the lockers to push back and meet his pumps, letting out horny little sobs of his name, her fingers busy playing with her clit? He couldn't have gone slow to save the world.

Have me however you want me.

"I want you everywhere. All the time," he rasped, breathing shallow, his hips slapping up against her incredible ass, watching it shake with a raw possessiveness that shocked him as much as it felt completely normal when it came to her. Only her. "Over and over and fucking over again, Josephine. I'll earn this hot pussy every single time, if I have to."

"You don't," she whispered.

And he wanted to hear her say that, watch her mouth form the words, so he wrapped her hair in a fist, drew her upright, and flattened the front of her body against the lockers. "Josephine?"

She turned her head, their mouths coming together like magnets. "Like you said, we're more than a sport. Some incentive." Heavy-lidded eyes searched his face. "Aren't we?"

"Yes," he exhaled, winded. From exertion. What was happening to him?

His emotions were cymbals crashing in his head and rib cage. He couldn't make sense of them now. Just knew this woman was his only method of breathing. He needed air. And he could get the most oxygen from her pleasure, so he knocked her fingers out of the way and stroked her clit with his own fingers. Middle and ring. Circling and playing in the wetness of her cunt, the place where they joined, that button that made her thighs dance anxiously.

"There it is, baby, let it happen. Right there on my cock this time."

"Oh my God, *please* God."

"Yes? I'm listening."

"Wells."

He drove upward, bringing her tiptoes off the ground, his fingers strumming her clit in a blur. "God? Wells? *Somebody* is giving it to you good, Josephine, because you're wet as fuck."

She slapped the locker with both hands, struggling to get her feet on the ground for leverage, but he wouldn't let her, instinct telling him she'd come harder if she didn't have that piece of control, and he was right. Her muscles locked up, fingers curling into fists, and she convulsed around him so tightly, he had to bite her shoulder to keep from shouting the ceiling down.

Mother Mary.

It cost him an ocean's worth of self-control to thrust deep and hold, letting her grind on his dick and draw out the pleasure, before he started pumping again.

"The things I'll do to keep you coming back," he growled into her neck. "Anything. God help me, I'll do anything for more of this."

She turned her mouth to meet his in a breathless kiss, her right hand leaving the locker, fingers spearing into the hair at the back of his scalp. Holding firmly while they devoured each other's mouths. "Let me see you," she whispered. "When you finish."

He didn't even know which part of his body was storing his heart right now. His stomach or his mouth. "That's going to make you want more?"

"I . . . think . . . m-maybe feeling close to you would—"

Quickly, in the name of self-preservation, Wells cut Josephine off with his mouth, because if she kept talking like that, he was going to start making a lot of premature vows. *I'll never kiss anyone else. I'll never touch anyone else.* Or asking her to come to Miami tomorrow morning, instead of going home during the break between tournaments. So he could see what she looked like in his bathtub and take her for long walks on the beach during sunset.

Am I romantic now?

When did that happen?

Wells didn't have a single clue. But if she wanted to look at him while he busted, it was the very least he could do.

Or so he thought. It was a lot more difficult than he imagined, in the sense that he could barely breathe in the face of so much intimacy.

She touched the tips of their tongues together and flexed her cunt—and he started naming saints. He wasn't even Catholic. Didn't realize he knew any of the saints, either. But he was obviously having some kind of religious experience, because the more she worked those muscles around his shaft, the more brilliant light flared at the edges of his vision, his body surging forward of its own volition, crushing her against the lockers. Hard. Thrusting. Thrusting.

"Oh Jesus. Sorry, baby. Sorry," he ground out, the slap of flesh, her halting breaths, the firmness of her ass against his stomach, it all blew him into oblivion, but her turning to lock their gazes together while it happened was like having his soul ripped clean out. Everything was green, like her eyes.

His entire universe.

His entire existence came down to her. Little gold flecks and the scent of flowers and her unruly auburn hair.

The dramatic release of tension happened in his lower body, but higher, too. In his chest. He was releasing himself *to* her. Just handing everything inside him over, and he couldn't stop, couldn't stem the desperation to bond with Josephine permanently, and that need took the form of rutting her up against the locker, her knees crashing into the metal, his own fist pounding it out of pure savage ownership.

Not only that, he was *being* owned.

Such a simple request. To look at her when he came.

But it was easily the most intimate leap he'd ever taken in his life.

Then she smiled at him toward the end and everything just kind of exploded into place.

The final scrape of sexual frustration left him, for now, exiting on a tide of raw, unparalleled relief, filling her body, her *body* that received him so perfectly, stroking him with fine muscles and sleek flesh, squeezing to a tempo only they could hear. His spend slowly dripped back out, coating their joined flesh while he groaned, working into her even as his erection subsided, because he simply couldn't stop, couldn't quit trying to get as close as possible.

Nothing had ever felt better than this woman. Ever.

"What are you doing between now and the next tournament?" he asked into her neck, voice uneven. "Come to Miami. I have a bathtub."

Color deepened on her cheeks. Wells just stared at the increase of pink in a total stupor. Like, how had he been living his life without realizing an angel was existing right under his nose?

"I . . . I mean, that sounds amazing," she started, visibly caught off guard by his offer. And why wouldn't she be? He'd just taken the postcoital leap from sex to spending nongolf time together. He'd prodded the relationship bear. At least she looked *mildly* interested in saying yes to coming to Miami. Right? "But I just . . . I really have to get repairs started on the shop—"

"Of course, you do," Wells rushed to respond. "That's . . . yeah. Obviously. The shop." Wells slid out of Josephine with a wince and pulled up his pants. He might have taken a moment to enjoy looking at the mess he'd left on her inner thighs, but he was in this odd place of feeling possessive, bonded with her, exposed. Was this how women felt after sex? Emotionally skinned alive and needing some kind of label stamped on the whole situation that said *permanent*?

Fuck, it was *terrible*.

Wells backed into the small bathroom and found a hand towel, returning to clean her up, compelled by some almighty force to kiss her shoulders as he did so.

All right, she didn't want to come to Miami. Maybe he could go to her? Help fix up the Golden Tee? But what if she wanted distance from him in between tournaments? Considering he was a mega asshole 90 percent of the time, that would be completely reasonable.

Why did the thought of Josephine wanting distance make him feel queasy?

He'd just test the waters to find out where they stood. "Today is Sunday. We'll need to leave for the Dominican Republic on Wednesday. That doesn't give you much time to sort out repairs on the shop." He let out a breath he'd been holding. "Maybe you need some help—"

"The Dominican Republic?"

Josephine had gone pale.

Wells's brows drew together. "That's the location of the next tournament."

"Oh my God." She pressed a hand to her forehead, slumping back against the lockers. "Wells, I'm such a ding-dong."

"I promise you, that's not true."

"I don't have a passport." She opened her mouth, closed it. "My parents were always afraid to take me out of the country in case we lost my supplies or had an emergency . . . I just . . . it never even occurred to me we'd have to leave the States." She crossed her arms over her tits, like maybe she was cold, so he found her bra and shirt, handing them to her, watching in fascination as she worked tiny, little clasps and straps, eventually pulling the garment on over her head. "I totally understand if you want to find a different caddie—"

His insides nearly became his outsides. "*What?*"

"Just for the next tournament."

Why did his pulse feel like it was going to pound straight through his skin? "It's you and me, Josephine. Or nothing. Period."

"But you won't be able to play in the next tournament," she pointed out. "There's no way to get a passport in three days."

"Then I'll withdraw, and we'll skip it." He thought for a moment, which was very hard to do when she'd just proposed that he find another caddie. "California is on the schedule after the Dominican Republic. We'll pick up there."

"But *Wells*."

"This conversation is over, Josephine."

She glared up at him, stubbornness on full display, and he couldn't stop himself from bringing their foreheads together, rolling right, then left. Licking gently into her mouth and kissing her, increasing the rhythm in degrees until their lips were moving at an eager tempo, her hands fisting in the front of his shirt in a way that proved she was affected as much as Wells, *thank God*. "A week and a half should give you time to make decent headway on the shop," he said gruffly, their lips damp and rubbing together. "I'm only sorry you're going to miss me so much."

She laughed softly. Shook her head at him.

What the hell did *that* mean?

Was it laughable that she could miss him?

Probably.

Definitely.

Maybe *he* needed a week and a half to get his heart in check. Because he'd most definitely fallen harder than a motherfucker for this woman, and he had no idea if she wanted anything with him beyond a professional relationship . . . that occasionally involved life-altering, rating-scale-shattering sex.

How was he going to last a week and a half without knowing where they stood?

God, she's beautiful. Those eyes. Her voice. Everything about her. Nope.

A week and a half wasn't happening. Life would be hell without some clarity. So he was getting some. Tonight.

"Is your flight in the morning?"

"Yes," she responded. "Early."

"Mine, too. Have a drink with me, tonight? We deserve to celebrate."

His invitation seemed to relieve her, lines softening around her mouth. Was that promising? "Yes. I'd . . . like that," she said, beaming up at him.

That's when he knew.

Holy shit, he was going to ask this woman—his *caddie*—to be his girlfriend.

CHAPTER TWENTY-THREE

Getting ready for drinks felt like a bigger deal than usual.

Josephine should have probably stopped zoning out, staring into the bathroom mirror, Beautyblender forgotten in her hand as minutes ticked by unnoticed. But memories kept occupying her mind. Sexy memories. Wells's tongue teasing her nipples, his hands unapologetically rough on her backside, the way sex with Wells was a surprisingly hot blend of disrespect and veneration.

"Might as well admit it," Josephine said to her reflection. "You want more. Badly."

In the past, she'd been treated like a fragile object in bed. Men who didn't take the time to understand her diabetes asked broad questions before they went to bed together like, are you going to be okay?

Um, yes. She was going to be fine. Blood sugar corrections were just a way of life. Fixing lows and highs. That was her normal. They never acknowledged that she could do everything a person with a working pancreas could do, they simply held back with her, worried her glucose monitor might rip off or she'd need sugar halfway through.

But not Wells. And not because he didn't care. In fact, she suspected he cared a great deal. She'd caught him checking her number on his app twice today. During a professional round of golf being broadcast *live on television*, money and respect hanging in the balance, he'd been thinking of her. Yes, Wells cared about her health. A lot.

He also seemed to recognize that her strength was more powerful than her condition.

Josephine swallowed, turning slightly to check her monitor where it always sat, attached to the back of one of her arms. If the darn thing didn't rip off during sex with Wells, it could probably survive anything, because wow. *Wa-how.*

She'd been nursing a growing crush on the man.

Their encounter in the private bag room had shot that crush into a whole new category.

Was she officially falling for Wells Whitaker? The real man and not the persona she'd been following for the last five years?

"Oh boy," she whispered. "I think I might be."

Her stomach flipped over with the anticipation of seeing him in the bar, which was crazy, since she'd been in his company all day long. But there it was. She wasn't looking forward to a whole week and a half without him, either. The shop desperately needed her attention, though. She couldn't shirk her responsibilities, as much as she'd wanted to accept Wells's invitation to Miami.

She looked down at her phone and winced at the time. If she was late for drinks, Wells would never let her hear the end of it. Allowing herself to enjoy the fizz of something exciting in her stomach—and it had nothing to do with the room-service club sandwich she'd scarfed down an hour earlier—she finished her makeup and put on the blue dress she'd worn to the welcome party at the beginning of the tournament, slipping her feet into heels and leaving the room.

In the interest of privacy, Wells was bringing her someplace off the resort grounds. Though she didn't know *where* they were going, she'd been instructed to meet him at the lobby bar and he would take care of the rest. Josephine took the elevator down and exited on the main floor, relieved to see that the crowd had thinned considerably, thanks to the conclusion of the tournament. She walked at a fast clip, certain Wells was already sitting at the bar, probably practicing a lecture about punctuality. But she didn't get very far before someone familiar stepped into her path just inside the alcove entrance, hindering her progress.

Buck Lee.

"Well, I have to give it to you, Miss Doyle," he started, putting out his hand for a shake. "You certainly proved me wrong out there this week."

Josephine kept her smile intact as they shook, although she couldn't stop herself from bearing down with a tighter than usual grip. "I didn't realize you were expecting me to suck."

He laughed. "I wasn't alone in that prediction, to be fair. Not because you're a *woman*, of course," the older man rushed to tack on. "Only because you're a newbie. An unknown one, at that."

"Right." *Go sell it somewhere else.* "It was nice to see you again, but I'm late meeting Wells, and he's prickly enough without giving him extra reasons." Immediately, she regretted saying that. It was a comment she'd meant to be good natured and fond, but it came across like she was commiserating with Buck and that wasn't the case at all. "Excuse me—"

"Prickly is one way to describe him, I suppose," Buck drawled, sipping from a rocks glass containing a golden liquid. "Belligerent, self-sabotaging, and stubborn. Those are a few others." It was obvious that Buck had been drinking for a while, which was the pot calling the kettle black, if you asked her. She wanted out of the conversation, but Buck kept going. "When he called and asked me to help him get back on the tour, I said no. Flat-out. I wasn't putting my reputation on the line again when he squandered it the first time."

She watched over Buck's shoulder as Wells approached through the crowd.

The closer he came, the more her stomach sank down to her toes.

Please don't let him hear any of this.

"If you'll excuse me, Mr. Lee, I really need to—"

"Then he gave me this whole sob story about your shop getting damaged in the hurricane. Throw in the fact that you're a woman—sorry—and we knew it would make our missing fans curious enough to tune back in. A real human-interest story." He gestured to the television above the bar with his rocks glass, chuckling to himself. "Look at that! They're talking about it right now."

Josephine was almost afraid to turn her head.

When she met Wells's eyes over Buck's shoulder, she saw shock and recognition, followed by regret. Oh God. Finally, she looked at the television, her mouth falling open when she saw herself on the course, the footage taken earlier in the day—she could tell, because of her ice-blue skirt.

Beneath her was the headline:

Golfer Gives Down-and-Out Diabetic Caddie a Helping Hand

Her skin turned icy, stomach roiling.

No. She had to be reading that wrong.

"Like I told Wells, the media loves an underdog story," remarked Buck. "Ratings, ratings, ratings, right? We knew this angle would get him back on the tour."

Josephine's heart pounded a hundred miles an hour.

Everyone in the bar was staring at her, obviously fascinated by her supposed sob story—and that sob story was her being a sickly charity case. Not someone who offered valuable advice. Not someone who was good at the job. No, instead she was a pet project.

Success and respect. Those two things were everything in this world—and she was obviously a million miles away from having the latter. What did that mean for her reputation? Presently, she was a caddie and she took that job seriously. Image mattered here.

And image would mean a great deal when it was time to re-open the Golden Tee.

"I'll tell you the truth . . ." Buck, oblivious to her acute distress, wasn't done talking. "I was shocked to find out that Wells had a heart. Didn't think he cared about anyone but himself, but obviously there's more to him than I suspected—"

Wells stepped up beside Buck. "That's enough, Buck." Urgently, he said, "Josephine—"

"There *is* a lot more to him," Josephine interrupted, looking directly at Buck and ignoring the hollow sensation in her chest that was growing worse by the moment. Oh God, had her parents seen this whole mess on the Golf Channel? Of course, they had; the television in their house was constantly tuned in to the network.

She wanted to be angry with Wells—and she was. She *was*. He'd gotten back on the tour by using her sorry situation as media fodder. At the very least, he'd allowed it, right? He'd put the information into hands that couldn't be trusted not to manipulate and twist it to their advantage.

That being said, *no one* trash-talked her golfer. Only her.

"There is a lot more to Wells. And maybe, when he called to ask for help getting back on the tour, he *was* playing for me. But he's playing for himself again now, too. He loves this game. He's great at it. And you're a fair-weather fan and friend, sir. In my book, that's the worst possible thing you could be. Excuse me."

Josephine spun on a heel and marched for the door on legs that felt wobbly, at best.

"Come back here, Josephine, *goddammit*," Wells growled, following in her wake.

Entering the bright lobby after being in the dark bar made her feel ten times more exposed than she was already feeling, but instead of heading for the elevators, she went outside. She just needed air to process everything. To decide what she was going to do about all of it.

God, now that the whole news story was sinking in, embarrassment scaled the insides of her throat, drying out her mouth.

She fought between the impulse to rant and the voice of reason in her head, reminding her that without caddying, she'd never be able to rebuild the shop. Wells had done her a huge favor—and he couldn't control the press. Still, she'd asked him that day in the Golden Tee, standing in a foot of flood water, to please not make her a charity case. But here they were—and it was so much worse than she could have predicted.

Wells caught up with Josephine right as she reached an outdoor patio and they emerged from the lobby together, striding in silence until they hit the edge of the golf course, as if by some tacit agreement that the green was where they would have it out.

"Josephine, you need to let me explain."

She took off her shoe and threw it at his head. "I don't need to do *anything*."

Wells ducked, watching the footwear sail over his right shoulder. "You're right. Let me start over." His silence extended longer than she expected. "First off, the fact that you stood up for me in there even after seeing and hearing . . . that bullshit. God, belle. I don't fucking deserve you. Okay? Can we just get that part out of the way?"

Her whole face felt as though it welled up. "And? Keep going."

Wells looked like a man walking on a tightrope tied between two skyscrapers. "When I called Buck for help, I just wanted to get back on the tour by any means necessary. I never thought it would go this far. Never thought you'd become some kind of ridiculous narrative."

"I'm not a charity case," she said in a strangled whisper.

"Damn right you're not." He slammed a fist to his chest. "*I'm* the charity case here. It's me. You're the one bringing me back from extinction."

Listening to Wells put himself down wasn't making Josephine feel any better. "What are they saying about the shop? Are my parents going to find out the insurance had lapsed? That needing the money for repairs and oh God, *insulin* is the reason I'm caddying for you?"

He closed his eyes. "Yes."

"Wells." She covered her face with her hands. "This isn't happening. Do you know how hard I had to work to make them trust me? To believe they could let go and let me handle the shop *and* my condition? Now they know I'm a fraud."

"You. Are not. A fraud. Don't you dare. You can't control hurricanes and a fucked-up health-care system, Josephine. You are the furthest thing from a fraud I've ever met in my life." He ripped at his hair. "I'm going to take care of this. I'm going to fix their misconceptions about you, about us, the first chance I get. Tonight."

"Leave it alone, Wells. Please. You're only going to draw more attention to the story."

He stared at her hard for a moment, before pacing away and shouting a curse up at the sky. "This is my fault. I shouldn't have trusted Buck. But you have to believe me, I never thought it would go further than the tour directors. I'm sorry, Josephine."

She exhaled sharply. "I know."

A heavy pause ensued. "I'm afraid to ask where this leaves us."

"What do you mean?"

"I mean . . ." He turned around again, but his eyes were a lot more haunted this time. "You'd be well within your rights to tell me to fuck off."

"I'm not going to do that. I might be mad right now, but I *know* . . . I know some parts of that story are correct. You *are* helping me."

"That pales in comparison to what you've already done for me, Josephine. You make anything feel possible. You woke me up again."

She took several deep breaths, trying to comb through her scattered pride—her optimism that had been shot full of bullet holes—and find a way forward. Taking some time to sit and think privately might have done her a lot of good, but this wasn't the kind of frustration that could be slept on. His words were beautiful, but they didn't change the situation—and it wouldn't look different in the morning.

Earning respect meant taking her job seriously *now*. Earning respect meant convincing people within the sport to take *her* seriously. Other caddies, golfers, officials, spectators. A romance with her boss could preclude her from that. In addition to the angle already taken by the media, being in a public relationship with Wells would only diminish her capabilities more.

Josephine could hear the speculation now.

She landed that job only because she's his girlfriend.

What a stand-up guy, taking care of her like that.

"I'll be at the tournament in California, but I think it's probably a good idea if we just back off on . . . whatever was happening between us. Okay?"

He closed his eyes slowly, jaw flexing.

"You know my plan is to reopen the Golden Tee. To compete

with the bigger courses in Palm Beach, and this is my chance. But I need to be seen as . . . as *capable* for that to happen. And that's hard enough for me without *also* being known for having an incurable disease and a flooded pro shop. Rescued and put back on her feet by Wells Whitaker himself. I don't want success that way. And imagine the slant on that story if we were also dating." Heat swamped her face. "I mean, I'm not making that *assumption*. I just—"

"Assume all you like, belle," he said, very adamantly. "I want to date the hell out of you."

Even after the upheaval of the last ten minutes, she wanted to say yes. It was totally possible they wouldn't be standing in that spot, wouldn't have been in Texas at all, if Wells hadn't been honest with Buck about Josephine's circumstances. He'd done what was necessary to get them on the track to making money. But after struggling every day of her life to be seen as capable on her own, the whole thing smarted. Badly. She was mad and helpless and sick over what her parents were thinking. And she just needed to step back for a while.

"I don't think that's a good idea right now," she answered, finally, her throat burning.

His chest rose fast and fell faster. "Come here, Josephine." He took a measured step in her direction. "Kiss me and tell me if you still believe that."

She backed up a pace, holding up her hand to stop him from coming any closer, as much as she wanted to do the opposite. With every cell in her body, she wanted to plant her face between his pecs, let him wrap his arms around her, and weather the storm together. Her irritation and worry and humiliation prevented her, though. "I think skipping the tournament in DR is good timing, because it'll give us a while to let the story die down." Swallowing took an effort. "We'll regroup and be ready for California."

Josephine could sense him wrestling with the need to argue. "I don't really have a choice, do I?" he drawled. Casual, when his eyes were turbulent enough to put Josephine right on the edge of second-guessing her decision.

She shook her head, holding firm. This was the right thing.

For long moments, he watched from beneath hooded eyelids. "At least let me get you safely to your room."

Her knees nearly dipped at the very idea of him standing outside her room. The golf course was safe. Ten yards from a bed was not. "You can bring me to my floor. But you stay on the elevator."

"Why?" He sauntered closer and this time, she didn't even have the wherewithal to stave him off with a hand, allowing him to press his chest against her, his breath feathering the hair at her temple. "Are you worried you'll forgive me and let me in?" He touched the tip of his tongue to the pulse pounding at the base of her neck, then lavishing it with a thorough lick. "Are you wondering what make-up sex feels like when it counts this much?"

"Yes," she breathed, her belly fluttering wildly, along with her heart.

"Thank God," Wells said on a gruff exhale. "At least that's something. At least that's hope. You're always giving me that." He cupped her face, alarming Josephine when she couldn't help but turn into the warmth, like a flower receiving water. "I have no right to ask, but give me a little more hope right now. Tell me I haven't blown my fucking chance with you."

"I . . . don't know," she whispered honestly. Not wanting to lead him on until she had a chance to think without his presence muddling her brain waves, crisscrossing them with hormones. "I'll try and have an answer by California."

"California," he repeated against her mouth, very concisely. "You're a lot more confident in my ability to spend that amount of time away from you than I am, belle. I'll tell you that."

Before Josephine could respond, Wells took her hand, cursed beneath his breath, and stormed through the lobby with her in tow. He was silent on the ride up to her room. She could sense him right on the edge, despite his nonchalant lean against the elevator wall. She expected him to try to kiss her again at any second and worried that she wouldn't be able to resist asking him to spend the night, because God, she needed comfort right now. Badly. More than she could give herself. But somehow, despite staring at each other right up until the elevator door closed and separated them, they stayed apart.

A week and a half isn't long.

You have more than enough to stay busy. Fires to put out. Pride to repair.

Somehow she knew, however, that he'd be with her every second of those ten days.

Close to her thoughts, waking and dreaming.

Maybe even closer than she realized.

CHAPTER TWENTY-FOUR

A week later, Josephine stood in the middle of the Golden Tee, surveying the progress she'd made cleaning and drying everything out with industrial-sized fans. Nearly all of the drywall would need to be replaced, as well as the warped hardwood flooring. As soon as her prize money from the tournament had hit her bank account yesterday, she'd given a local contractor the green light to start making measurements and ordering new windows.

The Under Armour sponsorship money was due to arrive in the next few days, but Josephine needed to see the dollars in her account before she believed it was happening. During her meeting with the contractor, he'd drawn a plan for a courtyard in front of the pro shop with putting greens and a covered deck, along with a window facing the fairway where golfers could approach and purchase supplies without even entering the store. The very first pro shop drive-through in Florida.

All he needed was the go-ahead.

Making those improvements would clean her out again financially, but unlike last time, the money wasn't going into a black hole. She wasn't plugging one leak, only to watch another one grow worse. One more successful tournament with Wells and she would figure out her health insurance. The fabric of her life was finally knitting itself back together.

And she'd never felt lonelier.

Every time Josephine blinked, a memory of Wells would dance on the backs of her eyelids like a taunt. The way he'd stood outside the bag room, waiting for her with that cantankerous expression, arms crossed. How he twisted his hat backward when hunkering down to check the angle of a putt. When he'd checked her mini fridge for juice boxes. The taste and texture of his mouth, the stubble of his chin and cheeks so abrasive, yet welcoming on her softer skin. Their feet drifting side by side in the green hotel pool.

How he drawled her nickname. *Belle.*

Wells made her feel like she belonged. Like she was vitally necessary.

Treasured. Important. Even when they were arguing.

And she missed him very, very badly.

It was Sunday. Three days remained before she was supposed to meet Wells in California. She'd distracted herself for the last seven with cleaning and gearing up to make major changes to the shop, but three more days seemed interminable now. That morning she'd considered getting in her car and driving the ninety minutes to Miami to see him, but wouldn't that contradict every decision she'd made on their final night together in Texas? She was keeping her distance for the good of her reputation. In the name of professionalism. Respect.

None of that seemed to matter at that exact moment, though, when she wanted to hear his surly griping so badly, her breastbone ached.

She would have given anything to call Tallulah. Just for five minutes, so she could tell her best friend everything. Tallulah would validate the decision she'd made. Or, at the very least, she'd ooh and ahh over the sex details. Life simply wasn't as fulfilling when there was no one to tell about the afternoon she'd hooked up in a bag room. That information was meant to be whispered and blushed about after three glasses of wine.

Although . . . calling those stolen moments in the bag room a hookup didn't exactly do them justice. Not when she could still recall the sensation of him inside her a week later.

Josephine slumped back against the damaged wall.

How had Wells spent the last seven days?

He'd texted her only once, with flight information. Just basic itinerary stuff.

Nothing else.

That's what you asked him for. That's what you wanted.

Josephine was saved from having to acknowledge the regret creeping in when she heard footsteps approaching from outside. If she needed any further proof that she missed Wells like crazy, it was in the way her heart rate spiked, her breath running short at the prospect of him walking into the shop.

Jim and Evelyn appeared in the doorway instead.

It took a considerable effort for Josephine to swallow the acute disappointment, which only led to a healthy dose of guilt. "Mom. Dad." She dropped the tube of cleaning wipes in her hand and approached them, their arms wrapping around her shoulders and drawing her into a double embrace. "I'm sorry I haven't been over to see you. I just wanted to get the shop cleaned up before you saw it in such terrible condition."

Evelyn rubbed a firm circle into the center of her back, squeezed her tight. "It's not your job to shield us from uncomfortable things, Joey."

Uh-oh.

She knew that tone from her mother. Loving, as always, but decidedly wounded.

Josephine exhaled and stepped back, studying the faces of her parents. They weren't the type to lay the guilt on thick, but they were guarded this afternoon. Hurt. And frankly, she deserved that reaction from them after being back in Palm Beach for a full week and avoiding the Big Conversation. "I'm not only sorry that I haven't come to the house. I'm so sorry about the rest of it, too." She wanted to rub at the discomfort in her throat, but her hands were covered in muck. "I don't know what exactly you've heard on TV, because I can't bring myself to watch. But . . . you've probably realized by now that I'm caddying for Wells because I . . . *we* need the money to repair the shop."

"You should have told us, Joey," Jim said quietly. "We have savings. You didn't have to shoulder all this responsibility on your own."

"I like the responsibility," Josephine rushed to say. "I *want* it. And it might seem as if you've misplaced your trust in me, but I promise, I'm going to build the shop back better than ever. All right? I won't make the same mistakes again."

Evelyn sighed. "You know the shop isn't the part we worry about most." She looked up at the ceiling and blinked several times, as if holding back tears. "It's you. You're a diabetic. You need health insurance. It's not some optional luxury—"

"Mom, I know. Can you please just trust me?" Josephine gave up on staying clean and massaged her aching throat. "I'm handling it. All of it. One problem at a time."

"How can I trust you when you lied?"

"Technically, she didn't lie," Jim interjected. "She just omitted the truth."

Josephine's shoulders slumped in relief. "Thanks, Dad."

He grunted, took a turn around the shop. "Do you have supplies? Sensors for your CGM? Insulin?"

"Yes. Enough to get me through until I can get a policy up and running. I'm not . . ."

"Rationing?" Her mother spat the word like an epithet. "You can't do that. We'd sell the house before letting you do that."

"I know! I know. That's why I didn't say anything." Immediately, she regretted her outburst, but her parents were staring at her, stunned, the words lingering in the air. She had no choice but to qualify them. To explain. With a sigh, Josephine turned over the crate she'd been using to transport cleaning supplies and sat down heavily. "What happens with the shop is one thing, my diabetes is another. I'm an adult, guys. I find my own solutions. I'm the one who has to live with this condition. It's mine. I don't want caretakers, because it makes me feel like I . . . I *need* them. It makes me feel sickly—and I'm not. I'm strong."

It occurred to Josephine that she'd been avoiding this conversation for years.

Smiling through the well-meaning warnings and advice. Nodding. Agreeing.

One tournament with Wells and she was no longer avoiding the uncomfortable topics. Maybe . . . she'd learned something from him? Or gotten used to facing problems head-on—bluntly and loudly. Whatever the reason, her short time with Wells had changed her for the better, hadn't it? Reminded her exactly how capable she was.

And that made her miss him even more.

Romantically, yes. Her gooey heart and sex feelings for the big jerk were undeniable.

But it was more than that. She missed her friend and fighting partner.

"You are strong, Joey," Evelyn said, voice quivering. "It was never my intention to make you feel otherwise. Sometimes I just can't shut off the worry."

"I know. I'm sorry you have to live with that, Mom. It's not fair."

Jim settled a hand on her shoulder. "You're worth ten lifetimes of it."

"Thanks." A watery laugh bubbled out of Josephine. "This conversation is getting way too heavy." She used the edge of her shirt to swipe at her eyes. "Quick, somebody say something funny."

"Good idea," Jim said quickly.

Her parents searched each other's faces for a moment until finally Evelyn snapped her fingers. "Oh honey, what was it Wells said this morning that had you in stitches?"

Wells? *This morning?* Josephine's mouth fell open.

Jim slapped his knee. "He told me there's a tree at the ninth hole at Torrey Pines where all the golfers go to drain the weasel. It's tradition! They call it the Pissing Tree. And it's the fastest growing tree on the course—he swore up and down!"

Josephine couldn't even begin to process that. They were going to be at Torrey Pines next week, though, so she pocketed the valuable information for future use. "Why were you speaking to Wells?"

"He calls your father every day, dear."

"He *what*?"

Jim crossed his fingers. "He's trying to wrangle me a ticket to the Masters."

"What do you talk about?"

"Golf. What else? Although . . . ," Jim hedged.

"What?" Josephine prompted.

"Well, he usually manages to sneak in a few questions about you, Joey-Roo." He paused, looking sheepish. "Come to think of it, that might be the real reason he's calling."

"Oh no, he *loves* you, honey," Evelyn assured him.

Jim's chest puffed up. "He does, doesn't he?"

"Yes."

Josephine stared at her parents. "What does he ask about me?"

"Well . . ." Her father scratched his head. "He's crafty about it. See, we were having a conversation about golf clubs and he says, very casually mind you, 'What kind of sticks does Josephine use?' And it goes like that."

Obviously, there was no satisfaction to be had from this line of questioning.

"He asked about her birthday," volunteered Evelyn. "Remember?"

"Oh yes. He wanted to know the date."

"Why?"

"Well, how am *I* supposed to know, Josephine?"

"By asking!"

"Wells doesn't like questions."

"Oh, for the love of—" Josephine pushed to her feet. "If he wants to know anything else about me, he can ask me himself."

Jim gave a firm nod. "I'll be sure to let him know that during our next chat."

"Good."

"Is there a romance brewing here, Joey-Roo?" asked her mother with a little shimmy of her shoulders. "I ran into Sue Brown at the supermarket yesterday and she seemed to think so. Said the broadcasters implied as much while you were in San Antonio."

"The checkout clerk at the plant store asked about it, too."

"Wow. More plants, huh?" Josephine sighed. "Did anyone ask about golf? Or caddying? Or was it all about whether or not Wells and I are—"

"I don't think I like questions, either," Jim blurted. "Don't finish that one."

"Dating. I was going to say dating."

"Oh." Jim coughed into his first. "Yes, it seems people are mostly interested in the possibility that our daughter is seeing Wells Whitaker. Also . . . that he's a class act for helping you get back on your feet."

Concerns validated, Josephine's nod was jerky.

Wasn't this what she'd been afraid of?

Being recognized as Wells's charity-case girlfriend, instead of for her abilities?

Apparently, she'd done the right thing by backing away and giving all the hype a chance to die down. Would it pick back up as soon as they were on television in California?

Only time would tell.

And inevitably, she'd have more decisions to make. Such as how much longer could she remain as Wells's caddie? More importantly, would any length of time serving as his caddie be enough to make people recognize her as an asset to the sport, instead of what had brought her on the tour? Would that talent serve the new and improved Golden Tee? Bring her family's shop the attention she was hoping for? Or was that only wishful thinking?

An hour later, Josephine was still mulling over these worries when she walked into her apartment. Before the door even closed, her phone started to beep.

Sensor expiring said the alert on the screen.

Time to change the site of her glucose monitor. One arm to the other.

With a yawn, Josephine showered and went through the practiced motions of removing the old sensor, unsnapping the transmitter that sent her blood sugar number to her phone, then attaching the new one to the back of her arm with a slight wince. No matter how many times she performed the ritual, a needle punching into the back of her arm never stopped being a little jarring. Blowing out the breath she'd been holding, Josephine snapped in the fob and tapped the screen on the app to begin warming up the new device, which usually took around an hour. She chewed a few tabs, just to make sure she didn't go low while waiting for the new device to kick in—and then she face-planted on the couch and fell fast asleep.

CHAPTER TWENTY-FIVE

Wells stepped off the treadmill and grabbed the white towel from the handrail, mopping the sweat from his face and bare chest. He dropped down on the mat and gave himself a few minutes to recover before working through a set of core exercises.

He hated every fucking second of it.

Honestly, he didn't like much right now. *At all.* Everything was annoying.

No matter how many times he adjusted the thermostat in his apartment, it was either too warm or too cold. Food was tasteless. Josephine had ruined jerking off, so not even that could relieve the restlessness plaguing him. Every time he started to rub one out, he got to thinking about how much better it would feel to be inside her and then his stupid chest started to hurt, *in addition* to his dick. Honestly, he was beginning to worry that something serious was wrong with him. Did he need to see a cardiologist or a urologist?

He'd worked out more this week than he'd done since the start of his career. Studied the course at Torrey Pines, poring over yardage books and perusing highlights from last year's tournament when, coincidentally, he'd sucked too hard to even make the cut. Not an easy thing to watch, but he was going to finish higher than he had in San Antonio. End of story.

Josephine was getting rich whether she liked it or not. Call it revenge for making him feel nothing but disappointment in his God-given right to beat off.

Finished working his core, Wells got to his feet and moved to the bench press. But instead of lying down, he slipped his phone out of his pocket. Whistling to himself, he pulled up a news segment he'd watched too many times. Not the one that had upset Josephine their last night in San Antonio. No, this one was from earlier that day. When he'd finished in the money and she'd jumped into his arms.

Please, God, don't let anyone trace these nine hundred views back to my IP address. Did phones even have an IP address? He didn't know, but surely the FBI could trace how many times he'd watched the same scene play out. How she'd smiled up at him with visible pride.

His jugular squeezed in the most alarming way.

What an angel.

Three more ridiculous days apart. Every second was absurd.

He was going to buy a new condo and move, just to have something to do besides working out and watching YouTube clips and calling Josephine's father, for Chrissake.

Wells hauled back, preparing to throw his phone across the room.

He stopped short when it started to ring.

No joke, he almost fell off the leather bench, thinking Josephine might be calling. *She changed her mind about taking time apart. She's coming to Miami and I'm about to raid a fucking Bath & Body Works to get ready for her.*

It wasn't Josephine, however.

It was Burgess Abraham. Also known as Sir Savage.

His professional hockey–playing friend, though neither one of them would *admit* they were friends. It was a completely healthy relationship.

Wells tapped the button to answer. "What?"

A low grumble of sound filled the small home gym. "Someone's in a mood."

"That's right."

"I live with a moody eleven-year-old now. Believe me, I don't need your shit, too."

Wells watched his own eyebrows rise in the mirror. "Your kid is living with you now? Like, full time?"

"Part time. And yet the whole apartment never stops smelling like Sol de Janeiro."

"What the hell is that? And how are things with her mom?"

"I didn't call to talk about this." Burgess sighed.

Wells chuckled. "Who's moody now?"

"Go to hell."

"Nice to hear from you, too." Wells switched the phone to his other hand. "Are you coming to Torrey Pines this week for the tournament?"

A hum came down the line. "I don't know. Do eleven-year-old girls like golf?"

"Christ, I don't know." Wells paused, trying to swallow the protrusion forming in his throat. "Josephine probably liked golf when she was eleven."

Even though Burgess didn't make a sound, Wells had a feeling he was amused by the abject misery in his tone. "Ah. The caddie."

Wells grunted.

Burgess made a thoughtful sound. "Can you ask her if it's advisable to bring Lissa to the tournament?"

"I could if she was here." He dug a knuckle into his eye and twisted. "Which she is not."

"You don't sound very happy about that."

"Nope!"

The hockey player was silent for several seconds. "She the one?"

"The one what?"

"Really?" Leather creaked in the background. "Don't make me say it."

"I'm afraid I need clarification."

Burgess cursed under his breath. "This always happens to me. The young people in my life think I'm wise because I've got a few gray streaks in my beard and I get stuck explaining romance and giving advice on how to handle women, when I'm obviously not qualified to do either one of those things."

"Hence the divorce."

"Remind me why I stay in touch with you?" Before Wells could answer, Burgess kept going. "Is she the one? As in, the one you want to be with forever. Or until she asks for a divorce with no warning, whichever one comes first."

Wells stared hard at his reflection in the mirror.

Was Josephine *the* one? It hadn't occurred to him to think of her that way, because he'd never expected to find *the one.* Hell, he'd never considered that *the one* existed. That term was a bullshit romantic notion that was used to sell Valentine's Day cards, right? But his bones were telling him—and they were dead certain—that he could spend the rest of his life walking the planet and never come across anyone that made him feel a *fraction* of the way Josephine did. Being away from her was making that all too obvious. "Yes. She's the one. Minus the divorce."

"Interesting."

"It's not interesting," Wells half shouted. "It's a shit show."

"If it's a shit show, it's probably your fault."

"Thanks, buddy."

Josephine's low blood sugar alert started beeping in his ear. She hadn't been exaggerating when she claimed it beeped constantly. High alerts had different tones, too. He'd been listening to them for the last week, wishing he could do something to help, but also confident that Josephine knew how to take care of herself. And frankly, it was a relief to have this connection to her. The shared app was an important link to her and he treasured it.

"What's that beeping?" Burgess asked.

"Josephine's glucose monitor."

"You said she wasn't there."

Talking about his caddie was making him feel better *and* worse. What sense did that make? "She's not here. It's an app. I can see—"

The beeping filled his ear again, but it was more urgent this time.

Urgent low.

Wells had never heard that one before. It was louder and sharper.

"Hold on." His pulse was skipping as he lowered the phone and opened the app, nausea swimming in his stomach at the sight of the dots plummeting. Plummeting down to the lowest number possible and disappearing altogether. "I . . . what the fuck?" His hands started to shake. "Something is wrong. I have to go."

"Bye."

After ending the call with Burgess, Wells didn't even hesitate to call Josephine. It rang five times and went to voice mail. *Hello! You've reached Josephine Doyle. Seriously? Who leaves voice mail anymore? If this is urgent, try me at the shop.* Beep.

"Belle, what's going on with your number? I–it just . . . there's nothing. It just flew down and now it's gone. Call me back, please. *Now.* Okay?"

Wells sat for maybe thirteen seconds, then vaulted off the bench and out of the gym, his hands extremely unsteady as he called Jim. No answer. *Really?* The guy usually picked up after half a ring. Was that a sign that something serious was going on? With Josephine?

"Fuck." He turned in a dizzy circle, seeing nothing, willing the phone to ring. "*Fuck.*"

He raced to the red emergency shot that was sitting on his kitchen counter, snatched it up, his car keys in his hands, too, before he knew his own mind. Scratch that, his mind had gone completely offline. His stomach was living in his mouth, sweat pouring down the sides of his face as he sprinted for the parking garage.

Ninety minutes. He was *ninety minutes* away from Palm Beach. If something was wrong, would he even get there in time? Christ, he didn't even have Josephine's address. Only the location of the pro shop. A fact that was straight-up mind blowing, considering she was *the one*.

What a cliché thing to call someone whose well-being had him this terrified.

Wells was in his Ferrari within minutes, tearing north on 95 toward Palm Beach with his heart ripping itself to shreds inside his chest.

"Why isn't anyone calling me back?" he shouted at the dashboard.

Against the leather seat, his bare back was slick with ice-cold perspiration, pulses hammering all over his body. If he got pulled over for speeding, so help him God, he would end up on the news in a high-speed chase, because he wasn't slowing down. Not happening. He could barely feel his foot on the gas pedal. Only enough to know it was damn near on the floor and every minute he drove felt like six hours. There was no music or talk radio, just the sound of his rasping inhales and shuddering exhales. And still, no one had called him back. Where the hell was he even going? He didn't have an address.

Wells smacked the phone symbol on the navigation screen. "Call Josephine."

No answer.

None from Jim, either.

Oh God. Something very bad had happened. He knew it. He *knew* it.

Unable to think of any other options, Wells called his manager. He was twenty minutes from Palm Beach at this point, having cut the drive time in half by illegal means.

"Well, if it isn't my favorite golden goose."

"Nate, please. I need help."

Two seconds of silence. "Oh Jesus, Wells. Don't tell me you're in jail again. You can't expect me to keep this out of the press. There are so many eyes on you right now—"

"I'm not in jail. I need Josephine's address." He couldn't even recognize his voice as it slurred out of pure fear. "Didn't she fill out some kind of form or whatever when she entered that contest?"

"I . . . yeah. But I can't share that information. I told you that already."

"It's an emergency, Nate," he growled. "Give me the fucking address!"

Something in Wells's tone must have gotten through to the manager, because a moment later, the sound of computer keys started to click. Wells pressed even harder on the gas pedal, weaving his car in and out of traffic, ignoring the outraged honks sounding in his wake.

"Okay, here it is," Nate came back, serious now. "Seven one one Malibu Bay Drive. Apartment six."

"Text it to me, too," Wells ordered, the address imprinting itself on his brain. "Thanks."

He hung up the phone and shouted the location at the navigation screen, surprised when it came up despite his frantic tone. Six minutes. He'd be there in six minutes.

Still no blood sugar number for Josephine on the app.

What was he going to walk into?

His brain couldn't even go there.

"Please, God, let her be okay." The air conditioner had turned the sweat to ice on his skin, but he barely noticed. "I'll be a nicer person. I'll sell this car and give all the money to charity. I'll never break another club. I'll donate both of my kidneys. Yes, both. Take my soul, while you're at it. Take everything. Whatever you want, *I'll do it*. Please."

Josephine woke up to the sound of her apartment door being kicked in.

She jackknifed on the couch, screaming so loud that it could be heard clear to Orlando.

This was it. Her *Dateline* moment.

A robbery gone wrong. *Or was it?* questioned Keith Morrison.

Who would rob *her*, though? She had nothing of serious value in the apartment. Her clubs were kept in a locker at the golf course. Jewelry? Did they want the locket from JCPenney her mother had given Josephine at her graduation brunch? Because she would stab first and ask questions later, if they went anywhere *near* that locket—

Hold on.

Wakefulness collided with reality, bringing life back into focus.

She wasn't being robbed. Not unless this shirtless, six-foot-two golfer with wild eyes had fallen on seriously desperate times.

"Wells?"

He didn't move. Not right away. He simply continued to stare at her, chest heaving, the door behind him hanging off its hinges.

Finally, he held up his phone and pointed at it. "No dots."

"What?"

He struggled through a swallow, his voice little more than a scrape. "There was an urgent low and then you just . . . went off the fucking map." His breath sounded more like a wheeze. "And you wouldn't answer your phone, Josephine. I thought . . . I thought you . . ."

At once, the situation clicked, the remaining sleep cobwebs dissipating.

The blood drained from her face.

"Oh Wells, I'm sorry." Slowly, she stood. "I should have explained this to you."

He dropped his phone with a loud bang, but didn't seem to notice he'd done so.

"I had to change the sensor. It takes a while to warm up and connect again with the app, so . . . there is no number for a while." He looked so shaken up, she was almost afraid to approach him. "It might have looked like I was crashing, but I was fine. I'm *totally* fine."

Wells doubled over, hands propped on his knees, sides puffing in and out.

"I'm sorry," she said, a chasm opening in the center of her chest. "I'm sorry that freaked you out. I fell asleep and my phone must have been silenced."

"Okay." He took several long, uneven breaths. "Just . . . let me get myself together."

"Okay." She shifted on her bare feet. "Would a hug help—"

"Yes," Wells rasped, barreling toward her like a cruise missile. Josephine was scooped off the floor and enveloped in a bear hug

that was so fierce, it made her eyes water. Wells buried his face in her neck and breathed deeply, gathering Josephine closer, closer, like he was trying to absorb her. "You and me not being together all the time is *fucking stupid*, Josephine," he roared.

"You're shouting in my ear."

No apology was forthcoming. Not from this man.

And honestly, Josephine didn't really need one. The way he was holding her like he was on the verge of breaking said more than words ever could. That was Wells, wasn't it?

No sweet nothings. Only actions.

Josephine stared over his shoulder at the brutalized door, piling more and more facts together. "Did you drive all the way here from Miami?"

"I'd have driven to the ends of the Earth, belle."

Oh wow.

Moisture washed into her eyes.

Hold that thought about sweet nothings—

"That's probably how long it would have taken you to simply return my call. *Christ*."

She started to laugh.

Holy cow, she'd missed him more than she realized. Like a hundred times more.

"Don't you dare laugh. I've been through hell. That was the worst hour of my life."

She wrapped her arms around his neck, sighing when he lifted her more securely against his chest, her feet leaving the floor. "I know. I'm sorry." Discreetly, she inhaled his neck, letting the combination of soap and sweat seep into her skin. "You're still paying for my door. Did you even knock?"

"Nope."

Wells walked them over to the couch and turned, sitting down heavily. And because of the way they'd been standing, she had no choice but to wrap her thighs around his hips, straddling him on the couch, her face smooshed in his neck.

Right. No choice at all.

"Listen, belle," he started a few seconds later, his palm stroking down the back of her head, still shaking slightly. "I remember what you told me. About your parents making a fuss about diabetes and how it reminds you there's something to fear. I know you can take care of yourself. This just threw me, okay? I didn't know what was happening."

"I understand."

"I won't lose my shit next time." He paused to let out a jagged breath. "But you should still answer your goddamn phone."

She nuzzled her smiling face farther into his neck.

"Because I don't wear matching outfits for just anyone, Josephine. I don't wear them for anyone but . . ." He jerked a shoulder. "You know who."

"Me."

A gruff grunt was his response. "Your dad didn't even answer my call," he said after a moment, sounding stunned.

"Oh? Were you calling him to ask more intrusive questions about me?"

Wells cursed. "I knew the old man wouldn't keep quiet."

She laid her cheek on his warm shoulder, almost moaning over the way his palm rode up and down her spine. The loneliness inside her had fled as soon as they were touching, and slowly it was replaced with relief, security, a sense of balance, and peace. Even if their default method of communication was bickering. "You wanted to know my birthday, I understand."

"That's right. It's the Wednesday we fly to California. I already have a present."

"No, you don't," she scoffed, lifting her head to make eye contact—

And caught the tail end of pure, undiluted affection before he hid it away.

"You'll just have to wait and see, won't you?" he said curtly, brushing Josephine's hair back from her face. His attention fell to her mouth, before he dragged it away. "Jesus, I can barely feel my arms. I think my adrenaline is crashing."

"Do you want to"—she sniffed him—"take a shower? Maybe it'll help with the nerves."

"Flattering as ever, belle," he griped. "I was mid-workout, you know."

"I'm sorry for interrupting."

He stood up, seemingly unfazed by a full-grown woman clinging to the front of his body. "You don't sound very sorry," he remarked. Was his voice deepening? "*At* all."

She dropped her legs from around his waist, patting his wrist to let him know he was still holding her in a death grip.

She had no idea what was going to happen between herself and Wells. After all, she still had the same concerns as the last time they were together.

Yet no matter what happened, Wells would always be the first person to crack the code to Josephine's safe. He was kind of an asshole, but in a way that made her feel . . . like an equal member of a team. People had shied away from challenging Josephine too much her whole life, no matter how often she proved herself capable or fought against the notion that she was weak. At the same time, she knew if she needed to lean on him, he'd hold her up without making a big deal out of it.

Kicking in the door didn't count—not knowing that she would suddenly go offline had been a legitimate reason for concern. He'd recovered and started giving her shit about it as soon as possible, too, which was weirdly . . . perfect.

"Wells."

Finally, he released her and turned for the hallway, assuming the correct way to the bathroom. "Yeah?"

"I'm glad I trusted you to follow me on the app."

For the briefest second, he couldn't quite disguise his vulnerability. It was fleeting, but potent. "Even after I kicked in your door?"

"Especially after you kicked in my door. You . . ." She searched for the right words, because the moment called for them. "You make me feel capable and healthy. But still like there's someone who has my back. That's not an easy balance and you somehow . . . know how to navigate it. Without me having to guide you. It's hard and you just . . . do it."

Visibly caught off guard, he opened his mouth, then closed it. "If you're trying to butter me up for matching pink outfits, you can forget it right now."

"Not even a soft pastel? Easter is coming up!"

He stomped away from her down the hall and slammed the bathroom door.

Wow. It had been a long time since her face hurt from smiling. She hadn't had that problem since the last time she'd seen Tallulah.

When the shower water started running, however, her smile started to vanish little by little, followed by a punctuated swallow. Her palms grew clammy, thighs tensing at the sight of shadows moving beneath the door.

Wells was getting *naked*.

In *her* bathroom.

To be fair, he'd barged into the apartment half-dressed, but the reality of those mesh workout shorts coming off was *extremely* hard to ignore.

Still, she wouldn't be spectating that big reveal. She'd been the one to put the brakes on their relationship. And for good reason.

This was her chance to take the knowledge she'd been digesting her entire life and put it to use. To make herself and her family proud by revitalizing and legitimizing their business. Dating Wells in the public eye would lead to her being pigeonholed as the strong woman behind the successful man.

Or worse, his pet pity project.

Uh-uh.

But they could be friends. Really good friends.

After all, she couldn't just send him home after he'd driven from Miami thinking she was a goner. As soon as he got out of the shower and they figured out something for him to wear, she'd ask him if he wanted to order takeout and watch a movie that didn't have Gerard Butler humping anyone in it. They could discuss strategy for Torrey Pines next week and gossip about the other golfers. It would be *great*. Maybe she'd even show him her high school yearbook so they could laugh over her humidity bangs, braces, and puka shell necklace trifecta.

Mind made up, Josephine wedged the broken front door closed as best she could and walked down the hallway toward the bedroom, intending to find an oversized shirt for Wells to put on. She paused only for the barest of seconds outside of the bathroom door. "Do you have everything you need?"

"No," he called back immediately.

Josephine frowned. "I just put fresh towels on the rack this morning."

"Yeah, I found those."

The bathroom door opened.

Steam rolled out in a dreamy waft.

There stood shirtless Wells, forearm braced on the doorframe. In a very brief towel. The sucker barely made it around his hips, leaving a very sizable slit running up his sinewy thigh. "This towel is more like Kleenex, belle."

"Oh," she rasped. "Is it?"

"Yeah." He tucked his tongue into his cheek. "It could fall off any second."

"Oh." A terribly wonderful tingle started in her breasts and slowly spiraled lower, lower, to her belly and the flesh between her thighs. Uh-oh. "Could it?"

"Afraid so." He dropped his forearm from the door and prowled toward where she stood transfixed in the hallway. "Listen, Josephine. I know you want to be seen as a professional. You need to be taken seriously to build your dream—and I get that. I want that for you. But, baby . . ." He crowded her up against the hallway wall and the horny sound that left her mouth would have been embarrassing if she could manage to think straight. "It's only you and me here. We can be professionals later." He leaned in, his mouth finding the pulse at the base of her neck and spreading warm air across that fluttering skin, kissing her there. "No one is watching us right now, Josephine. Makes you wonder why you've still got your panties on, doesn't it?" Slowly, torturously, his tongue licked all the way to her ear and bit down. "I know *I'm* wondering."

Wells grazed their lips together, held that position without kissing her for a beat, both of them already breathing like they'd just completed a swim to Aruba. Then he backed away, leaving her trembling against the wall, all sensitive hips, feverish skin, and jelly thighs, her mouth *dying* for the taste of him.

Turning, he sauntered back into the bathroom, letting his towel drop on the way into the shower, giving her a very generous view of that butt—and dear God, it was a golden, sculpted masterpiece. A sacrifice even the stingiest of gods would accept.

Tight, thick, round cheeks sprinkled with hair. Golf's most perfect bubble butt, right there in her home. Totally bare. And when he stepped into her shower, flashing her his balls and an erection, both of which, frankly, looked heavy and miserable, the temptation of Wells—being connected to him again, the way they'd been in Texas—had her taking a step toward the bathroom, hovering in the doorway. Should she? Or was this—literally—a slippery slope?

Two of them.

Wells crooked his finger at her from inside the steamy shower.

Then he dropped that hand to his shaft and stroked himself roughly.

And the possibility of saying no sifted right through her fingertips, like it never existed.

CHAPTER TWENTY-SIX

Was Wells playing it cool, as though his life hadn't flashed before his eyes today?

He was trying like hell, but in no way, shape, or form had he recovered from thinking something terrible had happened to Josephine. And honestly, he'd walked into that bathroom ordering himself to be respectful of her wishes. When he'd been damn near overcome by the need to kiss her on the couch, he'd reminded himself of what she wanted—and he'd refrained.

Unfortunately, Josephine's bathroom was like a cute little wonderland of her scents and personality. A combination of frilly and practical. Cheerful yellow soap beside an electric toothbrush. In a touch of whimsy, those glow-in-the-dark stars were stuck to the ceiling, but she had a ruthlessly arranged assortment of glass jars containing cotton balls and Q-tips. The kicker, however, was the baby-blue see-through bra hanging from the towel rack.

See through. With a white bow in between the cups.

At that point, Wells had reached the breaking point.

Do you have everything you need? his achingly hot caddie had called through the bathroom door, giving him zero choice but to accept the opening.

Now, standing in a veritable whirlwind of her scent—vanilla and lilacs, wasn't it?—he watched her approach through the open glass door of the shower, his dick swelling gratefully in his hand. *Come on, baby, don't stop. Almost here.* Honestly, Wells wasn't even sure fucking Josephine right now was a smart idea. His brain was still half fogged with the fear he'd lost her, his delirium compounded by the slap shot in the other direction when he saw her alive and well.

In *no way* would this be casual, despite how he'd made it seem.

Was he going to be able to have sex with this woman without professing his feelings and begging her to please, for the love of God, just cut the bullshit and belong to him?

Probably not. Maybe he should have kept his shorts on and left. Gone back to his lonely bachelor's apartment in Miami.

But Josephine.

Being around her again was like waking up after a lung transplant and remembering what it's like to breathe. He just wanted to get drunk on her oxygen. Was that so much to ask?

"Take off your clothes," he requested hoarsely, releasing his cock and bracing a hand on the wall of the shower. Otherwise, all his pent-up sexual frustration was going to end up on the shower floor as soon as he saw her tits. "Strip for me, belle. I need to see you."

She chewed her lip a moment, indecisive.

As a man who knew the strongest weapon in his arsenal—when it came to this particular woman—Wells turned around and let her see his ass. Eyes closed, he tipped his head forward beneath the hot shower spray, letting the water coast down over his back—and he held his breath, praying for Josephine to make the decision to climb in there with him.

Come on, belle. I need you.

Need me back.

His breath released in a gusty shudder when her palms slid up his wet back and Jesus, his cock saluted so fast, it nearly slapped up against his stomach. God *almighty*, the effect this woman had on him was unmatched. One touch and he had the urge to promise a bunch of ridiculous shit. *You want to be carried around town on a silk pillow, Josephine? Hop on. I knew I had these arms for a reason.*

Wow. He had problems.

Big ones.

Chief of which, he wanted to turn around and *demolish* Josephine where she stood. Just wrap those beautiful legs around his waist, lick his tongue into her mouth, and pound his way to heaven while she whimpered and clawed at him. But based on her tentative, featherlight touch, they weren't quite on the same page yet.

Stay cool. Calm the hell down.

Right. Easier said than done when his dick was stiffer than a flagpole in January.

And it only got worse when he felt Josephine's tongue trailing up and down his spine, her hands gripping both sides of his ass and massaging. Rhythmically.

A hot ripple passed through Wells, his hand dying to wrap around his dick again.

No, don't move. Don't do anything that might make her stop.

"That's yours if you want it, Josephine," he panted, his hands turning to fists on the slick tile wall. What was he doing? Offering her ownership of his *ass*? He didn't feel compelled to take back the proposition, though. If they weren't in a dark bathroom with stars glowing overhead, steam muffling their voices, his proposition might have come across . . . bizarre? Definitely bizarre. In the thick of the moment, though, giving Josephine her favorite thing about him came naturally. Giving her *anything* she wanted was the only way to live. "Matter of fact, it's been yours," Wells said, without thinking.

Words were just leaving his mouth without orders from his brain. Had his fucking filter been carried down the shower drain along with the water?

And then his thoughts scattered like beads on a wooden floor, because Josephine whispered, "I accept" into his neck—and she rubbed a finger against his asshole.

"What the . . . ," he said on a rushing exhale, his world tilting sideways. "Okay. Fuck."

Briefly, her hand appeared to his left, picking up a square yellow bar of soap—the handmade shit, like the kind someone bought at a farmers' market. Did she go to the farmers' market? Why was he thinking about this? Probably because he had no right enjoying what Josephine was doing back there. She'd soaped her hand up really well, based on the slippery sudsiness of her palm and she was . . . cleaning him. Rubbing three whole fingers up and down, up and down . . . there. Like, *right* there.

Motherfucker, that felt good.

Felt *great*, knowing Josephine was the one doing it. Enjoying the hell out of it, too, if her fast breaths against his shoulders were any indication.

The longer she kept at it, the more his hand itched to beat his cock and finally he couldn't hold off anymore, so he wrapped a fist around his inches, pumping hard. "Ohhh. Shit. What are you doing to me, baby?"

"Whatever I want." She sank her teeth into his shoulder, dug them in, then kissed the spot in apology. "Right?"

"That's right," he grated, sparks twinkling in the far corners of his vision. "But I can only take so much before I need to hit that pussy, Josephine. Please."

She did it. She actually did it. She pressed a finger inside him. Deep.

"What's the rush?"

His fists shook on the wall, his balls weighed down so heavy, the sexual pain was making its way into his stomach. "I don't . . . oh my God. Should you stop?"

"You tell me."

A soft thump on the shower floor had Wells glancing back over his shoulder—and down—to find Josephine on her knees, her lips tracing the valley of his ass, her eyes closed like she'd never tasted anything finer, and his pulse began hammering out of control, a new kind of serpentine lust uncoiling and slithering in the lowest region of his belly. What was happening here? Why was this the most turned on he'd ever been in his fucking life?

"What are you going to—"

Her tongue raked up the part of his backside—firmly—and traveled over the pucker of his asshole, sliding over it roughly once, twice, three times, while his knees verged on buckling and then, *holy shit*, she reached through his thighs and started to jack him off, her tongue still working and prodding and licking his rear entrance like her goal was to drive him fully insane. And she was. God help him, his right foot slid wider with a wet squeak of tile, so she could have more, and she moaned gratefully in response and nothing, nothing, could have prepared him for the animalistic surge of lust that tightened his balls and made him growl at the shower wall, without even really seeing it, because he'd gone fucking blind.

"You are in for such a fucking pounding, Josephine, I swear to God," he said hoarsely. "Enjoy being on your knees, baby, because you're going to spend the rest of the night on your back dealing with my dick. You've got *one more minute*."

He'd live to regret that. Or maybe the opposite. He didn't know.

She made the most out of that minute.

That grip of hers cinched up tighter around his painful erection, luxuriating in every single thorough stroke, while she did things with her tongue that he'd never even fantasized about. Had no idea he would even enjoy. She wet him down so thoroughly that when she entered him with her thumb, there was no discomfort, only this mind-blowing pressure in his balls that increased and increased the deeper she pushed, until he was shouting epithets at the wall. He probably made it only thirty seconds of that final minute before he was slapping off the shower spray, turning around, and scooping Josephine off the floor by her armpits. No sooner had he settled her on her feet outside the shower than he was tossing her up into his arms and kicking open the bathroom door, exiting into the hallway.

"Can I come inside you again?" Her desire-dazed expression only made him more desperate to lay her down and connect their bodies. Now. By any means necessary. He needed to get close and feel her have a goddamn orgasm. Watch her take his climax between her thighs and love every second. Every stroke. Every drop. "I've got seven days of frustration waiting for your pussy, Josephine. Can I take it raw? Yes or no."

She had to cross her legs, right there in his arms while he carried her. Squeeze them together tight. A good sign if he'd ever seen one. "*Yes.* You can."

"*Bedroom.*"

"There."

Wells stormed into the room she indicated, seeing nothing. He just dropped her onto the bed-shaped thing and lunged into the space between her thighs, fitting himself into her tightness and pumping home. Hard and deep, giving her every inch of the cock she'd made so stiff, he could barely breathe. "Son of a bitch," he growled, dropping down to roll his face around in her neck. "You have no idea what it's like to miss you, baby. *No fucking idea.*"

"I have some idea," she murmured, kissing the side of his face.

She lifted her knees and rubbed her inner thighs against his rib cage.

It was too much at once. Her words—the implication that she'd missed him, too—along with the welcome of her body was like a balm to his wounds. By some miracle, she seemed to know their exact location and how to treat them.

Mine. My Josephine. End of story.

Her fingers sank into his wet hair, her hips shifting and rising beneath him. And it felt so good, he had to roughly pin down her lower body or risk coming too soon.

"So smooth. God. Your body is so *smooth*," he praised in her ear, easing into the fuck with shallow thrusts of his cock, teasing her and testing himself, trying desperately to keep a grip on the pressure that needed an outlet so badly, he was on the verge of destruction. "That goes double for your cunt, Josephine. You ride so nice and smooth, don't you?"

And hot damn. Maybe he needed to stop talking to her like that, because she gasped and bucked beneath him, her intimate muscles seizing up in an erotic pattern, making his eyes roll back in his head. The way she squeezed him had to be illegal.

"Jesus," he groaned, his lips launching a sensual attack against her neck, sucking that spot beneath her ear. "Don't bother answering. Yes, you do, baby. Yes, you *fucking do*."

There was really no excuse for the way he took her on that bed.

It was savage and desperate. Wells wasn't exactly a stranger to hard, fast sex . . .

But this was not just that.

Every physical sensation had an emotional trigger point. He felt every thrust into her body like it was happening all over. In his chest, behind his trachea, deep in some unknown part of his gut. He couldn't get close enough to Josephine, couldn't keep his mouth off her delicious skin, trying to afford her as much pleasure as she was giving him, as if that were possible. He licked her neck, bit into the slopes of her shoulders, bruised her mouth with kisses, all while rocking into her body with a ferociousness he would have been ashamed of if she didn't have her nails dug into his ass, screaming at him to go faster.

He framed her jaw firmly in his hand, tilting her face up. "All right, baby. Just keep your legs open and I'll give you whatever you want."

They fucked like Armageddon was right around the corner.

And they looked right into each other's eyes while it happened.

Wells was on the verge of coming the entire time, because sweet hell, what she'd done to him in the shower would live forever in his spank bank, but he refused to let himself finish because then it would be over. And he never, ever wanted his time inside Josephine to be over. This full-body event that was shaking him, inside and out.

But then she started arching her back and making hiccupping sounds, her hands flying from his ass to the bedspread, twisting it in twin grips. He felt her pussy start to pulse with more insistence and there was no way he could hold off any longer.

Christ. He was done for.

She was the most beautiful goddamn thing he'd ever seen and *so fucking tight*, he was plagued with the urgency to fill her up. Mentally pleading with his balls to wait just a little longer, Wells reached down and used his middle and ring finger to play with her clit, shouting a curse when he felt exactly how soaked she'd gotten while he fucked her so unbelievably hard. She moaned at his touch, hands twisting and back arching, showing her bouncing tits off to him like a fucking meal—and thank God she hit her peak at that moment, because he went off like a bomb.

"*Fuuuuuuck,*" he dragged out, rubbing her clit as long as possible before he had to find his own anchor, planting a fist on the bed so he could get those final, deep strokes that were made a million times more incredible by her clenching flesh, her husky cries of his name. "Fuck taking breaks from each other, Jose-phine," he rasped in her ear, raking his mouth over it from side to side. "You feel how done I am with breaks from you, baby?"

"Yes."

He gave her one last, rough drive, making her gasp, the final dregs of hunger and pressure and misery leaving his body. "Say you're done, too," he demanded.

"I'm done. I'm done!"

"Damn right you are," he growled, licking the sweat from her throat like a certified wild animal freed from its cage for the first time. Wells collapsed onto Josephine, perspiration and water cooling on their skin for long, heavy minutes, before he tucked her into his side, wrapped them in the comforter, and finally, finally, got to hold his caddie in a bed.

They were asleep in seconds.

CHAPTER TWENTY-SEVEN

Josephine opened her eyes and stared at the outstretched man hand resting on her pillow. Perhaps it was her vigorously satisfied libido talking, but my goodness, that was the most beautiful hand she'd ever laid eyes on. Had it been sculpted by Bernini? Blunt fingernails and calluses and color from the sun. It was attached to the firm biceps beneath her cheek and she had the urge to sit up and study the rest of him, but that would require moving and that wasn't happening. Not yet.

The steady in and out of Wells's breath sifted through her hair and warmed the nape of her neck, every inch of his contoured chest rising and falling against her back. Their legs were tangled together, her bare butt tucked into his lap—and while the rest of Wells was asleep, there was a certain part of him that was wide awake.

Josephine was torn between the urge to rub her backside against him, to tempt him into a replay of what they'd done last night— and never moving again. Ever. Why wouldn't she lie there in the hazy dawn light as long as possible with someone she'd fallen for? If missing him horribly for a week hadn't been enough to convince her that Wells had wiggled his way under her skin, yesterday would have done it.

You have no idea what it's like to miss you, baby.

This human being had kicked down her door, both literally and metaphorically.

She'd never seen him coming. Not like this. Perhaps because she'd known him first as a celebrity, not a real person, the way she did now. How could she have known he would balance her like he'd been born for the job? Respect, challenge, arouse, and protect her, all at once. Make her feel passionate enough to fight and laugh in the same breath.

What was she going to do about him?

The screen of Josephine's phone lit up on the nightstand. Probably an alert from her glucose monitor, but she reached out anyway, careful not to move from her position against a sleeping Wells. Her breath caught when she looked at the screen, however, because it was not her monitor going off, it was an alert from her checking account.

The sponsorship money from Under Armour had landed.

The high five-figure amount was substantial, but not quite enough to cover the dream renovation. She'd reluctantly spoken with her parents about fronting the rest of the cost until their disaster relief funds came in—or Wells won big, and she received her cut. Whichever came first. Which meant that she could give the contractor the green light to make all of the improvements to the Golden Tee, effective immediately. He'd given her a two-week timeline and then the shop would be ready to stock with inventory. Shortly after that, it would be up and running again. But where would that leave her and Wells? Would she just . . . pass off her responsibilities to another caddie and go back to watching him on television?

They'd entered into this arrangement knowing it was temporary, but that was before . . . well, *before*. The former number one golfer in the world was asleep in her bed and he'd made it very clear he didn't want to take any more breaks. If Josephine was being honest with herself, she didn't relish the idea of spending long periods away from Wells, either. But her lifeblood, her family legacy, her heart, was here in Palm Beach and she couldn't ignore the Golden Tee forever. Furthermore, she didn't want to.

Worrying her bottom lip with her teeth, Josephine made the painful decision to disentangle herself from Wells and slide out of bed, releasing a breath when he grumbled in his throat. But he just rolled over in a bare-chested sprawl and went back to snoring quietly, his morning wood very prominently tenting the sheet.

The fluttering sensation in her rib cage was so intense, she had to turn away from the big, gorgeous sight of him and his sleep-mussed hair or she would never do what needed to be done. After putting on her robe and closing the bedroom door without a sound, Josephine made a cup of coffee, fortified herself with a few sips, and called the contractor.

Ignoring the dread in her belly, she gave him the thumbs-up to begin the work, effectively starting the countdown clock on her time caddying for Wells.

What other choice did she have? They had to pay rent to the club. A course needed a shop. Sure, they understood that the Golden Tee needed to rebuild after the hurricane, but they would eventually begin expecting monthly payments. Life moved on and it moved fast.

The coffee cup was halfway to Josephine's lips when a very familiar sound greeted her ears—the back and forth of her parents' bickering. And that sound was moving down the hallway toward her apartment door.

Dread pulsed in her stomach for an entirely different reason now.

She'd forgotten about brunch. They were there to pick her up for an early birthday celebration, because she was going to be in California on Wednesday, when she *officially* turned twenty-seven. They were not going to find their daughter ready for fancy eggs and mimosas; however, they were going to find her looking like she'd tossed a man's salad in the shower, before getting manhandled in a way that had probably taken the bounce out of several mattress springs. Which was all gloriously true.

She'd had stupefyingly good sex with a man who was still in her bed. Fully naked. And her apartment wasn't large by any stretch of the imagination, so the muffled snores of her boss/lover could be heard clear to the kitchen if one listened hard enough. Not ideal. This was incredibly not ideal.

I got this.

I can handle this.

If I can handle Wells's temper on the golf course, two retirees should be a piece of cake.

Wishful thinking, but okay.

They were knocking now. This was happening.

Josephine tightened the belt of her robe and gathered her hair into a knot, securing it with a stray hairband from her junk drawer. She took a deep breath, wished herself luck, and opened the door—

It promptly sagged on its hinges, thudding loudly on the floor. *Damn.*

She smiled brightly. "Good morning!"

"Josephine!" her mother sputtered. "What happened to the door?"

"Well." *Think. Think!* "Yesterday, while I was out. At the store buying goods." *Goods? Have you been transported back to colonial times?* "Someone in the building called in the smell of gas. So the fire department showed up and since I wasn't home, they had to barge in. It was a whole thing."

"The landlord doesn't have your key?" asked Jim.

"He was *also* at the store. Yup. I saw him there. Buying . . . goods."

This was why Josephine never lied. She was as translucent as a window. Both of her parents were staring at her as if homemade pasta noodles were oozing from her ears.

"Anyway, come in, come in." She ushered them through the doorway, corralling them in the direction of the small living room, snatching up the remote, and turning the volume on the television way up to drown out the snoring. "I'm sorry. I slept late, but I'll just throw on some clothes and we'll go. Give me five minutes."

Her father looked at his watch while reluctantly parking himself on the couch, along with his wife. "But the reservation is for ten o'clock."

Josephine groaned inwardly. Who had brunch at *ten* A.M.? "They'll give us a grace period. Also, no one is going to be there this early."

Jim did a double take. "Early? I've been up since five!"

"I'm going to get dressed. I'll get ready as fast as I can."

Josephine spun out of the living area, intending to wake up Wells and quickly explain the awkward situation while putting on some clothes—

Wells walked out of the hallway in a pair of white boxer briefs.

Never mind the incredible things they did for his godlike thighs—and almost definitely, his rear, though she didn't have the right angle, sadly—he was out in the open now. In full view of the living room. But at a glance, Josephine could see that Wells was still half asleep, a big dopey-smiled lion on the prowl . . . and quite unaware that her parents were sitting on her couch in the living room.

Otherwise, he wouldn't have scooped her up by the butt and planted a kiss on her mouth that was intimate and full of sensual promise. And tongue. Also known as the kind of kiss a girl never, ever wanted her parents to witness.

"Wells—" she gasped, pulling away. Attempting to set her feet back on the ground.

"The robe has got to go." He nipped at her neck. "I'm taking you back to bed, belle."

She grabbed the sides of his face and turned his head toward the living room.

"Oh." He put Josephine down but kept her close. As in, plastered up against his front. For obvious reasons, namely his erection—rather than saluting the whole room with it. "Fuck."

"Yup."

Her parents gaped at them to the soundtrack of the *Today* show.

"Jim and Evelyn. It's nice to finally meet you in person." Wells sounded surprisingly calm for someone trying to hide morning wood. "I'll just . . ."

"*We'll* just . . ."

Josephine and Wells started an awkward backward shuffle toward her bedroom. Why Josephine felt it necessary to throw in a polite wave, she'd never know. "This is sort of like . . . a team-building exercise," she called over her shoulder. "Like a trust fall, but we're moving as one entity. In the interest of golfer-caddie bonding—"

"You're fooling no one," Wells interrupted.

"I can't *believe* this is happening," she whispered furiously. "And seriously? It hasn't softened *at all* yet?"

He winked at her. "That's right, baby."

Josephine gave him a disappointed look. Or she tried to, anyway. A smile threatened to ruin the reproof. They were in the hallway now—and out of sight—so they ceased their shuffling and entered the half-dark bedroom together with twin lunges, closing the door.

"Which part can't you believe is happening?" Wells wanted to know. "Just out of curiosity."

"My parents aren't supposed to be aware I have sex!"

He raised an eyebrow. "That's . . . fucking ridiculous, Josephine."

She waved her hands. "I mean, they probably know on some level, but I'm not supposed to just . . . rip off their blinders like that."

Wells framed her jaw in his hand, tilting her face up. "Just to be clear, you're upset that they caught you with a male houseguest. Period. Not that it's . . . me?"

"What do you mean?"

"I mean . . ." He exhaled sharply. "We didn't really have a chance to talk about this last night, since we were otherwise occupied. But my assumption is that you want to keep our relationship quiet." Was it her imagination or did he look slightly worried. Exposed. "Does that mean from your parents, too?"

She was still stuck on the word he'd used previously. "Relationship?"

It took a full two seconds for his right eyebrow to reach its highest peak. "Was it not clear that we're in a relationship?"

"I-I mean . . . not abundantly."

His jawline ticked. "I don't *miss* people to the point of torment, Josephine. And I don't spend the night with women, waking up every couple of hours to convince myself they're not a dream. I do both of those things with you like it's my *job*. And a lot of other annoying things I'm not willing to admit yet, but they involve planning trips to Bath and Body Works and wondering if *Wellsophine* is a viable ship name." He slapped a hand down on the door above her head and leaned down until their noses were almost touching. "I was very happy being alone until you showed up. You've ruined me."

Her heart galloped in her chest. "I'm sorry."

"I'm not. I love being ruined by you. Bring it the fuck on." He kissed Josephine hard, slanting his mouth across hers and licking deep, his fingers sliding up into her hair and fisting. "We can be a secret for now. I understand your reasons. But don't ask me if we're in a relationship when I can barely think straight around you."

"We're in a relationship," she whispered against his mouth. "Of course we are."

He let out an uneven exhale into her hair. "Good girl. Now if you don't mind, I'd like to go spend some quality fucking time with my girlfriend's parents. Sound good?"

Swallowing proved impossible.

Oh God. She'd already admitted to herself that she'd fallen for this man, but her feelings were veering closer and closer toward love.

Let yourself fall. Just let go and take the dive.

That's what Josephine's heart compelled her to do. So what was holding her back from plunging down without a harness into the wind? Nothing.

Except the not-so-distant future when she'd have to put Wells's interests aside and focus on her own.

She trusted this man. More than she trusted anyone besides her parents and Tallulah. But she wasn't sure she trusted him to *let* her go so easily.

For now, though, *she* would let go, just a little more, and see where the wind blew her.

What choice did she have when Wells was looking at her like his next breath hinged on her answer? "Quality time sounds amazing."

CHAPTER TWENTY-EIGHT

Mimosas were not Wells's drink of choice.

The flute felt breakable in his grip. Champagne was for women.

But hell if he didn't knock back three of those suckers without noticing.

He was too wrapped up in the stories Evelyn and Jim were telling about Josephine to pay attention to anything else. The best part was Josephine blushing and begging them to stop. Goddamn, he wanted to hear it all again, but with her sitting in his lap next time so he could tickle her, kiss those pinkening cheeks and neck.

He really needed to get a grip on his hunger for his girlfriend. At least around her parents.

Girlfriend.

Had he bullied her into it? He'd been worried about that initially—and then he remembered that his Josephine didn't get bullied into anything. If she'd agreed to be in a relationship with Wells, that's because she wanted to be in one with him. End of story.

Although . . . maybe later, he'd just double- and triple-check.

God willing, it wouldn't be on the DL forever. He didn't know how long he could manage keeping the whole thing to himself. Even before they started dating, he'd been pretty obvious about his growing feelings. Warning Calhoun away from her like a possessive beast. Escorting her all over a family-friendly resort as if she might fall victim to an ambush.

And she didn't even *know* about her birthday present yet.

Would he be able to keep things professional in public? At all times?

Professionalism wasn't exactly his strong suit. Throw in the fact that he was officially dating a woman who made him feel purposeful and alive—not to mention hornier than he'd ever been in his twenty-nine years—and the ball of yarn could unravel fast. Even now, at brunch with her jovial but watchful parents, he was having a hard time stopping himself from yanking Josephine's chair closer so he could hold her hand.

They weren't keeping their relationship a secret from Jim and Evelyn, but Josephine wanted to let things settle after they'd walked in on him trying to drag her back to the bedroom for round two of sex.

That's fine. That's her right.

He didn't have to like it, though.

"Why are you frowning at me?" Josephine whispered to him out of the corner of her mouth.

"I'm just concentrating on the story," he rumbled back.

That wasn't a complete lie. Resolving to hold the shit out of her hand later, when they were alone, he crossed his arms, leaned back in his chair, and listened to Evelyn and Jim's story, amused by the way they traded sentences.

"Every single one of Joey's teeth has been lost in some traumatic way," Jim said, waving his hands around. "The first one came out the second day of kindergarten."

"The children left school that day traumatized."

"Like they'd just returned from war. Blood on their little shirts—"

"Older and wiser. They'd *seen* a thing or two."

"And the second one came out during a soccer game. A ball

hit her right in the mouth. We asked if she could be brave and walk off the field and she dramatically asked for a stretcher."

Wells laughed. A real, loud laugh that made Josephine look at him funny. "She's gotten a lot braver since then, I guess. Run her over with a golf cart now and she doesn't even flinch."

"Oh, come on, I more than flinched. I *howled*."

"Not long enough to stop yelling at me," Wells pointed out.

Josephine smiled. "Yelling at you always takes priority."

Christ. I want to kiss her and never come up for air.

"We just about died, seeing that happen on live television," Evelyn said, fanning herself with a limp cloth napkin, which couldn't possibly be producing enough wind to be worthwhile.

"That's when your whole turnaround started," Jim said, tilting his head curiously. "You birdied damn near every hole after the accident. Why is that?"

"It's a boring story," Josephine said quickly.

"No, it's not," Wells disagreed, unable to keep his expression from turning cocky. "She had my name painted on her toenails. I caught her blue-toed."

Josephine slapped her hands over her face.

"How delightful!" Evelyn split a glance between them. "But I still don't understand why that would spur you into such a comeback."

Now everyone was looking at him, waiting for an explanation.

Did he have one? That he could put into words?

"Well, uh . . ." He scrubbed at the back of his neck. "I don't know. I guess I grew up needing just one person on my side, you know? Just one. I finally had that for a while—someone on my side—but that experience only taught me that people come and go. Not Josephine, though. And I guess her toes reminded me that . . ." He blew out a breath. "Having Josephine on my side is more like having a whole army. And I wanted to fight, too."

Somewhere, ten miles away, a pin could be heard dropping.

Jim reached for his drink and took a long, healthy gulp.

Josephine stared at Wells with an unreadable expression.

Evelyn dabbed at her eyes with the cloth napkin. "Isn't that lovely?" She whooshed a breath up toward the ceiling and refocused on Wells with glassy eyes. "You said you didn't have anyone on your side growing up. Where were your parents?"

"Mom . . . ," Josephine murmured.

"No, it's okay." Wells reached over and squeezed her knee under the table, his chest expanding to twice its size when she wove their fingers together. "When I was twelve, my parents got jobs on a cruise ship. I'd been a lot of trouble, getting kicked out of school, refusing to come home when I was told, fighting. They just needed a break, you know?" He tried to smile, but it never quite formed. "Anyway, after that, they were always traveling. The times they were home, they needed to blow off steam, I guess. They partied a lot. I started staying with my uncle . . . and one afternoon, my parents docked after a trip to Mexico and . . . I just didn't go home. No one really addressed it. I just stopped going home."

A wave of embarrassment caught Wells off guard. Why was he ruining this brunch—his girlfriend's *birthday* brunch—by telling *this* sob story? The Doyles had never missed a milestone in Josephine's life. Probably never forgot to pack her a school lunch even once. His backstory probably sounded pathetic to them. So he tried to make light of it to alleviate the heavy mood he'd caused.

"I mean, if anyone understands blowing off steam, it's me. I'm sure you've seen the evidence of that on the news," he joked, no longer sure he should be holding Josephine's hand after reminding them he'd been in jail. Not exactly boyfriend material for their incredible daughter. But when he tried to take his hand back, she held on.

"Look what they're missing out on," she said for his ears alone, brushing a thumb across his knuckles. "Look what so many people have missed out on."

Someone started singing.

Several someones.

Wells was so busy looking into Josephine's eyes that it took him a moment to realize their table was surrounded by singing waiters and waitresses. They'd set a cupcake down in front of Josephine, a candle stuck in the center.

"That's the sugar-free one?" Evelyn mouthed to one of the waitresses, not so discreetly.

Josephine gave Wells a playful eye roll, before continuing to watch him steadily.

When the birthday song had nearly reached its end, she leaned over and settled her mouth against his ear. "Have you ever had a birthday party, Wells?"

What was happening inside his chest?

Pressure built more and more, crushing his windpipe.

He gave a stilted shake of his head.

She didn't let any pity show and she'd never know how grateful he was for that. "Blow the candles out with me?"

Wells barked a humorless laugh. "I don't need to do that, belle."

"I know." She gathered her hair in a hand, tilting her chin toward the flame. Inviting him to join. "I want you to."

That sealed it. Josephine wanted something—Josephine got it. Period.

With a sigh, Wells angled himself in his seat and leaned in toward the cupcake. Without counting down, they blew at the exact same time, extinguishing the flame. Somewhere deep inside him, a pothole paved itself over. Maybe the road was never going to be perfect, but it was getting better. Good enough to drive on.

"Your swing has been looking a damn sight better, son," Jim was saying.

Wells had to run that statement back several times to process it, because he was so lost looking at the man's daughter. Could anyone blame him? How did she always know the right thing to say? To do? Was she *actually* an angel?

"Thanks," Wells said slowly, narrowing his eyes to examine his girlfriend for evidence.

"Joey, how is your swing? You been keeping in stroke?"

Now *that* got Wells's attention.

He nearly got whiplash looking at Jim so fast. Then back to his girlfriend.

"Jesus Christ, Josephine," Wells started, hot irritation licking at his skin—but only irritation at himself. "I've never seen you hit a golf ball."

Jim's spoon clattered onto his coffee saucer.

A horrified and much deserved silence passed over the table.

"Never?"

"No," Wells said miserably. How was that even possible?

Josephine was laughing at him. "Calm down. We'll get to it."

"No, I don't think you understand, this needs to happen *to-day.*"

"Rolling Greens still hasn't opened its doors after the hurricane. And we don't even have a tee time anywhere else," his girlfriend sputtered. "Halfway through a day this beautiful? There aren't going to be any spots left."

Wells gave her a look that said *oh come on*. "My name has *some* pull, Josephine."

"So does yours, by now, Joey-Roo."

Joey-Roo, mouthed Wells with a smug wink.

Josephine kicked him under the table while taking a giant bite of her cupcake.

I'm going to marry this woman.

Done fucking deal. Someone direct him to the nearest ring shop.

"Call Lone Pine and see if they can slide you in, Joey. While you wait for your tee time to roll around, you can show Wells the progress on the Golden Tee." Jim clasped his hands, wringing them eagerly. "You won't believe how far the shop has come in just a week. Joey cleaned it up real nice, got it all set for construction to begin." He turned his broad smile on his daughter. "Did you talk to the contractor yet, honey?"

She stopped chewing. Swallowed thickly. "Yes."

"When?" Evelyn asked.

Wells watched her closely when she didn't answer right away. "This morning, actually," she finally said, sending a jolt of surprise to his gut. "I gave him the all-clear to begin working."

Jim could barely sit still in his seat. "Putting green, drive-through window, and everything?"

Josephine nodded. "That's right. We even discussed the idea of a consultation lounge where guests can look at drone footage of the holes and get advice on their strategy. I told him . . . to go for it." Her laughter was light. "All the bells and whistles."

The more Wells heard about the project, the more he started to relax. This kind of effort would take months, at least. He wouldn't have to give up having Josephine as his caddie any time soon. Right? "What is the timeline?" he asked.

When she took a sip of water instead of answering him right away, his palms started to turn clammy. "Two to three weeks," she said, searching his eyes. "The hurricane created such a need for rebuilding that they doubled the size of their crew. That should get us through the Masters, at the very least."

He couldn't be expected to speak when his throat was completely dry. "Yeah," he managed. *Two to three weeks?* "The Masters."

Something extremely worrisome was occurring to Wells.

A doubt that had been loitering in the back of his mind but with this revelation was making its way to the forefront, where it could no longer be ignored.

Could he even compete *without* Josephine?

When she left, who was going to talk him down off the ledge when he wanted to give up? Who was going to drop wisdom on him at the exact moment he needed it, in the perfect dose? No one, that's who. There was no one else who had Josephine's magic.

No one in the world.

When she left, where would that leave him? Sinking back down the leaderboard?

Would she want to maintain a relationship with someone who spent four out of every seven days on the road? Maybe she'd meet someone local. Another golfer, probably, since she worked at a pro shop. And *this* guy would be *nice*!

Dear God, he needed a distraction. Anything to keep him from begging this woman to stay with him on the tour, like a selfish prick, instead of realizing her own dreams. Thankfully, the waitress chose that moment to drop the bill in the center of the table and sail away.

Wells stood, ripping his wallet out of his back pocket, credit cards spilling out. "Let's go see that golf swing, belle. The fact that I haven't yet is bullshit."

"Ooh!" Evelyn patted her hair. "Now that's some language."

"Sorry, ma'am," Wells muttered.

Josephine hooted a laugh.

"No, no! I'm paying!" Jim half shouted.

"Yes. We insist!" Evelyn chimed in.

Wells and Jim lunged at the same time, proceeding to rip the check in half.

Evelyn buried her face in her napkin. "Lord have mercy on us all!"

"You can pay next time," Jim blustered.

"I can pay *every* time!"

"Oh, like hell you will!"

Josephine burst into a laughing fit, falling back in her chair. With sparkling eyes, she looked over at him. "Are you sure you want a next time?"

"Yes, belle," Wells growled, finally giving in to the unrelenting impulse to grab the leg of her chair and pull Josephine as close as possible, planting a firm kiss in the center of her forehead. "I want all of your next times."

And he was dangerously close to asking her to remain his caddie indefinitely.

As in, forever. Through the Masters and beyond.

Apparently he was more selfish than he realized.

"Don't think about the timeline," she whispered.

"Impossible. But I'm going to try like hell for you." *Don't kiss her mouth in front of her parents. You'll never be able to stop.* "Happy birthday."

"Thank you." She brought her lips to his ears and whispered, "Happy birth*days*, Wells."

And there was nothing else to grab onto. Nothing to anchor his feet or keep him from slipping down the embankment into love. Total and complete worship of Josephine Doyle. He landed hard and didn't even bother trying to get up.

Considering she'd just delivered her two weeks' notice, it was a dangerous place to be.

CHAPTER TWENTY-NINE

Josephine stood at the edge of the Golden Tee, watching Wells saunter through the space, hands in his pockets. He was not a hands-in-the-pockets type of guy. They were usually planted on his hips or his arms were crossed over his chest. She knew this man. Knew he was torn between being happy for her and apprehensive about the expiration date on their arrangement. And yeah, she was nervous, too.

Because when the shop was ready and the time came to return to real life, back in Palm Beach, Josephine wasn't sure she'd be able to leave him.

For the first time, she pondered the wild possibility of giving up the shop. Staying on as Wells's caddie until . . . when? Until he retired? He was only twenty-nine. Retirement might not come for well over a decade. And what if they broke up . . . personally *and* professionally . . . and Josephine no longer had the shop to return to? That was a lot of *what-ifs*.

And could she even physically leave the Golden Tee behind? Despite the flood, her family's history was still very much alive within these walls. Walking away would be like removing vital organs from inside her body and pretending everything was normal for the rest of her life. She would miss the place, of course, but mainly, she would miss the *meaning* of it.

Hard work, ingenuity, pride, tradition. Family.

At the same time, Josephine was growing increasingly worried that leaving Wells could prove just as difficult. Add two or three more weeks to the equation and . . . how hard would it be then?

Wells pulled Josephine from her dark thoughts by asking, "Where is the consultation lounge going to go?"

She pointed toward the back of the shop. "There. I'm thinking of two leather wingbacks, a big architect board with maps and yardage. I want it to feel like the captain's quarters of a ship. But . . . technologically modern."

He nodded for a long time, as though envisioning what she'd described. "It's going to be incredible, Josephine."

"Thanks."

"Where is the giant cardboard cutout of Wells Whitaker going to go?"

"In the bathroom," she said, without missing a beat.

He barked a laugh, then fell silent again.

Time to face the elephant in the room. Head-on. That's how they operated, wasn't it? "Why don't you just tell me what you're thinking, Wells?"

"Okay." He speared five fingers through his hair, before stuffing them back in his pocket. "I'm thinking . . . we just decided to be together this morning and already the situation is on the verge of changing." His eyes closed briefly. "I don't want anything to fuck with this, Josephine."

"Then we won't let anything fuck with it," she said, trying to keep her voice even.

Wells's chest rose and fell. "Yeah, except . . . you've met me, right? The self-destructive asshole who holds the record for breaking the most golf clubs on the tour? I've won more bar fights than tournaments." He shook his head. "I'm worried I'll backslide without you and . . . I'll stop being this guy who is worthy of you, you know? I'm on thin goddamn ice, as it is. I've finished in the money *once* in the last couple of years, belle. That's nothing."

"You're wrong. It's something."

"Yeah? I don't know." He swept the room with a glance. "What I do know is that this place feels like Josephine. It has your energy and spirit. Your love for golf. I can't deprive anyone of that, even if I'm inclined to keep you all to myself." A rigid line moved in his jaw. "We're going to spend the next few weeks kicking preppy ass on the tour, belle, because I want this place to be exactly what you want. I *need* that for you."

I'm in love.

I'm in love with Wells.

Oh . . . boy.

His ability to adapt and grow, his thoughtfulness, the way he cared about her without making her feel cared *for*. Now, his self-lessness had rolled through and knocked her down like a set of bowling pins.

Strike.

"Are you with me, Josephine?"

"Yes," she murmured. Then louder, "Yes, of course I am. Those preppies are toast."

And so am I.

"Glad we're on the same page," he said quietly, studying her beneath drawn brows.

Were they? On the same page?

There were still so many unknowns, but when he ran his tongue along the inside of his bottom lip and came toward Josephine, all those loose ends stopped flying wildly in the air and just kind of vanished.

For now.

"How long until we tee off at Lone Pine?" he asked, wrapping a gentle hand around her throat.

"Menty finutes." She winced. "I mean, twenty minutes."

One corner of his mouth jumped. "Flustered, baby?"

That was one way to describe the slow, delicious wind below her belly button, the need for friction making her nipples stand up straight. "Yes."

His hand left her throat, sliding down to knead her right breast. "Why?"

Pops of light went off in her vision, a moan building deep, deep in her belly. "I like when you talk to me. When you're honest with me."

"Oh yeah?" His lips dragged side to side across Josephine's. "I'm sorry you're the only person in the world I like talking to, Josephine. That must be a lot of pressure."

"I can handle pressure."

"Good. I'm going to give you a lot of it next time your panties are off."

A moan sung from her throat and he swallowed it with a hard kiss, his fingers pinching her nipples lightly through her shirt, drawing wetness between her thighs.

"There is no way I'm making it through eighteen holes of golf," he said hoarsely, his tongue flicking into her mouth, before suctioning her into a hard kiss, making her whimper.

"I signed us up for nine," she gasped.

He jerked Josephine up onto her toes, attacking her mouth from above. "Still too much."

"Two?"

"One, Josephine," he groaned. "I'm already hard just thinking about you teeing off."

"Wells Whitaker," she chided. "This is known as the *gentleman's* sport."

"Fuck being a gentleman." He walked her backward toward a wall, bent his knees, and slowly worked himself up between her thighs in a grind that made them both cry out. "I've been daydreaming about licking your beautiful pussy since this morning."

Everything inside her squeezed. "Let's cancel our round."

Wells pumped his hips and she screamed behind her teeth. "Should we?"

"Yes!"

"Nah," he drawled, tracing the curve of her neck with his open mouth. "First two times with you, I was too keyed up for foreplay. Not today." He sank his teeth into the slope of her shoulder. "Going to find out exactly how wet I can make my girlfriend." Turned on to the point of frustration, she tried to wrap her legs around his hips, but he blocked them, shaking his head. "Not yet, belle."

A protesting sound snuck out. "You really think I could hit a golf ball properly right now?"

He pretended to think about her question. "If you *could* visualize it, what would it look like, Josephine?"

She gasped in mock outrage. "How dare you turn my genius lesson back around on me?"

Without warning, a grinning Wells stepped back and tossed Josephine over his shoulder. He carried her out of the pro shop, smacking her butt soundly as they emerged and turned for the parking lot. "Maybe I've got a few lessons of my own up my sleeve."

CHAPTER THIRTY

When Wells and Josephine walked into the clubhouse at Lone Pine, jaws hit the floor.

Josephine didn't have access to her sticks and Wells had left his own in Miami, so they were forced to rent—but the chance to watch Josephine smack a few balls was well worth the extra effort. It wasn't lost on him that she'd stopped holding his hand in the parking lot—and he understood. As they walked through the lobby of the country club, past the bar and downstairs into the pro shop, every eye in the place was trained on them. Some people cheered, others wished them luck at Torrey Pines, but there was no way to miss the knowing expressions.

Wells wanted to wrap an arm around Josephine, draw her into his side, and shield her from those speculative looks, but he'd only make it worse, so he ground his molars and kept walking. He assumed that once they made it to the pro shop to pick up their equipment, the awkward moments would be over, but the worst was yet to come.

A young man wearing a name tag that read "Ren" slapped the counter and rocked back on his heels. "Wow. I thought you were pranking me over the phone." He knocked over a tiny brochure stand with his elbow. "You're really them. Wells and Fangirl."

Josephine's smile turned queasy. "Um. Hey."

As the greeting registered, irritation fired up into Wells's throat like a torpedo. He had not been keeping up on golf news.

He never did, because the endless speculation from the commentators could get into the head of the most seasoned professional. Somewhere along the line, had they started referring to Josephine as *Fangirl*?

"I'm sorry, what was that?" Wells said, planting a fist on the counter. "That's not her name, kid. Might want to try again."

"Josephine," he blurted, blotches forming on his cheeks. "I'm sorry, ma'am. That's just what they're calling you on golf X, formerly known as golf Twitter. I meant Josephine. Josephine Doyle."

She looked a little startled that the young man knew her actual name. "Oh! It's fine."

"It's *not* fine," Wells argued.

"It's just that . . . well, I finally got my girlfriend to watch golf with me, because of you two teaming up. She thinks it's so romantic." He rolled his eyes and blushed a little more. "She doesn't love the fact that you make Fangirl—sorry! *Josephine* carry your bag—"

Wells threw up his hands. "She's a caddie."

"It's my job." Josephine bit her lip. "Tell her it's not as heavy as it looks."

Ren scoffed. "Begging your pardon, ma'am, I work at a pro shop. They're heavy as shit."

"Is there anyone else here who could help us?" Wells asked through his teeth.

"Nope," Ren answered cheerfully, beginning to punch some buttons on the register. "You're the last tee time of the day. I'm heading out as soon as your round starts."

Wells bared his teeth in a mockery of a smile. "So sorry to see you go."

The kid nodded, obviously not picking up on Wells's sarcasm. "Do you want a cart? Or are you planning on making Josephine carry your bag around today, too?"

Josephine burst into laughter.

"We'll take a cart," Wells snapped.

Ren beamed. "Chivalry isn't dead, after all."

A few minutes later, as they were loading the clubs onto the back of the cart, Josephine elbowed him in the side. "You didn't take any of that personally, did you?"

He glared at her.

"The fact that you didn't question whether I was capable of carrying your bag is one of the reasons I . . ." Seeming to catch herself, she closed her mouth quickly. "It's one of the reasons I started to like you again," she finished, eventually.

"I hate the reminder that you stopped liking me," Wells grumbled.

"It was a very small window," she said, her fingertips tracing the back of his hand.

Kissing her mouth felt inevitable, but then she glanced over his shoulder, pulling back quickly at whatever she saw. "We have an audience."

Wells turned and squinted toward the clubhouse, unsurprised to see a group of people holding up their phones, filming. "That kid calling you Fangirl, Josephine . . . you were right," he said, suppressing the urge to rub at the hollow discomfort in his chest. "The way people minimize how important you are to me professionally. They would rather speculate on whether we're sleeping together than acknowledge how fucking good you are at your job." He stomped to the driver's side of the cart. "No one came up with a cute nickname for my last caddie. Or wondered if I was sharing a bed with him at night."

Josephine climbed into the passenger side, watching him closely. "This is really starting to bother you."

"Yes. Not only because it isn't fair, but . . ." He pinched the bridge of his nose, pressing down hard out of frustration. "None of their behavior stops me from wanting everyone in the world to know you're mine, belle. I'll never be able to turn that off. Does that make me a barbarian?"

Her look was one of pure understanding. Patience. Because she was an angel. Because she understood he was part caveman and didn't judge him for it. "I just think it means you like me, too," she said cheekily.

"Like you?" he echoed, witheringly.

They traded a look heavy with meaning. Wells more than liked Josephine and she damn well knew it. The vulnerability of her expression made him wonder—hope—those much deeper feelings went both ways.

Please God, let her love me back.

But neither of them said the words out loud. It had to be too soon, right?

Wells put the cart in drive and covered the distance to the first hole, stopping to the right of the tee box. They worked in silence, removing their drivers from their bags, the quiet hush of the course a thing of beauty as the sun dipped low in the sky, taking down the temperature and dusting everything in gold. He'd forgotten about these special moments on the golf course, forgotten why he'd found solace here as a pissed-off, neglected teenager, but Josephine had reminded him, hadn't she?

She did so again now, swaggering toward the tee box and bending forward to wedge her tee into the grass. The wind funneled past, fluttering the hem of her skirt to reveal a peek of white panties, and Wells bit the inside of his cheek, trapping an appreciative sound. Normally he wouldn't feel the need to keep his vast appreciation of Josephine's ass to himself, but after the whole Fangirl situation—not to mention the smug looks from the country club bar—he wrestled the groan back down into his belly.

Later.

He'd appreciate her later.

In so many positions, she would lose count.

There was more fluttering fabric as Josephine settled the ball onto the tee and Wells was forced to adjust himself. God, was he just as bad as everyone else? His girlfriend couldn't even tee off without him wanting to put his hands up her skirt. In his defense, he hadn't been inside her since last night—and only twice in his lifetime. Far from enough when he felt *this fucking much* for her. One hole, maybe two, and they were breaking the speed limit to get home.

Every single thought in Wells's head scattered when Josephine hit the ball.

He dropped the club in his hand, the weight slipping straight from his fingers.

Her form was perfect.

An actual miracle.

He replayed the stroke in his head, searching for a single defect and coming up empty—and then all he could do was watch the ball go sailing, landing in the dead center of the fairway. Bounce, bounce, then rolling to a rest. "Josephine."

"Yes."

His tone was pure reverence. "You had to have hit that two hundred and fifty yards."

If he hadn't already fallen madly in love with her, the cocky little smile she gave him over her shoulder would have inked the deal. "Jealous?"

His brain cells were still hanging suspended in the air—and honestly, his dick was now at full mast, because hell, Josephine had a more fine-tuned stroke than him, by a fucking mile, and her talent was so unforgivably hot, he just wanted to get closer to it. On top of it. *Her.* Now.

Maybe that masterful drive knocked some sense into him, though, because his thoughts reorganized in a new way—and suddenly he was thinking very, very clearly.

They had a problem. Josephine needed to be seen as capable and valued. She wanted success through her own merit and she damn well deserved that respect. The media had incorrectly labeled her as someone at the mercy of his kindness. Being in a public relationship would only compound the issue and yet, he already knew that pretending she wasn't his girlfriend on tour was going to eat him alive. Hiding was beneath them.

Did he have a way to solve these problems in one fell swoop?

Maybe. Yeah.

He just might.

But he needed to take action before he told her anything.

Otherwise, she might try to stop him.

"Do you trust me, Josephine?"

Her red ponytail whipped around. A second later she nodded. "Yes."

Gratitude spread through his limbs. "I won't let you regret that."

She shook her head. "What's going on with you?"

Being in love with you has altered my brain chemistry. Suddenly he could come up with solutions that would have eluded him before there were stakes involved. *High* stakes. Apparently when a man needed a woman the way he needed Josephine, he became a human think tank whose sole mission was to come up with numerous ways to keep her.

Wells ached to tell her his plan now, but he needed to *show* her he meant business. He wanted to give her proof he not only loved her but also understood her, so she wouldn't have any doubts about him when he said those three words.

Until then, though? He had another way to show her how he felt.

And it was about goddamn time they got down to it.

Wells slowly approached Josephine where she stood at the cart, checking something in her scorebook. The closer he got to her, the more goose bumps appeared on the slope of her neck, highlighted by the sunshine. Her body shifted at his increasing nearness, teeth sinking into her bottom lip, her gaze flickering over at him from beneath her lashes.

Awareness. She was so fucking aware of him.

They'd been like this since the morning after the hurricane, hadn't they? Thank God he had the freedom to act on it now. Mostly. They were still in view of the clubhouse.

Wells ignored the stab of resentment and leaned in slightly, enjoying the way his proximity made her chest rise and fall faster. "I can tell you want to wrap those gorgeous thighs around me," he said hoarsely, in the air above her shoulder. "And baby, I need to get under that fucking skirt so bad. Tell me a private place to take you—and it better be close."

She pressed her lips together to trap a moan. "Now?"

"Now."

"Um . . . okay. *Think.*" She shook her head, as if to unscramble it. "We're the last tee time, so no one is coming behind us. M-maybe . . . oh, I think the third hole has a thunder shelter?"

Wells had never moved faster, circling around the front of the cart and throwing himself into the driver's seat, while Josephine got in the passenger side—and he *gunned* that motherfucker toward hole number three. Thunder shelters were in place on a lot of golf courses for players to take cover if the weather took an unexpected turn and they were left inconveniently holding a bunch of metal sticks. But that's not what they'd be using it for today. Jesus. He couldn't even make it *home* with this woman.

"I didn't realize my swing was so inspiring," she murmured, dazed.

"Now you know, belle." He took a hard right to avoid a pin. "You ever want to win an argument with me? Just tee off."

"I told you I was qualified to give lessons."

"Oh, you're giving me lessons, as soon as I can concentrate on anything but getting you off. I want a swing like Josephine Doyle's."

She swept him a breathless, sideways look. "You really mean that."

Wells frowned. "*Hell yeah*, I mean it," he roared—just as the thunder shelter came into view.

He pulled up behind the structure, the distance and position taking them well out of view of the clubhouse, and he hit the brakes, preparing to climb out, throw Josephine over his shoulder, and carry her inside, where he would fuck the stuffing out of her. But she surprised Wells by launching herself across the cart and climbing onto his lap, her mouth capturing his eagerly, whimpers popping in her throat. And God bless her, she straddled him in that cocktease skirt, her pussy warm and firm where it pressed down on his erection, rubbing, *rubbing*.

He had to break the kiss to let his head fall back, his hands naturally finding the tight globes of her butt cheeks and kneading her forward, urging her to hump him.

"Fuck yeah, baby. Good, good girl. Just like that." He gathered up the material of her panties in a twist, turning the undergarment into a thong and tugging it roughly between her cheeks. Again, again, again. Noticing she humped him faster the harder he pulled, gasping into the kiss. "You want to trade lessons, Josephine?"

She kept right on kissing him, but made an affirmative sound in her throat, riding his lap with more eagerness, more insistence.

"I'll take that as a yes." He massaged her right cheek, then brought his hand down on it in a sharp slap. "Still yes?"

Her green eyes were glassy as she tried to focus on him. "Yes."

They never looked away from each other while he spanked her opposite cheek, then back to the right one. *Smack.* "Here's your lesson. You wear a skirt, you're going to get that pussy eaten and eaten good." He cracked his palm down on her backside, slightly harder than before, and she shuddered, her breath escaping in a rush. "It's very simple, isn't it, Josephine?"

"Uh-huh."

Wells meant every word of that lesson, too. He was starved for her. Needed to get a taste of that warm, wet flesh, *now.*

His own relief came secondary to the pleasure he'd get giving it to her.

Incapable of waiting another moment, he slid out of the golf cart seat with Josephine still attached to him and placed her sideways, sitting up on the driver's seat, falling to his knees in front of her. Shoving open her smooth thighs. Biting her through the damp, white panties, all of her, as much as he could cover with his teeth, moaning at the little jolt in her inner thighs. The way her hand flew to the steering wheel to hold on, her belly hollowing in and out.

The same way he'd done with the material of her underwear in back, he did at the front now, twisting the cotton into a thong and tugging it experimentally in the valley of her sex, licking his lips at the sight of her pussy plumping with arousal, parting, moistening. All while her ass writhed helplessly on the seat.

"*Fuck*, that is sweet," he gritted out, yanking the panties to one side and diving forward, French kissing her ripe cunt with a starving tongue. "Spread your legs a little wider than the last time I fucked it—you're my girlfriend now."

"You have no shame," she gasped. But her knees fell open another inch, didn't they?

Gratified to the point of pain, Wells dragged his tongue

through her flesh and found her clit, giving her several long strokes, until her thighs started to shake. "You let me act like this, because you know I would—and I will—humble myself in front of the whole fucking world for you, Josephine." He flicked his tongue against her clit while pressing his middle finger slow and deep into her slick opening. "Isn't that right?"

Her fingers gripped the leather seat so hard, it creaked. "Yes," she sobbed.

"I'm on my knees licking it like it's made of gold." He added a second finger, drawing them in and out, twisting, marveling over the soft clench of her. He'd never seen anything more beautiful in his life than the moisture she was leaving on his knuckles. "My woman comes first and hard, so she doesn't mind when I order her legs to open wide, does she?"

"St-stop," she chattered, her body shaking head to toe. "It's going to be over so fast."

God, so hot. Her honesty. The tremble in her voice. All of her.

"You don't want it to be over, belle?"

"No," she hiccupped, sinking her fingers into his hair and tugging him closer, hips lifting to meet his firm licks. "It feels too good."

Wells started to unfasten his pants with a grappling left hand— and he had no choice—because she was fucking his mouth now, mewling his name. She tasted like honey, clearly on the verge of an orgasm, and he wanted his cock out when it happened. Wanted to be stroking it and pretending it was locked in her snug pussy.

Fucking unreal. She had him *panting* for it.

On the verge of coming after one stroke.

Desperate for that final Josephine squeeze.

He added a third finger, the resulting wet sound like a hymn in his ears, and bore down with a firm tongue, rubbing her slippery clit until her fingers were twisting in his hair, her gasps growing closer together and then her fever broke at once, the taste of her coating his tongue and fingers, her hips shaking on the leather seat.

"*Wells*," she cried out, her elbow inadvertently hitting the horn on the cart, her thighs wrapping tightly around his head to ride out that last wave—and then she was sliding forward and off the seat, catching Wells off guard and forcibly pushing him onto his back in the grass.

She moaned when she saw his dick was already out, hard as nails. Still trembling from her climax, she straddled him, hooking her middle finger around the edge of her soaked, stretched-out panties to keep them pulled to one side, then sank down onto the shaft he offered in his shaking hand. A symphony of obscenities flooded his brain when she took him whole, planting her palms on his shoulders and starting to buck her hips.

"That was so good," she said breathlessly. "Oh my God, that was *so good*."

He had to dig deep for the ability to speak, being inside of her was so off-the-charts incredible. The flesh that welcomed him deep, deep, deep, was swollen from pleasure. *Juicy.* And there was something about this woman being hot enough for his cock to wrestle him onto his back that made one thing clear. This was going to be the best nut of his life. "What's this?" he rasped. "A reward?"

"One hundred percent." She shoved his T-shirt to his throat and raked her tongue over his right nipple, before biting it. Hard. "I guess I don't have any shame, either."

Wells was overcome by lust so fucking thick, he had no control of his body as he jackknifed into a sitting position, breathing out of control, both hands on her taut butt cheeks, yanking her as tight to his lap as she would go, while he plundered her mouth with his tongue. There was no such thing as too close or too frantic, they'd gone past any semblance of holding back or playing it cool. They went at it like mating animals in the grass, her hips slapping against him, their lips battling for the deepest taste, fingertips bruising flesh, his heart elevated to his throat and getting stuck there. Completely stuck.

I'm so gone for this woman.

She's not just the one. She's . . . the rest of me.

"How was I surviving before, baby?" Wells flipped their positions, rolling her roughly onto her back and hitting a breakneck pace, her knees damn near in her armpits. "What was I doing without you?"

He was afraid of her answer, afraid that he'd exposed too much, so he fastened his mouth over Josephine's and let the intense blast of relief hit him like a steamroller. It hurt so good, he roared brokenly into their kiss, his hips slamming down those final few times, before stiffening, his balls almost stinging from the sudden loss of pressure. *Sweet mother of God.*

Like before, he literally had no control of his muscles or intentions as he dropped, totally depleted of anything resembling strength, yet somehow he was the most powerful man alive, because this woman, this gift from heaven, his partner, had perfect breaths that matched his own. And she wasn't going anywhere. *She's not going anywhere.*

For now, whispered a voice in the back of his head.

CHAPTER THIRTY-ONE

Josephine woke up to find her boyfriend pacing naked in the living room, arguing into his phone. He hadn't even bothered to close the blinds, thus the Florida sunshine was bathing his backside in a warm, almost ethereal glow that made Josephine hold up her own phone and snap a picture. For posterity—or poster*ior*'s sake. Both maybe?

When Wells noticed Josephine had entered the living room, he gave her a slow grin that made little fairies roll around in her belly, giggling and firing pixie dust from finger guns.

Oh my goodness.

This was love. Adoration, affection, connection. And definitely lust.

She'd never actually had to change her sheets in the middle of the night because they'd gotten too sweaty, but there was a first time for everything. Since she didn't have to temper the desire to have a million first times with Wells, she smiled back at him, letting the welling sensation in her chest reach her eyes. And Josephine must have done a good job portraying how indescribably perfect and right it felt to wake up with this man, because he stopped pacing and stared at her, his Adam's apple unmoving beneath his chin.

"I was going to need to change my flight to California, anyway," he said into the phone. "I want to be on the same flight as Josephine."

In the wake of that gruff pronouncement—and the increasing storm of pixie dust in her belly— Josephine could hear the faint voice of a man talking on the other end of the line.

"Hold on, I'm going to put you on speaker," Wells interrupted, tapping the screen of his phone. "You're on with me and Josephine."

"Nice to meet you, Josephine. I'm Nate. You need a manager stat, honey."

"No, she doesn't. And don't call her honey."

An electronic snicker filled the apartment. "Sorry. *Josephine.* I was just telling your boy here that both of you need to get to California a couple of days early. Under Armour wants to meet with their new power duo to play kissy face. They also want to make sure Mr. Whitaker is still on the straight and narrow before they outfit the team for another tournament. You've also got some press to do. A practice round. I don't know who this fucker thinks he is, rolling into town the night before a tournament starts."

"Worked for us last time," Wells barked.

"Yeah, well, people actually *want* to see your disgustingly handsome face now, don't ask me why. The commissioner wants you and Josephine doing press, my man. You're the big human-interest story heading into the Masters. It's only two weeks away, you know. People love a comeback."

Josephine pressed a hand to her stomach to calm it.

Two weeks to the Masters. With all the changes in her life recently, the most prestigious tournament on the tour schedule by a mile had really crept up fast. Was Wells ready for that four-day pressure cooker, the competition to earn the almighty green jacket?

Yes.

She'd do everything in her power to make sure he was.

"How soon do we need to be there?" Wells asked, still completely naked and 100 percent glorious. "Does tomorrow work?"

Nate sighed. "It's going to have to be tonight if you want the commissioner happy."

"Since when do I give a f—" Wells stopped short when Josephine widened her eyes at him. "Hold on." He smashed a finger to the screen while crossing the room toward Josephine. "Josephine, quit looking at my dick. I can't concentrate."

"It's looking at *me*!" she sputtered. "*And* my neighbors."

His smile belonged on a pirate outlaw. "Just saving us time. We've got another set of sheets to ruin. As soon as we're done with this call, I'm going to—"

"I'm not muted, you know," came Nate's voice over the line.

Josephine slapped both hands to her cheeks.

Wells, not even remotely embarrassed, peered down at his phone and hit the correct button before refocusing his attention on Josephine. "Are you good with the schedule change? We'd have to drive to Miami for my clubs tonight and fly out from there."

She performed a mental inventory of her diabetes supplies. "Yeah, I can . . ." She trailed off when she remembered something. "Oh."

"What's up?" Wells asked, raising an eyebrow.

Why was she hesitating to tell him this? "I'm meeting with the contractor at Rolling Greens tomorrow morning. About renovations on the Golden Tee."

Some of the light went out of Wells's eyes, but he nodded without hesitation. "Okay, yeah. That's important. You need to be there."

"The project is going to start while we're in California and I won't be able to be here in person." Her palms were suddenly damp. "I just . . . I have to make sure we're on the same page or the job will be too far underway when I get back. Changes will require more work."

"I understand, belle." He walked around the kitchen island, pulled her into an embrace, and kissed her forehead. Once, twice. "I can do press on my own."

She pressed her face into his chest, rubbing her nose in the hairy patch between his pecs. "Thanks."

His big hand stroked down the back of her head. "That doesn't require a thank-you." After another few seconds, he shifted against her, bringing Nate back into the conversation. "Let everyone know it's just going to be me. Josephine can't make it to San Diego until Wednesday night."

Nate groaned. "Who is going to keep you in line?"

She imagined, rather than saw, Wells's eye roll. "I'll be fine."

But he was not fine.

He was not fine at all.

As soon as Josephine landed in California two nights later, her phone started to buzz, alerting her to the fact that she had three voice mails—and none of them were from her eternally anxious mother calling to make sure she'd arrived safely.

They were all from Nate.

Still waiting to exit the plane, she hit play on the first one.

Hello there, Josephine. Just checking to make sure you got on the flight. Nervous laughter. *We need you in San Diego, kid. The meeting with Under Armour went . . . fine? Notice my high-pitched voice when I say fine. Wells didn't like the shirt they asked him to wear. To be fair, it was lime green, but he didn't need to call it hell's official uniform. As you can imagine, they were a little insulted. I think I've smoothed it over, but . . . we sure could use you on the West Coast.*

Letting out a pent-up breath, Josephine moved on to the next voice mail.

You're on that flight, right? Ack. Wells and Calhoun exchanged words during a practice round. A lot of C-words being thrown around and none of them were my favorite C-word—condo, followed closely by capital gains. The commissioner called to issue a warning. Could you speak to the pilot about taking a shortcut or something? I'm only half joking.

With a weight increasing in her stomach, Josephine hit play on the third voice mail and wedged the phone between her shoulder and ear while hauling down her suitcase, carrying it off the plane clutched to her chest.

For the love of everything holy, Josephine. A reporter asked Wells a somewhat personal question about you. That reporter's equipment is now in the lake. We are on red alert here, my friend. Danger zone. Text me immediately when you land, please. I'll just be over here buying out the entire antacid section of Rite Aid.

Josephine set down her carry-on outside a Hudson News and started to tap out a text to Nate, but a message popped up from Wells before she could hit send.

Wells: You land okay, belle? Airline website says you should have touched down six minutes ago.

Josephine: I'm at the airport. How did your day go?

Wells: Perfect. I nailed it.

Josephine: Really.

Wells: I even helped a reporter clean his camera.

Josephine: WOW. What a Boy Scout.

> **Wells:** Man scout. Look for a guy in baggage claim holding a sign that says Wells's Belle.

> **Josephine:** What??

> **Wells:** He's your limousine driver. I don't fuck around when it comes to my girl.

Josephine stopped in the middle of the busy walkway, bouncing right to left on the balls of her feet for a good five seconds before continuing on her way.

> **Josephine:** You really didn't have to do that.

> **Wells:** Happy birthday, Josephine. Finally making it up to you. x

She frowned a little bit over that last message. What did he mean by "making it up to her"? She would find out when she reached the hotel, she guessed, but for now, she wanted nothing more than to get out of the busy airport. Sure enough, when she rolled her carry-on through baggage claim, a white-mustached man in a suit and jaunty cap was holding a sign that read WELLS'S BELLE. Despite her protests, he took over the duties of maneuvering her bag through the people traffic, leading her out onto the sidewalk, where a champagne-colored stretch limousine idled.

"Oh my gosh," she muttered, opening the door and throwing herself inside as quickly as possible, so no one would see her partaking in something so needlessly extravagant.

"Surprise!"

The interior of the limousine was dark, save for a row of blinking blue LED lights along the perimeter of the ceiling, so it took Josephine's eyes a moment to adjust enough to make out the figure sitting on the opposite side of the vehicle.

Even then, she didn't quite believe it. Her eyes had to be lying. *"Tallulah?"*

Josephine didn't know it was physically possible to have tears burst forth from her eyeballs, but that's exactly what happened. They *ejected*. Trembling and overcome, she crawled on her hands and knees to the front of the limousine, her best friend meeting her halfway. Laughing tearfully, they threw their arms around each other and toppled sideways onto the leather row seat. It took a full minute for Josephine to speak, words kept getting stuck in her throat. Was this real? Was this really, *actually* real?

"What are you doing here?" Josephine sobbed, pulling back to look at one of her favorite faces of all time, before diving back into the hug.

"Keeping the secret has been so hard. I've wanted to call you a hundred times."

"When? H-how?"

"Wells Whitaker, that's how. He emailed me a couple of weeks ago and asked what it would take to bring me in for a visit. When he finally convinced me he was *Actual Wells Whitaker*, I told him it would take an act of God to get me days off and a trip to California. And he said, 'Then you're in luck. Have your boss give me a call.' I think he promised her tickets to Augusta or something." Tallulah grasped the sides of Josephine's face. "You are caddying on the PGA Tour, Joey. I repeat, you are caddying on *the PGA flipping Tour.*"

"I know. I know, right?"

"You weren't joking on the phone!"

"Nope." Josephine plopped back on her butt on the floor of the limo, still swiping at the moisture in her eyes. "I can't believe he did this."

Finally making it up to you.

This was repayment for the time he'd hung up on Tallulah. Unbelievable.

He was unbelievable.

"I'm not even going to get mad at him for yelling the C-word."

Tallulah nodded in agreement. "Everyone has to yell it once in a while."

Josephine laughed. Reached out to trace her best friend's prominent cheekbones that, despite her time in Antarctica, still held the glowing, natural tan that heralded her Turkish background. She traced her dark brows and smoothed a palm down her long, brunette waves. "How long are you here for?"

Tallulah winced. "Therein lies the rub. Only one full day, I'm afraid."

Josephine's heart sank a little. "You won't even be able to watch one day of golf?"

"No," her friend said, straight-faced. "And I'm *devastated*."

"You're a terrible liar." Josephine shook her head. "Golf was never your thing."

"That might be true, but I wanted to see you in action, Joey. This research study is going to be over in a month, though, and then I'm there. Front freaking row."

Josephine didn't want to ruin the incredible moment by explaining she probably wouldn't be caddying for Wells in a month's time. It would start a whole conversation she wasn't ready to have yet. Not even with Tallulah. And those voice mails from Nate were still ringing in her ears. If Wells couldn't be on good behavior for one day without her, what chance would he stand without her . . . indefinitely?

"You okay over there?" Tallulah asked, perceptive as ever.

"More than okay," Josephine assured her.

"Good, because I'm going to need every scintillating detail

of this Wells Whitaker partnership. Don't even think about telling me you're *just* his caddie. You are more than qualified, but a dude doesn't track down your best friend and fly her to California from Antarctica unless romance is afoot." She tilted her head back and squealed. "Oh crap, you're already blushing! I'm going to flash a mounted policeman, I'm so excited."

"I'll never live that down."

"Nope."

Once again, moisture flooded Josephine's eyes out of pure happiness to be sitting next to her best friend. "Wells is . . ." She tried to search for the words that would adequately describe the waterfall of emotion in her chest when she thought of the temperamental golfer. "Well, he's my boyfriend *and* friend. We balance each other. I smooth out his rough edges and he makes me feel . . . stronger and more capable than I've ever felt. Ever. He respects me. Look what he did, flying you here. He's thoughtful. And he's so *mean*, but in a way that I love? Because *that's* normal."

Tallulah sighed gustily. "More. I need more."

"The sex is unparalleled," Josephine whispered.

Her best friend folded her hands and bowed her head, as if deep in prayer. "That's what I'm talking about. Continue."

"He's rough with me. No one has ever been rough with me."

"That's what you want, right?"

"Yes." She squeezed Tallulah's forearm to reassure her. "Apparently, it's what I've *needed* without realizing it. I'm not fragile. He reminds me of that, but somehow . . . I know if I wanted to have a fragile moment, he'd just whip out some glue and fill in the cracks."

"It sounds like he's been whipping out a lot of things," Tallulah deadpanned.

"I'm not complaining. Clothes are stupid."

"So stupid. Josephine." Tallulah turned, taking Josephine by the shoulders and shaking her. "Holy hell. You're caddying on *the PGA Tour.*"

"You already said that," she laughed.

"It deserves to be said again." She dragged Josephine back into a hug and she went willingly, sighing into her friend's shoulder. "I'm so proud of you. Not only because you're finally getting recognized for your talent. But because you're getting that sweet, sweet golfer dick."

"It's the opposite of sweet. It's like . . . monstrous—"

"Careful, you've got a sexually neglected future marine biologist on your hands."

"Fine, it's sweet."

"Liar."

"I'm so glad you're here."

"Me too, Joey. Now, I've been eating MREs for months. Someone take me to get some real food! And tequila. In that order."

CHAPTER THIRTY-TWO

Wells was in the middle of a press conference when he saw Josephine step quietly into the press tent out of the corner of his eye. His hand shot out involuntarily and knocked over one of the dozens of microphones in his face, sending a peal of feedback through the tent.

She tucked some hair behind her ear and smiled at him, and his concentration leaked straight out of his nose. Was that a new blue dress she was wearing? Josephine probably had a lot of items in her wardrobe he'd never seen before and that fact might have annoyed the shit out of him—a lot like this press conference—if his girlfriend hadn't been making moon eyes at him.

Last night, after getting confirmation from the limousine driver that Josephine had connected with Tallulah, he'd relaxed. Briefly. Then he'd gone for a walk through the lobby of the resort, on the off chance he'd catch a glimpse of Josephine. Sure enough, he'd seen her in the cocktail lounge looking so happy, he'd stood there grinning through the glass like a bozo, before eventually tearing himself away and going back to his room.

This was the first time he'd seen her in three days.

Which was not that long. But it might as well have been a decade.

Honestly, did she have *any* fucking clue how beautiful she was?

Beautiful and smart and adaptable and funny and adventurous. He could have sat there for a week listing her attributes, but the clearing of a throat into a microphone lassoed Wells, rudely pulling him back to the here and now.

"How did the practice round go, Wells?"

"Decent."

"Do you feel more confident coming into this tournament than say . . . a month ago?"

"Why? What happened a month ago?"

Laughter filtered through the tent. His manager all but slumped over in the back row, a relieved smile on his face. All it took to get his head together was Josephine showing up and smiling at him. Something about that nipped at the back of his neck, like a problem that was beginning to sprout teeth, but Wells ignored it. There were no problems to speak of when his girlfriend was wearing a blue dress and a smile.

The media waited for him to give a serious answer to their question.

Was this his moment to let it be known once and for all how indispensable Josephine was to their partnership? To make it clear that she was far from a charity case, but more like an untapped talent that he'd been lucky enough to find and benefit from?

Yeah. It was.

He'd done more than irritate their sponsor and tussle with photographers over the last two days. He'd drawn up a new contract with Nate. The kind of agreement that had never been executed between a golfer and his caddie before on the tour.

"Yes, I feel more confident," Wells finally answered. "A lot more."

"Would you say that's because of your good luck charm?"

Was it his imagination or did Josephine's smile falter a little bit?

Yeah. Definitely. But the change had been fleeting. Maybe being the subject of their question had just caught her off guard, because she was back to being her usual serene self now. "Why don't you ask her?" Wells jerked his chin toward where Josephine hovered inside the entrance. "She just showed up."

Every head turned at once.

A few camera flashes popped. Murmurs carried down the rows of reporters.

Someone in a headset rushed out onto the stage with a second chair and Wells stood, holding it for her. "And it's her birthday week, so everyone better have something to say about it."

A chorus of baritone happy birthdays rose from the gathered media while Josephine smoothed her dress and climbed the three stairs onto the stage. "Hey," she whispered, her green eyes turning any remaining waves inside Wells into a placid lake. "I was going to come see you last night, to say thank you, but Tallulah and I didn't stop talking until they closed down the bar. Like, we were *physically* removed." She took a shallow breath and released it shakily. "Wells, I'll never receive a better present as long as I live. I don't know what to say."

He didn't, either.

Who had filled his chest with sand?

"Uh-hmm." He grunted. Pulled her chair out farther. "Nice dress."

Her sides shook with silent mirth. "Thank you."

Another grunt, as they both took their seats.

Jesus, are you okay?

Was he feeling unbalanced because he hadn't kissed her yet?

"Miss Doyle! Do you think you'll inspire more women to become caddies on the PGA Tour?"

"I hope so."

"How has the reception been toward you on tour?"

"No complaints." She hedged. "I mean, there's always a little ball-busting in the locker room setting, but it helps that I don't have any balls to bust."

Laughter boomed through the tent—and some of it came from Wells.

There was nobody like Josephine.

In the wake of her joke, she turned and smiled at him, her eyes twinkling like twin lakes beneath a sunset, and he lost his ability to speak.

I'm in love with you, Josephine.

"I've got a question for both of you," said a man standing at the back of the tent. "The internet seems pretty determined to prove you're a pair on *and* off the golf course. How do you feel about the speculation about your relationship?"

Wells's ability to speak came roaring back. There was his opening. He leaned forward to speak into the group of microphones. "She's my professional partner. My *equal* partner. That's the only relationship that concerns anyone in this tent."

"What do you mean by 'equal partner'?" pressed the reporter.

"I mean, she's just as responsible for any success out there as I am."

Several beats of silence followed. They were visibly non-plussed.

"Are you going to give her fifty percent of the winnings, too?" asked the man, dryly.

Skeptical snorts followed that question. Most of the press, however, looked peeved by the reporter. A couple of them even threw crumpled-up paper cups at the man, which he batted away.

"Wells . . . ," Josephine whispered. "Ignore him."

He covered the microphone with his hand. "Do you trust me?"

Her brow wrinkled. "Of course."

Victory bobbed in his throat. She'd said it faster this time than last time.

Wells dropped his hand from the microphone. "I don't *give* her anything. She earns it. She's *that* good at reading a course. Making calls based on strengths and weaknesses I didn't even know I had. Hell, her drive is better than mine. To say I'm lucky to have her on my team would be an unforgivable understatement." He pressed his thigh against hers, where no one in the tent could see. "That's why I *am* giving her fifty percent of my winnings."

Silence abounded.

Josephine's head turned slowly, her eyelashes fluttering a mile a minute.

Everyone started talking at once, taking pictures and shouting questions, but he didn't have time for any of that. He needed to be alone with his girl.

"No more questions, you beady-eyed pack of vultures. We're out of here." He stood abruptly, sending his chair skidding across the podium, and waited for Josephine to rise, as well.

Which she did. On visibly wobbly legs.

He tried to gauge her reaction. Did she understand why he'd done it? She'd asked him to refrain from trying to correct the media's misconception of her and her so-called victim/hero relationship with Wells, because he might make it worse. But he couldn't do that. He couldn't stand by and let people believe Josephine wasn't the hero in this situation. And he *hoped*, maybe, once people stopped seeing her otherwise, their relationship could thrive out in the open.

Not now, obviously. Someday.

But Wells was shocked down to the soles of his feet when— right there in front of everyone—she reached out and took his hand, winding their fingers together tightly. Lights flashed, feet stomped, more questions were shouted, but they ignored all of it, communicating with nothing but their eyes.

I can't believe you did that, said hers.

His responded with, *You haven't seen anything yet.*

Side by side, they walked out of the tent.

And Wells only shot the reporters the briefest of middle fingers behind his back.

Wells stared at the dinner menu in his hands, the words blurring together in indecipherable lines. What did "braised" mean? He couldn't remember.

He was in the players' lounge having dinner with Josephine and Tallulah, but he'd barely managed a proper greeting for Josephine's best friend when they arrived.

Because he'd been rendered speechless by sex. Utterly fucking speechless.

"Wells, do you want one of these rolls?" Josephine asked, nudging the breadbasket in his direction. All he could do was look at the baked dough in confusion.

"Huh?"

Josephine pressed her lips together in amusement—because she knew exactly what she'd done to him. Scrambled his brain like a couple of farm fresh eggs, that's what.

She'd given him head. *Twice.*

Enthusiastically.

Were his legs even attached to his body anymore? He couldn't feel them. Couldn't hear or see anything but Josephine on her knees in that blue dress, telling him softly that it was okay to come in her mouth. That she really wanted him to.

You better not be doing this because of the press conference, he'd said, while flexing his hips toward her mouth. *Or because I flew in your friend, Josephine, I swear to . . .*

Can't I just miss the taste of my boyfriend's cock? she'd purred, kissing his crown.

And his brain went offline after that.

He'd literally passed out from the sucker punch of relief she'd given him. And when he'd woken up, she was back at it. *Moaning* as she sucked him.

No clothes this time. Not a single stitch.

Now he was supposed to make small talk. Chew things and operate utensils.

How.

Wells watched the waiter approach with a sense of dread. "Something to drink, folks?"

Josephine and Tallulah ordered glasses of white wine.

Wells helplessly gestured to the bar.

"A . . . beer, sir?" guessed the waiter.

Wells nodded, his neck so loose, he probably resembled a bobblehead.

He had no idea what he'd done to deserve the Cadillac of sexual favors, but he wanted to be a better person now. Volunteer more. Build orphanages with his bare hands. Save the bees. All of it.

"So, Wells . . ." Tallulah buttered a roll. "Do you have rituals you perform before a tournament starts? Like, is there a song that hypes you up?"

Both women looked at him expectantly. As if his brain wasn't still a pile of mashed potatoes on the pillow upstairs. But didn't he want to make a good impression on Josephine's best friend? *Get your head on straight.*

"Lately, I usually just argue with Josephine."

Tallulah snickered. "How long did it take you to realize she always wins?"

"Day two, I think. Maybe three."

"And yet, he keeps trying," Josephine said, squeezing his thigh beneath the table.

Making him think of how she'd held on to his thighs while she stuck out her tongue for his spend. "I'm never going to argue with you again," he rasped. "You win forever."

"Oh. This is a victory dinner?" Tallulah raised her glass of wine. "Aren't those supposed to come *after* the tournament?"

"Yeah. But we've always been a little unconventional," Wells said, and he could actually feel his fucking heart pounding in his chest as he looked at Josephine. "And I don't want to change a single thing."

Josephine's smile dipped a little, seemingly beneath the weight of the moment. "Me either."

"Holy shit," Tallulah said, setting down her glass with a clink. "Look at that giant man with a child's backpack on his shoulder."

Halfway through Tallulah's exclamation, Wells somehow knew she was referring to Burgess. In his panic to reach Palm Beach, followed by the rush to reach California early, he'd forgotten all about his phone call with the hockey bruiser. Now, Wells tore his eyes off his girlfriend and followed Tallulah's line of sight toward the lobby, where, indeed, Burgess was towering among a sea of people with a miniature, sparkly silver backpack on his shoulder, a very solemn young girl holding his hand in the check-in line.

"Wow, he actually brought his kid," Wells said. "To a golf tournament."

Tallulah raised a dark eyebrow. "You know him?"

"Yeah." Why was he shrugging so much? "*Casually*. Like, beers and the occasional phone call, but it's not a big deal."

Josephine tapped her temple. "Making a mental note not to fly him in for *your* birthday." She split a look between Wells and the lobby. "Do you want to ask them to join us?"

"With a *kid*?"

"Kids eat, too, last time I checked," said his girlfriend.

Suddenly, he was very fixated on what Josephine was saying. "Do you like kids?"

"Of course, I like kids."

"Do you want one?" he half shouted.

"Oh, I wish they had popcorn on this menu," Tallulah said wistfully, tipping her glass to her lips. "But I guess wine will have to do."

"Maybe," Josephine answered, finally. "Not yet. But maybe someday."

"I don't know a damn thing about kids," he warned her.

Josephine opened her mouth, closed it. "People usually don't know, until they have one. Not really." She very clearly kicked her friend under the table. "Right, Tallulah?"

The aspiring marine biologist choked on her wine, but recovered fast. "She's right. You have to *have* one to find out if you actually *want* one. It's pretty fucked. *Unless* your mother had one of your siblings late in life, like mine did, and you helped raise them." She rubbed her hands together. "That's how I know I want 'em. Bring me that child!"

Wells had the very distinct urge to witness Josephine around a young kid and he had no idea where it was coming from. "I'll ask them if they're hungry."

Josephine slumped, as if relieved to be done with his line of questioning. And he *was* done with it. For now. He'd never been remotely serious about a woman, the way he was with Josephine. It stood to reason that he should know her vision for the future. Obviously, she wanted to turn the Golden Tee into a premier destination in Palm Beach for golf, but beyond that . . . what did she want? A house? Did she want a split-level or more of a ranch style?

Unbelievable. He knew *nothing*.

When Wells reached Burgess, he briefly clapped a hand down on the man's gargantuan shoulder. "Hey, man. You made it."

Burgess turned halfway. Dipped his chin. "That's right. You better not suck tomorrow."

"Dad!" The little girl punched her father in the leg. "Normal people say hi?"

The hockey player grunted. "This is Lissa. She's eleven."

"Hi, Lissa who is eleven." Wells stuck his hand out for a shake. To his surprise, she didn't hesitate to take his hand and squeeze it firmly. "Do you eat? Food?"

"No, she eats tree bark," Burgess deadpanned. "Of course, she eats food."

"Look, I've had an *afternoon*. All right? I'm lucky to be alive right now." Wells jerked his thumb at the restaurant, his ridiculous heart skipping when Josephine waved. "We're having dinner over there. Me, Josephine, and her friend Tallulah. You're welcome to join. They've got a lot of things that are braised on the menu. That's all the information I have to report."

"Do they have chicken fingers?" asked Lissa.

Shit, that sounded good. "I don't know. But if they do, I'm fucking ordering them."

Burgess's left eye twitched. "Watch the language, Whitaker."

Lissa doubled over giggling.

Wells stared in stunned silence.

Holy shit. He'd made a child *laugh*.

Wells turned and made eye contact with Josephine, pointing at Lissa.

She's laughing at me, he mouthed.

Josephine sent him a double thumbs-up.

"We'll check in and come join you," Burgess said, already walking toward the attendant who was waving him over from behind the check-in desk. "Come on, Lissa."

Wells went back to the restaurant and sat down in his chair, feeling more than a little smug. "Pretty sure I was born to be a father."

"Wow."

"Wow."

"I'm as impressed as you are, ladies."

A few minutes later, Burgess and Lissa entered the restaurant, the hockey player required to duck to make it beneath the door-frame without smacking his head. Lissa looked embarrassed just to be alive, hugging her elbows and hiding behind her fall of blond hair as she wove her way toward the table and sat down, expelling a breath.

Wanting to keep his Cool Adult streak going, Wells picked up the breadbasket and dropped it in front of the eleven-year-old. Zero movement at the table. Why was nobody speaking? Wells traded a look with Josephine, who tipped her glass subtly at the hockey player . . . who was staring at Tallulah like she'd just arrived on a cloud, wreathed in sunbeams.

"You want to take a seat, B-man?" Wells asked, nudging a chair out with his toe.

Which just happened to be the seat beside Tallulah.

"I . . . yeah. Uh." Burgess made no move to sit.

Thankfully, Josephine set down her glass and sprang into action, because she was perfect. "Burgess, it's so nice to meet you. I'm Josephine."

"My girlfriend," Wells added, leaning forward. "And equal partner."

"Yeah, I saw a clip of the now-famous press conference." Burgess shook Josephine's hand. "You're the one."

A wrinkle formed between her brows. "The one what?"

"My one." Wells frowned at her. "Get on the same page, belle."

Josephine stared.

"And I'm Tallulah," blurted the other woman, leaning forward, while very clearly kicking Josephine under the table. Two, three, four times. "Nice to meet you, Burgess." When she got no response, she tilted her head at the eleven-year-old. "What's your name?"

"Lissa."

Tallulah reached out and gave her a fist bump. "Hey, Lissa."

Burgess finally sat down across from his daughter, very careful not to brush any part of himself against Tallulah. "Do you want me to see if they have a placemat you can color?"

"Dad, I don't color placemats anymore," she whispered, blushing furiously.

The man known as Sir Savage hung his head slightly, appearing to mentally berate himself. This was the first time that Wells had ever seen the athlete with his child—and there was no comparing the two sides of the man. Usually, he was dry-humored and relaxed. Right now, he appeared to be at a total loss. "Let's get those chicken fingers, right?" Wells said, not sure if he was helping. "But if anyone dips them in anything other than ranch, they can go sit somewhere else."

Lissa giggled again.

Wells gave Josephine a pointed look. *See?*

"I'm having the veggie burger. One of the hazards of studying animals for a living is I feel too guilty eating them. I can't chew without thinking 'poor George'!"

"What kinds of animals?" Lissa asked in a mumble, fiddling with the sugar packets in the center of the table.

"Emperor penguins, most recently. I love cold-weather animals."

"Like . . . polar bears?" ventured Lissa.

Tallulah beamed. "Yes!"

That got a smile out of the kid.

"Tallulah is part of a research team studying in Antarctica," Josephine said.

Lissa's jaw dropped. "Isn't it freezing?"

"Yes. I have to put on *eight layers* just to walk outside. I feel weirdly naked right now."

Burgess coughed. Snatched up his water and drained it. "How . . . long are you here for?" asked the hockey player, once he'd set down the glass.

"Just until tomorrow morning." Josephine and Tallulah traded a pout. "But the project runs for only another month and then it's back to school. I'll be working on my master's at BU."

"Burgess lives in Boston," Wells pointed out absently, while looking around for the waiter. "Remind me which neighborhood, man."

"Beacon Hill," Burgess said.

"Is that a nice area?" Tallulah asked. "Are there parks?"

"Parks?" Burgess echoed.

Josephine nodded. "My best friend loves a park."

"They're free," Tallulah explained. "You can sit in them all day. Reading, suntanning, people watching. It's a very underrated activity."

Lissa threw a sugar packet at Burgess. "Dad, there's a park on our roof."

Tallulah reared back slightly. "Okay, baller. I doubt I'll be able to afford a neighborhood that has roof park buildings." She grinned. "Not while I'm still in school, at least."

"Where would you live, instead?" Burgess wanted to know.

Tallulah shrugged. "Not sure yet."

Burgess made a long sort of grinding sound, like a car engine turning over and over and over. "We have space."

Josephine kicked Tallulah under the table. Tallulah kicked her back.

The athlete coughed into his fist, leaned back. "The roof park has a waterfall."

Tallulah pretended to faint.

"Dad, I thought you were going to rent that room to a nanny." Lissa rolled her eyes at the table. "He thinks I still need one."

"I'm going to be on the road, off and on, Lissa. Not to mention practices . . ."

"If you need to rent the room to a nanny, that's fine. I totally understand." Tallulah traded a conspiratorial wink with Lissa. "Lissa and I can still have a park date or two."

Lissa's spine snapped straight. "Unless *you* want to be my nanny."

There was a tremendous amount of kicking happening beneath the table.

Wells wondered if the women knew he and Burgess could see all of it.

"I-I guess . . . I mean, that would depend on what it entails . . . ," stuttered Tallulah.

"Fifteen hundred a week. Free room and board." Oblivious to the fact that Tallulah's mouth had dropped open, Burgess continued without ever once looking at Tallulah. "I wouldn't expect you there every second of the day, just mornings, evenings." He shifted in his seat. "Through the night. Especially while I'm not there, of course."

"Of course," Tallulah said quickly, she and Josephine trading some silent girl communication with their eyes, lips moving imperceptibly. Wells could only watch in fascination. "I'll be home most nights anyway, since I'll be studying. But I'll need to negotiate at least two nights for social activity."

Burgess squinted at her. "As in?"

"Partying, of course. Life can't be all work and no play," Tallulah said brightly. "Mornings are no problem. If my terms are acceptable, I'm . . . not sure I can say no to the offer."

"Fine," Burgess boomed. "Done."

Lissa clapped her hands.

Tallulah very discreetly sipped her wine while checking out Burgess's biceps.

Wells and Josephine turned to stare at each other.

What the hell had just happened?

Any why was . . . Josephine suddenly rocking in her seat?

Not just rocking, but kind of . . . shimmying.

Dancing.

She was *dancing*.

Spine snapping straight, Wells desperately tried to dig through the restaurant din to unearth the song that was playing. "California Girls." But not the one by Katy Perry.

Tallulah let out a hoot. "Oh, they knew you were coming, Joey!"

"Holy shit." Wells fell back in his chair. "The *Beach Boys*?"

"My grandparents used to play this on vinyl when I was little and went to visit. It's in my bones," Josephine said, wincing, but still dancing. "I'm sorry for what you're about to witness."

Wells grinned. "I'm not."

Tallulah grabbed Josephine by the wrist and hauled her toward a space between tables that was decidedly *not* a floor designated for dancing, but they were obviously determined to make it one. Both of the women gestured enthusiastically for Lissa to join them. When the eleven-year-old responded by bounding out to turn the duo into a trio, Burgess couldn't seem to hide his shock. In no time, Lissa was stepping side to side between Josephine and Tallulah, if a little self-consciously.

The Beach Boys.

A little old-fashioned, uplifting, positive, revolutionary, warm. It fit Josephine so well, he should have guessed it before.

"Wow. Look at you. You're a goner," Burgess remarked into his beer.

"I'm well past gone, man." Wells managed to tear his eyes off a joyful Josephine long enough to spear the hockey player with a look. "Looks like you're headed in the same direction. Enjoy the trip."

"What's that supposed to mean?"

"The only part of your new nanny you're supposed to check out are her references."

Burgess seemed to realize he was staring at Josephine's friend and ripped his gaze downward, growling into his beer. "She's too young for me. Probably . . . eight? Ten years?"

"Yup."

"Look, I play hockey, I raise Lissa, I stay home. I don't people watch. I *definitely* don't party," he spat, like the very idea was laughable. "She'll probably have a boyfriend—her age—before she's fully moved into my place."

"Okay."

Burgess bared his teeth. "Stop giving me one-word responses."

"Oh. Okay."

"I don't know what the redhead sees in you."

Wells laughed. Just let the happiness escape him in the form of a sound without trying to smother or temper it and Josephine met his eyes, her own softening at the sight of him enjoying himself. "Me either, man, but I'm not questioning it."

CHAPTER THIRTY-THREE

They finished in eighth place at Torrey Pines with five under par.

Out of 128 golfers.

Not too shabby. Especially when Josephine did the math on 50 percent of those winnings, got overwhelmed by the six figures of it all, and immediately attempted to give it all back while they packed their suitcases to return to Florida.

"It's too much, Wells. I can't accept it," she called through their open adjoining doors.

His chuckle drifted into her room. "You can."

"No, thank you."

"You have two options, belle. Take the money you earned. Or leave it with me and watch in horror as I spend it on you in the most frivolous ways."

Josephine paused in the act of sliding her toothbrush into her toiletries case. "Such as?"

"A skywriter comes to mind. Just think, you could see 'Wells's Belle' written in the clouds over your apartment building every day for a month. That's one option." He wasn't finished. "Maybe instead of buying every kind of bubble bath they sell at Bath and Body Works, I'll just buy you a whole franchise. Maybe a private concert from the Beach Boys—a cover band, at the very least. You want to hear more possibilities?"

"No, that's quite enough to prove you're financially reckless."

"See? Taking the money is the responsible thing to do. I can't be trusted."

Her phone signaled an incoming text and she picked it up off the bed, swiping to find a text from Jim. There were no words, just a picture of her father in front of the construction taking place at the Golden Tee, giving a thumbs-up—and Josephine's stomach dropped to her knees when she saw how much progress they'd made in just five days.

Drywall had been installed, shelves were in place. There was a crate in the background and she could see it contained the freestanding fireplace—decorative only, because hello, this was Florida. The windows were new, stickers still on the glass. Boxes containing the new display stands and furniture she'd ordered stood waiting to be opened. By her.

The shop was going to be done sooner than expected.

If Josephine was in Palm Beach right now, she would be putting together furniture, directing traffic, ordering stock from their supplier. Getting ready to open the doors. But she wasn't there—she was in California. And she'd agreed to fly into Miami and spend the week leading up to the Masters with Wells.

While the sweat cooled on their bodies in the dark last night, he'd kissed her neck and talked about all the places he wanted to show her in Miami. Restaurants, golf courses, the beach. His bathtub. When she'd hedged, preparing to tell him no, that she needed to get back to Palm Beach to check on the progress of the Golden Tee, he'd hit her with the knockout blow.

They could watch golf highlights in his home theater.

Her boyfriend had a home theater. With leather recliners and soundproof walls.

Josephine's life was no longer familiar and she couldn't discount the sense that reality, the one *she'd* built, was slipping through her fingers.

Another picture text buzzed its arrival on her phone.

The outdoor putting green was almost completed, too. Fencing had been installed.

Even the water feature was up and running.

At this rate, she could probably have the Golden Tee open for business in a week. Maybe even less, if she declined to let Wells whisk her to Miami.

Once she went back to Palm Beach, however, and got sucked into the reopening of the Golden Tee, she wasn't going to leave again. Josephine knew that fact like she knew the layout of Rolling Greens. Her heart was being torn in two directions, because as much as it beat for her family's business, it was beating for Wells Whitaker now, too.

And he needed her.

How many times today had she been called a good luck charm by the press? Not to mention all the idioms they'd assigned to her during television broadcasts. The one who turned it all around for Whitaker! The secret ingredient! Nate pretended to bow down to her every time they'd crossed paths during the tournament and at first, she'd laughed. Now she wondered if she had the strength to abandon this team.

Or if Wells would—or could—continue at this trajectory to the top without her.

Her thumb swiped slowly across the screen of her phone, a lump rising in her throat over the pride in her father's expression as he gestured to the new Golden Tee sign. Her roots were in Palm Beach. Were the ones she'd put down with Wells too new to be tested?

"Our ride to the airport should be here soon," Wells said, entering her room through the adjoining door—and Josephine quickly closed her texts and darkened the screen of her phone, the pit opening in her stomach. "What was that?"

"Nothing, just looking at pictures from Tallulah's visit," she lied, hating the acidic taste that sharpened on her tongue. "Trying to decide which one to frame."

Wells hummed knowingly and kissed her shoulder. "Not too long until she's settled in Boston. You'll see her again soon."

Lying to Wells was bad enough. Using her best friend to escape an uncomfortable conversation was even worse, and the guilt propelled Josephine into motion. She slipped free of Wells's potential embrace, desperately searching for any remaining item to stuff into her suitcase. "I'll, um . . . be ready in a sec."

After a couple beats of silence, she glanced up to find Wells watching her with his brows drawn, as if trying to read her thoughts. "Everything okay, Josephine?"

"Yeah, why?"

He regarded her closely, before shaking his head. "No reason."

Her phone buzzed audibly in her pocket and she had no choice but to ignore it, leading to a pregnant pause. "Ready when you are," she said, hurrying to zip her suitcase.

Wells took both pieces of their luggage and wheeled them out through her door. His clubs had already been shipped back to Miami and weirdly, she kind of missed the weight of them on her shoulder. Especially when they reached the valet—and were showered with applause waiting for their driver to pull around. At that point, she actually wished she was holding Wells's sticks as a prop. Just for something to do with her hands, because now she was alternating between awkward waving and tucking stray hair into her ponytail.

Had people actually been camped out, waiting for them to leave?

A security guard approached her with a bottle of champagne on behalf of someone in the crowd and Josephine smiled her thanks. Wells posed for pictures with a family in a rare moment of wholesomeness.

In the midst of the commotion, Josephine traded a glance with Wells and . . . he just looked so happy. Even his frown lines were less prominent than before. Compared to the golfer who'd quit mid-tournament over a month ago, he was a different man. Content. He laughed all the time. As a golfer, he was almost back to where he'd been at his peak, only now he had that relaxed aura of experience and maturity thrown in. He'd grown. With her.

They'd grown together.

She'd let someone else in to share in the ups and downs of her condition and she'd never, ever expected to do that. But Wells made it right.

They were a formidable team.

And she couldn't leave without knowing how far they could go.

Wells sat up in bed and looked down at Josephine, tracing the line of her bare shoulder with his gaze before standing reluctantly and heading for the kitchen. He poured himself a glass of water, set it down, then braced both hands on the counter without drinking a sip.

Something was off with his Josephine—around 10 percent of the time.

The other 90 percent of the days they'd spent together in Miami, she was her usual incredible self. Smiling, challenging him, melting him with her touch, stunning him with incredible insights as they watched old Masters footage in the dark, cuddled up on one recliner and wrapped in a fleece blanket. Quite frankly, Wells would have been more than happy to sit in that home theater listening to Josephine murmur observations in the dark, her hair still half-damp from a bath, for the rest of his time on this earth.

He was so fucking happy, he almost couldn't withstand the pressure in his chest. It built and it built and it *built* every time he looked at Josephine.

That 10 percent, though. It ate at him. Big-time.

Every so often, when she didn't realize Wells was watching, he caught her staring into space. Or lying awake in the dark, tense, when she should have been sleeping. Then there was the fact that she wouldn't swipe open her phone in his presence. He caught only the tail end of her phone calls to Jim, but she'd hang up before Wells could get the gist of the conversation.

Three times now he'd asked if something was wrong and she'd visibly declined to be honest with him—and that wasn't like Josephine at all. She was the most honest person he'd ever met in his life. It was one of a billion reasons he'd fallen in love with her.

Maybe she wasn't in love with him . . . back.

Totally possible. Totally understandable.

Wells couldn't even fault her for that. He'd probably join an order of monks, take a vow of silence, and go live on a remote goddamn mountaintop if that was the case, but he'd *get it*.

Or maybe he was just distracting himself with that horrible possibility.

Because deep down, he knew what her 10 percent withdrawal was really about and he needed to stop avoiding it. Or where confronting it would lead.

Wells hung his head and let the dread wash into his stomach.

Then he retrieved his phone from where it was charging in the living room. He stepped out onto his balcony into the balmy Miami breeze, hesitating only a second before calling Jim. It was late, just after eleven, so Josephine's father sounded concerned when he answered the phone. "Wells? Is everything okay?"

"Yes. Everything is fine. Josephine is fine. She's sleeping."

An exhale came down the line. "Good. Okay. What's up?"

Wells looked out over the Miami skyline, to the ocean beyond, but he wasn't really seeing any of it. He could see only the beautiful woman asleep in his sheets. His one.

The first and final woman he'd ever love.

"Have you talked to Josephine lately?" Wells asked, deep down already knowing the answer. If he was being honest with himself, he'd been blind to this moment, even though they'd been heading there since day one.

"Sure, I have," Jim responded, brightly. "Been keeping her in the loop on the construction. Although, I'm not sure you can even call it construction anymore, since the last day and a half has been all about finishing touches. Touchups and whatnot." Josephine's father paused, his tone losing some of its enthusiasm. "The place is good and ready for her."

Wells's heart dropped into his stomach.

Good and ready.

"Josephine knows that?" Dumb question. Of course, she knew. But he asked it anyway. Maybe to punish himself, because Jesus. The Golden Tee being rebuilt in the shape of Josephine's dream? It was the thing she was most excited about in this world. And she'd felt the need to keep the news from him. She hadn't shared her excitement with him. She'd hid it.

"Never mind. Obviously, she knows." Wells cleared the rust from his throat. "That's amazing, Jim."

"Sure is."

Silence filled the line.

"Thing is, Wells . . ." Jim hesitated, mattress springs creaking in the background, as if he'd risen from bed. "Damn the timing on this."

Wells swallowed hard. "What do you mean?"

"I mean, Rolling Greens has made their repairs and is up and running now, back to being operational. They need the Golden Tee to open their doors pronto, so we can start processing customers. Right now, they're renting equipment out of a tent in the parking lot and well . . . it's not what club members expect." A beat passed. "Basically, they're giving us until next week."

Next week.

Those two words landed on his shoulders like ten-pound sacks.

The Masters was next week.

"If Josephine is coming back, she'll have a lot of work to do before then . . ."

Wells's brows snapped together. "*If* she's coming back?"

He could sense Jim's discomfort without even seeing the older man. "Haven't you talked to Josephine about this?"

No.

No, he'd been too busy trying to pretend they weren't living on a deadline.

Not knowing how to answer Jim's question without sounding like a selfish asshole—and that's exactly what he was—Wells dodged. "Did she . . ." He shook his head. "I mean, obviously she's going back to Rolling Greens, right? It's her place. It's her . . . heart."

God help him, he sounded pathetic, and he didn't care one bit.

"I'm not so sure, Wells . . ." Jim trailed off. "I mean, it's the Masters, right? You need her."

The numbness crept into every corner of Wells's body as the crux of the matter washed over him like a ten-story wave. "She doesn't think I can do it without her." His legs wouldn't hold him anymore and he dropped into one of the chairs. "And why would she think any different when everyone has been telling her for weeks that she's responsible for my comeback. I reinforced that. Didn't I? I leaned on her too much and now . . . she's going to give up the Golden Tee to caddie for me. Is that what's happening here?"

Wells was going to be sick. *You selfish piece of garbage.*

Jim broke into his shame spiral. "She's trying to get an extension from the course—"

"An extension won't matter. It's only temporary. After the Masters, it'll be another tournament. Another one after that." It hurt to breathe. "She's too loyal to leave me."

Just like she'd always been.

Standing on the sidelines, his stubborn fangirl to the bitter end, no matter how badly he played. Holding up her sign. Wearing his discontinued merchandise. Rain or shine. *Of course* she wasn't going back to Palm Beach to leave him to compete in the Masters alone, especially after his continual bad behavior when she missed *two measly days* in California. How had he not seen this? How had he not recognized the pressure bearing down on Josephine?

No. He couldn't let this happen.

He wouldn't let the woman he loved give up her dream out of loyalty to him.

Otherwise, he was never worthy of that loyalty in the first place.

"I'll make sure she's home," Wells said, raggedly, ending the call.

And then he spent the night planning the hardest conversation of his life.

Wells wasn't in bed when Josephine woke up.

She frowned into the pillow, rolled over to stretch her sore muscles. If they continued having sex at this rate, she was canceling her gym membership.

"You don't have a gym membership," she yawned to herself, sitting up. Wanting to sneak one more look at the pictures her father had sent of the Golden Tee under construction, Josephine picked her phone up off the nightstand and scrolled through her camera roll, her stomach a combination of dread and excitement. More than anything, she wanted to show these pictures to Wells. He would be happy for her. He'd be interested and he'd probably have great suggestions, too, but . . . she was avoiding the conversation.

Not only with Wells.

She was avoiding it with herself.

She'd written an email to the owner of Rolling Greens asking for an extension on opening the doors of the new and improved Golden Tee, but although the owner had been following her journey with Wells on television, he'd apologetically declined. In fact, he'd seemed even *more* eager for Josephine to return to Palm Beach, now that she had some notoriety behind her, hoping it would earn him some clout with club members.

What was she going to do?

She didn't know. Every day, she woke up thinking the answer would have made itself clear, but she quickly became absorbed by Wells, by the magic they made.

By love.

Their relationship wasn't some temporary flight of fancy. It was built on rock. And she became more and more positive of that every minute they spent together. They'd seen each other at their worst and best, and they supported each other unconditionally. This man was the one great love of her life and she wanted to stay with him a little longer. She just needed to make sure Wells was solid and wouldn't self-destruct at the first sign of adversity.

Then she would go.

Yeah right.

She looked at the completed construction pictures on her phone one last time, no choice but to acknowledge the wistfulness in her chest, before setting it back on the side table, facedown. Quickly, she finger-combed her hair and pulled on Wells's discarded T-shirt, detouring to the en suite bathroom to brush her teeth before venturing out to the living room.

She stopped short when she found Wells sitting on the couch. Shirtless in sweatpants.

The television wasn't on. He wasn't reading or looking at his phone.

He was just . . . sitting there.

A finger of alarm traced down her spine, but she shook it off.

Maybe he was visualizing the course at Augusta. That wouldn't be unusual.

"Morning." She circled the couch and sat down beside him. "I'm usually the one who wakes up first. Everything okay?"

He didn't answer right away. "I don't know."

Nerves crept into her throat, but she laughed through them. "Why does it feel like I just walked into a breakup?"

Wells flinched. Just the slightest gathering of his shoulder muscles—

And the air evaporated from Josephine's lungs.

"Oh my God," she managed, pushing off the couch onto legs that were suddenly nothing more than cooked spaghetti noodles. "A-are you breaking up with me?"

Wells shot to his feet as well, looking pissed. "Are you serious, Josephine? I am not breaking up with you," he gritted out. "Don't even say those words out loud."

The roiling in her stomach settled. Slightly. "Then what's wrong?"

"What's *wrong*?" He shoved five fingers through his hair and took a deep breath, visibly calming himself down. "You've been hiding the screen of your phone, staring off into space when you think I'm not paying attention. And I think part of me knew what was going on, especially after days passed and you hadn't said one word about the Golden Tee. So I . . . called Jim last night." He took a step toward Josephine, where she'd frozen in place by the glass door that led to the balcony. "When were you going to tell me that the Golden Tee has to open its doors by next week, Josephine?"

It was all real now.

More than just words on her phone and a problem for tomorrow.

It was big and messy and she had to deal with it out loud. Right now.

"I'm going to call the owner of the course today and try to make him see reason." Her voice was veering toward high-pitched, apprehensive, but she couldn't seem to control it. "I can't miss the Masters, Wells."

"Josephine," he said calmly, though his eyes were anything but. "You should be in Palm Beach, getting the shop ready. I would have gone with you. I would have *helped*."

"I know," she whispered.

"Then why stay quiet about it?"

"I don't know."

"Yes, you do. We both know."

Josephine shook her head. She even had the impulse to run. Just run straight out the door and not have to hear anymore.

"Yes, we do," Wells continued in a gentler tone, closing the distance between them and cradling her face in his hands. "You're afraid to tell me you're not going to be caddying for me anymore. Let's just get it on the table, belle. We don't hide from each other."

With those meaningful words in her ears and his familiar,

beloved hands holding her cheeks, coupled with his nearness and the scent of him, Josephine was about to have a moment of weakness. A really, *really* big one. Someday she would look back and excuse herself for being a woman so in love, she was willing to give up everything to maintain the feeling. Keep the connection burning bright. To continue living the fairy tale no matter what it cost. To do what was best for this person she cared about, adored, *needed*.

"I'm sorry I hid it from you. It's just that . . . I've been thinking. Maybe I could hire a manager for the Golden Tee, so I can stay on tour with you." She forced a laugh, even as tears sprang to her eyes, and staunchly ignored the stab of self-betrayal in her abdomen. "I mean, I would look really cute in that white caddie jumpsuit at Augusta."

Wells looked . . . frozen.

"Hire a manager?" His hands fell away from her face and hung at his sides. "You must really believe I can't continue winning without you. If you're willing to do that. Let someone come in and live your dream. You would hate every second of it."

"I would get used to it eventually." Even she could hear the doubt in her tone. "And it's not that I don't believe you can win! I just think . . . I just. I can help, right? I help you."

"Of course, you do, baby," he said, passion evident in every word. "But I see what's been going on now. All this pressure that has been piled onto your shoulders." He shook his head. "Good luck charm this. The woman behind the comeback that. My manager hassling you to come babysit the golfer with the bad temper. Now you feel responsible. You feel obligated. And you are not. You're *not*."

A sound leaked out of her that sounded like air escaping a crushed balloon and that's exactly what she was. A piece of Mylar that had been filled past maximum capacity. As soon as Wells said the word "pressure" out loud, she recognized how much she'd been carrying around. But she was way too stubborn to let it all go. "I love the Golden Tee. I want to enrich my family's legacy, but . . . this can be my dream, too."

"Josephine. *Stop.*" He took her by the shoulders and shook her a little. "Listen to me. You're the most constant person I've ever met. You show up—*relentlessly*—for the people you care about. You showed up for me over and over and over, well past the point you should have. Because you are so fucking loyal, you don't know *how* to quit."

"I'm *not* quitting!"

He dragged in a breath. "Then you're fired."

The blow hit her out of nowhere, like a line drive to the stomach. Even as she reeled, however, her heart wouldn't quite let her believe what she'd heard. "Yeah, right. How many times have you said that? You're full of it, Wells."

He appeared winded, like he'd just sprinted the full length of a course. "I mean it this time, Josephine. You're fired. You're no longer my caddie. I'm *sorry.*" Wells reached for her and she flinched backward, numb, only remotely capable of feeling her hip ram into the wall. "I don't know any other way to do this. I'm doing what's best for both of us. You need to go run the pro shop of your dreams. And me?" He seemed to be struggling for an admission. "I think I need to know I'm capable of winning without you. No, we *both* need to know that. Otherwise, I'm always going to be an obligation, not the man you want to spend your life with."

A massive rupture took place in the middle of her chest. All she could hear was choices being made on her behalf—and she resented all of it. She'd claimed her independence a long time ago and no one took that away from her. No one. "Spend my life with you, Wells? You're *firing* me."

"Christ. I'm not firing you as my fucking girlfriend, Josephine. I'm in *love* with you."

Her heart got trapped in her mouth, but it was too broken and bleeding to get any enjoyment from those words. "I can't believe you're telling me this *now*."

"Yeah, I was hoping it would be a little more romantic, too!" Wells shouted, suddenly looking haggard. He paced away, hands dragging down his face, before wheeling back around. "Don't you think I want to be selfish? Don't you think I want to say 'Yes, great idea, hire a manager' so I can keep you with me on the tour? *Of course, I do.* I hate being away from you, Josephine. You *know* that. This is your fault for teaching me how to be selfless and wise and considerate. I want you to have your dream more than I want mine now."

Oh God, she could feel herself entering the bargaining phase of grief and she couldn't do anything to stop herself from going there. The more he spoke, the more she loved him and the more she was determined to stop him from being his own worst enemy. "You threw a reporter's camera in a pond last week. You're a beast with the media. We've come so far in just two tournaments, Wells. Imagine what we could do with one more? Maybe two."

There was so much affection in his eyes when he looked at her, she almost had to kneel down to shoulder it all. "You will never leave me, belle. I have to do it for you."

She shook her head, tears splashing down her cheeks. "No, you don't."

He closed his eyes for a moment. When he opened them again, a fine sheen had developed. "I had no idea what unconditional love looked like until you, Josephine. You taught me how to be like this. And I will love you whether or not you're helping me win some fucking game. We. Are bigger. Than a game.

Someday, when you're done being angry with me for this, I will be waiting to show you that. I'll *invent* new ways to show you." He covered his eyes with a hand and took a long shuddering breath. "But right now, you have to go."

The words were hardly out of his mouth before Josephine was moving blindly through the apartment, scooping her things off various surfaces, the floor, her legs almost too unsteady to hold her up. Was she mad at him? Unspeakably. He had no right to cut her off at the knees like that. Who did he think he was, making choices for her? *Calling her father?*

Throwing in her face how easily she'd been willing to abandon her own dream.

I have to get out of here. Before I try to convince him to let me stay.

Before I betray myself again.

Josephine was undoubtedly leaving personal items behind, but she didn't care. Eyes blurred with tears, she pulled on some jeans, ordered an Uber that would probably cost her a fortune, bundled her overnight bag to her chest, and speed-walked toward the front door.

Wells tried to step into her path, but she had too much momentum and easily skirted past him without braking. "Josephine, stop."

"You just told me to leave."

"Don't go like this," he growled, catching her around the waist with a forearm and dragging her back against his chest. "Tell me you fucking love me."

"I love you!"

Air burst out of him, followed by a ragged intake of breath, and Josephine knew that he hadn't really expected her to say it. That made two of them. Maybe when those three words were so unequivocally true, they couldn't be kept inside if someone invoked them. "Tell me we'll get through this," he begged into the back of her neck.

Now that, it appeared, was a request she couldn't grant. Not when she was this hurt, angry, and confused. "I can't see into the future, Wells."

"I can. My future is with you. That's the only future I'll ever want."

Anything resembling energy was ebbing from Josephine's limbs. The shock of being fired and told to leave by the man she loved was rendering her numb, like a small mercy. She needed to go, before she slumped back into his arms and cried like a baby. Her self-respect was full of holes after nearly abandoning her dream. Her pride was weak after having her offer to stay rejected. So she mustered up what little of those qualities she had left and wiped her eyes. "Don't be afraid to lay up on that par five at Augusta. Slow and steady, okay?"

She pulled open the door and left, closing it on an anguished rasp of her name.

CHAPTER THIRTY-FOUR

The night before the opening round of the Masters, Wells sat at the bar in the players' lounge, staring down into a glass of whiskey. He'd ordered it over twenty minutes ago, but hadn't yet taken a sip. The energy in the dimly lit bar was high and familiar, everyone buzzing about the tournament of the year. The Masters brought out all the legends, and they mingled with the young guns now, reminiscing about their glory days, holding court in their green jackets. Who would have the honor of winning one this year?

Josephine would have loved this.

That's what made his guts feel like they were in a miserable pile on the floor.

He no longer had insides, really. They had just kind of fallen out when she left.

Correction, when he *told* her to leave.

Before that thought could sprout teeth, Wells snatched up the whiskey and drained it, imploring the burn to work higher than his throat. To somehow singe away the memories of his fight with Josephine. Oh God, she'd been so hurt. He'd known she would be, but he'd underestimated. She'd gone white as a fucking ghost and he could *not* stop seeing that. It was like a horror film playing in his brain 24-7. On their first night in San Antonio, she'd told him having her help rejected hurt her feelings. It was her trigger—along with going to her parents for help—and he'd pulled them both.

But he'd seen no other way.

Did he do the right thing?

Did he?

He'd sat there all night trying to come up with solutions and he'd found only one no-fail way to combat Josephine's fierce loyalty. But, holy shit, was he suffering now. Not having Josephine around was like being dropped off alone on the moon, seven billion light-years from his beating heart. She hadn't stopped sharing her blood sugar data with him—that was the only thing that gave him hope that they would come out on the other side of this fight intact.

He could still see the rising and falling dots. He could still see she was okay. And thank God for that, because if she'd taken away that trust, he'd have crumbled.

As it was, Wells wasn't sure how he'd manage to wake up tomorrow and play a round of golf. He could barely feel his fucking hands. His whole life was mired in fog.

A ripple of murmurs moved through the crowd and Wells watched Buck Lee enter the room with his collection of pros, including Calhoun. He waited for regret and envy to drive up beneath his skin like twin spikes, as usual, but oddly . . . they never did. All he felt was a small sense of nostalgia, but it was layered under a giant heap of indifference.

"You want another one?" asked the bartender, gesturing to Wells's empty glass.

Did he? That would be his second double. The night before the Masters kicked off. He'd thrown a stick of dynamite into the middle of his relationship with Josephine so he could come here and prove to both of them that she wasn't some glorified crutch. That he could take what she'd so gracefully taught him and maintain his upward trajectory while she realized her own dream. One she wanted and deserved. And he'd meant what he said . . . at the time. A couple of days without her, though, and he didn't know if he could pull off anything resembling success.

Not when he was wounded and bleeding.

"Sure, I'll have one more."

A moment later the bartender set it down. He stared into the depths of gold, wishing he could see her green eyes. Just for a moment. Maybe then he could breathe.

A hand clapped down on Wells's shoulder. Without turning his head to look, he knew it was Buck Lee. On some level, he might even have been expecting the legend to approach him, though he couldn't put a finger on why. "There you are, son. I've been looking all over the place for you."

Wordlessly, Wells saluted Buck with his glass of whiskey. Set it back down.

Buck made a show of scanning the packed bar, Calhoun standing right behind him with a smirk. "I don't see your caddie around."

"Maybe she requested a separate lounge," Calhoun tacked on.

Violence fired down through Wells's fingertips. Hot breaths crackled in his lungs. It would have felt so good to punch that punk in his golden-boy face. Maybe he should. Tomorrow, he would pay for the mistake, but right now, it would be an outlet for his agony.

He's not worth it, Josephine whispered in his ear. *Don't give him what he wants.*

A wealth of threats and comebacks clogged Wells's throat. He couldn't find the energy to issue them, though. He'd been stripped of his bravado and rage. In its place, Josephine had left honesty. Genuineness. He wouldn't forget those things so soon. That would dishonor them.

"We both know you've already heard I have a new caddie. Why are you pretending otherwise?" Wells looked them both in the eye. "The fact that she's gone might be funny to you, but I promise, it's not funny to me."

To his surprise, both of them slowly lost their smug expressions. Several beats passed.

"What happened, man?" This, finally, from Calhoun. "I hope it wasn't something health related—"

"No, nothing like that," Wells said quickly, rubbing at his forehead. "She runs her family's pro shop down in Palm Beach—"

"The Golden Tee!" Calhoun supplied.

Wells eyeballed him. "Yeah . . ."

"They've been talking about her so much on the Golf Channel, I feel like I know damn near everything about her."

"You don't," Wells growled.

Calhoun held up his palms. "Fair enough."

"Let me get this straight," Buck said, shifting in his loafers. "She left the tour, where she was making hundreds of thousands of dollars, to go back to work at a pro shop?"

Wells sighed. "That's mostly right."

Buck tilted his head. "What did I miss?"

"The part where I fired her."

Calhoun spit out the sip he'd just taken of his martini. "You *fired* her?"

Everyone in the lounge was staring at Wells now. Silence descended over the room like a shroud. He could feel the horror the other golfers emitted in his direction and frankly, it made him proud of Josephine. She'd earned their respect. Of course, she had.

Wells turned in his seat to face the room at large.

It was right there on the tip of his tongue to shout at them to fuck off and mind their own business, like he normally would. He also had a threat or two lined up, just in case any of them got an ill-advised notion to try to hire her themselves. Or date her. Because he would rain unspeakable violence down on them. But the words got stuck in his throat when he saw genuine concern for the woman he loved on each and every face.

Even the waiter. And a busboy.

"She loves the pro shop more than she loves the tour, but she wouldn't go. She's too loyal." His explanation was growing weaker as it went on. "I had to *make* her go."

"Sweet baby Jesus, you fired your girlfriend," Calhoun drawled, almost fascinated. "How do you still have your balls?"

"Maybe I don't have them anymore. I haven't checked."

Calhoun . . . laughed?

Buck, too, the legend patting him on the back. A couple of the golfers in the room sent him drinks, which the bartender represented by lining up overturned shot glasses in front of his still full whiskey. It was more of a goodwill gesture, since he couldn't consume that much liquor responsibly on the night before a tournament or . . . ever, really.

Since when was he so responsible? And since when did the other pros give him anything but side-eye and trash talk?

It was the Josephine effect.

She wasn't even here and she was making things better. Brighter.

She'd changed *him* for the better in more ways than one. Not only on the golf course, but in the way he considered other people, not just himself. She'd changed the way he interacted with those around him. Calhoun and Buck had ordered seltzer water and were flanking him at the bar in some kind of . . . solidarity?

Holy shit, had *he* been the asshole all along?

Had he made an enemy, lost a mentor, and alienated a legion of pros . . . with the chip on his shoulder? One honest, vulnerable exchange and he had people at his back. Consoling him, even if they didn't agree with what he'd done to Josephine. Even if he didn't deserve it.

Fuck, that was humbling.

He wished so badly that Josephine were there so he could tell her about it.

He'd say, *Have I been the asshole all along?* And she would say something witty and Zen, like, *Wells, you've spent enough time giving people someone to hate, now give them someone to love.* Or maybe . . . he was saying that to himself. Right now. Josephine's voice would live rent-free in his head forever, guiding him, reassuring him, giving him shit, but the fact that he could conjure her wisdom on his own now? That meant something.

That meant he'd paid attention. Not taken her for granted.

That meant . . . maybe he *could* win on his own?

No, he would. He *would*.

There was a very real chance she'd never come back—and that would *gut* him. The view from his monastery in the mountains would be a bunch of grayscale trees and a pitch-black sky. But there was no way Wells would let the time he'd spent with Josephine mean nothing. If he had a sliver of a chance at getting her back, he'd have to prove he could stand on his own, without her constant support, because their relationship couldn't work like that.

Please let me still be in a fucking relationship.

Wells pushed the glass of whiskey away with his index finger.

"You're either going to play like dog excrement tomorrow," Calhoun mused, "or you're going to go out there and win the whole damn thing."

"Yup."

Calhoun paused. "You know, I have to at least make her an offer to join my team."

Wells had seen that coming, but the admission still drove into his eye socket like an ice pick. "Everyone in this room will probably make her an offer. The smart ones, anyway. She won't take it. She might hate me right now, but she's my . . . belle. Through and through."

If he listened carefully, he could hear his heart playing a tiny violin.

"You going to cry, son?" Buck asked, warily.

"Later, maybe." Wells exhaled. "In the bathtub with a nice pinot grigio."

They laughed. Wells didn't feel anywhere near better. But he wasn't alone.

And that was something.

"I'm going to head to my room," Wells said, standing up and laying some cash on the bar. "If you think giving me a little sympathy means I'm not going to gun for you tomorrow, Calhoun, you've wasted your time."

Calhoun held his hand out for a shake and, though he narrowed his eyes skeptically, Wells gripped the man's hand and shook. "I'll hate your guts through every hole," the blond man said. "But if I said it hasn't been inspiring watching you rise from the grave, I'd be lying." He shook his hand one final time. "Good luck tomorrow."

"Same to you. You'll need it."

Calhoun chuckled. "Enjoy your bath."

Wells decided to let Calhoun have the parting shot. His spirits were rapidly dimming and he couldn't think of a good rejoinder, anyway. The simple act of standing up and operating his wallet was as complicated as performing open heart surgery on roller skates—*and* they were each missing a wheel. He just wanted to go somewhere dark, lie down, and think of Josephine like the heartsick bastard that he was.

Before he left the bar area completely, Wells nodded at his former mentor. "See you, Buck."

"Night, Wells." He started past the older man, drawing up short when the man caught his elbow. "Let's have lunch sometime. All right?"

Some part of Wells wanted to break out the bitterness. *Now that I'm winning, you want lunch, huh? Nah, I'll pass.* But his eyes were a little more open tonight. Maybe clarity was a side effect of ripping out his own heart and throwing it into the ocean. It was possible—more than possible, really—that Wells was the one who'd been doing the wronging in the relationship with his mentor. Not the other way around. And if that was the case, he needed to own it.

"Yeah, Buck. I'd like that."

CHAPTER THIRTY-FIVE

Josephine polished a pint glass and set it on the wooden shelf behind the register, turning it so the course logo was facing forward. Without pausing for thought or rest, she flew to the next box of inventory, slid the X-Acto knife out of her back pocket, and sliced the tape, ripping the cardboard flaps wide. And did her best not to stare at the growing mountain of flowers, teddy bears, and bubble bath sets sitting just inside the door. Every time she turned around, another gift was being delivered. Accepting them was easy, but allowing herself to interpret their meaning was harder. She wasn't there yet.

So she kept stocking. Kept pushing.

She was so close to having the whole shop set up. They'd open the doors tomorrow.

Right on time.

She wouldn't have spare moments to think about what was happening in Georgia. In fact, she didn't even want to know. It was day three of the Masters. Jim had let it slip on the phone this morning that Wells had made the cut and Josephine had been almost alarmed by the rush of giddy pride that had rocketed through her bloodstream, but beyond that, she didn't even know his current score. That was fine. She needed to focus on the shop.

He didn't want her there. Otherwise she *would* be in Georgia. End of story.

But as much as Josephine wasn't in Georgia, Wells *was* in Flor-

ida with her in so many ways. As agreed upon, half of his winnings from Torrey Pines had been transferred to Josephine from
his accountant yesterday, and after reeling over her new financial
security, she'd promptly enrolled in a health insurance plan. As
soon as she paid the first premium, she'd burst into noisy tears.
The upheaval of relief made Josephine wonder if she'd suppressed
her worry over not having insurance for so long, she'd gotten
used to living with the stress. And that realization was something
she desperately wanted to share with Wells, which left her very
conflicted.

Mad at him. Missing him. Mad at him. Grateful.

Josephine finished the glassware display and moved on to
stacking boxes of golf balls, arranging them according to brand.
When the letters on the box started to blur a little, she remembered her glucose monitor had been going off for fifteen minutes
and forced herself to pop some tabs, chewing almost resentfully.

Breaks gave her time to think, and she really, really didn't
want to think.

Thinking made the center of her chest feel like the Grand
Canyon, just a yawning, arid place with acres of scorched earth
and sharp plants.

Tell me you fucking love me.

For some reason, that was the part of their argument she replayed most. Because it was so Wells. So *like* Wells to demand
something delicate with the roar of a king. That's what he'd been
doing all along. Shouting his insecurities at her and disguising
them as arguments. And she loved him so much for it. She loved
him so much she could cry enough tears to fill a lake, just for
missing his presence. The scruff of his chin, the scent of his de-
odorant, the roughness of his hips, those epiphanies that struck
his brown eyes when she said something that made sense on the
golf course, his villainous frown. His deep voice, his grudging

smile. The way he praised her, challenged her, coveted her. Spending a single second missing those things felt like a year.

And apart from that, apart from the razor-edged pining in her chest, she wondered if maybe, just maybe, he'd truly done the right thing. She was hurt and bitter and still in shock from the man she loved banishing her, but the Golden Tee would be empty right now if Wells hadn't sent her away. It would be a shell. Or maybe the course would be showing it to prospective replacements. People who wanted to give it a different name, maybe do a whole *new* renovation.

That would have killed her.

Missing Augusta was killing her, too. Slowly and painfully. Their cable had been installed this morning at the shop and the desire to turn on the television was high. But no, she was too afraid to find out he'd backslid and needed her.

Not when she wasn't there to help.

Josephine unstacked another box and got to work unpacking it. She was so absorbed in her task that she didn't hear Jim and Evelyn arrive. It wasn't until her mother planted a kiss on her cheek that she joined them in reality.

"Oh! Hey, Mom." She kissed Evelyn back, before giving her father's face the same treatment. "We're getting there."

"Oh, Joey-Roo, it's really coming along. It looks wonderful," Evelyn effused.

Smiling was agonizing but she attempted one anyway. "Thanks. We still have quite a bit of landscaping to do outside, but nothing to prevent us from opening for business. I'm stopping by the bank tonight for cash. The credit card machines are up and running."

Her parents nodded along with her verbal list of preparations. But when she finished and they simply stared at her without responding, it occurred to her how frazzled she must sound.

"Sorry for the info dump. I'm just excited."

"Of course you are, Joey," Jim said, affection shining in his eyes. "And we're so proud of you for . . . everything. Especially your determination to carry the Doyle torch. To keep it burning."

"Why do I sense a but coming?" Josephine asked warily.

Evelyn smiled. "When is there not a but coming with us?"

"Facts."

Her parents traded a look. "Far be it from us to meddle in your romantic life, dear," Evelyn said. "But we're wondering if you're just going to ignore the flowers."

Josephine squinted. "The flowers . . . ?"

"And the giant teddy bears," Jim added.

"I'm not following."

Jim nudged his wife. "Don't forget about the Bath and Body Works gift baskets." He winced. "Seventeen of them, to be exact."

"Ohhhh." Josephine figured she was abusing her tactic of choice, playing dumb, her gaze reluctantly tracking to the other side of the pro shop, where gifts from Wells were literally piled up to the ceiling. "*Those* flowers and bears and gift baskets."

Evelyn nodded encouragingly. "Yes."

"I haven't decided what to do about those yet."

"Dear."

"I'll have to clear them out for the grand opening, but—"

"Joey, have you turned on the Masters?" Jim broke in.

"We only got cable this morning!"

Evelyn just looked disappointed in her. "Honestly, Joey. Quit being such a pussy."

"Mom!"

The woman had the nerve to blush. *"Well. Stop!"*

Jim was slowly recovering from hearing his wife say the P-word. "Uh . . . I'm just going to turn it on. We can let Wells do the talking."

What was that supposed to mean?

Josephine didn't know, but she lowered herself onto a box and hugged her knees, bracing. Maybe part of her had known for the last few days that as soon as she turned on the tournament, the ice layer that had formed on her lungs when Wells said *you're fired* would melt. Just melt clean away.

And she was right.

There were a few minutes of footage of another pairing before the camera moved to Wells. But then . . . there he was.

Wearing pink.

That alone was enough to bring a watery, incredulous laugh tumbling out of her mouth, the shock that lingered inside her softening until it stung less. And less. But then he turned around to retrieve a wedge from his bag and she saw it.

Her caddie uniform from Torrey Pines hanging from his back pocket.

Josephine's heart squeezed so hard she gasped.

"Has he been playing with that the whole time?"

Evelyn answered. "Yes."

Josephine labored through a breath. A breath that hitched in her throat when the camera zeroed in on Wells's face and she saw the patchy, whisker growth on his cheeks, the sunken quality of his eyes, the grim lines on either side of his mouth.

In short, he looked God-awful.

And yet . . . he was playing well and holding his own. Knowing the man like she did, however, it was impossible for Josephine to miss the effort it was costing him to maintain his spot on the leaderboard. He looked tired and haunted. Haggard.

A lot like she felt.

"Honey, you've done the hard part," Evelyn said softly. "You've cleaned up the shop, restored it better than ever. We can rent clubs and sell merchandise for the first couple of days. Rolling Greens and the Golden Tee will be right here waiting when you get back."

"Back from where?"

Jim implored the ceiling for patience. "Augusta!"

"Dad, he needs to do this without me. He *wants* that."

"And I know you don't want to hear this, but that decision was fair enough, Joey. Relationships should be built on *even* ground." He squinted an eye at her. "Do you think that man wants what's best for you?"

Of course he did.

The answer came to her without delay.

Her heart knew the truth, as well as her mind. She'd never stopped trusting Wells, even in the thick of her anger. She'd just been too hurt by his seeming rejection to acknowledge it. Now, though, with his beloved image moving on the screen, and quiet proof that he loved her adorning his body, there was no more avoiding what she already knew. He'd taken that growth they'd achieved together and he'd done the selfless thing. He'd made the decision she was too scared to make herself. His turn had arrived to be the strong one and he'd risen to the occasion. Maybe she could have celebrated him for it if she hadn't been blindsided.

Now that she'd gained time and perspective, she had no choice but to see his actions for what they were. A man expressing his love the only way he'd known how.

"Yes, I know he wants what's best for me," Josephine said. "Always."

"Do you want what's best for him?"

"Yes," she managed. "Of course."

"That's love, honey." Evelyn tipped her head at the television. "And even when it's hard or you have to swallow your pride, love should always be celebrated."

It wasn't that Wells didn't know how to win.

In his early days, he'd won because being the best at something, being feared and revered, was like a drug after a lifetime of being ignored. Suddenly everyone loved him and that felt great. It was a relief to know the people who treated him like an afterthought had been wrong.

Then he started winning for Josephine. He'd barely taken himself into account when they'd joined forces. He'd wanted success only so he could share it with her.

But on the final hole at Augusta—day four, one shot off the lead—he didn't have either of those things to win for. Accolades and reverence were fleeting in sports. Was it nice to win and earn back respect? Yeah. But if all of that shit went away, it wouldn't break him this time. He'd let it send him into a tailspin once, but never again. He knew what real success looked like now—earning the love and loyalty of his soul mate.

Did he want to win for Josephine? Hell yes. Purely because she'd believed in him when no one else would. But she wasn't there. In his head, maybe, but not physically.

And he was out of fucking steam.

Earlier today, he'd rallied. Birdied nine holes, climbed to number one on the leaderboard. But he'd bogeyed the last hole, gone into the water two holes prior, and slipped to number two. Nakamura was lining up his shot now, twenty yards from where Wells stood. The veteran golfer was poised to win the Masters and he deserved it. He'd played four solid rounds.

And the guy probably wanted it so bad.

Look at that. His wife was waiting on the sidelines with the rest of the gigantic crowd, holding on to an older woman's hand. Probably her mother-in-law. They were bursting with pride, waiting for Nakamura to sink this final putt and take the green jacket home.

Good. He was welcome to it.

You're burning it all down, Josephine said in his ear. *Why?*

At the sound of her imaginary voice, Wells drifted back to a conversation they'd had in the dark one night in California.

"Which win do you remember most?" Josephine had asked.

"My second major."

"Really? Why?"

"I don't know . . . I guess, because I wasn't an imposter on the tour after that."

Josephine was quiet for a few moments, her index finger drawing circles in the middle of his chest. "So you remember it mostly because of how . . . other people would see you differently afterward?"

He'd been a little taken aback by that interpretation, but he couldn't completely deny it. "I guess."

"But what made it feel good for you?"

Another minute passed while he peeled back layers he didn't even know existed. That's what Josephine did. "The game . . . I was honored to become a part of the game. It's old and loved by people who've come and gone . . . and there's this beautiful ritual to it. I'd never had anything beautiful in my life before that and I guess I was just stunned when it loved me back."

Her appreciative exhale had roamed slowly over his body. "Remember that, Wells."

"I will, belle."

Recalling what it felt like to lie with Josephine in his arms and talk about their mutual love for the game had left his windpipe the size of a straw.

It shrank even more when Nakamura missed the putt.

The crowd let out an explosion of shock and disappointment.

A rush of fire blew over his nerve endings.

Holy shit.

That shot should have been a gimme.

But the guy had missed. Which brought them even at fifteen under par.

In other words, if Wells sank the next putt, he would win the fucking Masters.

And he couldn't even see the shot. His brain wasn't working. Lack of sleep, lack of her, too much of everything else.

Josephine, where are you?

Jesus.

He could recall her asking him, "If you could visualize the shot, what would it look like?" He strode to the quarter he'd left to hold his place, setting his ball in the same spot and pocketing the change. He turned his hat around, hunkering down and exhaling.

The crowd wasn't breathing.

The air had stopped moving. Not a hint of wind to dry the sweat beading on his forehead. His temples throbbed, along with the insides of his wrists.

It wasn't just a ball in front of him.

It wasn't just a hole.

Or some sport.

It was the only good thing he'd had in his life at one time. And he wanted to give this shot everything he had, didn't he? He had the right to want this win.

He'd gotten here because of love and that's how he'd finish it.

Wells mentally calculated the yardage, the angle, took stock of the wind and the grass and his breathing. He took the putter from his caddie and lined up the shot.

And he took it for Josephine, but also for the directionless kid he'd been at sixteen, the guy who'd lost his will to win at twenty-six but found his way back at twenty-nine.

And hell if the ball didn't curve high and right, then roll into the hole.

Wells dropped his club as the crowd erupted, his new caddie slapping him on the back, reporters rushing at him from every direction, the crowd surging toward the green as security attempted to keep them back, all under a totally airless blue sky. It was like something out of a dream, but it couldn't be, because Josephine wasn't there and he wouldn't waste a dream like that. She'd be—

There. She was standing behind the rope.

Wells free-fell right where he stood. The ground felt like it was rushing up to meet him, his heart thundering in his ears, but the image of Josephine didn't disappear no matter how many times he blinked or told himself it was a mirage. She was *right there*, smiling through tears.

Holding her WELLS'S BELLE sign.

The original.

She'd taped it together.

It fluttered to the ground when several fans boosted her up and over the rope, clearly recognizing her as his reason for living. His surroundings became a blur, because Wells was jogging. And then he was running. But he didn't make it far before he was brought down to his knees, right in front of her, by gratitude and love so full and vast and all-encompassing that it rocked him to a core he didn't even know he had.

One Josephine—and only Josephine—had reached.

Ten years from now, people would claim he cried like a baby as he wrapped his arms around Josephine's waist and buried his face in her stomach. And he would deny it.

But he did. He cried like a motherfucker.

"You won," she half sobbed, half laughed. "You won, you won."

"You're here," he rasped, inhaling her scent, his hands roaming over her back to make sure she was real. "You're here."

"I'm so proud of you," she whispered, her voice shaking with emotion. "Wells. Oh my *God*."

He buried his face deeper in her stomach for a moment, those words—her pride—making it necessary to gather himself.

"You were right. You did the right thing. I never could have done it myself." Her breath stuttered in and out. He held her tighter, trying to drown out the noise so he could hear. "I'm sorry I didn't see your act of selflessness for what it was. You love me, that's why you did it. Even though it was hard. And I'm just as proud of you for that, Wells, as I am of you winning today."

Every syllable out of her mouth was an embarrassment of riches. He'd woken up this morning wondering if she'd ever speak to him again. Now she was validating the hardest decision of his life. Not merely forgiving him, but *apologizing*? Gratitude and relief poured down over his head like a healing rain, even as the need to reassure her overwhelmed him.

"You have no reason to be sorry. No. None. I *hurt* you." He reached up and cradled her beautiful face in his hands, swiping away her tears with his thumbs. "You're forgiving me for that?"

"*Yes*. Do you forgive me?"

He started to issue another denial that she owed him an apology, but she laid a finger across his lips. "Fifty-fifty, Wells."

This woman. She was a wonder. Every second with her was going to be a dream. Thank God he got to have seconds with her. Minutes. Years. Decades. Every last one of them. "Then I forgive you, too." He caught another one of her tears with his thumb, the very sight of it wrenching his heart sideways. "And listen to me, we're going to be a team whether or not you're standing next to me in a uniform. When I'm not on tour, I'm with my girl. I'll move to Palm Beach so fast, it'll make your ponytail crooked."

She let out a watery laugh.

"Don't worry, I'll fix it for you. I'm an expert now."

"I love you," she sobbed with her eyes closed. "It's like, painful, you know?"

Fuck. His vision was blurring again, too. So much that he had to bury his face in her stomach again so her shirt could absorb the moisture.

After several centering breaths, he managed to separate himself enough to look up into the eyes of his best friend, his equal, the woman he wanted to wake up beside every day for the rest of his life, and he let the emotion in his chest pour out of him. "I love you, too. So much. I think deep down, I had faith we'd be together again, because love like ours doesn't just go away. It cuts clean through everything. It's start-to-finish kind of love, all right? You know it and I know it." He bowed his head a moment to find his breath. Looking into her eyes was stealing it clean out of his lungs. "While I'm down here on my knees, I'm going to ask you to be my wife. I can golf on my own, but I can't face a day where we don't belong to each other, all right?"

"I'll be your wife." She nodded, gulping in air. "Yes. I love you, yes."

Suddenly he had the strength to stand again. To lift Josephine in his arms and hold her tight, dizzy from his ascent to the highest heights this world had to offer.

Life with Josephine.

"I don't have a ring on me," he said hoarsely in her ear, before pulling back to finally, God, *finally* kiss her after far too long. "Will you accept a green jacket until I get you one?"

She shook her head. "I'll take you, Wells Whitaker. I'll just take you."

EPILOGUE

Eight Years Later

Josephine snuck a look at her watch. Ten minutes to closing and she still had customers in the shop, but that wasn't unusual anymore. Over the last eight years, the Golden Tee had built a reputation as a must-do experience on every Florida golf trip . . . and she currently had a waitlist for consultations a mile long. She'd let the guests finish navigating the drone footage they'd collected throughout the day before kicking them out. The upside to having the most original pro shop in Palm Beach meant a lot of customers.

The downside was they never wanted to leave.

And she adored the shop, but she also really, really loved being home these days.

She took a moment to marvel over the large number on the bottom of the day's credit card report before stacking the papers and heading to the office, which was a more recent addition at the back of the Golden Tee. As she passed the gathering of golfers, one of them whispered, "That's Josephine Whitaker. She owns this place." She pretended not to hear them, but once she stepped into the office, she allowed a smile to stretch her lips.

Let's face it, a lot of people mentioned her in the same breath as her famous husband, who'd climbed his way back to his rightful position among the top ten in the world. It was only natural. But just as often, she was recognized for building *this* place. Her love letter to her favorite sport.

She set the credit report down on the desk and looked around the office, her gaze drifting over the framed photograph of Wells proposing to her at the eighteenth hole at the Masters. Beside it, her caddie uniform had also been mounted in a glass box, along with her taped together Wells's Belle sign.

Josephine couldn't get enough of the reminders of that roller coaster series of weeks she'd spent falling in love with her husband—love that had only deepened considerably over time. But the picture sitting on her desk? She loved that one even more. Wells asleep on the couch in their living room, his golf cleats full of dirt and grass, a tiny baby girl sleeping on his chest. He'd wanted to get home so bad that afternoon, he hadn't bothered to change into street shoes before flying back from the tournament.

Josephine could relate.

She gently booted the remaining customers, locked up the Golden Tee, and drove home to Palm Beach Gardens. She and Wells had purchased the house before the wedding just over seven years ago and he'd immediately replaced the normal, perfectly fine bathtubs with the biggest, most obnoxious ones he could find. The one in their en suite played music and had twenty-seven jets and nine color settings. He'd also soundproofed the walls.

Suffice it to say they spent a lot of time in that bathroom.

She parked and headed for the front door, taking a moment to smile through the glass at the scene that greeted her. Wells, hat on backward, standing in the living room with an infant strapped to his chest. A portable putting green was spread out in front of him, their four-year-old daughter poised to take her shot with the miniature club he'd given her for Christmas. Her auburn hair was in its usual tangle, poking through the edges of her skewed princess crown, her toes painted a familiar blue.

They matched Josephine's.

As soon as Mabel finished taking her putt, Josephine walked into the soundless celebration—out of deference to the sleeping baby—and immediately had a four-year-old gunning straight for her, grubby arms wrapping tightly around her legs.

"Mommy!"

"Nice shot, Mabes! You're amazing!"

As she stooped down to hug her daughter, Josephine locked eyes with Wells a few yards away and couldn't stem the fountain of emotions that plumed inside her chest. Her breath ran short, hot pressure spreading behind her eyes. It was always like this when he came back from a four- or five-day absence during the season. He looked more than a little haggard and she knew it was from missing them. They'd been falling asleep on FaceTime for the last few nights and waking up the same way. But December was just around the corner, which meant a full month without traveling—and she was counting the days.

"Hey," she murmured when her husband approached, reaching up to cradle his stubbled face, her heart sighing when he closed his eyes and leaned into her touch. "You're home now."

He nodded. Opened his mouth to speak and closed it again. "Belle," he said raggedly, like it had taken all of his strength.

Something was up. He needed to talk to her. She could read him from a single word.

"Okay." She lifted onto her toes and kissed him, flutters carrying through her stomach and beyond as he slid unsteady fingers into her hair and deepened the kiss with a low, lingering groan. "Are you all right?" she whispered when they parted for air.

Wells kept their foreheads pressed together. "I'm so much better than all right. *You're* here. It's when I'm away that I'm not good."

"I know."

"My family is *here*."

"And we'll always be here." She looked him in the eye until he got through a deep breath, but something continued to weigh on his mind. "Let's get the kids to bed."

Wells nodded and the four of them climbed the stairs together, Wells taking their son, Rex, into one room, Josephine herding Mabel into another. Half an hour later, she went looking for her husband. He wasn't in their bedroom or the kitchen, but intuition told her where to find him, and she was right. Wells stood in the center of his trophy room, her gorgeous champion in sweatpants, no shoes, ink swirling high and low on his broad back.

If she tugged down his pants, she would find her name tattooed on his right butt cheek.

He'd threatened to do it for years and she'd assumed he was joking.

Nope. It had been her thirtieth birthday present.

Property of Josephine in bright blue ink.

Wells turned at her entrance with shadows in his eyes, but his arms opened automatically. On her way into them, she cataloged the changes in her husband over the last eight years. Lines fanning out from wise, contented eyes. The barest sprinkle of gray in his chest hair and stubble. He still radiated confidence, but it was quieter now, like he'd grown into it. And she had so much pride in the man he'd become, it almost hurt to breathe.

They swayed, locked in each other's arms for a few moments while Wells hummed the first few bars of "California Girls" into her hair.

He pulled back and looked her in the eye while tracing her cheekbones with his thumbs, and she couldn't help but fall even harder for this man, surrounded by accolades but directing all his affection at her. "Josephine." He smiled, kissed her softly. "I'm retiring."

A jolt passed through her. "You're . . . what?"

"I'm done with the tour. I want to be home." He stroked her hair, then whispered back the words he'd said to her eight years earlier. Words he said to her every time he returned from a trip. "You don't know what it's like to miss you, baby. No fucking idea."

"I have some idea," she said back, her chest swamped with bittersweet emotion. "Are you sure?"

"It's the second most sure I've been about anything in my life. You are the first." He pulled her into a bear hug. "I want to be home to love you more."

She blinked back tears. "I'll take all the love from you I can get."

"Good. I've got a lot of it."

"Me too."

They stayed that way for a long time, Josephine sensing he needed the anchor.

"Retired at thirty-seven," she said, finally, kissing his shoulder. "What are you going to do with so much time on your hands?"

"Coach Little League. Help out at the shop. Take the occasional commentating gig. Make love to my wife. Be her trophy husband." He sighed into her hair. "Golf."

They laughed their way into a kiss while he continued humming the rest of "California Girls" and they started to dance. And life stayed just like that.

Blissful.

Happy.

Together.

Forever.

Keep an eye out for Tessa's next sports romance, because one surly, single-dad athlete is about to fall head-over-hockey-stick for his live-in nanny . . .

THE AU PAIR AFFAIR

Summer 2024
PREORDER IT NOW!

ABOUT THE AUTHOR

#1 *New York Times* bestselling author Tessa Bailey can solve all problems except for her own, so she focuses those efforts on stubborn, fictional blue-collar men and loyal, lovable heroines. She lives on Long Island, avoiding the sun and social interactions, then wonders why no one has called. Dubbed the "Michelangelo of dirty talk" by *Entertainment Weekly*, Tessa writes with spice, spirit, swoon, and a guaranteed happily ever after. Catch her on TikTok @authortessabailey or check out tessabailey.com for a complete list of her books.

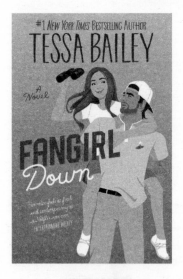